# Jewel of the Naga

Olivia Fields

Published by Rogue Phoenix Press
Copyright © 2016

ISBN: 978-1-62420-248-3

Credits
Cover Artist: Designs by Ms G
Editor: Christine Young

# Acknowledgments

Thanks go out to Ashley for endless moral support and data recovery, to Ghislaine for vetting the French, to Jeffrey the security guy for being generally awesome, to Rhea for insisting I add sacred cows and monkeys, to Paula for Google-fu, to Jennifer for helping on all matters of publicity and enduring my irascible bafflement therewith, to Rhonda for help with editing, and to a nice tall glass of moscato for working much-needed magic on a highly resistant scene.

Love always to my inspiration, who grabbed me by the hand and dragged me away from the nearly-finished novel originally intended to be my second. He insisted on pulling me all the way through this one instead.

# Prologue

Michelle sat on a stool at the bar, her heels hooked over the rail, her knees neatly pressed together. The place was one of those old-fashioned country beer bars full of smoke. Layers of drifting gray stratified in the air, lit up in dingy rainbow patterns by neon signs glowing in the windows and on the walls. The rearmost corner table hid in a pool of shadows. The man who sat slouched there appeared solely as a suit of clothes.

A weathered brown fedora shaded his features from her gaze. The hat went with battered leather boots, dark brown, and a pair of worn, travel-stained jeans. His legs crossed at the ankles, the sole of one boot propped against the round base of the table, which didn't yield to the pressure, its pedestal firmly bolted to the floor. His arms lay across the discolored wooden tabletop, one hand curled lightly around a bottle of beer, long fingers picking thoughtfully at the label. His sheepskin-lined leather bomber jacket looked as well-worn as his boots and his jeans. A waitress stepped up to his table. His hand dipped into his front pocket, coming out with a twenty casually tucked between two fingers.

His eyes gleamed for a moment, long enough to let Michelle know he was watching her. He tossed the bill onto the waitress's tray and she quickly whisked it away.

Michelle sat still for a moment, listening to the click of billiard balls and the low thumping whine of a Hank Williams tune on the jukebox. The song was obnoxious, but not loud enough to drive her out looking for a better place to spend the evening. Not with this man giving her the eye.

The stranger sat alone, but the waitress brought back two bottles for him, their brown sides glistening with condensation. She carried away the empty single.

His eyes still rested on Michelle as he waited for her response to his silent invitation. An intoxicating sense of power thrilled along her spine. The choice was up to her now.

She didn't think to look for her friends as she stood, adjusting her miniskirt primly. She made a fuss of it, delaying so he would have to wonder whether she would accept or decline. Her heart beat fast. She felt reckless, giddy, and hot. Wanted. She watched the man tip back his bottle without ever moving his head, without ever lowering his gaze.

Michelle made her decision. She approached him, her heels tapping slowly on the uneven wooden floor. He hooked the bottom rung of a chair with his toe, sliding it out for her.

She tried to breathe normally as she sat down, reaching for the extra bottle. The beer tasted nutty and tart on her tongue. His narrow, sensual lips curved in a small smile.

They drank without speaking. When he rose, she did also. His hand settled on the small of her back as he guided her out, warm and firm. Desire flared in the pit of her belly. She licked her lips, noticing the lazy way he walked, every sensual motion perfectly confident.

She didn't know quite how they reached a bed, but they fell into it together. Hands stripped off clothes in a frenzy of haste, mouths melting hot with passion as they met and opened, the kiss sinking effortlessly deep. His strong palms settled on her waist. His mouth burned its way along her jaw, slowly moving down to her throat. She fumbled her way inside his shirt, trying to push it off his shoulders, but he had to let her loose first. He resisted, filling his hands with her breasts, then following the same path with the burning press of his mouth.

She arched, whimpering and gasping. His knee parted her thighs. He followed it with one hand, lightly cupping her, discovering she had not worn panties. He groaned low and urgent against her breast. His thumb sank into her wet center, circling once around the little bud of her clit, finding her slick, ready for him, lifting against his touch. He drew back to fight free of his jacket, sweat starting to gleam on his narrow, tight-muscled chest between the wings of his shirt.

She lay open for him, waiting, watching with impatience as he stripped off his belt, flinging it aside. He popped the buttons of his fly. His thick cock pushed its way out, flushed rosy-dark. Long and straight, it fell free, pointing toward its goal with the unerring instinct of a compass needle. He shoved his jeans down, his eyes flashing up to rake over her body, burning with lust. Sinking onto her, he reached to stroke the blunt head of his cock against her, making her whimper and writhe.

"Please," she whispered, clutching at his shoulders, trying to drag him forward. He laughed softly. She had not heard his voice before: a soft tenor, rich, warm, and mellow. He purred approval, kissing her lips. She felt the throaty rumble of his chest against her breast a moment before he sank in, pushing her open with slow, steady pressure.

She tipped her head back, wailing as he stretched her, filling her. He slowly advanced his hips until he was sheathed, spreading her legs wide. Now his shirt had gone, his shoulders and back slippery with sweat. Her palms slid over the sleek muscles covering his ribs.

He drew back, then thrust home again. She cried out desperately, lifting her body to meet him. Her eager response unleashed his passion, and he thrust again fiercely. He rode her hard with a sturdy thrust of his hips, and she whimpered every time he claimed her. His teeth stung at her throat. She dug her short nails into his shoulders, bucking.

The bed frame groaned in protest. She was forced to let go of him to brace herself against the headboard with both hands. He found his rhythm immediately, making her small breasts bounce on her chest. One of his hands wandered. He pinched her nipple between his thumb and forefinger. The sensation zinged through her sharply. Michelle cried out, writhing beneath him, and came abruptly on his cock, shuddering with pleasure.

He laughed again, exultant, shifting his weight, pushing her thighs even farther apart so he could pierce deeper. Michelle clawed at the headboard, desperate. He never slowed. The starburst bliss of orgasm surged through her over and over, cresting anew with each powerful thrust. She shrieked until she had no air left, begging for more, pleading for him never to stop.

His laugh turned throaty, his chest rumbling with a growl. He reached down, withdrawing, and lifted her legs. He resettled her so her knees crooked over his elbows. She lay trapped under his weight as he fell on her again, mounting her with fierce speed, forcing the breath from her lungs.

The pleasure sparkled brighter, brittle and maddening, as she gasped for breath. She made a frantic, keening cry with what was left of her air, seeing stars, reveling in dizzy, lightheaded ecstasy, nearly more than she could bear. He caught her mouth with his for a long moment and stroked his tongue against hers, echoing the motion of his hips, a soft growl building in his chest. He drew back and froze, shuddering as he came, his teeth sunk in the narrow, perfect silk of his lower lip. She shivered against him, the crest finally receding, leaving her shuddering with aftershocks, completely spent.

He lay atop her in the aftermath, his breath gradually easing in his chest, and kissed her, then shifted to let her unfold herself before curling her against him. She snuggled with him wearily, not caring about the mess of sweat and semen on their skin.

Her last memory of the dream was of her lover's breath brushing softly against her ear as he murmured low, soothing words to her in a tongue she didn't know.

# Chapter One

*Two months later....*

"The sleep study was inconclusive. The main thing I learned is I don't need CPAP. You know, one of those nighttime breathing masks."

Michelle swiveled in her office chair, rolling her eyes at Elise, who paused in her typing to offer a sympathetic headshake. "They said my brainwave patterns were perfectly normal and my breathing was fine. I didn't have a nightmare or any other vivid dream all night. ....Mom, I have to do some work. Yes, I will. I know. Yes. Bye, mom." She escaped at last, setting her phone on vibrate, then burying it as deep as she could inside her purse.

Instead of returning to writing, she leaned back to stretch. Her long blonde hair fell down her back in loose waves, reaching nearly to her waist, where it caught between her back and the chair, giving her scalp a painful tweak. She swiped at her hair, tying it into a hasty updo with the ponytail elastic she wore around her wrist. Ugh. There was still some of the nasty goop on her scalp, the glue the technician had attached the electrodes with. "God, I want a shower."

"And about fifteen hours' sleep. You have bags." Elise ran an illustrating fingertip under her eyes.

"I had those already. That's why I went." Michelle flipped through the hardware engineer's illegible notes, trying to come up with a way to segue into the next paragraph of her technical manual. Her eyes felt grainy, hot and overworked. She'd slept even less than usual with all the wires and electrodes strapped onto her. Not to mention she'd been nervous knowing the sleep study tech was lurking next door, staring at her all night through the closed-circuit television.

"Damn it, if we don't start paying someone to transcribe Fred's notes, I'm going to go blind." She rubbed her eyes in frustration.

"Fred means well." Elise grinned wickedly, parroting the excuse Michelle always made for him. "He can't help it if he has the penmanship of a chicken on caffeine."

"Do I hear someone taking my name in vain?" Fred turned up right on cue, popping in through the door with a steaming mug in his hand. He blinked at them amiably, his eyes owlish behind thick glasses more than half fogged over by steam from his hot coffee. Unable to see, he stumbled over the edge of the anti-static mat beneath Michelle's chair, nearly spilling his drink. "Michelle, I have the notes you asked for on how to do a hard reset."

Confronted by Fred's earnest, sheepish look, Michelle's irritation melted away. She could never stay angry with him. Maybe it was because he tried so hard. She instinctively wanted to reach out and help him: to push his glasses further up onto his nose, straighten his collar, put the knot of his tie straight, or maybe muss his gel-slicked dark hair, freeing it from its rigid confinement. Keeping it slicked down against his head took so much product he was probably keeping the hair gel company in business all by himself.

"Sit right there." Michelle stabbed one finger decisively at the cubicle's single guest chair. "It's already 4:30. You can't do anything else by the time you get back down to the shop. Stay and read this out to me instead."

"All right." Fred seated himself meekly. As always, Michelle found herself trying to place his accent: something maddeningly faint on his tongue, elusive, possibly Celtic. For the life of her, she couldn't figure out where he'd lived growing up.

"To do a simple on/off, depress the power button for one cycle." He leaned forward and moved his finger under the words as he read.

"One cycle?"

"A second, give or take. Actually, 0.8765 seconds on average in lab trials." He blinked at her anxiously. "Should we round up?"

"Definitely." She suppressed a giggle. "What does the user do if the tablet freezes up?"

"Depress the power button for seven cycles. That's—"

"About six seconds." She interrupted his mental mathematics, watching Elise roll her eyes with exasperation. "How should I depress the button?"

"Play it some emo goth punk tunes," Elise wise-cracked. She offered Michelle a breath mint from the little tin in her purse.

For a moment, Michelle glimpsed a sparkle of real humor behind the glasses as Fred lifted his gaze. His lips curved, his temples crinkling with laugh lines as his steel-blue eyes flashed to her face to see if she would giggle.

"For Christ's sake, Elise." Michelle accepted half a dozen of the little flat, white candies, extending her hand to offer Fred some. The joke was an old one. Right now, the chance to pick Fred's brain before quitting time was more important.

"For a hard reset, you have to move the switch to the left before you push it in," he mumbled around the mints. "Hold it there till the screen goes black." He reached for the prototype on her desk to demonstrate.

"That's what I'm after." Michelle began to type rapidly.

She spent the remainder of the day making Fred translate his abominable handwriting, then wrapped up, hitting save on her document as the clock ticked over to five.

"You coming, Michelle? Some of us are heading for midtown to go bar crawling. Jenny wants to stop at Maelstrom for dinner." Elise pulled out a compact and started touching up her makeup, serenely oblivious to Fred's presence.

Michelle raised a brow at her friend's carelessness. Somehow none of the office girls ever seemed to notice Fred was a man. He occupied a sort of sexless status usually reserved for gay best friends. If he were sexier, or actually gay, Michelle supposed the group might make him a regular bar-crawling companion. However, she had no idea what gender he dated, and the girls all thought he was a total dork. Besides, the strongest thing she'd ever seen him drink was a cappuccino.

Michelle considered the offer, not too seriously. She needed a shower and a good night's sleep. She hated Maelstrom's gimmicky ambience, with its special "smoking allowed in the dining room" permit, its pictures of naked women festooned all over the walls like so much meat, and its surly wait staff. "If Jenny wants to meet supers, she shouldn't keep dragging us to godawful tourist traps. I can't think of any place less likely for a supernatural being to hang out."

"You never know where you'll meet a super." Fred pushed his glasses further up on the bridge of his nose. "I saw a banshee buying lettuce in the supermarket last week."

"Must have been noisy." Elise fished for a lip liner and touched up her fading mouth.

"Not really. She was quite soft-spoken, in fact." Again Michelle caught a quick flash of Fred's eyes. His expression looked mischievous. Maybe it was distortion from his thick corrective lenses.

"I don't think Jenny's as much into supers as she is into goths." Oblivious to his amusement, Elise tucked away her cosmetics. She made a satisfied duck face into her compact mirror.

"If she wasn't such a hipster, she'd know no real goths hang out at Maelstrom, either. The management makes the wait staff dress up, but that's as close as you get. There are no regulars; different tourists come in there every day. Anyway, I'll take a rain check. I'm heading home." Michelle stood up, cracking her neck. She grimaced, accidentally touching the electrode goop behind her left ear. "I had a restless night last night. At my sleep study," she huffed impatiently when Fred raised a brow. "The tech was a twerp, and he strung me up with about ten miles of electrical cable. You're on camera, and if you want to move, you have to call for help. Then a guy comes in to unplug you from the wall so you can go pee."

"You're having difficulty resting?" He blinked at her with concern, gathering his things. He couldn't have been in her cubicle for more than half an hour, but the contents of his messenger bag had already migrated across the left half of her desk and spread out all over the floor around his feet. "My mother always said drinking a glass of warm milk would put you right to sleep every time."

"Mine swore by sex," Elise inserted drily. Michelle couldn't help but giggle when Fred blushed and nearly dropped his half-finished coffee in his discomfort. "Not for herself, but for my father. She said he fell asleep halfway through the cum-shot, every damn—"

"Elise!" Michelle laughed out loud, watching Fred fumble hastily with his things. He struggled to escape through the door without dropping any of them. She dismissed him from her mind.

"You might as well try getting laid. If things with you and Kevin are still on." Elise gave her a sidelong glance, disturbingly keen.

Michelle stifled a sigh. "Sort of. Whenever he bothers to call." She hadn't taken many of his calls the last couple of months. Ever since she'd started having trouble sleeping properly, she had all she could do to e keeping herself clean, laundered, and fed. She did

y to maintain a casual boyfriend.

ids not good," Elise laid her hand on Michelle's

ire you don't want to come out for an evening with us girls?"

"This weekend," Michelle promised. "When I don't have to wake up at six AM and fight traffic for two hours on I-85."

"This weekend is Labor Day; we're all going to the convention." Elise stared at her in exasperation. "I can't believe you forgot. You're out of it, Michelle."

"All the more reason to rest up." Jenny was going to be in goth heaven; she lived for the con. "The convention will be a blast, but not if I sleep through all the parties." Michelle stuffed her things in her purse and left the building, stifling a yawn behind her palm.

# Chapter Two

Stuck behind the wheel of her car on I-85, Michelle hated her commute almost as much as she liked her job. She resented spending four hours every day creeping past every inch of what should have been a twenty-minute drive, watching huge chunks of her life evaporate before her eyes. Still, she couldn't complain; her current position paid well. She liked her co-workers too.

She got into her little apartment shortly after eight, neglecting to listen to the messages on her phone. She had a voicemail from Kevin, but she couldn't muster the energy to cope with him.

First on the agenda was a good hot shower to wash the rest of the gluey gunk out of her hair. Then she wanted a bathrobe, beer, and bed, maybe with a pause midway through to nuke a diet dinner. Better not to have the beer on an empty stomach. Trying to drink yourself to sleep was a bad idea.

Besides, she didn't have any trouble falling asleep or even staying asleep. Her problem was the dreams: vivid, brilliant dreams like IMAX movies filmed in full digital color, showing in 3D on four-story projection screens with surround-sound. Sometimes she had nightmares; other times... She'd never had such erotic dreams before. They lasted all night long; they left her exhausted. Day after day she woke to the insistent bleat of her alarm, wringing with sweat, her bed all but destroyed with the ground sheet pulled off the corners of the mattress and the covers wrestled all the way down to her ankles.

Michelle kicked off her clogs and dropped her clothes in the hamper then stepped into the shower. She set the water temperature as hot as she could stand it and ducked under the spray, sighing with pleasure, letting the heat soak into her scalp to melt the stubborn goop.

Her mind kept circling, nibbling away at her worries while she scrubbed herself clean.

She'd kept the sexy stuff to herself so far, just talking about the nightmares. Maybe embarrassment was why she hadn't had any dreams at the sleep study. She'd felt horribly self-conscious with all those wires plugged into her, thinking the technician might be able to read her mind and see the dreams as clearly as she could. She hadn't liked the smirking, too-jovial man from the minute she met him. She could just picture him snapping his gum as he stared at the closed circuit TV screen, rubbing his greasy palm against his fly, watching her get off in her sleep and coming along for the ride. Michelle shuddered.

The sex dreams had started slowly two months ago, coming at a rate of one or two a week, but now she had one almost every time she closed her eyes. The nightmares had only begun a couple of weeks back. Maybe if she could enjoy some rest in between them, she wouldn't complain, but they just kept getting more frequent.

She hated not knowing whether she was going to wake up screaming in pleasure or in terror. If Michelle didn't get some relief soon, she was probably going to fall asleep on the highway and wipe out, or maybe fuck up a document so badly her boss would let her go.

Michelle turned off the water. Stepping out onto the bathmat, she wrapped her long hair in a towel, squeezing until it stopped dripping. The beer sounded better every minute.

She made a face at the barren freezer compartment and pulled out a box of spring rolls, sticking them in their little paper envelope before putting them in the microwave to heat. She chuckled to herself. Time to go to the grocery store tomorrow. Maybe she'd meet a banshee in the produce department.

Her phone vibrated insistently inside her purse, and she opened the zipper, glaring inside. The phone made a low, irritated noise, like the bumblebees she and her cousins used to trap inside snapdragons in their grandmother's flowerbed back when she was a kid. Only two people it could be: her mom or Kevin. Sighing, she thumbed the touchscreen. Kevin.

She couldn't keep dodging his calls forever.

"Hey. Yeah. I'm still under the weather. I went to a sleep study, but of course I didn't dream while they had me wired up." She fished her steaming hot spring rolls out of the microwave and dumped them onto a plate, then sucked briefly on a burned finger. Grabbing a beer out of the fridge, she pressed the mild burn against the cold glass.

Michelle let Kevin ramble, her phone pinched between her shoulder and her ear. "Yeah, I know. I've been busy." Damn it, she needed rest too badly to go for a pussy call.

"How about I come over tomorrow. I'll bring a frozen pizza. We can let our hair down, watch some old action movies and snuggle up then see what happens." His voice sounded tinny, distorted by the phone's little speaker.

Michelle wanted to care for Kevin, she really did—but the problem was, she didn't actually like him very much. For one thing, he only offered to hang out when he wanted sex. Then he always played lowball with the plans. If he was serious about spending quality time with her, they'd go out to a nice restaurant sometimes, or go dancing, or to a new movie. He'd put up with a romcom sometimes for her sake instead of endless cop flicks.

If he were really worth keeping, Kevin would loosen his starched collar a little and go with her to a science fiction convention for once. But no, all he wanted was to flop on her couch, making her sit through the same old guns and explosions over and over until she got so bored she gave up and started to make out with him in desperation.

Her attitude probably wasn't very kind, but she was too exhausted and miserable to care.

"Look, Kevin." She felt embarrassed and rude doing this over the phone, but then again, maybe it would be even worse not to finish things now she'd made up her mind. "I've been thinking. You'd be a lot happier with a girl who doesn't have to work as much as I do. One who loves snuggling over shoot-'em-up cop films and staying in."

She paused for the deluge of denials, sighing, then tried again. "I just think we'll both be happier if we find someone more compatible. I don't like making you miserable. We're both unhappy like this." She was trying not to yawn in his ear, really she was, but weariness hung thick in her brain, threatening to drag her under before she could even stumble to bed.

"No, I'm going to the con this weekend with Elise and Jenny. Yeah, I'll come up with a time for you to visit so you can pick up your DVDs." She closed her eyes, feeling guilt settle heavily in the pit of her stomach. "I'm sorry, Kevin. I have to sleep, if I can. G'night. You're a great guy; you'll find somebody wonderful in no time."

She pushed the hang-up button on her touchscreen and set the phone on the coffee table then sat back, staring at the ceiling. That was the right move; she felt as if a weight had been lifted off her shoulders. The breakup wasn't all Kevin's fault, not by a long shot, but...yeah. No.

The spring rolls were already stone cold, but she ate them anyway, polishing off her beer. She had to catch up on some rest if she wanted to be fit for anything at all. She bit her lip. As if. She had to hope luck would bring the sex dreams tonight. At least they were fun.

~ * ~

Walking alone in the city always made Michelle feel ill-at-ease, especially at night. Tonight was even worse than usual; chilly with thick, misty rain falling. She sheltered under a convenient theater awning, glancing up at the sky. Droplets hung in bright, hazy halos around the streetlights. Multicolored signs caught in the mist, illuminating clouds of red, blue, or green fog.

She huddled into the collar of her coat, a gust of cold wind spraying rain over her face. If she could dart across the street, she might find a cheap umbrella in a shop on the other side so she could go home. But the sidewalk was jammed with people hustling to and fro. Taxis buzzed along at high speed, darting between buses and trucks. She couldn't find a streetlight.

The case at her back displayed a movie poster advertising one of the shows inside. She stepped back and leaned against the wall to let a woman with a wide umbrella pass by. The powerful lights illuminating the poster made the glass feel warm against her shoulders. Maybe she'd buy a ticket for the show. The rain might stop by the time she came out again.

As she hesitated, trying to make up her mind, a hole opened in the crowd. A man strode into the fuzzy circle of light cast by the nearest street lamp. He stared straight ahead, moving fast, his expression purposeful. He wore a black leather jacket with the collar turned up, black jeans, boots, and a mustard yellow turtleneck sweater. He cut through the crowd like a blade. Michelle blinked, almost convinced she knew him from somewhere, but the feeling passed as his pale blue eyes glanced aside and his gaze settled on her.

He slowed his brisk walk, veering his path to approach. He held a tight-rolled black umbrella. Before she could wonder why he wasn't using it himself, he offered it to her, the old-fashioned curved handle resting across the fingers of his left hand.

She dithered a little, realizing he meant to give it to her. "I couldn't take your umbrella," she protested.

His lips curved in polite, pleased response. "Then perhaps you'll let me walk you home." Again she felt a tilting sensation of unreality, as if she had forgotten something she should remember very clearly. "Is it far?"

"A few blocks." She should be wary of leading a stranger to her apartment. *This might be one of the nightmares.* Words ghosted through her mind, a brief awareness she was dreaming. His eyes distracted her, though. The thought vanished like a pricked soap bubble. He waited, a smile on his handsome face.

"All right, if you don't mind," Michelle mumbled, a little self-conscious.

He opened his umbrella with efficient grace and held it over her, gallant, as they set out together. Her feet seemed to know their path, though her mind didn't. He too walked as if he knew the way, never hesitating.

Now she had him with her, the street corners yielded traffic lights and crosswalks, always lit in their favor. The crowd thinned gradually until no one remained outdoors but them. Her apartment was nearby, a few blocks away, but no matter how far they walked, they didn't seem to be getting anywhere. Michelle began to feel uneasy, glad she had a companion.

"The street lamp's gone out ahead, by the vacant lot." The man slowed to a halt, his eyes narrowing. "I have a bad feeling about this."

She shrank close against his side. "Can we double back, maybe go another way?" She reached into her pocket for her phone, finding nothing except lint. Strange, hushed sounds filled the air, like a snake's scales slithering on concrete.

The man put the umbrella in his left hand, his right hand moving to settle protectively at the small of her back. "Too late. It's seen us." He lifted his voice. "You don't have any power in this place; I'm here to protect her. We'll pass on as we were. Go about your business."

With his warm, firm hand gently urging her on, Michelle

reluctantly stepped forward, nervous, trying to touch the ground as little as possible.

"Hold this." She clutched the umbrella as he fished in his pocket, drawing out a heavy flashlight. Its beam, strong as a headlight, pierced the mist.

The circle of light played over dismal, barren ground, scattered with an assortment of broken glass, dead weeds, and abandoned toys. She couldn't see anyone lurking behind the chain link fence separating the lot from the street, but the man hurried his pace as they passed, keeping the beam trained on a shadowed culvert.

A pair of eyes inside the pipe caught the light as they moved. Michelle stifled a whimper, covering her mouth with her free hand. The eyes hovered a few inches from the ground, tiny, like a rat's. They weaved back and forth as if the creature was swaying, but the beam of the flashlight revealed nobody, just the malevolent moving eyes.

"What is it?"

"I don't know. Keep walking." He remained calm. "I'll see you home safely."

The sense of menace faded gradually as they kept moving. The next street light was lit, so Michelle started to breathe again. The man tucked away his flashlight and reclaimed his umbrella. "I'm glad I found you tonight. Is that your building?"

Michelle nodded. He led her up the stair to the front door. "You should be safe now. I believe the creature has gone."

Michelle hesitated, her hand on the knob. Icy drops pattered off the cement lintel above her head, making unpleasant trickles of cold wetness on her head, but she didn't turn the handle yet. "You've been very kind. Would you like to come inside to have a hot drink and dry off?" She felt very small, her voice a little too loud, awkward. She blushed.

"If you like." His face lit with warmth at the offer. He followed her up the stairs, waiting as she unlocked her apartment. He glanced around. "Do you have a coat rack?"

He was dripping; he'd let her have most of the umbrella.

"I'll hang your coat to dry." Michelle fussed over him, covering her awkwardness. She stripped him to his sweater and jeans, hanging his coat. "This won't take long. The leather turned most of the rain. Is your sweater dry?"

"Wool insulates even when it's wet." He shrugged. "I'm a little damp at the collar, I suppose." His jeans were soaked, too, especially the left leg.

"Have a seat. I'll make us a drink. Would you prefer coffee or hot chocolate?"

"Chocolate sounds good." He put his hands in his pockets. "Can I help?"

"No, I won't be a minute." Michelle hurried into the kitchen to fill the kettle and put it on the stove. He followed her. Sitting down easily at her little table, he reached toward the lazy susan for a napkin.

"My name's Michelle," she told him, feeling more than a little silly, self-conscious. "What's yours?"

"I'm—damn!" his sleeve caught on one of her carnations. The vase toppled, spilling water everywhere. "I'm damned clumsy. May I have a paper towel?"

Michelle couldn't suppress a smile. "No harm done. Try next to the sink." She lifted the kettle off the stove and poured the hot water into mugs, then stirred a packet of cocoa powder into each, adding milk. He bustled around anxiously, mopping up the spill. Then he re-filled the vase and set the flowers back in the center of the table where they belonged.

She glanced at him as he wrung the wad of towels out in the sink before tossing the mess into the trash. "Want a nightcap in yours, Mr. Clumsy?" She held up a bottle of peppermint schnapps.

"I'd love one." His smile could have melted the iceberg that sank the Titanic. Heat kindled in Michelle's belly, a pleasant glow traveling all the way to the tips of her toes. She recovered quickly, turning away. She tipped a shot glass of the clear liquor into each mug, then puffed a little spiral of whipped cream on top of the drinks.

"I should really use a spring of fresh mint for garnish, but I wasn't expecting a guest."

"I'm fine as-is." He picked the cocoa up in both hands, warming his palms on the hot stoneware. His eyes closed with pleasure, lashes fanning out against his cheeks. Michelle tasted her own. The flush of renewed warmth sliding through her belly was a bit more than the schnapps could account for. His left hand wrapped around the mug. He wore no wedding ring.

She wandered to the window, gazing out into the night, enjoying her cocoa. The rain had thickened, pelting down in slanting lines, nearly obscuring the next building. She glanced at her wet coat, laid casually over the back of a chair, and at his jacket hanging over the vent. Drifting back toward the table, she stepped behind him. "It's a filthy night out. Do you have anywhere else you ought to be?"

She almost felt like she knew this man. Had he really been a stranger just a few minutes ago? She set her palm on his shoulder, her heart thumping hard. Tentative, she slid her hand lightly along his arm.

He sputtered a little with surprise, thumping his cocoa down on the placemat.

"I, er, no, not as such—"

"You're welcome to stay here tonight, if you'd like." Her hand lingered, fingertips circling on his biceps. "That is, if you want to." She slid her palm onto his chest, wanting to make her meaning quite clear.

He snatched a napkin, wiping hastily at his whipped-cream mustache. "I'd like that very much." He turned to her, blue eyes searching her face. "I mean, if you're sure." His hand found hers, twining their fingers together. "I didn't set out to seduce you when I offered my umbrella, you know." His gaze held hers, terribly earnest and a little anxious. Appealing.

"No, I'd hardly accuse you of planning my foolishness in going out without a raincoat." Michelle dimpled at him, unable to help herself. "You missed a bit." She leaned in to kiss a spot of whipped cream from the corner of his mouth, taking her time, leisurely tasting the sweetness of the cream and the pleasant masculine salt of his skin.

He rose, wrapping her in his arms, returning the kiss with devastating skill, drawing her up tight against his strong, slim body. He steered them into the bedroom without asking for directions, dispensing with their clothes so smoothly she hardly noticed they'd gone. She was gasping before they ever reached the bed, burning with need, half-drowning in his mouth. Her hands mapped the strong, hot lines of his bare shoulders and back. His muscles flexed with power as he lifted her, placing her lightly in her bed, then descended to lie atop her.

Her rescuer proved as kind as he was passionate, a considerate lover who tended to her pleasure before taking his own. Best of all, he stayed with Michelle after they were done to hold her as they rested. She snuggled against his chest with a soft sigh, feeling absolutely safe and protected.

She slept better than she had for weeks.

The strident buzzing of the alarm finally woke Michelle. At once, she missed her lover's warm embrace. Blinking open her eyes, she glanced groggily around, searching for him. No mess of scattered clothing on the floor. Worse, no head-print in the second pillow.

Lifting the sheet revealed pajamas. Her heart sank. Her lover had only been a dream.

Michelle forced herself to crawl out of bed, slapping at her clock until it shut off. Her coat hung in the closet, bone dry. The pavement outside was dry, too, the grass wilted and brown. No rain had fallen for days.

Michelle padded into the bathroom, dejected. Why couldn't she meet the man of her dreams for real? Sexy as fuck, but kind, loving, and gentle, eager to look out for her and be taken care of in return....

"He doesn't exist," she told her reflection, then stuck her tongue out at herself. Sadly, she began to brush her teeth.

# Chapter Three

Madhouse: the only way to describe a science fiction/fantasy convention as large as DragonCon. Michelle hung onto Elise's hand, dodging past a half-naked man who wasn't letting his beer gut prevent him from wearing a slave-girl bikini, then an impressively fearsome, tall demon with red muscular skin and a six-foot rack of black horns.

Hundreds of other convention goers had dressed up already, half of whom she couldn't even begin to identify. They hustled around in wide sweeps and angles, following their colored tape lines up to the front of the room to get their badges.

Giddy with excitement, Elise pinned hers on. "Tomorrow, this place will be crammed so full of people you couldn't squeeze in another person, not even if she was anorexic."

"That's not PC at all." Michelle disapproved.

"This whole convention isn't PC, honey. Oh, will you look at him!" She pointed to a man with black curly hair, his skin the color of burnt caramel. He wore gold harem pants and no shirt, showing off an elaborate tattoo of a cobra's hood stretching across his back. The ink was perfect, so detailed the scales seemed to shift, bunching as his muscles moved. Michelle eyed him with appreciation.

He turned and met her eyes, sensing her gaze. He wore a large blood-red cabochon set in gold filigree and affixed to the center of his forehead. His eyes glowed golden-brown through slitted contact lenses. He moved like the cobra in his tattoo, hips flowing with liquid grace. He gave her a knowing smile, then lowered one lid in a sly wink, making a frisson shiver down her spine.

Elise took off at a trot. Michelle followed in her wake, tolerant, winding through endless corridors passed room after room filled with outlandish people. Disorienting, surreal, incredible, the atmosphere reminded her of the dreamscapes she'd wandered so recently, both nightmarish and sensual.

You never knew who might turn up at the convention. You could run smack into a bona fide hunk like Nathan Fillion or a scary-looking actor who played B-movie villains or an old friend you hadn't seen since high school, dredged up somehow from three thousand miles across the continent. Why, if you squinted, that man over there almost looked like—

"Fred?"

He turned, pushing up his glasses, giving her a nervous smile. "Hi, Michelle. I didn't expect to run into you here."

Elise cackled. "I'd have expected to see you right here, Fred. Look, Shelly, we're smack in the middle of the Hall of Virgins."

"I didn't know you were a gamer." Michelle elbowed Elise irritably. "RPGs? MMORPGs? LARP?"

"I like a good first person shooter. But I don't intend to spend all weekend warming a chair and refusing to shower." He gazed at them with mild reproach. "I wanted to see the costumes, maybe take in a panel or two. I booked my room last fall. Do you have one?"

"No," Michelle admitted. "We were going to drive back and forth."

"You'll spend hours of your time fighting for parking. You ladies could..." he swallowed. "My room is a double. You could stay with me. If you didn't mind."

"We have a third, or we will tomorrow. Jenny's coming too." Michelle showed him the extra badge hanging from her lanyard.

"Do you snore?" Elise eyed him speculatively.

"Like a wounded bear, I'm told." He grimaced in apology. "I always carry earplugs. I'll lend you some."

Michelle considered the offer. "The cost wouldn't be bad if we split the room four ways, but I'd hate to inconvenience you."

"Not at all." He lowered his voice a little as Elise drifted away, drawn inexorably toward an impressively muscular superhero whose neon blue tights left little to the imagination. "If you don't mind, let's put Elise and Jenny in the extra bed. I'd rather you bunked with me. I'm not at all convinced Elise would take no for an...that is to say..." he shut up a moment too late, flushing. Michelle giggled.

"Your virtue is safe with me. More or less." He looked so worried she couldn't resist teasing. She gave him a bawdy wink. "Unless I get tipsy enough. Then all bets are off."

"I'll remember that." A seductive smile stretched his lips, sly and warm. Michelle blinked with surprise. He should definitely smile more often.

He fumbled into his pocket, pulling out a keycard. "I have room 4713 in the Marriott. The view is stunning, if you aren't afraid of heights."

"That's my favorite hotel. Isn't 47 a VIP floor?"

"Is it?" He blinked at her in mild surprise. "Maybe they made an exception for the convention."

"Didn't you mind taking room thirteen?"

He smiled again. "Thirteen has always been my lucky number." He gave her a wave before vanishing into the crowd. "See you later."

Michelle dragged Elise away from her hunky hero, ignoring her pleas. "He might really be the actor, like, in disguise, going incognito at the con!"

"As *if*," Michelle scoffed. They phoned for Jenny to join them as they hurried home to assemble their gear.

# Chapter Four

Around nine they trooped back downtown, managing to nab a decent spot in what passed for a reasonably priced parking garage. "Every place in town is charging through the nose this weekend," Jenny grumbled. "What a fucking rip-off."

"It's cheaper than parking under the hotel."

Michelle had to swipe her keycard in the elevator to make the button work for their floor. "It's a VIP floor," she muttered to Elise. "I don't know how he scored the room."

"It's going to cost a fortune. You should have asked how much before we agreed to share," Jenny complained.

The room lay empty except for a tidy set of bags standing inoffensively in one corner. Fred's open shaving kit occupied the bathroom vanity. Elise commandeered the luggage rack without apology and their gear all but exploded as they unpacked, taking over the room. Jenny's bag was especially bad. Half the costumes she'd stuffed in poured out all over the floor as soon as she unzipped the top.

"Do you always have to wear black?" Michelle eyed her gear with distaste.

"Yes!" Jenny shimmied into a pair of black tights with skulls woven in. She was still half naked when the door clicked open: Fred. She ignored him, not even bothering to turn her back. Michelle blushed somewhat uselessly on her behalf.

"I went over to Peachtree Center for some sushi." He ignored Jenny with surprising calm, offering Michelle the stack of boxes. "I thought you ladies would be hungry. Who likes chicken teriyaki?"

"You shouldn't have." Michelle peeked into the boxes anyway. "This stuff's expensive." She nabbed a segment of eel roll, dipping it in a

22

cup of sweet brown sauce. "You're too nice. Nice guys finish last, you know."

"Are you planning to take advantage of me for my sushi, then leave me to die old, alone, and forgotten?"

"Not until after I convince you to translate the rest of your documentation notes so I can write them up. The Marcuses are high maintenance."

"In that case, I'll have to keep translating for you." He gave her a shy grin, then chose a spear of tempura shrimp and bit off the end.

"So that's your secret. You're writing all your engineering notes with your left hand so you can sneak out of the lab on a regular basis to come gab with the tech writers."

"A brilliant deduction, Holmes." He dipped his half-eaten shrimp into her cup of sauce, but despite the double-dip, she couldn't muster the annoyance to make a fuss. This was Fred, after all. Where the hell was he going to catch anything contagious?

"Let's take up a collection, girls." Michelle spied the receipt sticking out from the edge of one box and nabbed it deftly before he could stop her. "Fifteen each ought to cover it."

The other ladies contributed without much enthusiasm, though they ate eagerly until the boxes were empty.

"That ought to keep us going for a while. We should go out and get pictures." Elise rooted around in her suitcase, fishing out a sparkly red mini dress.

"That's not a costume," Michelle protested.

"Who cares? The guys are gonna look. Aren't they, Fred?"

"Absolutely." In spite of his bold agreement, Fred wasn't actually looking at Elise, even though she peeled off without any more self-consciousness than Jenny.

Michelle settled on a Firefly T-shirt and jeans, ducking into the bathroom to change, but Fred didn't even take off his tie.

"If you're going to dress like a total mundane, you should at least wear a black suit and sunglasses. You could put one of those radio things in your ear, like a CIA agent," Jenny informed him.

"Should I?" He opened the door, ushering them out.

In the elevator Jenny put her back to the glass wall and shut her eyes as the stomach-rolling drop started. "Afraid of heights?" Fred asked Jenny as he stepped next to Michelle, protective. "Don't be. These things are carefully counterweighted. They can't possibly fall."

"Good to know." Jenny clung to the rail in spite of his attempt to reassure her, keeping her eyes clamped shut as they descended. Michelle settled for putting her back to the wall, watching the lights as they counted down.

They headed for the bar. Most of the seats were still empty, so they ordered drinks and chose a table where they could keep an eye on the crowd flowing through the hallway. Elise kept up a catty commentary, critiquing the outfits of anyone who passed. After a while, Michelle realized her sniping was wearing on everyone's nerves, so she tried to change the subject.

"Jenny, have you spotted any supers yet?"

"I think I saw a couple, yeah." Jenny drew herself up, self-important. "That guy, the really thin one in the black trench, did you see him?"

"I saw you staring at him." Elise tittered.

"Demon lord." Jenny wore a superior expression. "You can always tell."

"Really?" Fred raised a brow.

"This convention is a perfect venue for supers. They can gather here to be themselves without attracting any attention."

"I thought people who came to a science fiction convention in costume wanted all the attention they could possibly get." That was definitely a twinkle in Fred's eye. Michelle was abruptly sure he was baiting Jenny.

"Maybe so, but they can be accepted here. People who come to fantasy conventions are different. We like supers and want to be around them."

"That's possible, I suppose." Fred shrugged. "But humanity isn't very friendly to supers even at the best of times. I wouldn't say it's safe to go about openly as a super, not even here."

"It's safe to pretend to be one. Why shouldn't they be safe for real?"

"Because a super can't take off a costume to become human. If someone recognizes the super, then he's out of the closet. After supers are outed, they often have to change their identities and move on."

"How do you know so much about supers?" Jenny glared at him with irritation, obviously not liking the challenge to her authority.

"I knew one once." He looked down into his glass, swirling the whiskey and sniffing the sharp, woody bouquet. "I didn't realize what he was, not at first. We had a regular friendship. He seemed like a normal guy. He slept and ate. He had good days and bad. He watched television; he liked to jog. We played some pick-up basketball in the parking lot outside his condo on Saturdays. He had to work for a living. He actually went to the bathroom when he had to take a piss."

Fred's voice turned wry. "He was good at his job, but one of our co-workers learned his secret: he was a vampire. The next time his contract came up, it wasn't renewed. The company couldn't risk letting him interact with clients, they said. If word got out, it could ruin them."

He adjusted his glasses, blinking seriously at Jenny, then sipped his whiskey. "They kept thinking 'What if he killed someone for blood, a client or a co-worker or a family member?' Employers have a legal liability; they want to be proactive when they're aware of a threat among their workers. They can be sued if they aren't. He was classified as a threat, as if he were a registered sex offender. You know how some places have laws requiring sex offenders to warn everyone in the neighborhood when they move in so people can lock up their children? In a lot of cases, the neighborhood bands together to run the offender off."

He put down his tumbler, somber-eyed. "Supers don't have many legal rights. They've come out of hiding very recently. They aren't numerous enough to influence the outcome of elections. To most people, it doesn't matter if a vampire chooses to live on animal blood. There's always fear, a suspicion the vampire will snap at the earliest inconvenient moment and go after someone's teenage daughter.

"Vampires are the best-known example, but they're just the tip of the iceberg. At least they can survive without preying on humans. Some supers can't find an adequate substitute for their traditional source of food. They have to feed on something living in order to survive, much like humans have to consume plants and animals. Some supers have no option other than to harvest human blood or human emotions, which can be fatal to the human."

"There are some legal protections," Jenny protested. "Supers are covered by the Constitution now, at least here in America. They have recourse to the courts. The Supreme Court ruled the 15th amendment guarantees them the right to vote. It's a start."

"If they're willing to make their identities known, I suppose." He picked up his glass, leaning forward, intent. "But most have to create an elaborate, expensive false identity in order to sign up to vote. I've already explained why they don't like to go public with their real names. It's quite like being an illegal alien. The system is hard to join. Making the attempt carries so many risks and so few tangible benefits, most don't bother. They wind up on the periphery, where they're regarded as parasites."

"Who knew you were such a passionate advocate for supernatural rights?" Michelle spoke softly, taking a sip of her rum and Coke. "There's more to you than meets the eye, Fred."

"Really? Well—" he gestured broadly, spilling the remains of his scotch in the lap of his trousers, soaking his crotch. "Oh, hell!"

Elise collapsed into gales of unkind laughter as Michelle jumped up and rushed to the bar for a handful of cocktail napkins. Fred mopped himself as dry as he could, then excused himself to go back up to the room and change.

Fred always seemed a little clumsy whenever he wanted to change the subject. Michelle stared at his empty glass, frowning to herself, feeling a vague sense of *deja vu*.

"Quick, let's ditch Mr. Social Justice Warrior while we have the chance," Elise elbowed her stealthily. "He's a total downer."

"You said a mouthful." Jenny tossed back the last of her drink and set down her glass. "Maybe we'll find better action over in the Hyatt. I want to pose for pictures with as many hot men as we can find."

"No point sitting in the bar getting wasted," Elise giggled. "There's bound to be a few hot guys wandering around looking for action."

Michelle followed them reluctantly, sparing a guilty glance over her shoulder. She'd have to give Fred her number so he could text her when they were separated. He'd been extremely nice about sharing his room. He'd tried to buy them all an expensive dinner. It wasn't his fault Elise and Jenny were so shallow.

Though they found some costumers who agreed to pose for pictures, they didn't locate anyone interesting in the bar. It was destined to be one of those maddening evenings wasted hunting for the fun without ever finding any. After about three hours they gave up, deciding to return to the room.

"The con isn't properly underway yet," Michelle soothed Elise's sulks as well as she could. "Everything will be more fun tomorrow."

"Right. We should rest up for Friday." Jenny dumped her empty cup in the trash. "Let's go to bed."

Fred wasn't home when they arrived, though he'd rinsed his slacks and hung them neatly to drip dry in the shower.

Relieved, Michelle took advantage of his absence to change into her pajamas without having to feel self-conscious about changing. Of course, Elise couldn't let her wardrobe alone.

"Good lord, Shelly. Fuzzy pajama pants with feet and a long-sleeved shirt? Why didn't you bring a granny gown? You could put your hair up in curlers for a finishing touch. Then you wouldn't have to change into a costume tomorrow morning."

"Jenny always turns the air conditioning down to sub-zero." Besides, she wasn't about to wear anything to embarrass Fred. If Elise and Jenny wanted to tease him, it was none of Michelle's business. However, when her friend emerged from the bathroom, Michelle had to scoff. "What, you think you're a fashion model wearing a ratty old tank top and ripped gym shorts?"

"Fred's the only man who'll see." Elise shrugged. "Who cares?"

"You should. He's letting you share this room. He has to put up with your wet towels lying on the bathroom floor and your bra tossed on top of the air conditioner."

"Call the waaahmbulance. We're paying for our share," Elise snorted. She flopped down next to Jenny, who lay thumbing through a graphic novel. "Listen, there's our truant boy now." The door whirred as Fred triggered the lock with his card. He stepped in, adjusting the knot of his tie.

"Where were you? We didn't ever spot you coming down the elevator, so we eventually went on over to the Hyatt." Elise gave Fred a big cheesecake smile, making Michelle roll her eyes with exasperation. "I hope you were able to hook up with some people. Did you have a nice time?"

"I've been to a room party over at the Hilton," he confessed. "Nothing fancy. A few guys like me." He gave a self-deprecating shrug, pushing nervously at his glasses. "A little bit of talk, a few beers, planning our convention. Did you know the con chair is going to auction a date with Katee Sackhoff at the charity event? A bunch of the geeks want to pool their money and force her to go out with all of them. I've heard of job interviews by committee, but dates by committee? Needless to say, I wouldn't join the consortium."

Fred rummaged in his suitcase, then went into the bathroom with his pajamas in his hand. He came out after a minute or two wearing a sleeveless white undershirt and a pair of loose gray sweatpants. He dove for the bed as if he had nothing on, but not before Michelle enjoyed a pleasant peek at the layer of muscle on his arms and chest. He was wiry, very lean but not skinny, a lot more cut than she'd have given him credit for. Who could have guessed geeky Fred would be so easy on the eyes?

The mattress was a good one, barely moving as he lay down. He settled himself on his pillow, shyly keeping his back turned to her, so she turned hers to him as well. Nestling down to get comfortable, she closed her eyes against the glare of Jenny's reading lamp.

She'd promised Fred she wouldn't challenge his virtue. She had to pray she wouldn't wake up from one of her erotic dreams humping his leg or something. How embarrassing! Michelle bit her lip.

"Pleasant dreams," Fred murmured gently, setting her at ease. She nestled into her pillow.

"You too." It took a while to fall asleep in the unfamiliar bed, but mercifully she didn't have any dreams at all.

# Chapter Five

Michelle woke late the next morning, exceptionally well-rested. She swiftly became aware of Fred lying propped on one elbow, gazing at her, still wearing his pajamas. He didn't give the moment enough time to grow awkward.

"Good morning, sleepyhead. The other girls have gone out already. Want to head down for a coffee?" He rose without waiting for an answer. She watched as he negotiated the obstacle course to his suitcase, pulling out a pale blue button-down shirt, a T-shirt, some dark slacks, and black socks: his everyday work clothes.

She hardly noticed them, though. Fred was *built,* in a subtle way, his body lean but powerful, like a gazelle. He kept his fitness hidden under his geek uniform, but without the camouflage of a fussy shirt and tie, his shoulders looked broad in comparison to his trim, tapered waist. Her mouth went dry as she watched the play of muscles visible at the armholes of his tight white undershirt.

"Yeah, okay," she managed when he glanced back at her. She forced herself to climb out of bed. For fucksake, what was wrong with her if she was so pathetically horny even Fred turned her on?

Michelle wandered into the bathroom to spruce up a little, brushing out her hair. After a glance in the mirror, she patted on a touch of makeup. She felt good, well-rested. She pulled on her favorite Totoro T-shirt over a pair of shorts. A quick visual inspection confirmed she could get by for at least one more day without shaving her legs or borrowing a pair of Jenny's tights.

Adjusting the hem of her T-shirt, she emerged to step into her sandals. Fred looked alarmingly dull. His one concession to the convention's informality was the absence of a necktie. He put his wallet in

29

his pocket, beaming at her through thick glasses.

"Patrick Stewart's doing a panel this afternoon. Do you want to take in a thing or two this morning, then go stake out his line with me?"

"Sounds like a plan."

They bought coffee, then wandered through a few random events, pausing to hear half a concert on the Hyatt concourse before shuffling out to stand in line on Peachtree. Fred fetched them hotdogs from a vendor's cart while she held their place in line. They ate sitting on a set of concrete steps in the sun, laughing and chattering. He sunburned a little, the skin on the bridge of his nose turning pink, before they were let inside.

"I need a shower," he admitted after the panel. "I got pretty hot waiting in line."

"You should wear some jeans and a T-shirt for once," she teased him. "You'd feel cooler. I can't smell you, so you're all right for now." In fact, she was lying. He smelled of aftershave: a little musky, a little spicy, not bad, distinctly male.

"Are you having a good time?"

"Yeah," she admitted, suddenly feeling a little shy. "Let's go check out the Crüxshadows show on the concourse. I bet Jenny will be there."

They rode the escalators down. Sure enough, she spied Jenny in the audience, gyrating frantically amidst a sea of black. Elise leaned against one of the pillars some distance away, waiting for her. She made a wry face as they approached.

"They sound a lot better here than they do when you're doing the circuit of the band tables with all the sound systems going hell hallelujah," Elise conceded. "But they aren't my genre."

"Who's up next?"

"Some little Celtic band." Elise stuck out her tongue. Two guys were already unpacking their gear over to the side of the stage. Michelle couldn't figure out what their instruments were supposed to be, but they had on kilts.

"Fred, you should buy a kilt," Elise needled him. "There's a booth in the dealers' room."

"I'm not showing off my knobby knees in a kilt," he protested.

Jenny's arrival interrupted Elise before she could goad him further. Jenny streamed with sweat, gasping for breath. "Good set," she said. "Love it, love it, love it." She bounced in place, manic with energy, as if she could still hear the driving beat even though the band was swiftly clearing their gear off the stage.

The next band started before Crüxshadows finished packing. Michelle winced. "Oh god, this guy can't sing. Let's get out of here."

They took off, escaping onto Peachtree. They strolled down the road to a busy cafe, where they managed to score an upstairs booth. Fred sat next to Michelle, listening to the girls chatter without talking much. He kept dipping his french fries in a mix of mustard and ketchup, making Elise wrinkle her nose. Michelle poached a fry to go with her chef's salad. He grinned at her, turning his plate so she could take more if she wanted.

"There's a *Hobbit* actor panel in the Marriott in an hour with some dwarves or orcs or something. Whatever. Then we could go buy drinks."

"I want to take more pictures of hot guys," Jenny insisted. "The Hyatt's the best place."

"Not since they banned photography on the ballroom floor." Elise scowled.

"Then we'll go up to the next level."

"I'll need to change," Michelle made a face at her T-shirt. "Let's go back to the room."

They did, towing Fred with them. Again he ignored Jenny as she peeled off her clothes, wandering around in her underwear while she chose a costume to put on. She selected a black leotard, tutu, tights, and a pair of strappy platform boots whose thick soles raised the top of her head nearly to the level of his chin.

"Don't break an ankle in those," Fred advised her when she was decent again. "Shouldn't you put a light on top of your head to alert low-flying air traffic?"

She stuck her tongue out at him as she calmly started weaving rubber snakes into her ponytails.

Michelle showered quickly, then hastily changed into a white silk top paired with a black leather bolero, matching miniskirt, and high heeled boots. She managed to dress while Fred was still taking a shower of his own. He came out wearing yet another button-down and slacks, making her laugh with fond exasperation. "Is that all you brought to wear? Maybe we *should* take you to try on a kilt."

"I'll model one for you, if you like." He gave her a merry sidelong glance. "Afterward, I think you'll be silent on the topic forever more."

Michelle didn't believe his modest claim after seeing him in his undershirt, but she kept her opinion to herself. They managed to reach the dwarf panel shortly after it started, sitting down near the back. Fred vanished for a few minutes, then re-appeared in triumph, carefully balancing a little cardboard tray full of plastic cups.

"Orange juice?"

"Vodka screwdrivers." He distributed them to the ladies, keeping one for himself. Onstage, the men started singing a song about dragons and gold. Their low baritone voices sent a pleasant shiver down Michelle's spine. She tasted her drink, approving of Fred's choice as the slow, growing warmth of the alcohol hit her belly.

"Fred, I'm starting to think you know how to do this convention right after all," she murmured. A small smile curved the corners of his mouth, a spark passing between them.

She turned her attention to the stage, sipping from her cup. Fred settled in at her side, taking a drink from his own. She could see his smile from the corner of her eye, making her heart flutter a little.

After the panel let out, they wound up lurking in the lobby at the Hyatt, where Michelle was put in charge of taking all the pictures Jenny and Elise wanted. Fred didn't seem to mind lingering at her elbow, helping her keep her things together, even carrying her purse for a while.

"My fucking phone is full of pictures," Jenny wailed at last, her words a little slurred. "I need to go back to the room to dump them on my laptop."

"That's because you insisted on all the video of you with the guys dressed as dragon trainers."

"The tall one was hot!"

Michelle giggled, swaying a little unsteadily. "You said that about the old man with a walker, too. You're drunk."

"Like you're not?"

They staggered back toward the Marriott together, letting Fred break the path. Michelle was relieved to escape from the press of the crowd. The quiet of the room felt sane and orderly by comparison, despite the abandoned clothing scattered everywhere.

She stole a sidelong glance at Fred in spite of herself. Either she was drunk off her ass, or...no. She'd started seeing him differently before she ever started drinking. She was attracted to Fred. She could tell he felt the same way about her, too. It was a thing, and it was happening.

Elise flopped into the desk chair. "Let's do my phone when yours finishes."

"I'm bored. We should play truth or dare." Jenny crunched on the last bit of ice out of her glass.

"Ohhhh yes. We have a man with us. Or we've got Fred, anyway. He'll have to do." Elise tittered. "What do you say, Shelly?"

It was one of those ideas you regret in the morning, but the vodka in Michelle's glass tasted deceptively smooth, and she'd drunk plenty. That was Fred's fault. He'd stood at her elbow with a fresh drink all evening. God only knew how much he'd spent at the cash bar back in the Hyatt. Maybe after they ditched him last night, he thought he had to buy her off to persuade her to spend time with him.

She sat down on the bed, her head spinning, trying not to spill her last swallow. Fred was already on the phone with room service, ordering two bottles of top-shelf vodka and a gallon of orange juice. Apparently he believed intoxication shouldn't come cheap.

"Truth or dare is a children's game," she muttered.

"That's right. Grown-ups don't waste time on the truth part," Elise crowed in triumph. "We could play dare."

"Quadruple dirty dare," Jenny refused to be outdone.

Michelle glared at Jenny woozily, watching the light glint off the rhinestone in her labret, which sparkled under the bow of her black lipstick. "That's way too much bling for a goth. If you want to fit in with the emo set, you need to wear a spike."

"Get you a masochistic emo sub. Spike him right in the balls when you go down on him," Elise agreed, making Fred wince.

Michelle listened to the sliding scrape of Fred pushing back the curtains so they could see the cityscape glittering through the glass.

"I think you're a faker," Michelle sat up, swaying. She jabbed an accusing finger vaguely in his direction. "You come on all geeky and wide-eyed, but you're an operator if I ever saw one. Fancy room, gorgeous view, lots of booze... You talk me into sleeping in your bed, then keep a full drink in my hand all night. Now you have three women trying to convince you to play quadruple dirty dare with no truth. You must think you're gonna get laid or something." Her mouth was running away with her, but she couldn't seem to stop talking.

"Don't look at me. I wanted to go to the *Rocky Horror* show. Elise and Jenny were the ones who wanted to regroup in the room." He still looked dorky, awkward like always, but she could tell he wasn't really uncomfortable. She would've expected him to be sweating bullets at the idea of quadruple dirty dare, but he seemed very calm. She glared at him suspiciously. How much had he drunk? Had he been faking with a plain glass of juice?

"The *Rocky Horror* show doesn't start till, like, four or five AM. They say it starts at midnight, but then they fuck around doing other stuff for hours before they run the movie." Elise drained her cup, then tossed it toward the trash can. She missed by half a mile, spraying ice all over the carpet. "Sorry about your security deposit, Fred."

"Coming out of your share of the credit card if they ding us, Elise." He still didn't seem upset. "I'm paying for the booze."

Abrupt banging at the door announced the impossible, or at least the very unlikely: room service had already arrived to deliver the drinks. Michelle decided VIP floor mojo was made of awesome. Fred tipped the waiter while Elise picked up the spilled ice to toss into the sink, wavering unsteadily as she stooped.

"Let's *start*," Elise whined. "Jenny, give us a dare."

"I think Fred needs some education." Jenny wandered over to the window, pressing up against the glass and gazing down at the interstate. Apparently, her fear of heights limited itself to elevators. "He's too dull for this convention. Look at the man. He still has on his work clothes, for fucksake. He practically screams 'pocket protector.'"

"We should give him a makeover."

Fred laughed, pouring himself a generous measure of vodka. He topped up his glass with juice. "That sounds appalling."

It didn't, Michelle thought, trying to picture him in something other than his normal dork suit. He wore a button-down oxford with a fussy white tee-shirt underneath, and big thick glasses. They looked like they ought to be taped up like in *Revenge of the Nerds*. As usual, he'd slicked his hair back with way too much styling gel. She wondered what he'd look like in jeans and a dark blue Henley, with his hair styled by someone who didn't hate the very idea of volume.

Maybe he should go punk and wear a bit of black eyeliner to make his eyes pop. He might actually have very nice eyes. Definitely, he needed to lose the glasses. She'd like to put him in big clunky boots and a black kilt, with thick wool socks. Add a white T-shirt, then spike his hair up like a punk. He'd look damned fine.

Her world spun a little as she studied him. She realized he was holding out another cocktail for her.

"You're trying to get me drunk," she accused. His eyes widened with innocence. She knew the truth, though. She hadn't forgotten telling him she might sleep with him if he got her drunk enough. The knowledge combined with the booze to give her a delicious tingle. She was buzzing, flying high, just drunk enough to think she could accomplish anything without edging over the peak and dropping into depression.

Dorky little Fred wanted to sleep with her. The thought warmed her belly, making her feel sexy.

"Why would I need you to drink more alcohol? You're drunk already." He sounded reasonable. She accepted the glass, determined to sip slowly. A little more wouldn't make any difference, not if she paced herself.

Satisfied, he turned from her, setting his hands on his hips. "If we're going to play dare, I have one ready. I think Jenny and Elise should make out."

"You dog!" Elise poured herself two fingers of vodka. She didn't fuck around with any orange juice. Jenny barked a laugh at the window, still pressed up against the glass as if she wanted to levitate right out into the sky.

"Dorks are always the biggest perverts." She didn't sound too upset. "We'll kiss if you and Shelly agree to go to second base."

The very idea made Michelle laugh at the ceiling, trying to picture herself at second base with Fred. A day ago, she would have snorted at the idea. Now it was more intriguing than alarming. As she remembered the glimpses of Fred in his pajamas, a soft glow ignited in the pit of her belly.

"Don't stab me in the balls with that thing in your lip," Elise warned Jenny. "No photography, Shelly."

"Hot girl-on-girl action," Michelle imagined the captioned photo on a social media website. "What happens at DragonCon stays at DragonCon!"

"Does it, now." Fred sat down next to her on the bed, his knee nudging at her thigh.

"I don't know. Does it?" She was going to let Fred touch her breast. Michelle giggled nonsensically up at the ceiling for a second time, her stomach soaring with giddy anticipation. Maybe Elise was right. Maybe he did need an education. She'd like to shock him into showing some more of what he was hiding. Maybe he was as randy for her as she was starting to feel for him. Yeah.

A wet sound revealed her friends were kissing, but she paid no attention. Neither did Fred. He still gazed down at her, a smile crinkling the tender skin around his eyes. He obviously didn't give a damn about Jenny and Elise and their half-assed, bi-curious, drunken tonsil hockey.

"Bastard," she announced without anger. She struggled upright, balancing unsteadily on her high heels. If she was going to make a pass at Fred under cover of the game, she was going to make it spectacular.

"Lie down on your back," she ordered. His eyes flared, but he obeyed without hesitation.

"You're supposed to wait till we can watch," Elise broke the lip-lock to complain, then yelped when Jenny bit her to reclaim her attention.

Michelle shrugged out of her bolero, then reached for the hem of her blouse. She snagged it with both hands, skimming it off in one quick motion, leaving only her bra to cover her top half. Fred's eyes went wide behind the horrible glasses. His adam's apple bobbed as he swallowed hard. Excellent.

She shook out her hair and advanced on him, predatory. She put one knee up, crawling onto the mattress. She still had on her little leather mini and panties, but the skirt didn't cover much, not from this angle. He stared at her, eyes roving hungrily. In spite of his passivity, his expression still didn't reveal the kind of panic she'd expected.

"Our little Fred is a faker," she crooned. She flung her knee over him and sat down right where it would do him the most good, carefully judging her position so she nestled snug and tight over the ridge of his cock.

He swallowed again, his hands lying half-open on the pillow, resting on either side of his face. He was warm, hot even, much more so than she'd expected. Lust fairly baked off him. She felt his cock swell under her, the sensation delicious even through the fabric of his slacks. She shifted again to savor the feeling, appreciating his size—quite substantial, still growing. She ought to have guessed he was hiding a nice one.

She reached for his glasses, delicately grasping the frames, then lifted them off his face, setting them aside on the pillow. They'd pinched the bridge of his nose, leaving red marks on either side, but she barely noticed. Without the barrier, his eyes were stunning: steely ice blue, the irises surrounded by a thin rim of gold, the hint of color echoed by another golden ring at the center around the pupil. Flecks of gold scattered at random through his irises. When they caught the slant of light from the bathroom, his eyes turned tawny green for a moment, like a cat's, before he shifted slightly and the pale blue reclaimed them.

She studied him as he lay passive, unmoving, letting her have her way. His brows were heavy but neatly trimmed, his nose perfectly straight. His narrow lips stretched in a small smile, his teeth even, very white. She set her fingertip into the cleft of his chin, studying his mouth for a long moment, hypnotized. She had the oddest feeling she'd never seen him before, as if she had climbed onto a total stranger, someone devastatingly handsome, not her dorky friend Fred at all.

His gaze caught hers again; this time, it held her. His eyes burned, the fierce gold rims like simmering flames around the delicate blue, the same hue as pale water bubbling in volcanic pools. She sank deeper, drowning, sensing his lust building like magma welling toward the surface, threatening to explode into devastation. She realized she had forgotten to breathe when her chest heaved, forcing her to inhale.

His hands stirred at last, sliding down to rest on her thighs, then stilled, so hot against her skin she wondered vaguely if they would leave the prints of his palms branded into the flesh when he removed them. He waited patiently. The corner of his narrow little mouth curved upward in the slightest smile.

Michelle reached for herself with trembling hands. She dipped into her bra, pushing down the strap to lift out her breast. His eyes moved then, breaking the stare before his gaze overwhelmed her. They fixed on her nipple.

She leaned forward, guiding her breast toward him, offering it cradled in her left hand. His lips opened, welcoming her. His cock pulsed beneath her, hot and swollen; he exhaled softly, almost a moan.

He wet his lips, then softly suckled her in.

Michelle could not stop the wail escaping her throat; the touch of his mouth sizzled on her like a bolt of lightning. Pleasure exploded, going supernova at the core of her. She shuddered, coming helplessly without warm-up or warning as her body betrayed her, wracked with fierce pulses of shattering ecstasy. She felt shocked and embarrassed, horribly exposed. His lips tugged at her: soft, wet, steaming hot, wicked.

After a long moment, he finally withdrew his mouth, leaving her nipple wet, puckering taut at the cool rush of air. He laid his head back down on the pillow. His fiery gaze caught her once more, holding her locked. He lifted his hips once, pushing up at her center. The tease sent renewed shocks of pleasure quivering through her overloaded nervous system.

She realized Elise and Jenny had stopped what they were doing to fix startled stares on them; she could almost hear her frantic cries still echoing in the too-silent room.

"The *fuck* was in that vodka?" She muttered, scrambling off Fred hastily, clumsy in her embarrassment. She managed to tuck her breast back into its cup, scrabbling with the bra-strap until it rested over her shoulder. The six staring eyes were simply too much to endure. She stumbled out of the room without putting on her shirt, staggering up against the waist-high wall shielding the walkway from the open atrium.

She clung to the cold iron bars lining the walkway, her head spinning. An ocean of vague sound echoed hollowly in the empty space: music, voices, and the song of the building itself as the air flowed through the atrium.

"Michelle." Fred spoke behind her, gentle. She turned reluctantly, embarrassed, but he had shielded his devastating eyes behind his glasses again. They were their normal mild selves now, distorted a little by his thick lenses. He held a peace offering in one hand: her blouse, which she'd forgotten in her panic. "You're drunk. Don't fall." His arm slid around her shoulders and he guided her away from the edge, then helped her put on her blouse. His hands felt like any other hands. They were warm, but nowhere near hot enough to burn. She must be a lot drunker than she'd thought. Fucking vodka.

"I'm dizzy," she managed, trying not to cling to him, but mostly failing.

"Elise and Jenny are going down to dance. Do you want to?" Her friends were emerging from the room, gazing at her with eager curiosity.

"No." Suddenly she wanted to sleep; she needed it worse than anything ever. "Go ahead without me." She clung to Fred until the girls cleared the door. After a doubtful look, they set off down the aisle toward the elevator.

"Did you drug me?" She leaned on Fred as he guided her in through the door. "Are you going to fuck me after I pass out?"

"No. You've just had too much to drink. You'll be fine. I won't touch you, I promise." He seated her on the edge of the bed, then helped her out of her shoes. "Unfasten your bra. Now slip it out from under your shirt. Good." He tossed the garment away. Lifting her legs onto the bed, he nestled her under the covers before turning her on her side.

The last thing Michelle felt before sleep dragged her under was the press of Fred's lips against her forehead, burning hot.

Then dreams claimed her.

# Chapter Six

Michelle awoke with a pounding head, still dressed. She even had on her panties. The leather skirt had shifted a little, binding her. Adjusting it to ease the tension, she turned onto her back. For a long moment, she blinked woozily up at the textured ceiling, trying to orient herself. She'd spent the night with Fred fucking her up against the window. No. That was a dream.

Fred had put her to bed, kissed her very chastely, and turned out the light. There he was on the other side of the bed, fast asleep. Innocent as a lamb, he still wore his undershirt, his trousers, even his socks. The unshaded window filled the room with soft illumination from an overcast sky. The other bed still lay empty, neatly made. The window glass was clean; the waxing light revealed no smudges except the ones Jenny had left when she leaned against the glass to look out.

Michelle's dreams seemed more vivid in this moment than the pale reality of anything else she'd ever done.

In her dreams, Fred had led her into the room after Jenny and Elise went away, but she hadn't been drunk. Instead of putting her to bed, he'd kissed her. When she'd guided his shy hand between her thighs, he'd found his confidence. He'd pushed her up hard against the window with his narrow, strong body. The burning heat of Fred's hands on her waist had been a stark contrast to the chill of the plexiglas. He'd yanked her clothes off her, then fucked her long and hard from behind. Right there, in front of the glass so the whole city could see if they bothered to look, his hot hands branding her waist, his cock setting her alight from inside.

It had definitely been Fred in the dream; her memory was very distinct on that point. He'd had her several times, with all the unnatural endurance of dreaming. He'd taken her standing up tight against the window with her breasts and belly pressed to its cool surface while his hot cock rammed into her, lifting her onto her tiptoes with the force of his strength.

When they were done, she'd gone to her knees on the carpet, sucking the taste of herself right off him, swallowing him down eagerly when he came. Afterward, he hadn't needed to rest. He'd picked her up and laid her out over the fussy little work-desk on her back. She'd locked her ankles behind his waist, clinging desperately to the edges while he fucked her so hard the desk groaned nearly as loudly as she did. Then she'd spent a blissful eternity with her legs resting loosely over his shoulders while he buried his face between her thighs. He'd made her come on his tongue so many times she'd nearly gone mad with pleasure, shrieking and pleading through a supernova of white-hot sensation.

They'd made love in the shower, too, their bodies steaming wet, slippery with sweet-smelling shampoo. He'd held her up with her back against the wall, impaled, clinging to his neck, her legs clutched behind his thighs. His cock had been so thick she'd nearly thought he would split her in two.

"Hair of the dog that bit you?" Fred sat up, looking abominably well-rested and alert. He opened the mini-fridge, reaching for their jug of orange juice. "You'll feel better afterward."

Damn, but she was glad he couldn't read her mind. Unfortunately, her mouth had other ideas.

"Did you f-fuck me?" The words came out awkward, with a hint of stutter. She honestly didn't know what answer she needed to hear.

"I didn't touch you." He gazed at her sadly, a little hurt, reproachful. "I promised not to." He stepped forward, helping her sit up, putting a glass in her hand.

She swallowed a mouthful, tentative, then touched her forehead, where the sensation of his lips lingered. "I got too drunk."

"My fault. I'm sorry." He sounded sincerely contrite. "I hope you'll forgive me."

"Where are Jenny and Elise?"

"Still off dancing, presumably." He shrugged. "I don't much care about them, I'm afraid." His accent, usually faint, sounded stronger than before, his voice throaty and melodic.

"You should fuck me now."

He stared at her, startled at last. Then he laughed, a sound of pure delight she had never heard him make before. His head tipped back as the laughter poured from him. She sat very still, not quite sure whether to be flattered or offended.

"I'm afraid that's not a good idea." He regained control of himself at last, stepping forward. His fingertips brushed her cheek, feather-light. "Workplace romances, you know."

"We could have a convention romance." The drink made her feel better, restoring an acceptable equilibrium between her head and her stomach. She reached out to hook her fingertips into the waistband of his trousers, trying to tug him forward.

She couldn't move him; he was stronger than he looked. "I don't have a condom."

"I don't care."

"Jenny and Elise could come back any minute."

"Fasten the deadbolt. We'll ignore the knocking." She reached for his hand, pressing his palm flat against her breast.

"I don't think I could leave you afterward," he said softly. He gently pried her fingers loose from his wrist. He lifted her hand to kiss the knuckles, his lips very warm.

She dithered a little, blushing, then looked away. "So, don't leave. We'll be an item. You can fuck me every day of the week and twice on Sundays. Just fuck me."

"I'm very sorry." He squeezed her fingers lightly, compassionate. "But I can't." He withdrew into the bathroom, leaving her blinking with dismay, her cheeks hot with humiliation. The door latched behind him with a soft snap. After a minute or two, the shower started.

Jenny and Elise staggered in while she was still paralyzed with humiliation. They looked absolutely wasted, their makeup smeared, their faces lined with fatigue.

"What happened?" Elise's eyes lit up as she spied Michelle. "Did little Fred get some? Did you show him a thing or two? Tell all!"

Michelle shook her head. "Nothing happened." The words tasted heavy, disappointment bitter in her heart.

"We stayed out all night just so you two could fall asleep?"

"You stayed out all night dancing, drinking, and having a blast." Michelle refused to be baited. She was already upset enough. "I'm going out for breakfast. You two should get some sleep so we can dance all night tonight." The hell if she'd hang around mooning over some pathetic tech nerd who had the nerve to turn her down. She snatched her bra and a pair of jeans.

Michelle managed to escape the room before Fred could emerge from the shower. Relieved, she relaxed as she caught the elevator down to find a cappuccino. The convention was so large it might as well be a city all its own. She could vanish into the crowd, where she wouldn't have to see Fred again until she was ready to deal with him.

# Chapter Seven

Twin shadows of disappointment and embarrassment stretched gloom across Michelle's morning. Deciding she wasn't interested in any of the scheduled panels, she toured the walk of fame, then wandered through the dealers' hall without enjoying herself.

Her feet hurt in her boots by the time she made her way to Peachtree Center to eat a chicken sandwich. She muscled in next to a group of post-adolescent fanboys with a spare seat at their table. They tried to flirt at first, but she answered shortly, then ignored them as much as possible, focusing on her lemonade.

She was nearly finished when a hand appeared in front of her, holding a brownie on a paper plate. Fred had found her.

"You left before I could explain." He looked miserable.

"Forget it." She didn't accept the peace offering, picking up her cup instead. "You need a table? I'm almost done here."

"You know, if you were a natural bitch like Elise, I wouldn't bother apologizing. But you're not." He got down on one knee at her side, grave and elegant. "Pardon me, if you please, Michelle? I was quite rude. I didn't expect you to be interested, or I'd have been better prepared. I'm sorry. I should have responded more politely."

"Get up. People will think you're proposing. For heaven's sake. I accept your apology. Now stand up!" She managed to tug him to his feet, terribly flustered. "I've been turned down before; I can deal. Besides, you're right. Workplace romances are a dreadful idea. Now let's never mention last night again. Pretty please?"

"I'm not sure I can promise that." He gazed at her, his eyes troubled, a shaft of sun from the skylight catching their crystal blue. They filled with radiance, threatening to hypnotize her again in spite of the glasses.

"You're so damned...awkward." Michelle rubbed her palm over her face. The fanboys stood up to leave, jostling past Fred and Michelle in the cramped quarters. When they had gone, Fred sat down opposite her, folding his hands. He laced his long fingers, pulling nervously at his knuckles until he realized what he was doing. He forced his hands to be still, placing them flat on the table.

Michelle sighed. "If you won't agree not to mention it, then at least agree not to bring it up to anyone but me. Can I have that much?" She tried to smile, but her lips trembled a little.

"Of course. I don't kiss and tell." He bowed his head, smiling a little. The light still shone on his face, making faint highlights of auburn glow in his dark hair in spite of the gel. She felt her throat go dry. She knew a lot more now about the good looks he was hiding, and she couldn't forget either the fiery pleasure of his mouth on her breast or the devastating dreams afterward.

"Why don't you stop wearing those damned glasses, Fred? Wear contacts or choose better frames. Do something else with your hair. Buy some flattering clothes. You could be stunning with just a little work."

"Do you really think I should?"

Michelle didn't answer, but actually no. She'd rather keep Fred as her own little secret. She could imagine how Elise would make an ass of herself trying to bed him. God forbid! Michelle looked away, not quite knowing what to say.

"I cultivate this look because I don't like having to turn anyone down. I hate hurting their feelings." Something raw and tight in his voice drew her gaze back to him.

"Are you asexual, or gay or something?" He had to be. God damn it all. "God, Fred, all you had to do was say so."

"Asexual? That might be one way to look at it." Fred scrubbed his hand through his hair, disarranging the carefully-combed strands. "I'm not able to take a lover for reasons I'd rather not discuss at this time."

Erectile dysfunction, catastrophic groin injury? But she'd felt him respond to her. Religious vows? A dead wife? A survivor's guilt complex? Maybe he was sick. Did he have AIDS or something? Michelle unwrapped the brownie, breaking off a corner. The chocolate tasted rich and bitter, still a little warm in the center, with bits of caramel and nuts. "At least it's not me."

"No." His warm fingers covered hers, very light, sending a spark shooting through her. "Not at all. If I could make an exception, believe me, I would do it for you."

She blushed, and somehow everything was all right again. Fred regarded her steadily, his expression soft. His fingers stroked hers, a little wistful.

"Friends?" She smiled shyly. He nodded.

"Friends." He squeezed her fingers. A slow smile stretched his lips. "I'm glad I caught up with you, Michelle. I've been worried. But I'm afraid I have to go. I'm speaking at a panel this afternoon."

"Hang on." She scratched around in her purse, tearing a strip off a deposit ticket. She scribbled her number on it. "Here, in case you need to text me about the room or something."

"Thank you." He tucked the scrap of paper into his wallet with care, then departed. Her heart felt lighter, the shadow of gloom dispersing as she finished her brownie.

# Chapter Eight

Michelle enjoyed her afternoon much more than the morning. She reconnected with Elise and Jenny after they finally woke up around four.

"Let's go to one of the Brazilian steakhouses for dinner. I want to escape from this madhouse for a while," Elise grunted. "Then we'll come back to dress up for Jenny's Voltaire concert. There's a rave afterward; we'll dance all night like you said."

Michelle agreed, privately vowing to turn in before three if she could sneak away. At twenty-eight, she was getting too old to enjoy all-night dance parties the way she once had. She wondered what Fred was up to, but couldn't bring herself to mention him. She didn't need Elise figuring out she had a crush. He was right: the woman could be a bitch. If she found out, Elise would never stop bringing up Michelle's misplaced feelings at embarrassing moments.

They went off to dinner. It cost more than Michelle could afford even though the small servings of various meats tasted so savory and tender they melted in her mouth. Sitting with Jenny and Elise, listening to them planning their night at the dance, felt oddly dissatisfied without Fred by her side, balancing their cattiness with his quiet humor.

Fred was nowhere to be found when they went up to the room to dress. Michelle frowned with frustration, but at least she didn't have to hide in the bathroom to dress up. She put on goth makeup, borrowing one of Jenny's black wigs to go with a skin-tight sparkling minidress, high-heeled boots, and tights. They left for the concert together, pausing frequently as they threaded their way through the hotels to let people take their picture.

Voltaire entertained with wit and talent, a fine comical singer with a handful of celebrity guests. After it was over, though, Michelle was glad to let Jenny fight the crowd alone as she tried to score face time with him. She drifted to the edge of the seething crowd, watching the audience mill about, waving luminous wristbands or glow-light necklaces or fake lightsabers of every imaginable color.

A familiar man caught her eye: the man with the cobra's hood tattoo leaned against the wall only a few yards away. He wore black jeans and biker boots, but no shirt, still showing off his tattoo, which gleamed as if it had been oiled. He didn't move to leave as Voltaire's groupies filed out and ravers poured in.

He smiled at Michelle, familiar, a little insolent. She flushed, caught staring for the second time in a weekend. His eyes remained fixed on her face as he advanced toward her, his smile widening.

She felt decidedly odd under his slit-eyed stare, as if she were a mouse too hypnotized, too paralyzed to flee the predator stalking closer to pounce and feed.

"Hello." His voice was flavored with a thick Hindi accent, deep and resonant, a little sibilant. "I am Saakaar."

"Michelle." She gave him a polite, nervous smile, shifting back slightly on one heel to reclaim a little space. She wondered suddenly whether Jenny would think he was a super. Michelle was almost sure of it. Would Fred agree?

"You like my tattoo, yes?"

"It's very beautifully done." She lifted her chin. "But your eyes are wrong. Thinking all venomous snakes have slitted pupils is a common mistake. Cobras' pupils are round."

"You are knowledgeable about snakes, which makes you unusual. Especially for an American woman. However, if I do not wear slitted pupils, ignorant folk think I have not a proper costume." Saakaar's English had an odd lilt and an exotic turn of phrase. She expected to see fangs spring forth from the top row of his even white teeth. She realized she was staring, transfixed, waiting for them to emerge. She wrenched her gaze back to his eyes, swallowing hard.

"I am sorry the contact lenses make you uneasy. I have seen this before." He turned aside slightly, looking toward the stage, where a DJ was testing the mic preparatory to starting his first set. "People cannot meet my eyes. Little children hide behind their mothers' skirts."

"Sorry." Michelle laughed a little, trying to regain her composure. He was just another guy in contact lenses, though he had a lot more ink than anyone else she'd ever met. "The effect is disconcerting."

"Yes. Will you forgive my eyes and dance with me?" He extended his hand. This time his smile was more charming than threatening, so Michelle accepted.

"I'd love to."

He led her out to the center of the floor, every motion confident. If Fred was built, this man was *ripped*. He must spend hours every day working out in the gym. Every muscle was distinctly defined, sliding gracefully in concert with the others. He moved like water, flowing from pose to pose with a rapid, sleek economy of motion that drew the admiration of everyone who saw him.

Soon a small space formed around them as people stopped their own dancing to watch. Michelle began enjoying herself immensely. Some part of her pride still stung from Fred's rejection, and she liked being the partner of a man who drew so much attention from the girls in the crowd.

"You are a good dancer." He flipped his dark curls off his forehead then stepped closer, heating up the dance, undulating against her. Michelle laughed, matching his motions, flattered by the compliment. The rhythm of the song changed, growing faster. She felt herself loosening up, sharing her partner's energy, freeing her hair and tossing it back to flow over her shoulders.

"Very beautiful, little Michelle." He pulled her against him so she could hear his voice in her ear over the music. His hands slid along her back and around her waist, molding her against him. "I thank you for the dance."

His mouth settled against her forehead as the song ended. She felt his lips burn there briefly. She stumbled at the sudden stop, then swayed dizzily, closing her eyes against the strobe lights flashing over the crowd. When she recovered, Saakaar had vanished. Abruptly, she clutched at her stomach, suddenly near vomiting. A new song began, the dancers surging into motion, closing in around her.

No one paid any attention to Michelle as she staggered, falling to her knees, lost among the press of wildly moving people. A heel came down savagely next to her fingers and she snatched her hand back against her chest. She was in serious danger of being trampled.

"Michelle? Michelle!" She recognized Fred's voice shouting her name over the music, frantic. His hands fell on her shoulders, tugging her up. He held her against him, dragging her out of the dizzying press of the crowd into the relatively bright, cool lobby.

"Michelle, what the hell happened in there? Holy fuck." His fingers touched her forehead to gauge her temperature, but they burned her. She jerked her head away, then moaned as cramps seized her stomach, swaying in spite of his support.

"Danced," she managed. "Got sick."

He stared at her, shaking his head, his face white. "I'm taking you back to the room."

Nobody paid them any attention as Fred half-carried Michelle back to the Marriott. She was just another over-indulger among many, leaning on her partner for help walking. Fred didn't speak, focused on getting them to their goal.

After the door shut behind them, he carefully settled her on the bed, pulling off her shoes and her wig. He fetched a packet of wipes from her bag to clean the heavy goth makeup from her face.

"Do you want your pajamas?" He finished cleaning her face, tossing the used towelettes in the trash.

Michelle's stomach hitched without warning. Desperate, she rolled to the edge of the bed. He moved like lightning, and the wastebasket appeared under her mouth before she could soil the carpet. She threw up, heaving painfully even after there was nothing left in her stomach.

"He couldn't have roofied me. I didn't drink anything." She moaned. "I got food poisoning, maybe."

"Maybe." Fred didn't sound like he believed her. He stroked her hair off her shoulders, lifting it out of her way.

When she was done, he peeled off her clothes, his expression tight with worry. He gently helped her into her pajamas, dressing her like a child.

"I'd take you to a hospital if I thought it would do any good." He fetched a damp washcloth and bathed her overheated face. "Can I fetch some medicine to soothe your stomach? I think some of the hotel shops are open all night."

"No." She didn't want him to leave. She groped for his hand, clutching his fingers. "Thanks for taking care of me."

"I should have stayed with you all evening. I thought..." He pinched his mouth shut, shaking his head once, savagely.

"I hope Elise and Jenny are okay. We all ate at the same place."

"I'm sure they're fine." Fred waved off her concern. "The guy you danced with did this to you."

"Snake."

"Yes." Fred's voice fell, grim. "I saw him leaving the ballroom as I went in."

"Need to sleep." Michelle couldn't hold her eyes open any longer; her stomach emptying itself had taken the last of her strength. "Don't leave me, Fred?"

"I won't." His hand squeezed hers lightly. She felt him settle protectively at her side as she slipped away.

# Chapter Nine

Snakes slithered after Michelle wherever she went, their scales scraping on the pavement, on the concrete steps to her apartment, on the tile in the building's empty lobby. She fled, stabbing frantically at the call button for the elevator, hoping she could shut them out of her home.

After she selected the number of her floor, the door closed the snakes out. She sagged, near sobbing with relief—but then serpents began to wriggle in through cracks in the elevator car. They even forced their way through the control panel, pushing out the numbered plastic floor buttons and flowing in through the holes in the wall. Others rippled in from the ceiling vent. She screamed as they converged on her, writhing their way up her legs, slithering around her throat and under her clothes. She screamed again, struggling frantically as a large python worked its way between her thighs to violate her, but the serpents wriggled their way into her mouth and nose. They choked her until she couldn't call for help or even breathe.

Hands seized her, ripping snakes from her face. She nearly collapsed with relief as she dragged in a gasp of breath. Fred.

He fought the snakes grimly, his eyes blazing, crushing them between his fingers and under his heels, ignoring their fangs when they scored his arms or fastened in his ankles. As soon as they were all dead, lying in a twitching heap on the floor, he pulled her tightly against him. He dragged her out of the elevator when the doors opened, half-carrying her to her apartment. He set her on her sofa, then laid his finger over her lips to quiet her, stroking her cheek until she calmed.

After a few minutes his mouth sought hers, his tongue urgent; he unbound her hair and buried his bloodied, bitten hands in it. She closed her eyes, glad he was touching her instead of the serpents, his tongue in her mouth, his fingers sliding inside her waistband. Reality warped, changing around her, but she couldn't keep track of what was happening. Confusion seized her. Fred's eyes turned dark, his face pinched with worry. She sensed a terrible sadness in the desperate way he kissed her.

"What's wrong?" she asked, pulling back a little, then nestled her cheek against his face, distressed by his expression. He petted her hair, soothing her gently.

"Do you trust me to take the nightmares away?" he asked. When she nodded, he drew her close, savoring her mouth softly, kissing her until she couldn't breathe, couldn't think. She welcomed him eagerly, loving every touch of his fingers and his mouth as much as she had loathed the scaly writhing press of the serpents attacking her.

She tried to speak, meaning to ask him what was happening, but by the time her mouth opened, she couldn't quite remember what she'd intended to say. She blinked, confused. Fred laid his palm over her lips lightly. "You're still dreaming, Michelle. Let me help you with the nightmares."

She nodded consent despite her confusion. Fred nuzzled against her throat, his free hand sliding over her body, stirring pleasure wherever it traveled.

Michelle sighed, forgetting the vague sense of unease that lingered. Fred kissed her earlobe, his hard cock pressing against her hip, then moved to cover her. His weight pressed her thighs apart and he slid inside her body.

She nipped lightly at his fingers as his hips stirred, moving him inside her in a slow, sweet glide, lust burning away her doubts, leaving her floating in ecstasy. Soon he filled her entire world and she lost herself in the joy of taking what he offered, giving everything she could in return.

# Chapter Ten

"Will you look at them?"

Michelle blinked awake at the sound of Elise's voice, her eyes feeling grainy, her body aching. She realized she was lying tangled with Fred, arranged as she had been in her dream. His arms cradled her and his face pressed against her throat. One of his warm hands rested lightly on her breast; his thigh lay tucked between hers. Both her arms wrapped tightly around him as if she feared he might try to pull away to escape.

Never mind they were both fully dressed. Elise smirked at Jenny, who covered a satisfied titter behind her fingers.

"I owe you twenty bucks." Jenny elbowed Elise. "I'll pay up after we sleep."

Fred tensed against Michelle subtly as he awoke. Like her, he lay unmoving until Jenny and Elise had gone to bed, then for a little while longer. Finally, Jenny's soft snoring revealed she, at least, had gone to sleep.

"Do you feel well enough to get up?" The murmured words vibrated against Michelle's collarbone. He detached himself carefully from her, trying not to make any noise.

"I think so." Michelle didn't feel sick to her stomach anymore, but resting hadn't done her much good. She felt cold wherever Fred's body pulled back from hers. All she really wanted was to close her eyes and sleep some more.

"Let's dress and go out, then. We need to talk." He disentangled himself, taking care not to pull her hair as he stood up. She blinked at him, abruptly realizing he was wearing jeans and a long-sleeved, pale gray T-shirt. Had he been wearing them when he came for her last night? She'd felt so sick she hadn't noticed. His hair was tousled, soft and loose around his face, a deep, rich brown without its usual handful of styling gel. He didn't bother to put on his glasses before he started hunting for his wallet.

He realized she was staring at him and gave her a wry look. "Come on. Clothes now, then coffee, then we talk." He scrubbed his fingers through his hair, reaching for his shoes. He glanced in the mirror to see her struggling to sit up on the bed as he pulled the loafers on over his socks. "Do you need me to help?"

Michelle didn't answer, groping for her own clothes. She jammed her feet into a pair of sandals, then brushed out her hair in the bathroom, grimacing at the red-eyed, worn face waiting in the mirror. God, this had turned into a weird fucking weekend.

When she stepped out of the bathroom, Fred stood waiting with the door held open. He shut it lightly behind them, sealing their friends inside, remaining silent as they walked toward the elevator. The perpetual hum of the hotel atrium sounded muted and strange, the noise more mechanical than human. She listened, half-mesmerized by the pulse of the building: a thousand air conditioning units, elevator motors, vacuum cleaners, and housekeeping carts mingled with a few echoing voices. She glanced over the balcony. A handful of early birds were already circulating far below, bright-eyed and bushy-tailed, purposeful.

For once the elevator came almost as swiftly as it was summoned, announcing its arrival with a cheerful ding. Fred slid his arm around Michelle's waist to steady her as they slid downward with stomach-lurching speed, not stopping on any extra floors as they descended.

They went to buy an iced coffee, then rode back up to the lounge on the tenth floor. The whole area lay empty, with a variety of abandoned fliers, used cups, and bottles littering the floor. A single lazy employee in a rumpled uniform slouched around, slowly picking up the detritus of the previous evening with a gripper clamp. Lethargic, he stuffed the junk piece by piece into a huge black plastic garbage bag. Fred led her away from the man, toward the back of the building. He tucked her away in a carpeted spiral staircase by the rear wall.

She perched on a step, gazing silently up at Fred. She sipped her coffee quietly, trying to reconcile this sober, devastatingly handsome man with the relatively unattractive but appealing geek she'd once thought she knew. He seemed as though a shade had been lifted, revealing a bright light hidden underneath. He looked stunning, even more gorgeous than she'd guessed he might, but he seemed absolutely unaware of the difference. He held his cup without drinking, pacing like a caged thing, his brows drawn down in a scowl.

Finally, he raised his gaze to her as she swallowed the last of her coffee. She tensed in response to the sternness of his expression.

"We have a serious problem, Michelle. It's all my fault." He ran his hand through his hair. For a second, she glimpsed the nerdy geek again, the shy, insecure man she'd been growing so fond of. "I need to explain some things I've done. I know you won't like them. Please hear me out before you go off the deep end."

"All right," she agreed slowly. She set her empty coffee cup aside for the cleaner to deal with, folding herself up with her chin on her knees. She laced her fingers together over her calves. "Is this about me asking you to have sex? Because I—"

"No. The problem is something else entirely." Fred shrugged helplessly. "Let me talk for a while, if you'd be so good." His accent thickened with his distress; in any other circumstances his voice would be soft with music, but now he just sounded guilty and miserable.

"All right," she encouraged him when he didn't continue right away.

"There's no simple or kind way to put this, Michelle." His white teeth savaged his lower lip. "I'm a super, an incubus. I have to absorb sexual energy regularly in order to survive." He held her gaze steadily, meeting her startled expression with apologetic resolve. "I've been entering your dreams for perhaps two months now, harvesting your emotions for sustenance. I take only enough to stay healthy without harming you."

"The dreams were from you?" Her voice broke in an indignant squeak. "All the fucking, the nightmares—?"

"Not the nightmares." Fred closed his eyes, his expression wracked with pain. "Never those. I didn't even know about them until you mentioned you'd done a sleep study. You looked more tired than you should. That worried me. The next time I touched your mind, I did a little looking around. I found the nightmares in your memory. Do you remember the vacant lot?"

Michelle rubbed her forehead, struggling to extract the foggy memory from her brain.

"I walked you home in the rain. We saw eyes. I knew then some other supernatural entity was visiting you. He was waiting in your mind. I warned him away, but I knew I'd better keep a close eye on you in case he came back."

It was too much to comprehend all at once; Michelle needed to focus on one thing at a time. "You were...feeding on me." She shuddered, wrapping her arms around herself even tighter. The iced coffee was suddenly too cold in her belly. Her stomach lurched again at the thought of the dreams.

"I was." Fred stared down at the intricately patterned carpeting.

"You were fucking me in my sleep."

"I wasn't. I was suggesting you dream I was. It's quite different." Fred's gaze pleaded with her, his clear blue eyes intense as a laser. "If I'd actually been fucking you, you'd probably be dead by now." His expression turned bleak. "That's why I couldn't accept your offer, Michelle. Having sex with an incubus involves an energy transfer that can grow too intense for the human to handle. I don't want to kill, so I avoid physical intimacy. Feeding off dreams instead of making love is like drinking water instead of single malt whiskey, but it keeps me alive. I believe my visits aren't entirely unpleasant for the lady involved. At least, I hope you didn't find them so."

He looked forlorn, pushing his sleeves up to his elbows. Some remote portion of her mind that wasn't occupied with stomach-churning panic noticed his hands with a detached, clinical interest. She hadn't ever paid much attention to them before, but they were beautiful, finely shaped, slim and strong.

"I won't argue with any complaints you have regarding the violation I committed when I fed on you without permission. Important though that is, there's something much more urgent we need to discuss right now: the other entity."

His sober words stopped Michelle short before she could spiral into hysterical accusations. They hit her like a splash of cold water.

"The snake." She knew suddenly, without doubt.

"Yes." He lifted his head, meeting her gaze unhappily. "Saakaar." He glanced toward the nearest bank of elevators. "I've asked some of my friends to meet with us this morning to help explain. They're coming now."

# Chapter Eleven

Three people approached, two men of about Fred's age, accompanying a much older woman with pure white hair. She shuffled slowly, leaning on a carved black walking stick. One man held his hand under her arm to guide and support her. The other walked a little way in front, nodding gravely at Fred as they drew near.

"Fredric." His accent sounded different than Fred's, thicker, possibly German.

"Karl." Fred inclined his head politely. "Michelle, Karl is a distant relation of mine, a cousin several times removed. This is Erik. They have brought the sibyl."

The old woman raised her eyes toward Fred. Michelle flinched before she could stop herself. The woman had no pupil or iris in her eyes, merely white sclera.

"Your past has finally returned to haunt you, Fredric." Michelle expected the wheezing rasp of an old crone, so the woman's low, silky voice came as a surprise. The sibyl turned her sightless gaze on Michelle. "Of course an innocent is involved. Another innocent." She stepped forward to lay her fingertips on Michelle's forehead, pursing her lips, her brow creasing in a frown. Michelle felt a pulse of heat flare at the touch. She gasped, flinching away to break the contact before it burned her.

"You have been marked," the sibyl spoke bluntly. "First by Fredric, then by Saakaar. First as a protection, then as prey."

Fred spat words in a language Michelle didn't know. It sounded like swearing.

"Can someone please tell me what the—what's happening?" Michelle abruptly reached the end of her rope; she had to bite back a curse of her own out of respect for the woman's age.

Fred sighed. "The sibyl has confirmed my fears, Michelle. Saakaar intends to make you the means of his vengeance on me."

Karl slouched against the inner post of the stairwell, smiling without humor. "Let us begin at the beginning, shall we? The human is still confused. Fredric, what have you told her?"

"Nowhere near enough." He scrubbed his hand over his face. "I've confessed my nature, and I explained she was also visited by another entity."

Michelle glowered at him. "Tell me what I need to know." Vengeance? This all sounded ludicrous, like the plot of a bad B movie.

"Saakaar is a naga, a powerful Hindu shapeshifter, a magician whose primary form is a cobra," Fred explained. "That isn't a tattoo on his shoulders; it's his own skin. Before I saw him leaving the rave, I couldn't be sure who else had interfered with you."

Fred sighed. "I hoped the other entity wouldn't be a problem. But I needed to observe your dreams to see if you had any more nightmares, so I arranged for us to share a room.

"You shine like a flame in the dark, Michelle; you draw attention without meaning to. At first I thought it was a coincidence when another supernatural being found you interesting. I could tell the being was cultivating your fear, but some entities have to absorb fear to survive. It yielded immediately when I intervened, so I didn't believe its interest was very serious."

He moved to sit on the floor, where he wrapped his arms around his knees. "When your friends dared me to touch you, they gave me the opportunity I wanted. I established an energy transfer through our intimate contact. I used it to leave a psychic trace on you, one any supernatural being would sense immediately. I made my mark more of a warning than a claim. Not 'this woman is mine' so much as 'this human has a powerful protector and friend; don't interfere with her.'"

He surged to his feet again, pacing aggressively until he reached the wall, then sagged to let his forehead rest against the concrete. "I should have known the matter wouldn't be so simple. If the other entity hadn't been deliberately hiding from me, I would have sensed it much earlier. But Saakaar was clever. He only sought you out when I left you alone to sleep. No wonder you needed medical help. You had no rest at all. He drained you whenever I didn't visit."

"Why are his actions your fault?" Michelle set her anger aside with an effort, trying to understand. "You said this was all your fault. I don't understand."

"It's my fault because the other entity is Saakaar." Fred rubbed the bridge of his nose miserably. He would no longer meet Michelle's eyes. "When I was still very young, I fed on a mortal woman who was of special interest to him. I was undisciplined, and I lusted for her." He squared his jaw. "She was incredibly beautiful, with long black hair—I have a weakness for beautiful hair. That's part of what drew me to you."

"Enough." The sibyl spoke, silencing Fred. "You mean well, Fredric, but you are burdened with guilt. You do not speak fairly on your own behalf. Leave us for a time."

He nodded once, defeated. He stepped away, his hands in his pockets. Erik went after him. Michelle watched unhappily as they walked to the windows together. Erik spoke to him so quietly she couldn't hear. Fred didn't answer. He slid gracelessly into an isolated armchair, burying his face in his hands.

At a look from the sibyl, Karl continued Fred's tale.

"Fredric went to the woman's bed one night as a corporeal man. He feasted on her pleasure until she died." Michelle shuddered, her hand flying to cover her mouth. Karl waited politely until she composed herself enough for him to continue. "She did not suffer in dying, but when Saakaar learned Fredric had taken her life in his hunger, he flew into a passion of fury. He loved the woman, and he made a public vow to have his vengeance.

"Among our kind, revenge is his right by tradition. Yet Fredric's indiscretion took place five hundred years ago. Until now, Saakaar made no move against him."

"Even I hoped he had forgotten," the sibyl confessed, her fingers tracing the carved patterns in the handle of her walking stick. "But he will have an eye for an eye."

"You mean he wants to kill me to avenge the death of the other girl." Michelle didn't feel real; this had to be another one of the nightmares. Surely her alarm would shatter the illusion any minute now. She would awaken drenched in sweat, grateful to find the horror wasn't real.

"Yes," Karl agreed. "Our idea of justice is a simple one, though such harsh measures are rarely practiced in the modern world. Such extreme forms of revenge have more consequences for us now than they once did. Yet, in spite of the consequences, I believe Saakaar means to destroy someone Fredric loves."

Michelle turned troubled eyes toward Fred. "But he doesn't love me. We hardly know each other. I'm his... food." The words made her shudder, bone-deep and uncontrollable, all the way up her spine.

"I assure you, he feels more than that." Karl's voice turned wry, a little bitter. "Fredric has entered your mind. He knows your mind and spirit intimately. Though some of us are fated to live as predators, supernatural beings love as deeply as humans. We often come to love our human prey more than our own kind, though your life spans are cruelly short."

"Fredric loves." The sibyl spoke in her low, breathy tones. Goosebumps rose on Michelle's arms. She rubbed them, unthinking, folding herself up tightly. Even after all this, a little flutter stirred in her belly. Her heart warmed at the knowledge in spite of her fear.

"Fredric underestimated Saakaar. The naga spent centuries biding his time." Karl remained where he was, unnaturally still. "He has been watching, waiting for Fredric to love a woman. When Fredric marked you for protection, that gave Saakaar proof of the deep bond he suspected. The naga knew the time had come to take his revenge. He sought you out and overcame the protective mark Fredric made with one of his own, a curse marking you as his to destroy.

"Saakaar is far stronger than Fredric, much older than anyone here except the sibyl. None of us knows the full extent of his magic."

He moved from his pose against the wall, then sat down at her feet, moving slowly. Perhaps he meant to give her time to shy away if she wanted. "Saakaar almost certainly means to kill you. Like a serpent, he is not an evil creature by nature, but his power renders him a significant threat to those who do not respect him properly."

Karl glanced aside as the sibyl shifted. "The sibyl would remind me to say Saakaar is aware the tradition he follows is not in keeping with human law. At this time, supernatural culture forbids one of us to take the life of a human. We could lose the fragile progress we have made toward making peace with our human cousins. All the advantages we have gained could be taken from us. We don't want to be reduced to a life of fear and hiding again, which would happen if we were declared a menace to humanity. We would be pursued to our deaths.

"Make no mistake, your race has the means to exterminate us all."

His manner shifted, ominous. Michelle shrank back from the sudden hostility in his face.

"Silence." The sibyl spoke again. "This human means harm to no one."

"Yes, sibyl." Karl bowed, reclaiming control of himself. He rose, returning to his place against the wall.

The sibyl laid her hand on Michelle's knee, her touch surprisingly light and dry, as if a puff of air could blow her away like dust. "You are angry. I can sense your fear, too. Yet in your heart, there is love for our young Fredric."

Michelle flushed, biting her lip. "I don't know."

"You know enough in your heart, but I will also tell you enough for your mind." She lifted her head, extending her hand towards Fred, as if her fingers tasted the air. Her voice fell into a singsong tone. "His given name is Fredric. Supernatural entities take no surname, though most attach one to their identities for convenience in today's world. He was called after his maternal grandfather, Friduric, who was born in the vicinity of Berlin in the second century after the birth of Christ.

"Fredric himself was born in what is now Wales some six hundred years ago. His father was an incubus and his mother was a cambion. That helped her survive their repeated mating. She gave birth to Fredric." She paused when Michelle eyed her, doubtful. "These thoughts are taken directly from his mind, child. Attend me."

"A cambion?"

"The female offspring of an incubus and a human being. Such things can happen, though they are rare." She blinked her sightless eyes. "Perhaps they will be less rare in the future, now our peoples are at peace. But this peace we now enjoy was a long time coming. Like the vampire, the incubus and the succubus were favored targets of Christian monks in Europe during the Dark Ages.

"They were hunted without mercy, and are a scarce breed now. This is the case even though most of the tales of incubus visitations throughout history have actually been attempts to disguise forbidden sexual encounters between humans, in the same way holy men blamed succubi for the frailty of their own flesh when they experienced nocturnal emissions. Wet dreams."

Her blind gaze reminded Michelle of an owl's; her empty eyes seemed wider than they should. "Most incubi choose to feed through dreams, as Fredric does. Rarely do they take a woman in corporeal form. Yet, humans used to blame them whenever a supposed maiden found herself embarrassed. How distressful for a family to admit a young woman's pregnancy came from sinful lusts or even rape, usually at the hand of a trusted uncle, a family friend, or even her priest, her spiritual confessor. Surely, some evil supernatural being must have been responsible instead. The family honor could remain intact if others believed the shamed woman had been visited unwilling by a demon in the dark of night, as she slept."

The sibyl's white eyes held Michelle transfixed; she drew a deep breath, unable to stop listening. "Though their crimes were exaggerated, such beings conveniently existed. The Christian mystics named them incubus, demon, minions of the devil. They sought them out and killed them to cover for humanity's sins."

Another voice spoke at her elbow, Michelle flinched, startled. Released from the sibyl's hypnotic stare, she looked up to find Fred's sad gaze waiting for her.

"I don't know what you believe, but those religious words are mostly meaningless when applied to supers. We don't automatically serve Satan or defy the Christian God. Those are labels applied by unsophisticated humans to explain things they didn't want to confront.

"All I know is I am a creature who can—who must—manipulate energy differently than humans. In spite of my species' long lifespan, I can be injured or killed. I have a spirit, just like humans do. I have a body as well. If God exists, I am one of His creations as much as any human. I can starve, hate, hurt, and love. I live, though you have no reason to be glad I exist."

"I can't take it all in." Michelle stood up to move away from them all, wandering slowly out into the open, where she tipped her head back, staring up through the shaft of the atrium, tracing the latticework of balconies as they stair-stepped toward the narrow top of the building. "I'm going to wake up on Thursday night before DragonCon. I'll be in my bed at home. I don't think I'll go to the convention this year after all."

"This isn't a dream." Fred followed cautiously, approaching her with slow, measured steps. "I'm afraid this nightmare is real. Saakaar would still be targeting you even if you never attended the convention." He hesitated without touching her, hovering at her shoulder.

"They say you love me. Is that the same way Jenny loves

cheeseburgers?" She was surprised at the bitterness in her voice. "Or like Elise loves ice cream?"

She sensed him step back, turning away. He walked toward the locked doors keeping random hotel guests from venturing onto the open balcony. "Like a connoisseur loves vintage wine or fine, aged whiskey. Like a Browncoat loves Joss Whedon." His voice turned wry and self-deprecating. She turned, finding him standing silhouetted against the morning light, his hands tucked into his pockets. "Like a geek loves a goddess. Like a man loves a woman."

"I don't know how I feel. I can't even be sure I know who you are." Michelle dug the nails of her right hand into the skin of her left arm, leaving deep pink grooves in the pale flesh. "I don't even know if I'll live long enough to find out." The threat sounded ridiculous, unreal...but she remembered the burning pain on her forehead all too clearly.

"I don't know how much I can protect you," Fred admitted. He gently pried her fingers free, stopping her from hurting herself. He pressed her hand between both of his own. "I was able to force Saakaar out of your dreams last night. That's a good sign. If I can find a way to stop him, Michelle, I swear I'll do whatever I may."

"I need some time alone to think." Michelle couldn't look at him. She couldn't bring herself to meet his earnest, worried gaze. "I trusted you, Fred, while you used me and hid the truth."

"I understand how you feel." Fred swallowed hard. "I'm sorry I wasn't honest with you, Michelle. I wish I could tell you to take all the time you need, but I'm not sure how long we have before Saakaar moves again."

"I want a few hours." Michelle shuddered at the thought of re-encountering the snakes from her dream. "Till dinner."

"If you won't let me come, will you at least take Erik?"

Michelle hesitated before nodding agreement.

"I'll wait for you in the room at dinnertime then." Fred looked aside, murmuring to Erik for a moment before returning his attention to Michelle. "He doesn't speak English, I'm afraid, but I guess you don't want anyone to talk to."

He was right; she didn't. Michelle accepted her silent companion reluctantly, turning away to head for the elevator, feeling terribly alone and vulnerable in spite of her guardian.

After the elevator spat them out, she wandered through the lobby out onto Peachtree Street, trying to ignore Erik's silent presence at her shoulder.

The man of her dreams was real after all...but was Fred a good dream or a nightmare in disguise?

The streets felt much friendlier by the light of day than they did at night, the sidewalks mostly empty. Sunday had dawned bright and sunny, the sultry heat in the air combining with plenty of fluffy cumulus clouds to promise afternoon thundershowers. The time must be something after eleven; church would let out soon.

She led Erik into a small, mostly deserted coffee shop a few blocks from the convention hotels. Michelle asked for a coffee with cream, venti. Erik managed to negotiate the ordering process by virtue of pointing at the menu, getting himself coffee and a cookie. They chose a table, sitting down behind their steaming cups.

Michelle pulled out her phone to check her email, methodically deleting the spam, trying not to think. The diversion didn't work. Memories paraded through her brain: dozens of dream scenes, as explicit and vivid as if she had actually lived them. She felt like a fog had lifted.

In possession of the truth at last, she could recognize Fred as the man in each one. Not her shy, geeky Fred, with his thick glasses, his pocketful of pens, and his ridiculous talent for knocking things over as soon as the conversation grew awkward so he could have an excuse to escape. This was another Fred; a beautiful sexy Fred who had deceived her. She didn't know yet which one was the truth of him.

*He had to eat to live.* She understood the necessity, in the same way she now understood why he'd refused to make love with her for real when she asked him to. *He believed I wouldn't agree to let him feed, if he asked permission.*

Would she have consented to let him visit her dreams? She thought of Fred's thick lenses and his awkwardness. She couldn't deny her dismay at the thought of being fed on like some kind of cattle. She wouldn't have understood how much her rejection would cost him. His secret revealed, Fred would have been forced to leave his job. She could picture him going in search of a new place to settle, trying to find another woman to ask in hopes she wouldn't reject him, leaving him to starve.

Michelle wiped furtively at her eyes, distressed by the notion of Fred wandering alone and hungry, rejected by woman after woman whose kindness and sympathy he desperately needed in order to live.

Could she reasonably expect him to ask permission from his partners under those circumstances? It would be unthinkable for a human to force a woman and take what he wanted for fun, but maybe it wasn't fair to judge Fred by human standards. He had to eat. By the rules of the supernatural community, he'd done what he must to keep himself alive without harming her. He'd always repaid his debt by ensuring she took pleasure in his visits.

If Fred had been granted the time to build their relationship naturally, he could have revealed his true nature to her when she was ready instead of being forced by Saakaar's interference. How would she have responded? She'd have been upset at first, certainly, but the dreams had been amazing. He'd always taken great pains to construct a fantasy she would like, giving ecstasy in exchange for sustenance. She liked his personality, too, at least as much as she'd been allowed to see. She'd always longed for him to be real.

He was nothing like she'd have expected a super to be. Legends and media images made supernatural beings out to be the ultimate in seductive menace, demonic entities to be mistrusted, fought, and destroyed. No wonder they hid whenever they could.

Michelle gazed at Erik, who sat sipping from his cup, gazing mildly out the window at the street. He seemed very human, as Fred always had. Patrons milled through the shop behind him, buying sandwiches and eating lunch. He chewed his chocolate chip cookie, smiling kindly at her.

These were people, not demons.

*You're forgetting the girl Fred killed.* The voice of good sense intruded, cold. She looked away, trying to recover her self-possession.

Yes, she was forgetting the danger, and she couldn't afford to. It would be difficult to have a satisfying romantic relationship with someone who could quite literally sex you to death. Michelle tittered a little in spite of herself, feeling hysterical. There were lots worse ways to go. The girl hadn't suffered, Karl claimed. Anyway, she'd survived two months of the dreams Fred sent, hadn't she? Crazy as it sounded, the two of them might have been able to make a relationship work somehow.

*Now you're forgetting Saakaar's curse.*

Regardless whether Michelle could trust Fred, she needed help getting out of this mess. She was going to have to rely on Fred and fight fire with fire. That was the bottom line.

The pragmatic cynicism of the thought oppressed her, making her heart ache. Deep down, part of her still believed Fred was the kind, considerate man he seemed. It might be seventeen different kinds of stupid, but the sibyl was right: she wanted to give Fred a chance to earn the love she'd already begun to feel.

Finally, Michelle stirred and reached for her cup. Her coffee had gone stone cold. She glanced at her watch. Her worries had occupied the entire afternoon. She drew a deep breath as she spread her hands on the scarred, greasy formica tabletop. Her body ached, stiff and sore from sitting still so long.

"We're going, Erik." She grabbed her purse, pausing half a block down to dart into a storefront to grab a carry-out pizza. The soft, puffy clouds of the morning had coalesced into a steely gray threat, massing tall and blotting out the sun. The air felt thick, like hot soup on her face. Thunder grumbled loudly, rattling the windows of the looming downtown skyscrapers.

They hustled along the sidewalk and arrived at the Marriott as the first cold drops of rain plopped down, painting dark spots the size of quarters on the sidewalk. Michelle ducked into the dark entry garage with relief, pressing ahead without waiting for her eyes to adjust to the dim light.

Erik's hand fell on her shoulder, stopping her. He stepped up protectively, glaring over her shoulder. She glanced at him, uncertain, then followed his gaze to a bench near the door. Saakaar sat at ease, leaning back against a cement column with his ankles crossed. He clasped the long, rough white cylinder of a hand-rolled cigarette between his forefingers and smirked at them, taking a deep drag off the cigarette. He blew a puff of smoke in their direction. Michelle could smell burning cloves.

Erik spoke, his tone urgent. Michelle didn't need an interpreter. She hustled through the door at his side, avoiding a clattering knot of stormtroopers. Her heart raced with fear, her stomach clenching. She glanced over her shoulder, but Saakaar didn't follow. Still, she longed for Fred's comforting presence at her side.

Her watch read five o'clock sharp, and the hotel lobby seethed with people. They wasted several minutes trying to catch an elevator with enough vacant space to let them ride up together. She fidgeted, sweating a little, but finally the numbers counted all the way up to forty-seven and the door slid open.

Fred was waiting, leaning against the concrete wall opposite the elevators, his face pale and strained.

"I feared you might not come back." He stepped forward to meet her, his whole heart in his expression.

Tears gathered unexpectedly in Michelle's eyes, blurring her vision. "Yeah." She cleared her throat, embarrassed. "Coming back seemed like the right thing to do." She blushed a little, glancing down at her toes. "I brought us a pizza. Let's go back to the room."

Fred reached to caress her cheek with a shaky hand. Accepting the box, he led the way. "I told Elise and Jenny to go on to dinner without us. The sibyl has called a gathering at seven o'clock to discuss the situation with Saakaar. His actions could potentially affect all the supers, so everyone has a right to witness the discussion. We should have plenty of time to finish before we head down."

# Chapter Twelve

By the time they ate and freshened up, the clock read fifteen to seven. A soft knock at the door turned out to be Karl. Michelle stood timidly next to Fred as they rode down to join the sibyl on the tenth floor. The elevators around them all opened in a staggered burst. A wild parade of outlandish beings pouring out.

Fred offered Michelle his hand. After a moment, she reached to clasp his fingers. They tightened warmly around hers and she clung to them, gazing around the crowd. Ordinarily, she would have assumed the people were ordinary convention-goers wearing a variety of exotic costumes and displaying striking, unusual physical features granted by chance or by surgery, but these beings needed no costumes or makeup. They were exactly as they seemed.

The crowd parted a little uneasily, forming a corridor to let the sibyl pass. A small empty space cleared for the meeting, situated midway between the two narrow ends of the building. People milled uneasily and a second corridor formed between the clearing and the opposite elevator. Saakaar strolled through the crowd toward them, never glancing aside, stopping beyond the forefront of the assembled crowd.

Fred stepped forward protectively, partly shielding Michelle with his body. Saakaar smiled a tight, mocking smile at them. His tongue flickered out, licking his thin lips; Michelle realized it was bifurcated, split at the tip. She shuddered.

"I think no one here is fool enough to say I have gone beyond my rights in marking this human as mine to kill." Saakaar gestured slightly and pain flared on Michelle's forehead. She gritted her teeth, trying not to react. "None should deny I may do as I please in finishing her. Least of all you, Fredric."

"I may have no right, but nevertheless, I'll do everything I can to stop you." Fred squeezed Michelle's hand, then released her, stepping forward to block Saakaar's path. Muscular like a bodybuilder, with a golden glow to his olive skin, the naga made Fred look terribly slender and frail. However, Fred stood firm. A subtle aura of menace radiated from them both. The assembled crowd drew together, for all the world like a ring of high school students closing in around an impending fight.

"Your rights have precedent, but they are secondary to a greater matter: the welfare of us all." The sibyl interrupted quietly, but her voice silenced the muttering. "You should not kill this human, Saakaar. Give your vengeance another form."

The naga didn't draw back, neither in response to her words nor to Fred's threat, standing at ease while he surveyed them, smiling coldly.

"Perhaps this is the time to bring up another matter of concern," he turned, including the entire company in his glare. "Someone has stolen my jewel."

A gasp went through the supernaturals, who stared at him and drew back subtly; some crossed themselves or made a sign to ward off the evil eye.

"None of you, at least none who matter, needs to be told what this means, I'm sure." Saakaar flicked a contemptuous glance toward Michelle. She vividly remembered the blood-red stone he had worn when she first glimpsed him. He'd worn the jewel at the dance, but now the broad expanse of his forehead lay exposed.

"Saakaar's jewel is a sacred relic. It contains both an elixir of life and a deadly venom. With it, the naga can confer death on any individual, or grant immortality," Fred told Michelle softly. "Some humans would pay anything for those powers."

The sibyl hobbled toward them, shaking off Erik's protective hand. She beckoned to Saakaar. He obeyed, leaning down so she could place her palm upon his forehead. "He speaks true; the stone has been stolen. It must be restored before humans can misuse its power."

"I will find the stone," Fred blurted, stepping forward again. "And I will set it against the debt I owe Saakaar. If I can retrieve his jewel, he must let Michelle go free, unharmed."

Saakaar laughed, a soft, sibilant threat. "I will not interrupt my own efforts while I wait for an ignorant upstart like you to bungle the retrieval."

"Stop your attacks on her, then, while both of us search. We'll see who finds the jewel first." Fred lifted his chin boldly, stubborn.

"Very well," Saakaar snarled. "The sibyl has asked for my concession, so I will grant this one. We will both seek the jewel. While we do, I will spare your woman. If you find my jewel and restore it to me, I will accept the jewel in exchange for lifting my curse. But I will find it first. Then I will kill her." He bowed slightly.

Fred stepped forward, extending his hand to shake on the bargain. Their eyes locked as their palms met. Both their knuckles went white as each struggled to make the other wince. Hatred blazed from Saakaar's hard black eyes, meeting with icy resolve from Fred.

"I think you'll find this search a challenging one," Saakaar whispered, mocking. Michelle could see the bones of Fred's fingers grinding together inside his savage grip. "Do not forget—you will have to eat." He smiled pure malice, letting go. Fred pulled his hand back, rubbing his fingers slowly to restore the circulation.

"Let's go, Michelle." Fred reached for her with his left hand and drew her away. She stole a last glance back at the sibyl, who stood leaning on her stick, looking after them through her cloudy white eyes. Then they escaped into the elevator, where Fred pressed the button for the forty-seventh floor. "I'd better go right away, without saying anything about my plans. I don't want to waste time trying to create a lie to explain why I'm leaving."

"I don't either," Michelle lifted her chin, her voice shaking. "I'll text Elise. She can take our baggage home when she and Jenny leave."

Fred turned to her, his eyes wide with surprise. "Michelle, I don't expect you to come with me. The search will be dangerous."

"I'm not going to sit at home wondering what the fuck's happened to you, waiting for those snakes to come back and eat me alive." She swallowed hard. "My life's on the line. I want to go down fighting."

Fred bit his lip. His hand squeezed hers. His voice thickened with emotion. "Do you have your purse, your credit cards, your phone?" She nodded. "Good. Hold the elevator while I go to the room to grab my computer. We can worry about clothes later. If we take the time to pack up, we'll be stuck explaining to Elise and Jenny." The door opened on the empty waiting area and Michelle blocked the door with her body while Fred trotted away.

He reappeared in a few minutes, holding his briefcase. By then the

71

elevator had begun to protest, buzzing a loud alarm insisting Michelle clear the door. They stepped inside, then hit LL to take them down.

"I'll pay our share of the bill at the desk; we can settle up later. Then we have one more stop to make before we go." Fred looked grim, determined.

"Go where?"

"I don't know yet. The stop is to find out."

# Chapter Thirteen

Michelle texted Elise while Fred approached the front desk to settle their share of the bill. 'Emergency. Leaving with Fred. We paid our half. Please take our stuff home with you,' seemed too little, but she didn't know what else to say. Probably Elise would think they were too horny to wait any longer for some real privacy.

Fred tucked away his wallet as he hurried back to her. "Come on. We're going to the Sheraton." He led her through the melee of costumes through skywalks and along wet, steaming sidewalks until they arrived, then took a shortcut up the emergency stairs, exiting into a utilitarian corridor. He pulled Michelle to a stop in front of a featureless door.

He glanced around, then darted a few steps down the hall, coming back with a discarded room service tray. Setting aside the used glasses, he hid the messy silverware under the plate-cover, then gestured Michelle to stand aside. He composed himself before tapping at the door. "Room service!" Fred looked down, adjusting the tray on his hands, obscuring his face from anyone using the peephole.

After a short pause the door opened. Fred thrust his foot in swiftly. "Got you, Robin." He pressed through, levering his shoulder against some token resistance.

Michelle hurried forward to support him. A short elfin woman with untidy long red hair glared furiously at him, her arms firmly crossed over her chest.

"That's not fair." Her voice sounded very high-pitched, petulant and more than a little peevish.

"Are you saying you wouldn't do the same?" He radiated visible charm; Michelle frowned a little at him, watching closely. Was this how he wove his spells?

"Of course I would. But I'm supposed to be the trickster. No one is supposed to pull a trick on *me*." Her pout intensified.

"You didn't come to the gathering this evening." He gave the little woman a slow smile, his eyes twinkling.

"Those big meetings are boring." She didn't seem at all intimidated, despite Fred looming half again her height, looking handsome enough to make a beauty queen do a triple-take. She put her fists on her hips, glaring up at him. "If you've come to trouble me for doing as I please, I'll give you cause to regret it."

"Michelle, this is Robin Goodfellow." Fred gave up his efforts to charm Robin, at least long enough to shoot Michelle a wry look. The name tickled her mind, but didn't turn anything up until Fred continued. "Otherwise known as Hob, Goblin, or Puck if you travel in learned Shakespearean circles. The one and only."

"Really?" If she remembered right, Puck was a household spirit, a minor prankster, even a prince among mischief-makers, depending on which legend you listened to. She'd always thought of Puck as a man, but maybe the distinction wasn't consistent or even important with a super like this one.

The flattery of the Shakespeare reference softened the little woman slightly. She lifted her chin with pride. "So what if I am?"

"The rumor mill says you take a professional interest in every mischief that's done. Even if you weren't behind a prank, you know how to find out who did it. I need that now." He sat down, facing her eye to eye. "For centuries my kin have taken the blame for maidens you've tormented in your satyr form. No doubt we'll aid you again in the future. Plus I know you have no cause to love the naga."

She pouted again. "They're spoilsports. Snakes don't have a sense of humor."

"No, they don't." He cut to the chase. "Who stole the naga's jewel?"

"I knew that's why you're here." She turned her back on him, padding over to her bed on bare feet. "I didn't steal Saakaar's gemstone. I'm already immortal. If I want to kill someone, I know lots of better ways." She crossed her arms over her chest and flopped onto the bed, where she crossed her legs into the lotus, turning up the soles of her bare feet.

"You know who stole it?" he wheedled.

74

"Of course I do." She leaned back, narrowing her eyes at him, ignoring Michelle completely.

"What do you want in exchange for the information?"

Robin's grin turned nasty. It stretched so wide the sight truly alarmed Michelle; it looked as though the top of the girl's head would fall off.

"Entertainment," she smirked, stretching. "I want to come along to watch the fun."

"You'll have a laugh at the expense of whoever loses?"

"Of course."

He sat back to consider her, his eyes narrowed. "No double-crosses. You'll stay neutral, or I won't agree."

"I can follow you anyway."

"I can make following quite difficult for you."

"You?" Robin scoffed. "You'd best conserve your strength, I'm thinking." At last the girl shot a sharp look at Michelle. Her eerie, predatory smile reappeared. Michelle flushed, embarrassed, and looked away. She didn't like everyone meddling in her business.

"Let's speed up the negotiations." Fred pressed Robin, visibly annoyed. "I'm not made of time."

"The thief isn't here any longer. Only a fool would linger close to Saakaar after making him angry." She cut a sly smile at Fred. "The jewel was stolen by a thief working for a very wealthy human who wants immortality." She snapped her fingers. An hourglass appeared, with a quarter of the sand already poured out. "You're this far behind your thief. His buyer is waiting in Manhattan."

"How much time will pass before he gets there?"

"Four hours, give or take."

"How far are we behind Saakaar?"

Robin laughed. "Since he didn't have the wit to ask me? You're ahead of him."

"Will you take us to Manhattan?"

Robin snorted. "Already the fun is starting. That would hardly be neutral of me." She flicked her fingers at them dismissively. "You'd better go now. There's a non-stop flight to La Guardia you might catch if you hurry." She picked up the clicker and turned on her television set.

Fred led the way out, shrugging when Michelle gazed a question at him in the hall. "Robin will follow us in her own way."

"Can we trust her?"

"Insofar as we keep her entertained." He gave Michelle a wry look. "That is to say, not far at all, because she'd be nearly as pleased to see us fail as she would be to see Saakaar lose. I'd say we can trust her for a distance of approximately one ten thousandth of a nanometer."

Michelle chuckled; the remark sounded absolutely like the dorky Fred she knew. "We'll need an electron microscope to keep an eye on her then." He glanced at her, surprised, his expression warming at her amusement.

"She'll regard 'neutrality' as helping or hindering both sides at random. We should always assume she's toying with us for her own purposes. However, the same will be true of Saakaar when she offers him her assistance. She's probably doing that this very minute. Still, I believe she likes him less than she likes me. Her preference should give us an important edge. Come on." Fred offered his hand. Michelle twined their fingers shyly, trotting along behind as they hurried toward the parking garage where he'd left his car.

Sitting down behind the wheel, he strapped on his seatbelt, then fumbled in a pocket for his glasses, pushing them up on the bridge of his nose. "I really do need these," he said sheepishly, "if you want me to be able to read road signs."

He looked more like himself with them on, she had to admit. But now the genie was out of the bottle. She could still see his attractiveness in spite of the camouflage, like a visual puzzle you couldn't unsee after you'd discovered the truth. Now she knew how to penetrate the disguise, it was absurdly easy to see Superman half-hidden behind Clark Kent.

"Can you book our flight while I drive?"

"Sure." Michelle fished out her phone.

"No telling when we'll be back. This is going to cost a fortune," Fred sighed as they parked in a long-term lot and boarded the shuttle bus to the terminal.

By the time they cleared security, they had three minutes left before their scheduled departure. They wound up running through the terminal frantically, dodging pedestrians as well as they could. If they'd had to check bags they would never have made it, but they boarded the plane just before the door closed.

# Chapter Fourteen

By the time they made their final descent into La Guardia, Michelle was tired. She stared wide-eyed out the window at the panorama of city lights spread out beneath the wing of the plane, reaching for Fred's hand again as the landing gear thumped down. The aircraft swooped in so low over the East River she feared they would fall short and ditch in the water instead of reaching the runway. Fred squeezed her fingers gently, comforting. "First time flying in to La Guardia?"

"Yes," she admitted. "My first time in New York, actually. Please don't think I'm silly."

"Of course not. Coming in over the water like this is always nerve-wracking. So is the rest of New York, at least the first time you visit."

To Michelle's relief they landed safely on solid ground. Fred bought them a couple of spare T-shirts in a souvenir store, then they paused next to baggage claim to debate their next step.

"Don't know where to go?" The shrill voice behind them was already familiar to Michelle, even after such a short acquaintance. "What a pity."

They turned to find Robin sitting cross-legged on the tiles behind them, leaning against a wall. She still appeared barefoot and tousled, exactly as she'd been in Atlanta, holding a tablet computer in her hand. "That's all right. Even if you made a plan, you'll have to change it. The original buyer fell through." Her wide smile stretched again, this time with the seeming innocence of a cherub. "He encountered an unfortunate accident, you might say."

Fred scoffed a little. "Unfortunate? I'm sure the thief thinks so, but I don't believe you agree. She'll probably get a little more entertainment now," he muttered to Michelle. "Where is the jewel?"

"Things have grown a little more complicated," Robin admitted, not looking regretful at all. "The thief is trying to arrange an auction through a service offered by an auctioneer of rare and valuable commodities."

"How far behind us is Saakaar?" Fred continued, suspicious, making Robin's big wicked smile stretch across her face again. She extended one arm, pointing. Fred turned to see Saakaar standing not fifteen feet away, a small suitcase in his hand. He glared at them all irritably.

"He flew first-class," Robin giggled merrily. When Fred turned back, opening his mouth to reproach her, she was gone.

"I might have known you'd be fool enough to bring Robin into this, Fredric." Saakaar's dark eyes had no slitted contacts in them now. A crisp white button-down shirt hid the exotic cobra hood on his shoulders, but he still looked menacing. Probably he had trouble with racial profiling by the TSA when he flew. To Michelle, he looked exactly the sort of man a nervous guard would suspect of being a terrorist.

Saakaar glared at Fred. "I can't thank you enough for making this quest an order of magnitude more difficult for us both." Next he bowed toward Michelle, mocking. "Since your protector has chosen to enlist the help of other supernaturals, surely I will not be condemned for doing the same." He glared at them both before striding out toward the cabstand.

Fred frowned, reaching for Michelle's hand. "Let's rent a room where we can hole up for the night. Robin gave us a clue, but I'll need to do some research online to figure out the details. Then we'll have to go hunting." He pulled a notepad out of his pocket and began to scribble. "I'll start with Sotheby's. Possibly Christie's, if they think a gem in a setting is an artwork. I don't think they'd host anything this dodgy, but we can't risk passing them up. A couple of other auction houses have a specialty service for supernatural items, too. They might be more likely candidates for this sale."

"I'll have to pose as a buyer to make inquiries.... If I could get an inside line on which auction company has the jewel, I could try to be there for the seller's demo. The house will want proof the item has the promised characteristics before they agree to go to the expense—and the risk, in this case—of holding an auction." He fretted, scowling at his notes, then dug out his smartphone.

"Let's move; we won't accomplish anything standing here." Michelle tugged him out through the double doors into the honking madhouse of the arrivals pick-up area. There was no sign of Saakaar, so she pulled Fred into the taxi line. She dug in her purse for her phone, hastily pricing a hotel or two. She winced at the results.

"Tell the driver to go here." Fred told her absently, flipping open his wallet. He gave her a tattered, dog-eared card printed with an address in Greenwich Village.

She tucked away her phone and accepted the card, steering Fred into a cab. She read the address to the cabbie, who put it into his GPS, then forced his way out into the nasty traffic. They set out toward the sparkling skyline in the distance. Michelle spent the ride fretting while Fred remained absorbed in his phone. When they climbed out, Michelle paid the cabbie. The street was narrow, with a few scrubby maples set into grates interrupting the sidewalk. They were on the southeast side of the Village, according to Fred. She'd never seen this part of Manhattan on television.

"Let's eat some dinner, then hole up for the night." Fred led Michelle around a couple of turns to a quiet little brick oven pizza restaurant serving dinner late. This would be her second pizza of the day, but Michelle hadn't eaten much of the first one, so her stomach growled with hunger.

Starting to relax a little, Michelle watched Fred as he ate. He remained so preoccupied with his phone he barely spoke, raising his head every so often to take a bite of pizza or a sip of beer. He seemed to enjoy the meal, folding his pizza like a proper New Yorker. She wondered if he actually benefited from eating human food.

She ate her share quietly, much more neatly than Fred, passing him napkins whenever he needed them. She savored the tall glass of draft beer accompanying the meal.

One of the busboys had begun wiping tables, moving steadily closer to them. She had to prod Fred with her toe to alert him. He gave her an apologetic, sheepish grin, then led her away, twisting and turning through progressively less welcoming streets. He finally ducked into a narrow alley, still moving with confidence. Though Michelle normally wouldn't have touched the place with a ten-foot pole, she followed him. The tall buildings on either side shut out most of the light and puddles of oily water stood on the pavement. She thought she heard a rat scratching through the trash somewhere nearby.

"Are we still in the Village?"

"No." He approached a red-painted door, tapping at it. A little panel slid open, reminding Michelle of a speakeasy. After Fred spoke through the slot for a moment, the door opened to admit them into a sumptuous but small lobby furnished in gilt, dark wood, and crimson velvet. The attendant who waited inside wasn't even trying to look human. She had shimmering gossamer wings and a pointy, elfin chin. Her capricious, hostile manner reminded Michelle of movie fairies. Her eyes narrowed as she moved to block Michelle's path.

"No mortals."

"The human is with me," Fred said pointedly. He gently drew Michelle onward, bypassing the pixie's outstretched arm.

"Then no corpses in the morning, incubus." The pixie smiled, malicious. "Dispose of your own trash."

Michelle felt goose bumps rise on her arms. She glanced nervously at Fred, who patted her hand lightly, reassuring.

"No corpses at all," he said patiently, accepting the key the sullen pixie offered. They climbed three flights of dark, narrow stairs, then walked all the way to the end of the corridor, where their key let them into a corner room. Michelle ventured inside, nervous, feeling vulnerable. However, the place seemed quite normal inside, like any nice hotel room. The room was surprisingly spacious, furnished in mild shades of beige. She was glad to see a soft, wide bed and a comfortable sitting area next to an unlit gas fireplace. A single window overlooked the main street. Fred drew the shade, hiding the harsh lights and dingy concrete walls of buildings across the way.

"I didn't think to bring my toothbrush or toothpaste or shampoo," Michelle murmured.

"There should be some waiting in the bathroom. Supers usually travel light. When things go bad, there isn't always time for us to pack a bag." He cracked his neck loudly, making her wince. Then he went to the sitting area where he pulled out his laptop, his fingers flying over the keyboard.

# Chapter Fifteen

With Fred engrossed in his research for the duration, Michelle gave up on talking. She went instead to investigate the bathroom. Sure enough, shampoo and lotion soap sat beside the sink in little bottles. She sniffed one neatly-wrapped cake of soap: lavender. A disposable razor, toothbrush and toothpaste, and a small black comb lay opposite them on the countertop. The tub came outfitted with a modern showerhead, adjustable to several massage settings. The tub and toilet seemed acceptably clean.

Glancing over her shoulder at Fred but receiving no response, Michelle decided to take a shower while he worked; she hated the way flying made her feel grubby. Latching the door behind her, she climbed into the shower, setting the water as hot as she could stand. She scrubbed herself pink with a rough washcloth and the slim bar of lavender soap. If Fred was going to kill her, she might as well be clean for the mortician.

She grimaced into the shower spray, reminding herself to be fair. Fred was out there right now trying as hard as he could to come up with a way to help. The pixie's casual threat had given her the heebie-jeebies, that was all.

Finished rinsing her hair, she turned her back to the spray, letting the stream of water work the tension out of her shoulders. She felt good, luxuriant and sensual. She tweaked the temperature up a notch, bracing her palms against the wall so she could stretch her back. Rolling her shoulders, she luxuriated in the clean, hot water cascading over her skin. She hummed softly, absorbing the sensation, rubbing her palms over her belly, enjoying the wet silk of her flesh. When the water started to cool, she turned off the shower and toweled herself thoroughly, humming a little. Dry, she wrapped her towel around her hips to cover herself, pulled on her T-shirt, then stepped out quietly, hoping not to disturb Fred.

She could have saved herself the trouble. He sat quite still, his hands poised to type, but the laptop sat idle, its screen powered off. His eyes fixed on her, wide and dark. A sheen of sweat gleamed on his forehead.

"You had..." his voice husked a little, so he cleared his throat before continuing. "A good shower, I take it."

She dithered for a moment, trying to understand his expression. Maybe she needed to wear more clothes. "Yes. The water pressure is nice and strong." She clutched at the towel, wishing she'd put her shorts on instead of leaving them to air out.

"I could tell." He flushed suddenly, dropping his gaze. Michelle felt herself color also.

"You felt that?"

"Showering was obviously very pleasurable for you," he mumbled. "Nothing unreasonable or perverse. Please don't feel uncomfortable. I was just...." His adam's apple worked as he swallowed. "A little distracted."

"I'm sorry." Michelle retreated to the room's single bed where she turned back the covers. Sitting, she slid her legs under them, concealing herself carefully before discarding the damp towel. "I hope I was at least a decent snack." She felt shy and exposed.

Fred closed the laptop. "I've found what I can for now, but there's no point calling anyone until the auction house offices open tomorrow." He stepped over to the bed lightly, giving her time to adjust to his presence. "Michelle, don't be afraid. The pixie was being a bitch. They often are. Haven't you read J. M. Barrie? They're very jealous, very petty, exactly as he characterized them." He shrugged, helpless, reaching for her hand.

"She was rude because she was angry a human was here with a super. This place is fairly exclusive. Not too many humans know this kind of hotel exists. Even fewer have ever set foot inside one. It pissed her off that I brought you here." He smiled apologetically, rubbing his thumb over the back of her hand, savoring the texture of her skin. "You're safe with me, Michelle. I'll do my best not to leave you alone with anyone like her."

He sat down on the bed. "As for the shower? Think of it like this. Sometimes you find yourself next to a kitchen where all kinds of wonderful dishes are being prepared. You don't have to sniff the air. You can smell them whether you try to or not. You can imagine how heavenly they'd taste. The scent in the air makes your mouth water. You'd love to have a bite of everything, but you're in control. It isn't impossible to stay on your diet."

He helped her lie down, then pulled the sheet up, tucking her in with gentle care. "It's very similar to being around someone you desire, but having the courtesy to keep your hands to yourself." Fred gave her a sheepish smile, one she couldn't help but return. He removed his hands from the bedclothes and replaced them in his lap. Michelle watched, concerned, as his expression closed and he withdrew inside himself, tucking the moment of openness neatly away. He put on a brisk, businesslike mask to replace it.

"Did you leave me any hot water?"

She dropped her gaze, embarrassed. "I ran the shower till the water went cold. I'm sorry."

"The water won't take long to heat up again." He rose to investigate the closet. "We have extra pillows and blankets in here, if you need them. You might want to go online while I'm in the shower; you need to email Robotidata. Tell them you want to take sick leave for the next few days. I'm sorry, but I don't know how long. I've already sent an email request to HR for myself. Elise will gossip, I'm sure, but it can't be helped."

"I'll email too." She hesitated until he reached the door. "Fred?"

"Yes?" He turned slightly, the bright bathroom light catching in the lenses of his clear blue eyes, picking up a hint of red in his dark hair.

"A diet is different from starving yourself. You can't do that."

"I'll be all right for a few days. Maybe this will be over by then." His smile stretched a little too wide, doing little to deflect her concern. "When Saakaar has the jewel, we can go back to normal."

"Improper power charging will keep the unit from functioning at peak capacity." The familiar jargon of their job eased the urgency of her statement, but they both knew the truth.

"We'll talk about me when I need to feed." His voice turned husky for a moment, his eyes softening. "I'm going to rinse out a few things while I wait for the water to heat." He made his escape into the bathroom. The latch clicked shut behind him.

Michelle stood up when she heard the water start running. She went to Fred's computer, logging into her work account to compose the email he'd suggested. She couldn't resist the impulse to prowl a little when she'd finished, glancing guiltily at the bathroom door before she did. His browser cache looked innocent enough, at least if you knew what he was. His desktop wallpaper featured a picture of her. Mildly startled, Michelle examined the photograph. She sat bent casually over her desk with her hair pulled back in a ponytail, typing. He must have taken the picture the day she transcribed his notes.

She swallowed hard, struck by the familiar calm of the scene. The woman in the picture had no idea what was about to happen to her. She had no clue she was loved. Michelle shifted her legs, self-conscious. The picture could give no other message. He had captured her in a moment of oblivious grace, then put the shot on his desktop. She flushed, embarrassed by her intrusion. But could she commit an unfair invasion at this point, given how often he had entered her dreams without telling her what he was doing or asking permission?

Maybe she had a right to snoop, but she felt better when she'd maximized the browser window again to cover the desktop. She shut the laptop, leaving it lying on the coffee table.

She went back to bed, slipping under the covers, gazing at Fred through slitted eyes when he emerged from the bathroom a few minutes later. He wore white briefs and a sleeveless undershirt, his hair a messy nest of damp strands, wildly tousled. As he turned his profile, she could see the curve of his ass, spare but sweet, a tempting shape inside the tight cotton fabric.

He combed his hair in front of the mirror, blinking a little at his reflection as he constructed his part with care. Then he came to bed, setting his glasses on the nightstand before climbing in slowly, trying to arrange himself without disturbing her. He kept to his side, carefully polite, lying on his back and gazing silently up at the ceiling.

Michelle could imagine the pixie's contemptuous disbelief if she were to see the two of them now: chaste, untouching. Fred lay stiff. It looked like he was trying not to breathe, his hands folded over his sternum like a corpse arranged for burial in a coffin. He reminded her of a nervous virgin on the first night after the wedding ceremony.

She stirred, nowhere near sleep. "Fred?"

"Yes?"

"What will we do when all this is over and we go home again?"

She raised herself on one elbow, gazing down at him. "Will we go back to work? Are you going to..." she hesitated. "Stick around?"

"I didn't think you'd want me to." He blinked up at her, his eyes half in shadow, holding very still.

She raked her hair back, frowning. "You should ask before you make an assumption like that." She sat up, crossing her legs, and covered her lap with the sheet. "I don't want you to quit your job and vanish, if that's what you think."

Fred hesitated for a long moment before speaking. "Would you want things to go on as they were?"

It was her turn to consider. "I don't know if they have to go back to how they were before. I mean, if an incubus always kills his lovers, how do cambions ever happen? How do you get a baby incubus?" She gestured awkwardly. "I don't know. What kills the girl? Does she have to die? Is the damage sudden, or is it cumulative?"

"I'm not certain." Fred sounded gruff with pain. "I don't think any scientific studies have been done to quantify the phenomenon." He took refuge in clinical jargon, still staring up at the ceiling. "My own observations indicate both a physical and psychic drain occur even in dreams. The effect can become extreme over time. The victim experiences reactions ranging from fatigue to unconsciousness. When actual sex is attempted, an additional physical strain is imposed on the woman's body. I think that's more likely to be fatal. The less energy transferred, the less the psychic drain. The less...." he hesitated. "The less physical response the woman experiences, the less likely she'll experience a fatal heart attack or stroke."

"Physical response. You mean orgasm?" She shivered, remembering how hard she had come for him when he touched her.

He scrubbed a hand over his face wearily. "Yes. There's a reason they warn human men who want medication for erectile dysfunction to ask the doctor whether they're healthy enough for sex. Normal sex can kill a human with a heart condition. I think excessive orgasm puts a strain on even healthy individuals." He cleared his throat with awkward care, still trying to sound clinical and detached. "That sort of response is an expected outcome of relations with an incubus."

"There have to be ways to work the problem. We could try—"

Fred sat up, turning away from her, putting his feet on the floor. "When I killed Mishti, it was the most horrible experience of my life. I didn't intend to harm her, but I was ignorant and careless. She wasn't in distress, or so I thought. But after we finished, she fell unconscious. When I realized she wasn't merely sleeping, I felt her wrist. She had no pulse. I tried to revive her, but her death happened centuries before I learned how to perform CPR. I couldn't wake her. She died in my bed."

He stood, abruptly retreating to the bathroom, turning back briefly at the door, his face white. "I was so devastated I nearly chose to end my own life. I haven't touched a woman sexually since then—at least, not until I marked you. I won't risk your life, Michelle. In case your curiosity is stronger than your caution, please consider this, too. I would not choose to survive causing your death. Not for long." He vanished abruptly into the bathroom, turning on both the sink and the shower, but she could hear him vomit in spite of his efforts to cover the noise.

Michelle grimaced to herself, her stomach rolling in sympathy. She rose, tucking the towel around her body so the sight of her bare flesh wouldn't torment him. Then she went to care for him in his misery, just as he had tended her in the hotel. He looked terribly pale in the stark light of the vanity mirror, his hands braced on the seat of the toilet. A scattering of freckles dusted his shoulders. The harsh light made him look too thin, his ribs forming prominent ridges under his skin.

Fred wiped his mouth, then bent to retch again. She gently supported his forehead as he emptied his stomach, then seated him on the lid of the toilet. She wet a washcloth in the sink, squeezing it out thoroughly, and wiped his face with the cool cloth, continuing until he regained his poise. Slowly, the color returned to his cheeks.

"I'm sorry," she said quietly. "So sorry, Fred. I'm sorry you've never found someone who could be a proper mate to you. I can't begin to imagine spending five hundred years alone, hiding in dreams without ever letting anyone come close enough to return your feelings."

He gave her a tired smile and laced their fingers, running his thumb along hers. "I don't suppose this is much consolation, but that's a future you won't ever have to face."

She laughed a little, rueful. "I suppose not." She patted his face lightly. "Come back to bed. I promise I won't upset you again tonight with my foolish questions."

"They aren't foolish at all." He met her eyes soberly. "You deserve to know these things." He rose to his feet, hesitating a moment, then kissed her cheek softly. "Go back to bed. Let me brush my teeth and check a few more websites before I join you."

She lay down, hoping he wouldn't take long. However, he sat up very late. She fell asleep long before he kept his word.

# Chapter Sixteen

A shaft of morning sunlight penetrated the curtains and played across Michelle's face, making her squint. She rolled to escape, settling against Fred's warm body. She snuggled in, sighing, before remembering she shouldn't.

She opened her eyes as his arm came around her. His face looked drawn, but the evening's accumulation of stubble appealed to her nonetheless.

"I've come up with a plan for retrieving the jewel," he murmured. "You aren't going to like it."

Michelle frowned at him. She stirred sleepily, rubbing her eyes. "Why not?"

Fred stared up at the ceiling as he spoke, stroking her arm with absent affection. "Because it's too risky for you to go in with me. I'm going to pose as a buyer to gain access to the auction. If I can't come up with a way to steal the jewel before the sale, I'll trail the actual buyer home. Then I'll incapacitate the buyer with an extreme energy drain while he's sleeping and take the gem before he recovers. Dreamwalking is a useful skill. I can find out any secrets I need, such as the combination to a safe, then use them to my advantage."

"He? You can do that even if the buyer is a man?"

Fred snorted a little wryly, amused. "I can. There's little gender difference in the mechanics of dreams, actually, though I much prefer having relations with women."

"Your plan sounds risky." She didn't like the idea of him having sex with someone who wasn't her, either, not even in a dream. Michelle made herself push her worries aside to consider things practically. "What if Saakaar is there first?"

"Saakaar won't condescend to purchase his own jewel. He's been worshipped as a god for centuries in India; it's done dreadful things to his ego. His dignity won't allow him to buy back a possession of his own, especially if he can manipulate someone else to do his dirty work for him. He could stop the auction by saying the gem was stolen, but he's so arrogant he won't want to show weakness before humans by admitting thieves stole his most precious possession. He would have to prove his claim, too, which would be difficult." He hesitated. "At least, I hope he won't bid, but this is all guesswork."

"What will I do while you're gone?"

"You'll wait with one hand on your phone. We may need to travel fast to keep up with the buyer. If that's the case, I'll pick you up on my way out. You can run interference for me and take care of logistics while I handle the actual theft. I may need you to guard me while I'm projecting myself into the thief's dreams. If I'm not in a safe place, I'm vulnerable while I'm feeding." He stirred uncomfortably. "I'm hoping I won't have to carry things so far."

"I hope not." Michelle nestled her face against his shoulder, pensive. "You're right. I don't like your plan. I thought we were going to stick together."

"The auction house will run an extensive background check on anybody who tries to gain access to the event. You won't be considered an acceptable candidate because you aren't exceptionally wealthy. I'm afraid we don't have time to construct a false profile for you to present for the buyer inspection." He cleared his throat, sheepish. "I always keep several fake identities ready, as a precaution in case I need to abandon one of my personas in a hurry."

"What about Saakaar? He threatened to enlist other supernaturals in the search. There's Robin to worry about, too."

Fred shrugged. "I didn't say the plan was perfect, but I couldn't come up with a better one." He turned toward her, his arm sliding around her waist. Michelle's heart began to hammer with anticipation as he drew her close, but he withdrew after touching their noses together lightly. "I'll leave you here. This place is a safe house of sorts, a refuge when a super is in trouble. We sometimes use it as a place to hide out from human pursuit, but it's also considered in very poor taste for supernaturals to attack or interfere with one another's business while they're inside. You should be safe here if you're safe anywhere. Don't agree to let anyone come inside the room. Don't venture outside by yourself, either."

His hands were warm on her back, his chest firm against her breasts. Michelle wanted a kiss so badly she ached. She held herself back with an effort, afraid to upset him again.

Fred studied her expression for a long moment, as if he sensed her feelings. Then his eyes closed. He leaned in, brushing his lips lightly across hers. The delicate touch sent a delightful flare of bliss coursing through her. She slid her arms around him, savoring the sweetness, but the kiss didn't last long. He withdrew quickly, touching the tip of her nose with his again. Then he rolled out of bed and vanished into the bathroom.

She flopped over onto her back, straight into the sunbeam. Scowling, she shaded her eyes and climbed out of bed to adjust the drapes. Before she succeeded, he emerged to find her struggling in vain to make them overlap.

"We obviously need to buy you some more clothes," he chuckled. Michelle blushed, caught with no pants on. "After I finish making arrangements with the auction house, I'll come back to take you out shopping. Neither of us can go around forever wearing just one pair of underwear, jeans, and a couple of cheap T-shirts." His eyes lingered on her appreciatively. "Even though I don't have any complaints with the view at the moment."

"Tease." Michelle dimpled at him in spite of herself. She escaped quickly to the bathroom, secretly pleased when his eyes followed her every step of the way.

"I'll need to get fitted for a business suit, too." Fred clicked his tongue. "I can hardly attend the auction posing as a wealthy bidder if I'm wearing an 'I ♥ New York' T-shirt. I suppose Brooks Brothers might agree to do a rush job if I tip handsomely enough."

By the time Michelle came out, he was on the phone, making arrangements to meet with a representative from one of the auction houses. He managed to sound impressively formal and austere for a man wearing just his tighty whities. She tried not to giggle at him.

He gave himself enough time to dress and travel to his appointment on time. On his way out, he grabbed a banana from the big bowl of fruit sitting on the coffee table, hesitating for a moment with his hand on the doorknob. "I'll call if I won't be back by three." He closed the door and she latched the deadbolt behind him.

# Chapter Seventeen

After Fred departed, Michelle felt uneasy, somewhat let-down. She hated passivity, but there seemed little other choice in this case. There was nothing good on TV, so she settled on a cartoon channel and sat back in the leather easy chair to brood, tucking one knee under her chin. This kind of helpless waiting was exactly what she'd intended to avoid when she refused to stay behind.

After a few minutes, she realized Fred had left his laptop, so she grabbed it and curled up on the sofa to begin searching the web. Thousands of people online were completely obsessed with supers, just like Jenny. There had to be something online about how to have sex safely with an incubus.

The number of results on her first search made her eyes go wide: incubus sex was a wildly popular topic. She'd have her work cut out for her trying to separate the wheat from the chaff.

Several hours later she set the computer aside, shaking her head. From fantasies to fanfiction to roleplay, she'd located very little usable information, mostly speculation from women who wanted to try sex with an incubus but who'd never met one, or from men pretending to be an incubus to try and get laid.

Everything she'd found agreed on two things. First of all, an incubus had to eat. That didn't mean steak and potatoes. Fred had to have regular sexual contact, either telepathically or physically, if he wanted to survive.

The second thing? Apparently sex with an incubus was the ultimate in pleasure. She thought again of the woman who'd died. 'She didn't suffer.' She could still hear the words in Karl's heavy German accent. She chose an apple from the bowl, chewing thoughtfully.

"I guess Mishti *didn't* suffer," she murmured to herself. If Fred could make her come so hard just by kissing her breast, what would sex be like with him? The leather of the easy chair felt cool against her skin. She folded her legs, slowly eating her apple. For Fred to have avoided sex for centuries except the pale imitation to be had in dreams? It was a wonder he hadn't given himself some sort of psychic malnutrition. No wonder he'd been so aroused by sensing her pleasure in the shower.

She felt ashamed of her shyness from before. They'd already done nearly everything imaginable, at least in her dreams. There was really no point in being prudish. In their shared dreams, he'd already seen her a hundred times without a stitch on: up close and exceptionally personal.

But now he was trying to be noble, refusing to feed. She was simply going to have to persuade him to eat. If he felt too guilty to visit her while she slept, she'd have to try something else.

She wandered over to the window, gazing out restlessly onto the street to watch for him. Finally, she spotted him walking briskly along the sidewalk. Somehow he seemed much smaller there than he did when he was near her, slim and self-effacing, studying the ground in front of his feet as he walked. He moved fast through the crowd, deftly managing not to touch anyone.

He ducked into the alley, vanishing. Michelle felt her heart race with anticipation as she waited. She glanced into the mirror, hastily running a brush through her hair, then arranged herself casually in front of the television. Should she be wearing her shoes? She had one in her hand when the lock clicked. The door pushed open, but the deadbolt stopped it after half an inch.

"Michelle, it's me." His musical voice sent a shiver of delight through her. She dropped the shoe, hurrying to let him in. Fred smiled at her a little wearily. "The jewel is at Superlatives. They're an underground auction house specializing in items of paranormal significance." He lifted a cluster of grapes from the fruit bowl. "They're running a check on me before they let me in, but there shouldn't be much for them to find on the ID I'm using. If they won't admit me to the auction after the check, I have another idea or two on the back burner." A small frown creased the skin between his eyebrows. "Did you have a good morning?"

"My morning was very dull." Michelle stepped to his side, brushing his arm with her hand. "I'm glad you're back."

Fred drew a soft breath in response to the touch and offered her a grape. She lifted his hand with the bunch still in it, catching one between her lips. She tugged the grape off the stem, blushing a little when her flirting startled him, making his brows shoot up toward his hairline.

"I'm looking forward to escaping from this room. I can't wait to get some lunch and a new outfit." She pretended she hadn't been teasing outrageously, flipping her hair off her shoulders before scooping it up in a ponytail.

"Then let's go now." His eyes sparkled, warm with happiness. She felt as if she were dancing on air when she left the room at his side, his hand resting lightly on her shoulder.

# Chapter Eighteen

Fred whisked Michelle into a cab, directing the cabbie uptown. They spent the afternoon in a whirlwind of shopping, sticking to small, off-brand boutiques, hovering uneasily between chic and reasonably priced. They ended up at Brooks Brothers, where Fred chose a suit off the rack, then arranged for alterations.

Michelle went along to the fitting room. She watched the tailors measure him, then pin the jacket and trousers to fit him, amazed at how the simple change of clothes transformed him. Her familiar companion had entered the room, but within five minutes, he'd changed into someone formidably handsome, looking so polished as to be downright intimidating.

"Very flattering, if a little conservative," she commented shyly after all the adjustments were done. He examined the results in a three-panel mirror. "You don't look yourself at all."

He glanced at her, thoughtful. "Is that good or bad?" He straightened the lapels, frowning a little at his image.

"You look ravishing." Not precisely the answer he'd asked for, but maybe he'd let her get away with an evasion.

He chuckled a little wryly, lifting a brow, so she knew he'd spotted her ploy. "My looks make you uncomfortable." He ran his fingers through his forelock, disarranging a few strands, somehow transforming himself from stunning to downright devastating in the process.

"Uh." Michelle rose, fiddling with the strap of her purse. She turned away, feeling her cheeks heat. "They remind me how much I still have to learn about who you are."

"I'm always me." She watched in the mirror as the tailors stripped the suit coat off him, leaving him standing in his shirtsleeves. Then the trousers followed. She swallowed hard. Even in his briefs and socks, the tails of his shirt dangling loose, Fred's charm hadn't faded. The attraction lingered in the intensity of his eyes, in the slow lift of one corner of his mouth as he smiled at her, in the casual disarray of his hair, in the delicate strength of his hands as he loosened his tie, pulling it from his collar.

"I know you are. I just keep seeing more of you. It makes me realize how little I know." Michelle twisted her purse in her hands, anxious, then made herself stop.

The tailors slipped out, taking the pieces of the suit with them. Fred stepped to her, laying one palm on her arm.

"I think I know what the problem is." His palm moved slowly, his thumb stroking lightly beneath her sleeve. "Good looks are something I usually try to cover up, but I can't help having. Attractiveness comes naturally to my species. Humans call it a glamour. They think we're casting a spell, using a kind of magic. If we are, it's a type of magic not exclusive to supers."

He shrugged, self-deprecating, then let her go and turned to study their reflection the mirror. "A number of humans can generate a glamour too, some more powerfully than others. The spell is strongest when people are in love. Then it works both ways." His gaze fell to the floor, then lifted again, seeking hers in the glass. What she saw there made her breath stop in her chest. Her heart began to race. "They each see the other as more beautiful than seems possible." He studied her face, searching her eyes. After a moment's hesitation, he turned to face her again, reaching delicately for her waist.

Michelle's belly fell into her toes, a swooping, melting heat, as he leaned forward, tilted his chin, and closed his eyes. Her lips parted instinctively to meet his. Then he was kissing her with slow-building hunger, his lips pressing hers open, his tongue darting in to tease hers lightly, his hands steady on her back.

Delightful heat soared through Michelle and she swayed, leaning against him. The kiss wasn't the same devastating flash-fire as the night when he marked her, but she lost herself anyway, pure want destroying sense. Her arms rose, locking behind his neck, and she buried her fingers in his hair. He groaned into her mouth, his embrace tightening to crush her breasts against his chest. His tongue played warmly with hers as she rose up on her tiptoes. The whole world turned hot, wet, and sweet.

The soft sound of a throat clearing drove them apart. One of the tailors stood in the doorway, wearing a scandalized expression, carrying a pair of trousers folded over his arm. He held a slip of paper in his hand. Fred let Michelle go reluctantly, nuzzling her cheek for a last sweet moment, then reached for his jeans. He pulled them on and zipped them up with some difficulty. He kept his dignity though, unabashed, accepting the proffered paper when he finished. He pulled on his T-shirt before they went out to the counter to pay their bill.

"I arranged for the suit to be ready before the reception tomorrow night," Fred mused as they rode the elevator down to the street level. "I'll have to come pick it up after lunch tomorrow."

"I want to go to the reception with you."

"I wish you could." Fred raised his hand to hail a taxi. "But I couldn't come up with a better option. At least you should be safe back in the room."

She acquiesced with reluctance, feeling a little out of her depth. "Let's not go to a restaurant tonight." She didn't want to deal with the noise or the crowd. "Is there a delicatessen or a specialty food store we could visit instead? Let's buy some wine, cheese, and fruit to take back to our room."

"Maybe we could picnic in Washington Square Park. It's not a long walk from our hotel." He smiled, catching her hand in his. "We'll find something in the Village."

They located a deli, where Fred chose a variety of cheeses while Michelle picked out a luscious mix of fresh berries and fruit. They ended up sitting on a slatted wooden bench in the park, shaded from the sun under the arching branches of a tall tree, nibbling squares of cranberry cheddar cheese on crisp wafers. The tart red wine Fred had selected complemented the meal perfectly in spite of being served in paper cups. Even though the park bench dinner wasn't the intimate event Michelle had originally envisioned, she liked being outside so much she couldn't regret the change of venue.

Fred seemed preoccupied, eating silently. He frowned a little to himself, not looking at anything but his food. She let him think, alternating bites of apple and cheddar as she watched children frolic in the fountain a few yards up the path.

After a while he lifted his gaze and found hers waiting.

"I expected you to be very angry with me for feeding on you without permission, but you don't act like you are," Fred spoke quietly.

"May I ask why not?"

Michelle finished chewing a bite of pear, using the time to consider her response. "I thought about what you did from your point of view," she said at last. "I remembered what you said about supers having to abandon their lives when people find out what they are. I understand you have to eat. You were doing the best you could with an impossible situation. I happened to be handy."

Fred studied her, his expression sober. "You're wrong. In fact, I chose you quite carefully." He swallowed hard, as if bracing himself for an outburst.

Michelle blushed. "I'm flattered," she murmured. "What were the criteria?"

It was Fred's turn to flush with embarrassment. "I already told you I could feed off nearly anyone if I had to, but I don't like to. I daresay you wouldn't enjoy eating scraps pulled out of a dumpster. The principle is similar."

Michelle couldn't help but giggle, picturing Fred wandering through a sexual buffet populated with individuals straight out of photos posted on the 'People of Walmart' website: the incubus equivalent of dumpster diving.

Fred chuckled with her for a moment, then grew serious again. "Your hair attracted me at first. Also, you're very pretty, but I didn't find just your looks attractive. I'm afraid I spied on you for a while before I fed to learn more about your personality and found it appealing as well." He gave her a worried glance, but she remained calm, gesturing for him to continue.

"You needed someone who deserved you." Fred grinned a little, wry. "I didn't assume I was good enough to replace your boyfriend, but I didn't want to interrupt a happy relationship, either. In the end, I admired who you are. That's what I meant when I said your soul shines inside you. You're happy by nature. You work to see the best in people. You aren't all knotted up in the dogma of religious intolerance, but you're highly moral. You're kind and compassionate, very giving. I thought if I dared to ask you outright, quite politely, you might actually take the time to think things through, then agree.

"Not out of prurient interest in fucking an incubus to find out what all the hype is about," he grimaced, "but because you understood the need. I thought if I told you what I was, you would keep my secret even if you didn't agree to help me, because you'd believe it was the right thing to do."

Fred fell silent for a moment, brooding. Michelle tossed the pear core in a nearby trashcan, wiping her fingers on her jeans. "Then why didn't you ask?"

He stared down at the toes of his shoes. "Because I was afraid you wouldn't like me enough to agree because you desired me. I didn't want you to let me feed only because you felt a moral obligation."

The silence stretched for a long moment, broken by the barking of a dog and the raucous honk of a taxi in the street nearby. Then Fred raised his head, drawing a deep breath and gathering resolve. "Why did you come back to me after you learned the truth, Michelle? Were you afraid of Saakaar? He probably would have lost interest in you if you'd abandoned me."

Michelle took a moment to look away, thinking. She rummaged in one of the shopping bags to choose another piece of fruit. "No. I came back because I liked you enough to trust you in spite of everything." She drew her hand out of the bag, holding an enormous strawberry.

Fred reached for the bottle to pour her a little more wine. Her answer seemed to satisfy him. The quiet moment lengthened between them, somehow comfortable.

Michelle bit her way slowly down to the cap of the berry. A mist of water droplets refracted the setting sun into a shimmering rainbow over the fountain. When Fred finished his drink, he kicked off his shoes to wade in, balancing with both arms out as he walked around the arc. Michelle laughed, charmed by his playfulness.

He came out after a few minutes and padded over, leaving wet footprints in his wake, to reach for her. She batted at his arms, giggling, but let him pull her up. She kicked off her sneakers, following him in. Soon they were running and shrieking with the children, getting splashed by the jets of the fountain, laughing whenever one of them tagged the other.

As the sun sank, the children gradually vanished with their parents. People wandered off until Michelle and Fred were left alone, walking around the circle of the fountain, hand in hand. Michelle was soaking wet, her hair hanging in bedraggled strands around her face, but the warmth in Fred's eyes said he still found her beautiful. He was so handsome he made her heart skip a beat whenever she looked at him, even with his hair plastered flat on his forehead and his wet T-shirt clinging to his ribs.

They left the fountain together without speaking, sitting down on the hexagonal concrete cobbles to put on their shoes. The lantern lights came on overhead, followed rapidly by floodlights igniting from the ground, bathing the arch in warm light as they wiped their feet dry with their socks. They pulled their sneakers onto bare feet, stuffing the damp socks in their pockets. This time Michelle reached for Fred's hand as they set out. He smiled as he accepted her shy touch. They strolled slowly back to the hotel, each with a plastic shopping bag of leftovers dangling from one hand.

Fred seemed a little quiet, but not unhappy. Michelle assumed he was tired and hungry. He had to be. He'd always visited her every other day, but tonight would make the third night in a row with nothing to sustain him.

She was not about to let this state of affairs continue.

## Chapter Nineteen

The second-shift pixie gave Michelle a withering glare when they entered the hotel, but Fred intercepted the look and backed her down with a warning stare of his own. Interposing himself between the two of them, he guided Michelle through the lobby and up to the room, then went for a bucket of ice.

She rinsed herself off quickly in the shower, choosing a butter-soft cotton nightshirt to wear. The top buttoned down the front, barely covering her bottom in back. She stared at herself in the mirror, debating her plans, then firmed her jaw, committing to them. She didn't bother with a bra or panties, but went out as she was.

Fred glanced at her, giving her a welcoming smile. However, he didn't respond to her state of dishabille quite as she'd hoped. Her pajamas were hardly a sexy lace teddy and stiletto heels, but she'd expected to provoke at least a little more reaction. Still, she had faith in her ability to tempt him.

She changed the channel on the TV, giving Fred a good look at her bottom as she bent over to take the clicker off the table. When she glanced up, he deliberately looked away. His adam's apple bobbed in his throat as he swallowed hard. That was a little more like it, but still not enough, so she upped the ante, moving to sit next to him on the sofa.

"Do you like action movies?" Michelle hunted through the channel bank, looking for something a little more romantic than the latest news of the Middle East.

"They're okay, I suppose. I prefer science fiction or a good comedy."

Michelle smiled a little, shifting closer, leaving the television tuned to an old episode of *Star Trek* on BBCA. Fred sat like a lump;

everything about him implied fastidious, polite disinterest. God, she felt awkward, putting the moves on exactly the same way Kevin would have.

"You're a hard man to help, Fredric." That caught his attention. He gazed at her, frowning a little. Michelle reached, mustering her courage, and threaded her hand into his hair, tugging him over for a kiss.

He softened for her a little, letting her tug at his lips with hers, but his hands stayed put in his lap. *Stubborn bastard.*

"Geek rule number one: no sex during *Star Trek*," Fred joked, then gave in, shifting to pull her into his lap. "What am I going to do with you, Michelle?" He stroked her damp hair out of her eyes, then lifted his mouth for a real kiss.

"Lots of things, I hope," she mumbled against his lips, then lost herself in his kiss, twining her arms around his neck.

"Not too much, though," his attempt to sound stern was spoiled as he slid his hand up over the soft cotton shirt to cradle her breast. He touched his nose to her throat, inhaling and running his tongue along her skin to her collarbone. Michelle shivered with pleasure, arching into his hand. Fred made a low, urgent sound against her flesh, his teeth touching her skin lightly.

"You're going to spoil my diet."

"I mean to." She laid her hand over his, pressing it against her, squirming suggestively deeper into his lap. She loved the sensation of his body against hers, a little warmer than a human male.

"We can't afford to do this." Fred drew back, his eyes dilated, his face flushed. "I'm sorry, Michelle, but I need a cold shower before things go too far. We'll talk later?" He gently lifted her, putting her back on the couch. He stole a last lingering kiss as he rose, then pulled away.

He spent an unnecessarily long time in the shower, even longer than she expected. Thwarted, Michelle fumed on the couch, glaring at Michael Dorn's prosthetic forehead until David Tennant replaced him. She remained patient, but Fred didn't emerge from the bathroom, not even after the credits ran for *Dr. Who.* He was definitely hoping she'd go to sleep while he delayed. She checked her phone: ten PM. She chuckled, both amused and irritated. He might have succeeded the previous evening, but delaying tactics weren't going to do the trick this time. If he wouldn't let her touch him, then she'd have to fall back on plan B.

She composed her mind to calm, opening the plastic bag holding the leftover fruit from dinner. She pulled out a carton of kiwi slices, nibbling one while she waited. Finally, the bathroom door opened, emitting a puff of steam. Fred came out, his hips wrapped in a towel. He had another one draped over his shoulders, partly concealing his chest.

She heard him inhale sharply when he spotted her sitting up, waiting.

"You're amazingly shy for an incubus." She held her ground, taking bites out of the slice she held until she finished.

Fred hesitated, seeming uncertain what to do. He finally picked up the remote and a weather report, then turning the volume down until it was a soft drone in the background. He tousled his hair with the spare towel, moving to sit on the other side of the lounge from Michelle, returning the towel to its place on his shoulders.

"Do you really need to preserve that much modesty?" She raised a brow at him, tilting her head at the protective towels. "We've been intimate already."

"I suppose we have, in a sense. But we mustn't risk sex for real, not skin to skin." He turned aside, looking back toward the television. He didn't doff either of his towels.

"If you can sustain yourself from sharing dreams, you should be able to absorb what you need in other ways that don't involve physical contact. I can feel pleasure without you touching me; you felt me enjoying my shower, so you could feel it if I touched myself." Michelle watched him carefully as she spoke. "Can you feed that way?"

"It should be possible, though I've never tried." His ears turned pink. He tried to cover his embarrassment by tousling his hair dry again, but she wasn't fooled. He kept his head turned firmly away from her.

"Five hundred, six hundred years alive, but you've never had a girl offer to touch herself for you to enjoy?" Her voice sounded almost too light, falling into the sudden silence between them. "I want to try, Fred."

"I wouldn't ask you to."

"I'm offering." She brushed his scruples aside impatiently. "Don't you think it's time to forgive yourself?"

He bit his lip, seeking an answer, but she wasn't finished. "Have you ever asked me for what you want, Fred? I don't remember you asking. No, I don't mean you took whatever you wanted without permission," she assured him hastily when he turned to her to protest, pain dawning on his face. "What I remember from every single dream is seeing you and deciding you were attractive, then approaching you myself. Time after time, you turned up in my dreams. You were obviously interested in me, but you waited until I made the first move. You let me come to you. You never demanded. You never even asked to take. You always let me make up my own mind to give."

She stood up, deftly snagging the uppermost of his two towels in her hand, pulling it from around his neck. "I kept choosing you because I always enjoyed our dreams. I always loved whatever we did together." She walked away to give him some time to calm while she hung the towel neatly over the bar in the bathroom. The mirror showed her a brief glimpse of her face. She looked a little pink-cheeked, her hair still damp, but her expression was resolute, her chin firm. She was ready.

"My mind is made up; I want something real." She emerged from the bathroom again, stretching with her hands clasped behind her head, making her nightshirt ride up nearly to her hipbones. The soft cloth dragged against her tender nipples, making them stand up. Fred froze like a deer in headlights, caught halfway between standing and sitting, his wide eyes locked on her.

"Get ready. The table is set." She couldn't keep from smirking a little, giddy now she had him where she wanted. "Dinner is served." She sat back down on the leather armchair. Her nipples drew tight in response to the cool, smooth surface against her skin. She felt pleasantly aroused from the rush of acting on her plans.

He might be the sex demon, but she was driving now. He wore the stunned expression of a man who'd been offered everything he ever wanted, who found himself helpless to listen to good sense or conscience or anything else except the urgent demands of his hungry cock.

Michelle gazed at him, enjoying the dusting of dark hair on his chest. Even and crisp, not too thick, the nice symmetrical thatch led to a tantalizing trail that vanished into his towel. She let her hand wander across her chest, undoing a few buttons, then dipped inside her nightshirt to caress her breast. She watched his eyes darken. His response gave her the daring to continue, so she lifted her other hand, kneading her breasts, pinching the nipples lightly between her fingers.

He gave a low groan and slowly eased back, lowering himself onto the couch, his eyes fixed on her. His eyes began to glitter as he settled. His tongue darted out, wetting his lips. He moved silky-smooth, like a stalking cat, seeming unconscious of the change as instinct took over from intellect.

She shivered, lifting herself in response to the intensity of his stare. She let her knees part slightly, imagining the hands on her were his. By now she knew what he liked; the months of dreams wouldn't mislead her.

He touched her mind without verbal communication, not even an exchange of images. The electricity between them simply jacked up from one-ten to two-twenty in the blink of an eye. She gasped, uttering a low whimper. She flicked her nipple with her fingernail. Fred echoed the sound she made, growling deep in his chest, his eyes burning.

That was all she needed to lose the last of her self-consciousness. She arched and lifted for him, moaning. Deliberately, she let the shirt slide off her shoulder, then lifted her breast for him to see. Cradling her breast in her palm, she alternated between rolling her nipple between her fingers and pinching it, sending little zings of pleasure sizzling through her nerves. Her knees spread wide apart for him.

Fred licked his lips, predatory, gazing so intently she thought the touch of his eyes might burn her.

She let her free hand drift down, teasing herself open. She touched herself lightly with one fingertip. Fred groaned again, his hands flexing, both fists opening and closing, the knuckles turning white. She could sense how urgently he wanted to touch her himself. He was boiling with lust and need, his cock straining at his towel.

She wanted him inside her; she wished she could feel the heat, hardness, and strength of him. Moaning, she slid her hand down farther, two fingers pressing inside her body. She rode them, squirming, then lifted herself, kneeling so she could move more easily. She sank against the back of the couch and spread her knees wide. "Tell me what you want," she commanded him, stilling herself, waiting.

His teeth sank in his lip; he quivered, his breathing loud, harsh in his chest. "Take off your nightshirt?" She obeyed, dragging it over her head and tossing it away hastily, loving the sound of his quick inhalation as she bared herself for his eyes. "Now touch yourself again," he said, so she ran her hands all over her breasts and belly, moaning. She slid them down to stroke herself inside and out. She closed her eyes, imagining him riding her: harder, faster. She tossed her head, her hair cascading over her, tickling at her breasts. Her skin felt on fire, alight with the intensity of his focus. Every whisper of air against her flesh sang through her nerves with the sensual clarity of a caressing hand.

She began moaning, whimpering as her thumb circled her clit, imagining his tongue on her. "Yes," he whispered, husky. "Make the pleasure last, Michelle. Not too quickly."

She obeyed, slowing, catching her breath. He began to whisper, soft burning words. "There. Now. Slower. Both hands, yes. Touch your breast. With your hair; stroke your nipple with a strand of your hair." The soft stream of instructions continued. She sank away from self, letting him guide her, feeling almost sleepy as she obeyed, hypnotized by his desire.

His voice resonated in time with the beat of her heart. She could almost see his words imprinted on her retinas when she closed her eyes to listen. His voice ached, rich with lust and rough with need as his words touched her in place of his hands. She writhed, gasping for breath. Her heart was racing now, beating frantically in her chest.

"Now, Michelle," he purred. She went off like a firework, pleasure searing sparkling trails through her nerves. She shrieked once, then collapsed like a puppet with her strings cut, shuddering against her fingers. A series of aftershocks wracked her nearly as hard as the original orgasm.

When her eyes opened, he sat with his hand closed around the thick shaft of his cock, stroking himself lightly. She stared at him, feeling another aftershock of pleasure ripple through her at the sight. He was hard and red, the tip of him dripping wet, but apparently he had not come. His eyes were shut, his face slack with pleasure. He breathed deeply, as if inhaling some rare perfume.

He opened his eyes after a few moments, blinking with what looked like confusion. Then his gaze settled on her. He smiled.

"You didn't come," Michelle murmured with dismay. Her throat was raw. She hadn't realized she'd been making so much noise.

"No, but I don't have to come. I feed on your pleasure, not my own. I feel much better now." He looked healthy and robust, some of the weariness smoothed away, his color high. "But you're spent. I can tell."

She tried to protest, but found she couldn't raise herself to sit again. Her arms and legs felt shaky when she tried to make them answer her mind's call.

He stood up, leaving his towel forgotten on the chair. Lean and lithe, he stepped over to her. Michelle's mind didn't want to function properly. Impending sleep gathered around her like storm clouds sweeping in, eclipsing the sun on a summer afternoon.

Fred gathered her in his arms, lifting her off the couch. Cradling her against his chest, he carried her to the bed and settled her under the coverlet, then slid in behind her. He pillowed her cheek on his shoulder, wrapping his arm around her waist. Carefully, he tucked her head under his chin. His bare body nestled against hers: solid, very real.

"Rest, Michelle." His voice breathed love into her ear. Unable to resist, she slipped away into dreams she would not remember in the morning.

# Chapter Twenty

Michelle roused without knowing when she crossed the boundary between sleep and waking. She didn't move, content, wrapped in perfect comfort. Slowly she realized Fred held her. She blinked into his face for a moment, admiring the dark fans of his lashes against his cheeks. He lay very still, breathing evenly.

The nagging shaft of sunlight from the window was back, making its way across Fred's head toward his eyes. Intense light caught in his dark hair, picking out a narrow glowing stripe of skin, highlighting the fine down of hair on the curve of his ear.

Michelle nestled closer, not wanting to have to face the day. His arms tightened as he turned his eyes away from the light, burrowing tightly against her. She felt him come awake, the rhythm of his breathing and his heartbeat changing subtly, his body shifting as he transitioned from the heavy stillness of slumber to a gentle awareness of lying close to her. He shifted, accommodating her more comfortably. His lips brushed her cheek.

"Mmmm," she told him, half in approval, half in protest. "Don't want to get up."

"Do you still feel tired?" His voice sharpened with concern.

"No. Too comfortable to move."

He chuckled, relieved, and nuzzled at her again, his legs shifting to part hers as he drew her even closer. "Any other time, I'd agree. But today I have urgent things to do. I have to retrieve the jewel so Saakaar will remove his curse from you."

Michelle winced; she'd been enjoying Fred so much she'd all but forgotten her problem.

He kissed her slowly but lightly. However, he drew back when she opened her lips for him. "Mmmm, another time. I'm sorry." He stroked her cheek, then rolled out of bed. She indulged herself, watching him moving around the room. He seemed gracefully unconscious of his nudity. He moved with brisk efficiency as he chose his clothing, then vanished into the bathroom. How could anyone ever find him geeky and unattractive?

She crawled out of bed as soon as he was gone, rummaging through her clothes. She made it as far as sitting on the couch holding a crumpled T-shirt in her hands before he came out. He trailed his palm over her bare shoulder.

"We'll be all right," he murmured softly. "I'll retrieve the jewel and deal with Saakaar. Then..." he hesitated, his fingertips drifting along her collarbone. He laid his other hand on her opposite shoulder, massaging her neck. "Then you can decide what you want without anything pressuring you. You can have all the time you need to make up your mind whether you want to risk being with me." He bent to kiss the crown of her head. "Remember, don't go out or let anyone in. I'll be out late tonight."

That meant she'd be eating her meals from the fruit bowl, the mini-bar, and the remains of their supper. "I don't guess I can order pizza delivery here. Bring some hot food back with you?"

"I will." He stroked her hair for a moment, then withdrew abruptly. "I love you, Michelle. Thank you for last night." The door closed behind him.

She sat very still, his words echoing in her ears, her hands trembling, her heart pounding hard with exhilaration. Then she made herself rise. Very deliberately, she drew the deadbolt. She thought of calling her mother, but what would she say? "Mom, I'm in a relationship with a super. An incubus, to be exact. We're very much in love. He's a bit of a dork, except he's totally gorgeous when he wants to be. By the way, if we have actual sex I'll probably have a heart attack and die from all the hyper-orgasms."

She cringed away from the very idea, so she set her phone decisively out of reach.

Not feeling much like dressing, she stripped the duvet from the bed, wrapped it around her, and curled up on the couch, turning on the television. With Fred's laptop on her knees, there was at least something to keep her occupied.

Her phone buzzed against the table, nearly startling her out of her skin. Elise. Michelle thumbed the answer button. Might as well face the music.

"Hey."

"Where the hell are you? Jim's having kittens. The Marcus project is stalled without you and Fred. The clients are pissed as hell. Jim has me trying to read Fred's notes so I can put together a stopgap manual to show Harold while you two are off in Bermuda or wherever you went, balling the jack."

"I'm sorry, Elise. Go on my computer and get my files. You'll want to look for the Marcusdocs folder on my desktop; I've already done a lot of what you need."

"Thanks." Elise sounded a little mollified. "Where are you, anyway?"

"Fred had a family emergency. I came along to give him some support," she lied. "We're in New York."

"What the hell did he need you for?" Elise sounded highly skeptical.

"Balling the jack, what else?" Michelle retorted, dry.

"With Fred. Dorky little Fred who won't take off his tie even for DragonCon. The same guy who wears a pocket protector and tapes his glasses together?"

"No, he doesn't."

"He might as well." Elise paused. "Does he at least have a big one to go with his sunken chest?"

"None of your business." Michelle kept frosty, maintaining her dignity. Sunken chest? Ridiculous. Surely even Elise had eyes.

"What about Kevin?"

"I broke up with him the day after my sleep study. We weren't compatible."

"You think you and Fred are?" Elise sounded dubious.

"I don't know." She sighed explosively. "We're finding out."

"Have you really had sex with him?" Elise kept pushing, titillated. "Is he any good? When you two made out in the room, you were shrieking like a banshee. Tell all, girl!"

Michelle wasn't about to tell her a thing, not unless she wanted everyone at Robotidata to hear about it in five minutes or less. "Look, Elise, not now, okay? I really appreciate you stalling the Marcuses. I owe you one. I'll be back as soon as I can. Tell Jim to hang in there. I'll log in remotely and send you everything I can." She pushed back her hair. "Maybe I can come back to the office early next week."

"Yeah, that would be good, but—"

"I have to be going. I'll give you a call in a couple of days. Thanks again, Elise." Michelle hung up. The phone immediately buzzed again, but she let voicemail take the call. So much for reconnecting with the real world. Doing actual work on the Marcus files would suck, but at least she'd have something worthwhile to do while she waited for Fred.

# Chapter Twenty-one

Michelle settled in to endure a long wait. After half an eternity of work, the shadows began to stretch. Then the sun set, fading from the window, gradually replaced by street lamps and flickering neon. Michelle shut the drapes to protect her privacy. She wandered somewhat forlornly around the room, peeling an orange as she tried not to fret. She fucking hated waiting, feeling powerless, reduced to hoping Fred was all right. There was nothing whatsoever fit to watch on television, she'd sent Elise everything she had on the Marcus project, and she was sick of surfing the web.

Her phone buzzed again. The number status displayed 'unknown.' She hesitated, but it might be Fred. He'd never actually remembered to give her his information. She thumbed answer cautiously, prepared for a telemarketer. "Hello?"

"Michelle." Fred's warm voice made her heart flutter. "Sorry I'm taking so long."

"How are things going?"

"They let me attend the reception after they inspected and verified the gem this afternoon. As far as I can tell, they have the real jewel. I've seen no sign of Saakaar. Did anything happen to you today?"

"No, I sat staring at these four walls." She folded her legs under herself anxiously. "Did you expect trouble?"

"Not really, but I'm glad nothing bothered you. I'm leaving the auction house. Would you like Thai, Chinese, or something else?"

"Chinese would be heavenly." Michelle's mouth watered. "I hope you can get the takeout fast. I want you to hurry back."

She could hear the smile in his voice when he spoke again. "All right. I'll try not to take too long, but traffic in midtown can be a real pain in the ass."

Michelle showered, dressing rapidly, but she had plenty of time. Another hour passed before Fred burst in carrying two big bags of steaming cartons: wonton soup and fried noodles, fried dumplings, chow mein, beef with broccoli, egg rolls, crab rangoons, even a couple of dishes she'd never seen before.

He peeled out of his formal suit, hanging it up carefully, then joined her for dinner wearing his undershirt and a pair of pale blue boxer shorts. They sat cross-legged on the floor next to the coffee table to eat. Michelle tried not to talk with her mouth full, but she was too curious about his day to stay quiet for long.

"What was the auction house like? Did they give you a hassle? What kind of price do you think the jewel will go for? Did you meet any prospective buyers? Why wasn't Saakaar there?"

Fred fielded her questions, but though he smiled, his good humor seemed too shallow to suit her. She sensed an unaccustomed quietness in him even though he provided thorough answers.

"I missed you today, Fred." She curled up next to him on the sofa, where he was flipping through the channels idly, grimacing whenever he passed a particularly dismal show. "You left in such a hurry I didn't have a chance to answer what you said."

He glanced up at her with alarm. Their gazes caught and held. Michelle slowly eased closer to him, tucking herself under his arm and draping her legs over his lap. "I think maybe I love you, too. I want to find out for sure," she murmured, nuzzling the pulse point below his ear. "I want to see how we work out together. We can be as careful as we have to, but I want to be with you."

"But you need a real lover—"

"And you don't?" She nuzzled her way toward his lips. "If you can do without, so can I." She kissed him carefully. His arms came around her, nestling her close. "We can be lovers in our dreams."

He sat up, shifting her. She moved until she was kneeling over his lap, gazing down into his face.

"You have bichromia," she murmured, tracing his cheekbone with her thumb. "I can see so many colors in your eyes."

His hands slid along her back, supporting her. He smiled a little shyly. "I don't deserve you."

Michelle narrowed her eyes at him to make him stop. She

shrugged out of her thin T-shirt, then worked the clasp of her bra. Unfastened, it dangled over her chest, barely covering her. She smiled seductively down at him, then shrugged the straps down over her shoulders, leaving herself bare. His eyes didn't leave hers, shining with love.

"You're wearing far too much," she leaned in, snagging the hem of his undershirt, enjoying the slow revelation of his flat belly and his pretty pink nipples. Fred had to fumble off his glasses underneath the cloth before she could tug the shirt off his head, which reduced them both to giggles. After his glasses were safely set aside on the coffee table, he dragged her against him, his eyes gleaming.

"I think you can probably handle a little stress," he murmured, his voice warm like smoke. "At least enough for one more kiss." His mouth fastened on her throat. She gasped, her head falling back. The kiss wasn't instant flame, but his mouth was hot, wickedly skillful, his teeth just sharp enough. Soon she was squirming and whimpering on him, his chest hair a rough friction against her tender nipples. Fred's cock pushed eagerly up at her through his boxers, when she ground down against him. He lifted his hips, thrusting against her in return. He suckled at her throat hard enough to leave a mark. His hands wandered gently over her back, tangling in her luxuriant hair.

Then they fell sideways. Their underclothes remained as a protective boundary, but the rest of their skins pressed together. He turned her, sinking between her thighs, then resumed kissing her, exploring her mouth. The pleasure grew sharper as his control was tested. The world slid sideways in response to the sense of connection, every pleasure doubling. She felt drawn tight with anticipation, every nerve flaring, every part of her needing him, craving more.

"Sleep, Michelle." Fred's voice seemed to come from everywhere. She slid under without warning.

# Chapter Twenty-two

Michelle knew she was dreaming this time. She still lay underneath Fred, but everything shifted in a subtle way. She couldn't feel the scrape of stubble when he kissed her. A variety of other small irritations had vanished without a trace, too. The elastic of her panties no longer bit into the inside of her thigh. She had plenty of room for her leg between him and the back of the couch.

"Fred," she murmured against his lips. He drew back a little, caressing her face with his palms.

"Yes," he acknowledged. "You're dreaming. I'm with you." He lifted his hips, pressing the hard ridge of his cock against her. "We can do whatever we want while we're here."

"Mmmm. Want you," Michelle purred. "Lots and lots of you."

He grinned then, showing straight white teeth—the first big sexy grin she'd ever seen on him, purely mischievous. "That can be arranged. There *are* advantages to dreaming."

Michelle blinked. During the brief instant while her eyes were shut, they relocated to the bed without ever moving. Her pillow lay tucked snugly under her neck. Fred had re-imagined them on their sides, face to face. His body felt subtly hotter against hers. She realized they'd left their underwear behind on the couch.

Someone stirred behind her. Michelle flinched, turning to see who owned the unexpected body. She was startled to find another Fred. He now embraced her from both sides. His cock hardened against both her belly and her backside, four of his hands exploring her at once.

"You can have as much of me as you want," the Fred behind her breathed as the one in front kissed her.

"Oh my God," she moaned into his mouth, arching between them.

His hands went everywhere. One ventured between her legs and two covered her breasts. One slid to her knee, lifting her thigh so the Fred behind her could enter her body. His caresses glided over her skin with slow care, reverent and tender. Everywhere they went they trailed sparks of pleasure in their wake, making her moan. He pushed into her slowly. She cried out, arching her spine, loving the feel of him sliding deep inside her. He moved steadily, plowing her open, making her his own.

"Good?" he purred against her shoulder and began to thrust in earnest: long, slow strokes driving every millimeter of his cock deep.

She cried out, muffled. The scene shifted again. This time the bed grew larger and more copies of Fred appeared. She lay atop him, face up, with his cock buried deep inside her. Three more of him knelt nearby. As the scene settled, they moved forward, laying their hands on her. Two gripped her wrists and drew them up, pinioning them over her head. The last began to suckle her breasts, tormenting her nipples with sweet liquid fire. The two who held her put their cocks in her hands. She stroked them eagerly, each palm wrapped around a cock, sliding tissue-thin skin over a blood-hot core. The copies made soft, satisfied sounds driving her wild with need. One of the Freds unstoppered a bottle from the shelf. He drizzled something slippery over her hands, heedless of the bedding.

She speeded her strokes, bearing down hard on the cock inside her. All of them groaned in response.

"On your knees?" Fred suggested, caressing her cheek. She gasped agreement and they maneuvered her gently until she was positioned the way he wanted, every touch considerate. Then he mounted her again. Two mouths returned to her breasts while Fred—the one who had been there from the beginning—moved to kneel in front of her.

He gently lifted her chin in his palm, positioning her to accept him in her mouth. He still had his foreskin. It cradled the head of his cock, the thin skin pulled back enough to let the tip emerge, gleaming red like a ripe plum. She guessed he would be more sensitive than a man who'd been cut.

The thick, straight shaft thrust toward her lips, nestled in a tuft of dark wiry hair. His balls hung high. If she could, she'd have reached to cup them in her palm. She wanted to feel their weight and enjoy the way the smooth round centers shifted inside their soft purse of skin.

His erection flushed a dark, rosy pink, so beautiful her mouth watered. Belatedly she realized he was waiting patiently while she examined him, as if there must be a verdict, as if she might not choose to do what they both wanted.

Michelle opened her lips eagerly. Sucking him in, she swallowed him deep. The Freds fell into an effortless rhythm, fucking her steadily from both ends at once. She could hear herself whimpering, moaning helplessly. Satisfying them both was too much, impossible. Yet she could breathe; she could manage. The mouths on her breasts drove her mad as the cocks claimed her, hot and hard. Then another Fred joined them all, slipping beneath her, his hot skillful tongue finding her clit.

She cried out shrilly, coming for him, the unexpected liquid shock of his tongue eclipsing all the other sensations that threatened to overwhelm her senses. The Freds held her steady. They kept on taking her, merciless and hot, gentleness giving way to urgent need as the pace turned demanding. She knelt helpless, enjoying their hands and mouths all over her, feeling eager cocks pushing deep inside, claiming the pleasure she had to offer.

She'd always fantasized about this, wondering how many men she could satisfy. She could reach out blindly to touch hot male skin everywhere around her. She reeled, intoxicated with a sense of power and euphoria from knowing so many men wanted her so badly. She'd never expected the chance to try anything like this. Six or seven extremely trustworthy, attractive men didn't come wandering down the hall every day looking for a bored technical writer to join them in a hot session of group sex. Even if they had, Michelle would have been too cautious to accept.

She couldn't think anymore, though, not with Fred's tongue circling. Wicked and deft, he knew exactly what she liked, teasing exactly the right spot with the tip. Her nerves were insanely sensitive so soon after coming, but he barely touched her, not letting sensation recede, ensuring she would come much harder the next time he brought her off.

The soft little touches were almost more than Michelle could bear. She made throttled sounds around the cock in her mouth, helpless. A scrape of teeth on her nipple made her buck. The Freds chuckled softly, appreciative, but didn't stop what they were doing, pushing her toward a second overwhelming crest with impossible speed. They played her like a virtuoso coaxing a perfect symphony out of his most beloved instrument.

Her whole skin buzzed with sensation. The world exploded into sparkling white light as she came a second time on Fred's tongue, helpless, completely claimed. When she was able to think again, she could feel hard hands holding her wrists; others braced her ankles, restraining her. The sense of being unable to move made her whimper around Fred's thick cock, a little worried. He caressed her cheek lightly, understanding. "I can feel what you're feeling. If you don't like what I'm doing, I'll change it until you do," he murmured, reassuring. "Let go. You're safe."

She did, abandoning herself to the hands, mouths, and cocks touching her. Moaning, she entrusted herself wholly to Fred.

Afterward, things slowed down, but even so, he still gave her as much sensation as she could contain without bursting, finding hazy, half-guilty fantasies waiting in her mind to fulfill for her. The next time the Freds fucked her, she lay outstretched, helplessly pinioned to the bed by gentle, immovable hands while cock after cock filled her, one after the other. Finally, she accepted one after another of him in her mouth, all of them standing clustered around her face, painting her cheeks, lips, and eyelids with the wet, salty tips of their cocks while they waited for their turns.

His hands traveled along her body, trailing bliss in their wake, opening her, touching her, penetrating her. Hands tangled in her hair, fingers pressed into her mouth, lips and tongues painted her with kisses. They were all him, eyes loving, hands gentle, bodies eager. She had never felt so deeply bathed in affection, every touch perfect as he ravished her, driving her to the crest of ecstasy over and over again.

The original Fred remained in front of her, directing the scene. Eventually, Michelle grew conscious of his dominance, of his careful restraint. He focused on her, controlling the dream, his goal her pleasure rather than his own. She reached for him when she had a free hand, pulling him forward very carefully, using his cock for a leash. He chuckled, amused, and cooperated. She licked the tip of his cock, tasting bitter salt. He was flushed, his balls drawn very tight against his body. She didn't think he had come yet.

"You need to come," she murmured huskily as she began kissing her way along his cock. "I want to taste you. Come for me, Fred, in my mouth."

His eyes sank shut; a shiver went through him. The other copies of him drew back a little, letting her focus on him. She stroked his cock, loving its solid weight in her hand, then went down, sliding forward until her nose touched his belly. She looked up to find his gaze as she withdrew, trying to communicate her love and desire without speaking. He smiled fondly, brushing her hair out of her eyes with trembling fingers. Then she remembered he could sense her emotions; she didn't have to speak to tell him the depth of her feelings.

She focused on his cock, running her tongue over the shaft. She strummed her tongue at the sweet spot beneath the head, making him gasp. Grasping the base in her hand, she sucked and bobbed her head, humming around the shaft. This one felt real; this wasn't the too-easy orgasm the others had given up without her ever needing to try.

He let her work, holding her hair out of her face. She could hear the involuntary hitches in his breath whenever she pleased him. She let the sounds guide her, learning he liked long slow strokes varied with a few short quick ones. When she cradled his balls in her hand, he shuddered, his fingers bracing lightly on her shoulder as he swayed. She sucked harder as he began to surrender control, falling into the pleasure she offered. Coarse hair tickled her nose. If this were real, her jaw would ache as she grew tired.

But it was a dream, so she didn't. She withdrew to let him watch her kiss the tip and paint her lips with pre-come. "So beautiful, Fred." She sank down on him again, sucking the luscious head of his cock, teasing at the foreskin with her tongue. His head tipped back, his adam's apple working in a harsh swallow. She pulled off briefly. "So good." her lips slid against the head of his cock as she spoke. "Your turn to let go." She swallowed him down again. Sliding her hand back behind his balls, she pressed lightly with her thumb, seeking the sweet spot buried inside him. He spasmed suddenly when she found her goal, choking out a shocked gasp.

His cock jerked out of her mouth and a single stripe of come painted across her face before she could recapture it. She savored the way he trembled for her, the taste of him flooding her mouth. She swallowed eagerly, milking him until he gently disengaged. He reached for her, pulling her up against him to kiss her, murmuring husky words of love against her lips.

Once he had come, Michelle sank to the bed, exhausted. Fred seemed to understand. He wiped her face clean gently, then the copies moved in again. They all lay down with her and tangled her in between them, kissing her softly until the dream faded. She stirred then, feeling the real Fred holding her. In spite of her drowsiness, she recognized a sharp distinction between dream and reality: all the little discomforts were back. Fred snored lightly into her ear.

Perfection.

Michelle snuggled closer, holding him tightly, before she slid back into slumber.

# Chapter Twenty-three

Michelle woke to the inevitable sunbeam in her eyes. She hid her face against Fred's neck, feeling sated, sensual, without the aches or stickiness she usually felt after a really great night of sex. Somehow, she missed them.

She grimaced a little, freeing her numb arm from its warm prison beneath Fred's chest. He blinked into her face, grimacing against the light. "Morning," he murmured, deep and husky. "Feeling all right?"

She felt foggy, a little sluggish, didn't want to admit her fatigue. "Mmmm. Wonderful." She stretched, tangling their legs so she could press herself against him, rubbing herself lightly against his thigh. "Well-fucked and satisfied." She stroked a wisp of hair off his forehead. "But ready to go again any time you like."

He chuckled, stroking her shoulder. "I think I made the perfect choice. You're insatiable." He kissed her lips, but his body pulled back subtly, disengaging as he retreated from the intimacy instead of deepening it, exactly as he had the previous morning.

"Don't make me wait for you here today," she begged. He rolled onto his back with a sigh.

"I'm sorry. If I could take you with me, I would." He stared at the ceiling, his brows drawing down in a fierce frown. His moods were still unfamiliar to her, a discovery in process. She hadn't yet seen him scowl before. Quietly, she studied the lines of his forehead, the creases between his heavy eyebrows, the way the clear blue of his eyes darkened and turned cool. She didn't think he was angry with her, but the expression sent a shiver down her spine.

Michelle climbed out of bed to pull on her T-shirt and panties. "Will today be the last day?"

"At Superlatives? I hope so." His ferocious expression didn't soften, threatening to burn a hole in the ceiling. "I can't wait until this is over. Then we can spend time relaxing together." He reached out to clasp Michelle's wrist, stroking his thumb against the pulse point. His scowl finally melted as his eyes sought hers, earnest. "There will be time for us. I promise."

Michelle chewed her lip as she watched him get up to dress before he kissed her goodbye. She hoped he was sincere.

She sat back down, folding her legs in the lotus, half-covering herself with bedding. Not another eternity of shitty daytime TV!

Michelle sighed. Maybe she wasn't such a good partner for him after all. In spite of her promises, she wanted him for real, buried deep inside her: all the imperfection, mess, and awkwardness. She wasn't satisfied with the half-impossible haze of pornographic imaginings, all the rough angles carefully left on the cutting room floor, glorious though the dreams had been.

Michelle needed him to be more than a flawless, impeccable sex god. She wanted her dorky, sweet, insecure Fred, smiling shyly at her through his ridiculous thick-framed glasses, with his stubble scratching her lips, his chest hair tickling her nipples, his body sweaty against hers. She wanted to watch him sitting at his computer and wonder what he was thinking. She wanted him to raise his blue eyes to look at her, his expression a little uncertain, his gaze searching her face, checking to be certain she was happy.

She wanted to feel their teeth clicking as they learned how to kiss, working to find a fit for their bodies. She even wanted to drag herself out of bed to make breakfast for him, find out how he liked his eggs and bacon. She craved real intimacy: loving someone, learning to relate to one another. That wasn't going to happen if Fred pulled away every time they drew close to waking intimacy.

She got up and went to the shower. Time to shave her legs and make herself presentable. No point letting herself hang around being a slob. She never knew when she might be needed.

# Chapter Twenty-four

She was almost finished in the bathroom when a tap on the door made her jump. Had Fred forgotten something? She stood up, tossing back her heavy, wet hair, eagerly opening the door to greet him.

Robin beamed up at her instead, arms folded over her chest, eyes sparkling with delight—or possibly malice. "How are you this morning?" She seemed almost obscenely cheerful, bouncing on the balls of her feet. "A little tired? A little worn out? Such a pity. Human skin is so fragile; it shows every little thing. What do you call them? Those things on your face. Crow's feet?"

Shit; she hadn't set the deadbolt. Michelle blocked the door with her foot, setting her heel into the carpet. She didn't know how much of a barrier she could create against a super. Still, Robin showed no sign of forcing her way in. Instead, she went for the direct approach.

"May I come inside?" Robin tilted her head, trying for a winsome expression. "I have information I think you'd find very valuable."

"Fred's not here." Michelle kept her answer short.

Robin's smile stretched wide—too wide. "I know. Don't you want to know what he's doing?"

"You aren't supposed to meddle with another supernatural's business. Not here."

"But you aren't a supernatural." Robin spread empty hands, trying to look harmless. "Besides, I don't meddle. Not me! I help. There's a difference." She beamed and Michelle sighed. Fred had told her not to let anyone in, but they were already dealing with this being. Besides, maybe Robin did have information Michelle needed. Her curiosity threatened to eat her alive.

"All right, but on one condition: you have to leave whenever I tell you to."

"Deal." Robin darted inside before the door was properly clear, almost as if she had turned to smoke to slide through the crack. She marched straight to the sofa, making herself at home, singing to herself in between snitching a pear and taking dainty bites. She nibbled the fruit as if she had all the time in the world, volunteering no information.

"What do you want?" Michelle approached her warily, tolerating the interrupted strains of "Michelle Ma Belle" with considerable patience, given the circumstances. "You're hardly Paul McCartney."

Robin merely kept singing, ignoring the complaint.

Michelle frowned. "If that's all you have to say, you can leave now."

"Fredric is trying to buy Saakaar's jewel himself. Don't you want to know how he's planning to pay?" Robin grinned at her, then devoured a big bite of pear, chewing messily.

"He said he didn't have enough money to buy the jewel."

"He doesn't." Robin said with her mouth full. Her eyes gleamed with triumph. "But he does have something to barter with."

"What's that?" Robin's obvious excitement bothered Michelle.

"Himself." Robin squealed with glee. She abandoned the mangled pear, dancing around Michelle with an excess of high spirits. "Do you know how much a human would pay for a night with an incubus? Maybe you do," she gave Michelle a decidedly insolent look. "But you don't have to, do you? You can wait here and watch television while he whores himself out for you, then comes back home in time for *dinner*." Malice danced in Robin's expression.

"He shouldn't have to sell himself too many times," Robin continued airily. "Even set against immortality, really good sex should bring a hefty return. Five, maybe ten sales at most. The auction house thought he was a fine barter. They'll make an intangible fortune from the PR and a very tangible one from the sales. Of course, they don't have time to advertise. Fredric may not go for as much at a quick auction, but the death-by-orgasm crowd are already standing in line." She snapped her fingers.

The television came on, showing Fred standing on a dais in a dimly lit lobby, picked out by spotlights. He stood tall, dapper in his new suit, his hair coiffed to an artful tousle, his eyes glittering in the bright light. People milled around him, commenting quietly to themselves, lust shining in their faces. Fred looked a perfect devil, poised and sultry, but she could glimpse the carefully hooded misery lurking behind his eyes. She couldn't bear to think of her beautiful, shy Fred, up for sale, exploited to satisfy a racial stereotype for her benefit.

"A certified incubus, a pretty one in his prime? For sale by the night? Get ready to spend a lot of time watching soap operas. You're going to be stuck here for at least a week." Robin's voice fell. "He'll be working until they make the appraiser's predicted value for the jewel, plus overhead."

"Why are you telling me this?" Michelle struggled to keep her voice even.

"I thought you should know." Again Robin smiled her shark's smile. "True love is so terribly sad when things don't go smoothly. I'm almost tempted to intervene."

"How much was the appraisal for the gem?" Michelle thought uselessly of her IRA, her parents' ancestral farm in Virginia, the family silver....

"Around a billion US dollars. The appraisal isn't of the jewel, per se. The value lies in its power to grant immortality. That's the number Fredric persuaded them to settle for, anyway, after he pointed out how much they'd save on overhead, insurance, and risk of customer dissatisfaction if nobody could figure out how to make the jewel work. Immortality is a seller's market, I'm afraid."

Michelle slumped onto the couch, staring dazedly at the wall. A billion dollars. How many zeroes was that? Nine? She couldn't manage as few as six, not even if she sold or mortgaged everything she and her parents ever owned.

"What do you want?" Michelle asked. She turned to stare at Robin, feeling bleak. "Did you come here to rub my nose in misery, or do you have something useful in mind?"

The shark was back, Robin's smile stretching to reveal an impossible number of teeth.

"There's always more fun to be had." She rubbed her hands together, her stubby fingers flexing with glee, then pulled her palms apart. A bag stretched out of nowhere between them, its top gaping open. Michelle spied a glint of gold inside. "Wouldn't you like to save your pretty Fredric from all those nights of noble martyrdom?"

Michelle eyed her warily. "If you have enough gold and are

willing to help, why didn't you give this to us in the first place?"

"That wouldn't have been any fun." Robin's eyes danced, mocking her. She tilted the bag, making the gold inside slither around with a tantalizing jingle. Michelle couldn't help but peek inside. No way could Robin have lifted so many gold coins at once, not even if she were a bodybuilder twice as tall.

"That isn't real gold, is it?"

"It is, at least for now." Robin tittered to herself, smug. "It's temporary, of course. There's no telling what you'll find in the purse tomorrow." She clapped her hands shut; the bag vanished. "I will personally guarantee any potential problem with this gold is undetectable by human spellcraft. At least until tomorrow morning. Even the best spells wear off after a while."

"If I bid on Fred, I can have enough gold to pay for him?"

"Yes. Then Superlatives will give him the jewel. Their only remaining concern will be what to do with their vault full of frogs the next day," Robin confirmed happily.

"I don't trust you," Michelle said slowly.

Robin looked wounded. "Oh, but I am an honest Puck." She pouted, twisting her toe into the carpet. "Shakespeare said, so it must be true." She stood up straight, throwing her shoulders back. "I hereby solemnly swear on any power you like: I'll give you enough gold to buy Fredric's services. If you do your part, the two of you will have the jewel, free and clear of all obligations to Superlatives. Afterward, you'll have to handle Saakaar yourselves. He doesn't care very much for me."

Michelle could see the demon imp of amusement dancing behind Robin's eyes in spite of the solemn oath. "You aren't telling me everything," she said slowly.

"I hardly have time to recount the history of the universe for a mortal," Robin shot back rapidly, dimpling a mischievous smile.

Michelle rolled her eyes. "I meant you haven't told me everything I need to know."

"Nobody ever knows everything they need to."

"What are you going to demand in return for this favor?"

"What I always ask." Robin shrugged elaborately. "Fun, of course."

'Fun' sounded far too vague to be a satisfactory answer. Michelle hesitated, but Robin opened the sack again and shook it. "Limited time offer. Going once...going twice...."

"All right, all right." She couldn't leave Fred to do this on his own. They'd simply have to deal with the consequences of Robin's trickery later. She reached for the sack, but Robin twitched it away.

"Patience," she chided. "We can't go as you are. Hmm." She snapped her fingers. Michelle found herself garbed in a little black dress made of sumptuous velvet. A glance in the mirror revealed a matching feathered pillbox hat. The dense veil obscured her features. Her hair was dry, twisted into a tight chignon with a few wisps escaping to frame her face. A single ebony hair stick tipped with a faceted ruby pinned the coil of hair firmly in place. She held a small leather clutch purse with the gold gleaming richly inside.

"That purse contains as much as you'll need," Robin chirped. "Just keep reaching inside. The money won't run out."

Michelle snapped the clasp and looked up, taking a tentative step in her stiletto pumps. They hurt immediately. Robin now wore a dapper black tuxedo and ruffled white shirt with a black satin bow tie, an ensemble that looked vaguely ridiculous on such a short woman. Her long coppery hair trailed down the back of the suit coat. She too wore pumps—rather less stiletto-heeled and pointy-toed than Michelle's. They looked quite comfortable by comparison.

"Time to go," was all the warning Robin gave before she snapped her fingers again.

# Chapter Twenty-five

Michelle stumbled as they landed on deep pile carpet, her heels sinking in, making her wobble dangerously. They stood in the foyer of a large building amidst a crowd of tastefully dressed people, mostly women. Small clusters grouped together, conversing in low tones and sipping from glasses of wine. A few of them wore more flamboyant clothing, less tasteful but still obviously expensive. No one seemed to have noticed the newcomers' sudden appearance.

Michelle turned to scan her surroundings. A runner of red carpet led toward the exit, passing between a pair of security men diligently guarding a velvet rope. The carpet path continued out into a small lobby fronting on a busy city street. Where she stood, the ceiling rose high, elaborately plastered and painted, inset with tasteful recessed lighting. The inevitable bulbs were carefully hidden behind the frieze-work, but the reflected light was bright enough to make jewelry sparkle on the people who milled around her.

Michelle accepted a glass of burgundy from a waiter and sipped to cover her nerves. Through a gap in the crowd, she glimpsed the dais where Fred had been standing when Robin showed him to her. The platform stood empty now.

A subtle but steady flow of people drifted toward the left. At Robin's silent beckon, Michelle followed them to a bank of elevators. A courteous, liveried attendant ushered half a dozen patrons inside a car, then pressed a button marked "Private lounge" as he swiped a keycard through a magnetic reader. The elevator dropped downward instead of rising, startling Michelle. She steadied herself on the brass rail, looking at her pale face in the mirrored wall. This close, she could see her eyes through the veil, but at any distance, only her lips and chin would show.

The ride seemed to take an unusually long time. Robin began singing again, irritating Michelle. Again, no other patrons seemed to take notice.

The elevator finally settled, and the door slid open with a smooth, discreet flourish. Michelle blinked. For a moment, her mind didn't want to resolve what she saw. The smooth baroque polish of the lobby had been replaced with a much more primitive atmosphere. Rough-hewn stone walls held sconces of wax candles, and a chill mist clung to the floor. The effect was beautiful but eerie, reminding her of a phantom's lair. People stepped out of elevators carefully, a little hesitant, but the floor was smooth and solid underfoot despite the fog.

An amphitheater had been carved into the rock. Steps descended into the shallow bowl, leading to rows of thick, crimson velvet cushions on a curved stone bench. A small paddle with a number embossed in gilt lay waiting at each place. Fewer people had come down than Michelle expected. These must be the serious bidders, people who meant to buy.

Fog poured over the lip of the bowl from the back, following the stairs down for a few steps before dissipating. Michelle carefully descended to take a seat, glad to find she was quite comfortable without a wrap. She turned her bidding paddle over in her hands. The numerals read thirteen.

"Superstitious?" Robin's voice carried across the company. Michelle shook her head no. This was all showmanship, a sales pitch to raise Fred's price by titillating the bidders, immersing them in the whole gothic mystique humans inaccurately associated with supers.

"How much gold is in this purse?"

"Infinity." Robin made no effort to keep her voice down. The little woman wriggled with glee. "Bid till you win."

Michelle wondered how such an easily assured victory qualified as fun for Robin. Her thoughts evaporated when a subtle vibration went through the ground. A spotlight shone down on the stage, the smoky illumination showing hints of flickering red and orange. In the middle of the pool of light stood Fred, as smartly put together as she had ever seen him.

He no longer wore his Brooks Brothers clothing. For the sale, Superlatives had exchanged the conservative outfit for a more dramatic one. The sharp Italian suit featured daring retro tailoring with wide lapels and long tails and a deep crimson rosebud as a boutonniere.

Michelle couldn't help but admire the effect: his black serge coat stretched to his knees. A short cape attached over his shoulders, making them seem broader. He wore no hat, his hair artfully styled, gleaming in the light. A top hat and a pair of white gloves lay on a spindly table standing to one side of him, suggesting he had been disturbed in his home. A half-full crystal decanter and a bell-like snifter of brandy increased the illusion of a private residence.

Fred's face looked unfamiliar, his expression hard, almost fierce. He gazed out at the bidders, his eyes narrowed in the eagle-eyed, sharp gaze of a predator. He held himself haughtily, unmoving, leaning on a gold-handled cane with one leg slightly advanced. A low murmur of appreciation, almost a moan, rustled through the house. Michelle felt her own belly dip, fluttering with an undeniable erotic thrill. The glamour was in full force, enhancing his appearance to an unbearable, tantalizing degree.

"Ladies and gentlemen." A low, resonant voice—a recording of Fred himself, his accent more pronounced than usual—silenced the murmur, commanding attention. "Superlatives Auction House is proud to present this limited specialty item for the true connoisseur. A demon of the underworld has come forth to offer himself for your delectation, and for his own." His voice deepened, taking on a smoky rasp, seductive. "Be certain your heart is bold, should you venture to bid. Rest assured, as the demon sates your appetite for pleasure, you will certainly satisfy his."

Onstage, Fred licked his lips, turning his head so his level gaze swept across the bidders. Again the ghost of a moan rippled through the crowd. He shrugged lazily out of his coat, then a snap of his wrists spun it in a circle, the black fabric flowing around him like the beating wings of a bird of prey. He let the garment swoop to crumple at the edge of the stage in a puddle of inky darkness. He was slim as a blade underneath, wearing a close-tailored dark waistcoat. It caught the lean lines of his body and displayed them to devastating effect. Even his shoes gleamed, reflecting the floor in their perfectly polished surface.

Several uniformed stewards entered the bowl from the back. They spread out among the bidders, offering clipboards loaded with stiff sheets of paper and shiny black fountain pens. Michelle accepted hers, scanning the words. The document combined a contract with a liability waiver, specifying winning bidders were obligated to pay as they bid, on pain of lawsuit and seizure of assets. Michelle swallowed hard. Her assets would not even begin to cover her debt, should Robin prove false.

The second half, requiring a separate signature, stated the buyer would hold Superlatives blameless of all negative outcomes resulting from the purchase, then explicitly stated the risks the buyer assumed upon successful purchase of the commodity. To the winner, Superlatives promised one night, not to exceed twelve hours, of mutually consenting sexual congress with an incubus, the consequences of which were deemed likely to include severe bodily injury, permanent physical or mental incapacitation, and a strong potential for fatality.

Michelle signed on both dotted lines, her functional handwriting crabbed in comparison to the graceful, archaic font. The steward made a note of her bidder number on the contract, then produced a seal, notarizing the paper. He swiped the raised imprint with a sheet of carbon for legibility and tucked the document into a gleaming leather folder, then vanished.

On stage, Fred picked up the snifter of brandy and sipped, the bell of the glass cradled gracefully in his palm. He gave every appearance of bored ease, waiting for tiresome formalities to be finished so the real business of the evening could begin.

Michelle swallowed hard. The butterflies in her stomach had grown to the size of starlings. She thought they might be turning cartwheels. She had to pray whatever mischief Robin had up her sleeve wouldn't prove catastrophic.

# Chapter Twenty-six

The start of the auction interrupted Michelle's worries. A heavy-jowled auctioneer wearing a red cummerbund and a black tailcoat stepped up to a microphone at one side of the stage. A spotlight struck the area, highlighting the Superlative logo embossed on the front of the tasteful brushed-chrome podium. He cleared his throat, shuffling through a small handful of notecards.

"Now, ladies and gentlemen. The bidding will begin at a million dollars. Raise your bids in increments no smaller than $100,000.00. Will anyone bid one million dollars US for this unique item, never before offered here or elsewhere?" He twirled the curl of his handlebar mustache with one finger, attempting a winning smile.

Half a dozen paddles shot up. Michelle clutched the handle of her own, but didn't bid yet.

"One million, yes. Can I hear ten? Ten million. Fifteen? Twenty. Twenty million. Twenty-five? Thirty." The bidding shot up rapidly.

Michelle resisted the impulse to gnaw on one scarlet-lacquered fingernail as she watched the other bidders, trying to plan her meager strategy. "Bid till you win" sounded all right in the abstract, but what she really wanted was to win so decisively Fred would never have to sell himself again. If she could establish a personal rivalry with a determined bidder, she could drive the price up quickly. For now, she would bide her time.

She awaited her moment, fidgeting, eyeing the others. She sat only a few seats to the side of one, a bored looking, statuesque woman with burgundy-tinted hair in a shade nature never intended. Jenny could probably identify the dye both by manufacturer and color number.

The woman affected very pale foundation with dark crimson

lipstick. She'd drawn her brows onto her face with narrow, sharp black lines. They arched too high, making her cheeks look as round as a chipmunk's. Michelle figured her for a rich goth, or a goth poseur of some sort, one with more money than sense. She flicked her paddle casually, without even looking.

A slender man sitting far to the left caught her eye as well. He sat neatly, straight-backed, and had slicked-back blonde hair and a deeply cleft chin. He raised his paddle with twitchy, nervous gestures, licking his lips. He had a fey manner to him, quite self-conscious. He would have pinged Michelle's gaydar even if he weren't bidding on a night with a male incubus. She suspected his visible agitation meant he might drop out soon.

Various other people put in random bids, but not so consistently as those two. Several of them were middle-aged bottle-blonde bombshells or redheads with cold, calculating eyes. She guessed they must be jet setters who'd had every experience money could buy, so bored and jaded an incubus was about the only novelty capable of stirring them to show interest in a man who didn't have money. One seemed to be an older version of the same type, perhaps sixty. She smoked a vapor cigarette and sat with her legs neatly crossed. She flicked her paddle up any time a lull occurred in the bidding process.

The bidding slowed a bit at seventy million. Michelle started to sweat, fidgeting with her paddle. At this rate, Fred would have to sell himself more than fifteen times to buy Saakaar's jewel.

The auctioneer paused for a sip of water. As if on cue, Fred bestirred himself. Every eye in the room riveted on him as he casually set aside his brandy and began to flick open the buttons of his waistcoat. Unhurried, one by one, he opened them with theatrical twists of his wrists.

"Seventy-five, do I hear seventy-five? We have seventy million. Do I hear seventy million, one hundred thousand?"

Michelle raised her paddle, her hand trembling, her fingers cold, clumsy with nerves.

"Seventy million, one hundred thousand!"

"Seventy-five," the goth spoke, sounding bored, flipping back her hair.

"Seventy-five, do I hear eighty?" The auctioneer cajoled. The slim man raised his paddle fretfully, giving the goth a nasty glare.

Even at a hundred million, Fred would have to sell himself ten times. Michelle winced. His waistcoat hung open now. He shrugged his shoulders, making the cloth slide back, a calculated tease.

The room quieted except for the auctioneer's drone. Every eye fixed on Fred as he slipped the waistcoat off his shoulders and tossed it lazily toward his opera coat. His close-fitting shirt seemed to shine in the light, the pale blue emphasizing the icy depths of his eyes. She could see a hint of definition on his chest where the shirt clung artfully close to his skin. Even though she'd seen him bare-chested, the teasing hint left her dry-mouthed with lust.

"Eighty, eighty. Eighty and one? Eighty and one. Eighty and two?" Michelle raised her paddle. Fred's eyes turned toward her. He slid his fingers behind the knot of his cravat and tugged, leaving it hanging loose. He unfastened the top button of his shirt, holding her gaze with smoldering eyes.

"Eighty and three? Yes, to the lady there. Eighty and four?"

"Ninety," the slim man spoke up impatiently, his voice nearly cracking. The goth scowled at him, tapping her paddle against her teeth with irritation. Michelle saw she held the number six. Six was not a lucky number. Not at all.

"Bid him up," Robin urged Michelle, her shrill voice insistent. No one else reacted.

"We have ninety million dollars, a bargain price for such a rarity." The auctioneer's ostentatious tones rang out too loudly, booming inside the enclosed space. Fred tugged at his cravat, which slithered free, the hiss of silk against cotton loud in the absolute silence. He rolled his head a little, easing his neck. The shirt collar parted, revealing a tease of flesh at the hollow of his throat.

He stepped forward, running the silk cravat between his fingers, gazing speculatively out at the crowd. He turned his gaze to the nervous blond man first, challenging him with a smoky stare.

"Ninety-five? Ninety-five to the lady in the veil. Thank you, miss. Do we have a hundred?" The auctioneer began to sweat, his fleshy face gleaming.

Fred challenged the false redhead next. He smiled a little, sultry, his narrow, sensual lips never parting. He began to roll the silk between his fingers, making a neat packet.

His stare traveled again, back to Michelle, who dimly heard the blond man make a bid of a hundred and five as Fred's gaze fixed on her, challenging.

She raised her paddle for a hundred and ten, provoking an angry explosion of breath from the blond man and earning a scowl from the redhead. Fred smiled at her, though, lifting his fingers. He blew her a kiss, then tossed her his cravat with a gentle underhand pitch. It arced over the first few rows of the crowd, unrolling a little before it fell neatly into her hands. The fabric was still warm.

Michelle flushed, finding the exotic scent of expensive cologne on the cloth. He liked her best, not even knowing who she was. The certainty warmed her belly. She ignored Robin's titter, lifting her paddle again to bid a hundred and twenty-five.

Fred unbuttoned his cuffs in the ensuing silence, folding them back neatly. His posture changed to a relaxed slouch, almost insolent, and his lips parted. He reached up, tousling his hair exactly the way Michelle liked, a few wisps dangling down before his eyes.

"A hundred and fifty!" The blond man snapped, peevish. He glared at Michelle, challenging her to raise him again.

"Two hundred." Michelle stared at him, her stomach flip-flopping. By raising so much, had she put a premature end to the competition?

Silence greeted the auctioneer's next query. She feared the worst, but a stir at the top of the bowl distracted them all before the gavel could fall, and a new arrival stepped down the stair to join the bidding.

# Chapter Twenty-seven

Saakaar. Michelle inhaled sharply. He moved slowly, casual in an olive polo shirt and khaki slacks, somehow dominating the room with a casual indifference hinting at supreme confidence. "Three hundred," he announced, signing the attendants' legal documents with a lazy flourish. He reached for a paddle, stifling a bored yawn.

Michelle blinked at him in dismay, then turned to look for Robin. Predictably, she was nowhere to be found. Michelle bit back a curse. She struggled to keep her composure, glad the veil covered so much of her expression.

In for a penny, in for a pound. Her fingers tightened on her paddle as she prepared to raise.

"Four hundred," a new voice chimed in. Michelle turned to see the sixty-ish lady raising her paddle, seeming bored.

Saakaar smiled and sank down onto a cushion, arranging himself with every evidence of enjoyment. He snapped his fingers and a concierge brought him a shot glass full of some amber liquor, which he tossed back quickly, replacing the empty glass on the salver.

The burgundy-haired goth girl glared daggers at Michelle as she set down her paddle with a decisive snap. Likewise, the slim blond man looked crestfallen, tucking his paddle inside his breast pocket. Michelle couldn't help feeling sorry for them both.

The bidding progressed, once again dropping back to increments of a hundred thousand. Two more bidders entered the fray. Michelle sat back, clutching the silk cravat in her hand. She watched the amount go up, not bothering to put her two cents in again—at least, not yet.

Fred put his hands in his pockets, listening for a moment, then stepped down from the stage, easily passing into the crowd. Heads turned to watch him strut past, longing eyes following him as he moved among the bidders with easy grace. First, he went to the forlorn gentleman who had so hoped to win him, setting a hand lightly on his shoulder to commiserate. Then he continued his transit of the audience, smiling faintly at a few people who looked up to meet his eye. His smile remained reserved and cool, but Michelle understood: He was a compassionate man who couldn't help but feel flattered by the bidders' admiration.

The goth girl came next. Fred laid his knuckles against her cheek, brushing her skin lightly, giving her a more sympathetic smile. He stepped away before she could reach out and clasp his hand and climbed over the bench toward Michelle. She had not bid again, so he must believe she was out of the race.

Her heart kicked over, thumping guiltily as he drew near. She held out her hand, opening her fingers to reveal the scrap of silk she cradled in her palm. He picked the cravat up thoughtfully, shaking it out, then stretched it between both of his hands to drape it around her neck. The scent of cologne was much stronger with him near. Michelle's eyes fell shut as she inhaled. She felt his fingertips trail softly along her jaw, sparking sweet starfire through her nerves.

"Five hundred million," Saakaar chuckled, derisive. Michelle opened her eyes in time to see Fred stiffen subtly, taking a half-step back from her, his gaze locked on her face. Michelle flushed, feeling her skin heat and go crimson.

Of course. The rush of pleasure she felt at his touch had revealed her to him.

Michelle lifted her chin to smile at Fred, apologetic, then raised her paddle, hearing the auctioneer call a query. "Five hundred and fifty." She had no idea why Saakaar wanted to drive the price up, and no time to think, but she would outbid him if it killed her.

Fred's eyes sank shut for a moment, the most overt expression of emotion he had yet allowed himself. He recovered quickly and moved on, leaving Michelle to dither, hoping he wasn't angry.

Saakaar laughed, mocking them. Robin had reappeared, standing anxiously behind him, wringing her hands. She flicked her fingers at Michelle, urgently indicating Michelle should keep bidding, trying to smile in spite of her obvious association with the enemy.

Fred, at least partly oblivious, targeted the older lady for his next visit. His posture remained graceful, but Michelle could perceive subtle hints of tension in the way he held his head.

"Six hundred million," the woman barked sharply, raising her paddle. Fred smiled at her politely, reaching to shake her hand. Michelle winced. The lady had no way to know the stakes, but if she didn't win, her bid couldn't hurt her. And regardless of Saakaar's attempt to muddy the water, Michelle intended to win. She couldn't bear seeing Fred compromise himself this way for her. No more.

"One billion dollars," she snapped, tiring of the ruse. A shocked hush fell over the room. Saakaar laughed aloud, breaking the silence, and set his paddle aside. Pushing back his long, curly hair with both hands, he stretched, luxuriant.

The older lady gasped, glaring at Michelle with open hostility. The auctioneer gazed at them both, holding his breath. Then the lady released Fred's hand and set her paddle down with a decisive click.

Michelle groped at her side, trying not to look frantic. She almost collapsed with relief to find Robin's purse there, still reassuringly fat.

"Going once. Twice. Three times...sold to number thirteen for one billion dollars!" the auctioneer breathed. Conscious of all the eyes fixed on her, Michelle stood up with great dignity to accompany the attendants who converged on her, fussing and clucking, to lead her out.

# Chapter Twenty-eight

Fred fell in at Michelle's side as they climbed out of the bowl, seeming quite poised, but a single sideways flicker of his eyes said otherwise.

"Robin is responsible for this, no doubt." He looked straight ahead, speaking very softly, offering Michelle the crook of his elbow to hold. "I told you not to let anyone in."

"I couldn't bear to sit helpless after she told me what you were doing." Michelle's voice shook.

"I'm grateful for your good intentions, but we've no idea what game she's playing. Rest assured, Saakaar is controlling her. She may like me, but she's afraid of him."

"Would you rather I'd let him purchase you?"

"Trust me, he had no plans to." Fred's voice turned wry. "He wanted you to win. I daresay Robin didn't tell you about the geas."

"What's a geas?" Michelle looked up at him, troubled, as the elevator arrived.

"It's a spell of obligation." Fred ushered her into the elevator, where a number of Superlatives personnel joined them, silencing further conversation.

"I want the jewel now, Mr. Barton," he told a slim, hatchet faced man in Superlatives livery. Barton gave him an unimpressed look.

"As soon as the transaction clears from our winning bidder."

"I'll be paying in bullion," Michelle asserted herself.

"We'll bring in an assayer." The man pushed back a wisp of his white hair and tapped at a radio nestled in his ear. "You can have your armored car come tomorrow—"

"Bring him now. I have the gold with me." Michelle hoped to hell she did; Robin's clutch purse still weighed reassuringly in her hand. She earnestly hoped it wasn't already stuffed with frogs.

Barton paused, giving her a narrow look. "Certainly." He spoke softly into his radio, issuing orders. "If you please, we'll settle you in the executive lounge. You can have a bite of lunch and a drink while you wait."

"That will be quite acceptable," Fred told him firmly. "We'll both wait there. Bring the jewel immediately. Set a guard on us if you like, but I want to see my purchase now."

"Yes, sir." The man eyed him with distaste, but he vanished to do Fred's bidding. Fred escorted Michelle into a wide lounge with a dozen mahogany tables scattered about the room. Sunlight played over a balcony extending the floor beyond the rear wall, the brightness making Michelle blink. Even though she'd come in near noon, the dim of the underground auction house had fooled her into expecting darkness outside.

After a few minutes, a pair of guards stepped in, pushing a heavy cart with a built-in display case. One of them flipped up the lid, revealing the jewel. Then they retreated, one taking up a post on the balcony, the other discreetly standing outside the door. Fred scrutinized the cabochon carefully, sighing with relief.

"No funny business here, at least. What's in your bag?"

Michelle peeked inside worriedly. "I had gold coins. Now I have gold bars," she pulled one out.

"Those will be easier to count, I suppose." He set the purse aside. "Michelle...." He hesitated, shaking his head. "I understand why you came to help me. I admit, I'm even grateful. The dowager would have won otherwise. She wanted to die, and she came prepared to bid all she had." He frowned. "I couldn't read more in the brief time I could touch her. I think perhaps she is very ill. Regardless, I would not have wanted to take a partner who desired me to kill her."

He fidgeted, rubbing a miserable hand over his jaw. "Still, I fear your choice will bring unpleasant consequences."

"You mentioned a geas, an obligation."

"Yes." Fred went to the bar to mix them both a drink. Michelle remained quiet, giving him time to gather his thoughts. She accepted the tumbler he handed her, but set the drink aside on the table, reluctant to cloud her thoughts.

Fred sipped his own drink, closing his eyes to savor it before speaking. "When dealing with supernaturals, mortals have found a number of safeguards are required. We'll have to trust Robin is sly enough to deceive the assayer with her bag of tricks." He gestured wryly to Michelle's purse of gold.

"I don't want you to have sex with anyone but me," Michelle confessed in a low voice. "But if you don't want to, if they're forcing you to—"

"Superlatives was afraid I might try to renege on my portion of the bargain," he explained. "They worried I might use telepathy to convince a woman we had lain together rather than risk killing her. They wanted me to give value precisely as promised, so they put me under a spell. I must have corporeal sex with the winning bidder." He bit back a swallow of his drink. "If I resist, the geas will make me a puppet. I'll be forced to do as the agreement specifies regardless of my wishes."

"Then this is no better than rape." Michelle's hands trembled a little as she spoke the word.

He barked a pained laugh, silencing her, laying his hand on her knee to soothe the sting of his response. "That is not the issue." His hand burned hot on her skin. "Believe me, I want you. I have wanted you desperately since I first laid eyes on you." His palm stirred, traveling up slightly, his thumb sliding back and forth along the inside of her thigh. Michelle's body lit up in response, desire pulsating through her, burning sweet in the pit of her belly.

"I could damage or even kill you, Michelle."

"You won't." She put her hand over his, leaning forward, intense. "You said yourself you were careless before, thoughtless and inexperienced. You also said incubuses can produce offspring with human women. That means the woman has to live at least nine months after the act, so corporeal sex doesn't have to be fatal. We'll be careful."

"I don't like to risk you. This is supposed to be about saving you."

"We have no other choice." Michelle swallowed hard. "I prefer this option to the alternative. I trust you, Fred. I'll let you know if I'm in trouble."

"This is what Saakaar wants." Fred bent his head, his eyes closing. "The sibyl asked him not to kill you himself, so he's arranged for me to kill you instead."

"You won't." She laid her hand against his cheek, almost pleading.

"I won't let you." She smiled at him, her lips trembling a little. He slid his arm around her waist, pulling her close.

# Chapter Twenty-nine

"Such a pleasure to see the two of you getting on already." An oily-looking man with a Windsor knot in his discreet gray tie approached them, seeming to glide on casters. "We do so like for our clients to find their transactions pleasant and amiable." He bowed to Michelle, taking her hand to kiss her knuckle. "I am Mr. Smythe, representing Superlatives in this transaction. Delighted to be of service to you, Miss...Jones?"

"Yes," she confirmed, reclaiming her hand. "Thank you very much."

"I understand you would like these tiresome business matters dispatched with all speed," he smiled at her politely. "Let's begin, shall we?" A bevy of subordinates trailed in his wake, and he directed an overly elegant gesture toward one of them. "Our assayer, Mr. Baker, as you requested."

"Thank you, sir." Michelle rose to shake hands with the man he indicated. His beard was so heavy his dark stubble had already started to come in despite the early hour. "How do you do, Mr. Baker. Let's start, shall we?"

"By all means, miss."

Michelle reached into her purse, drawing out a 400 oz. ingot. Her nails marred its soft surface, which had been stamped with the crest of the Bank of England. She took a deep breath, hoping Robin was as clever as Fred believed, and handed the gold over.

The fussy little man accepted the ingot and transferred it to his companions, who examined the gold carefully, passing an electronic wand over it. They put their heads together to discuss the results on the readout.

"I don't believe this bar has been magicked," one of them decreed at last. "There's a reading, but it's very low. I think we're just picking up residue from the magical purse Miss Jones is using. Now let's see if the metal is pure." They swiftly set up a scale and a small chemistry set then began to work.

"You do realize you'll need over three metric tonnes of pure gold bullion to constitute a billion US dollars," the man eyed her little bag with doubt.

"How much weight is this floor engineered to take?" Michelle asked the manager calmly, reaching into her bag again. "Perhaps you should arrange for additional security and an armored vehicle, Mr. Smythe."

"We have sufficient vault space in another part of the building." He snapped his fingers for an assistant. "Have Mr. Barton prepare for incoming funds. We need security guards with carts. Miss Jones, if you'll move this way? This portion of the room is directly above our strongest foundation. I trust it will suffice."

"Perhaps you'd care to enter competition with the Federal Reserve Bank of New York, Miss Jones?" The assayer quipped dryly as she pulled out more bars. His wit earned him a brief frown from Mr. Smythe.

Michelle busied herself stacking ingots. Even with Fred's help, it took nearly an hour.

The assayers seemed pleased with the results of their poking and prodding, so security guards began piling ingots onto carts under the keen, suspicious eye of Mr. Barton. The assayers renewed their check on the gold, selecting bars at random for testing, pronouncing each of them satisfactory.

Finally, Mr. Smythe reached into his pocket for a key, unlocking the display case housing Saakaar's gem. "Mr. Fredric, if you'd care to claim your property? May I trouble you to sign this receipt?" Smythe himself signed a receipt for Michelle, affixing the assayers' affirmation stating her gold was acceptable. He directed one of his men to notarize both documents.

"That's settled," he pronounced at last, with evident satisfaction. The guards and assistants departed in the wake of the last cartload of gold bars, leaving the three of them alone. "Now we can proceed immediately to the more pleasant portion of our transaction."

His oily manner worsened with the addition of innuendo, raising Michelle's hackles, but Fred laid a calming hand on the nape of her neck.

"Miss Jones and I would like to inspect our room. Then we'll go out for dinner. If the lady saved back one of those gold bars?" He smiled at her, impeccably handsome, taking the heavy ingot she fished out of her purse. "Could you cash this for us and call a car? We'll be going out for *omakase* before we retire."

"Of course, of course!" Smythe scuttled away to speak with a guard, then returned to lead them to the elevators. "The cash will be ready in a few minutes. For now, please follow me."

They rode all the way to the penthouse floor. Fred put a possessive arm around Michelle's waist as they disembarked, strolling along a corridor with one glass wall. The vista filled with lengthening shadows as the sun sank in the west. Artificial lights began to illuminate the windows of all the skyscrapers.

"The penthouse faces southeast, with a rooftop garden and small heated pool. Indoors you'll find a jacuzzi for your enjoyment. The facility also features a sumptuous bed and bath. I personally ensured the room is stocked with every delicacy from fresh berries to caviar, so you may wish to use the fully functional kitchenette in the morning. By all means treat yourselves. Stay to brunch tomorrow after your transaction is finished, with the compliments of Superlatives."

Smythe shot his cuffs with a twitch of his shoulders. "This is a room we reserve for our most illustrious patrons." He unlocked the door by swiping a card, ushering them in. "Guests of especial distinction such as yourself, Miss Jones."

Michelle blinked at the luxurious room. Lush throw rugs dotted the palazzo tile on the floor, matching fixtures lending the room an Italian flair. Potted plants thrived in corners or on tables, several hanging gracefully from the ceiling. One corner held the promised sunken jacuzzi tub, designed to fit two comfortably. The wide bed lay in the opposite corner, piled thickly with puffy coverlets topped by satin pillows. Two of the walls were made of glass, one facing the sunset, which boiled orange and red in the cloud-scattered sky. Vertical blinds lay folded against the walls, waiting to be drawn to create an intimate, private apartment.

A turf of grass covered half the roof. Potted palm trees grew in corners, and exotic orchids had been tucked in nooks and crannies everywhere. Lianas trailed over a long, narrow pool. A bench sat tucked in a shady corner, and two lounge chairs stood waiting on the small lawn. A latticework of dark iron guarded the edge, twined with ivy.

"This will do," Michelle glanced at Fred, feeling a little shy.

"It's exquisite." He stepped forward to kiss her cheek, heedless of Smythe's presence.

"Intimate luxuries may be found in the cabinet by the bedside. We furnished them specifically for this auction. They are sealed and unused." Smythe's smile looked a little too sly to suit Michelle.

"I suspect we won't be needing them," Fred gave him a haughty glare, reaching to lay his hand on the small of Michelle's back. "But thank you for your thoughtfulness."

Smythe cleared his throat deliberately, reaching to touch an elaborate antique telephone. "This is the house phone. For your convenience, we have a physician on call, should your activities prove overtaxing."

Michelle flushed, but she felt relieved nonetheless.

"We'll require a key to access our lodging later."

"Certainly," Smythe fished in his pocket. "This will activate any of the locks you need: the exterior door, the elevator, or the door to this apartment."

"Thank you." Fred tucked the key card into his pocket. "May we have our money?"

Smythe radioed for his assistant, who delivered Michelle's cash, passing the envelope over politely. She accepted the packet without counting its contents.

"That will be all," Fred said, mingling courtesy with firm command. Smythe bowed his way out in haste.

Fred finally located the closet, where his Brooks Brothers suit awaited; pants, coat, and shirt all freshly pressed, hanging in a neat row. Michelle moved shyly away from Fred as he changed, folding back the coverlet of the bed. The sheets were cotton, but with such a high thread count they felt almost like silk. The pillow-top mattress yielded slightly to her pressing hand, a delightful mixture of soft and firm. She put the coverlet back in place, then went to peek into the bathroom. The place was so clean it sparkled, with more palazzo tile, plants, and gilt plumbing fixtures.

She stepped inside, marveling at the size of the room. The shower featured a built-in bench and several different styles of showerhead. The stall could easily have accommodated five bathers at once. A linen closet stood half-open, shelves filled with huge fluffy white towels. Two thick terrycloth bathrobes hung on the door and plush slippers lay waiting under the vanity. Even the toilet paper was multi-ply, lavishly quilted. She guessed the second commode must be a bidet.

"Let's go eat," Fred's voice purred in her ear, silky. His hand descended lightly onto her shoulder. "Then we can try out the jacuzzi."

"All right." Her stomach fluttered with anxiety and pleasure as she thought of sharing the night with him in this beautiful room—of making love with him for real, despite the risks.

# Chapter Thirty

Fred led Michelle out to a fancy sushi bar where they sat at a table by the wall, not far from the bar, which seemed to be carved from a single huge piece of wood. The head chef himself stood on the other side of the bar, not far away. He flowed like water as he moved, deftly assembling the dishes he would serve. Fred ordered the *omakase* for two from the host, asking for sake on the side. Michelle's mind darted from thought to thought, her heart fluttering with anxiety.

"We should talk," Fred looked at her kindly. "However, this may not be the best place."

It wasn't; the food began to arrive quickly. "White truffle nigiri," Fred said shyly when she didn't recognize the dish. The sushi melted on Michelle's tongue almost as wonderfully as Fred did in her dreams. She closed her eyes, savoring every bite, content to let the talk wait for later.

"O-toro and caviar," Fred pressed another piece on her as the courses continued to arrive. "I have to admit I'm glad I'm here with you, not with someone else." He smiled warmly.

She was glad to be with him, too. The tuna with caviar was incredible, but nowhere near as good as being here with Fred, seeing gentle heat warming his face. She wished there were less worry behind the smiles.

She reached for his hand, twining their fingers, squeezing to reassure him, but no words came. Instead her throat closed, tears prickling at the corners of her eyes.

He reclaimed his hand to pour her two fingers of sake, inviting her to drink. The courses kept coming, spaced far enough apart for their palates to cleanse between flavors. By the time their slice of melon and green tea ice cream arrived, Michelle was ready to go back to their room,

147

a promising glow of arousal building in her belly.

They departed the restaurant, hailing a cab back to their lodging above the auction house. The building echoed with quiet, no one inside, but lights had been left on for them to find their way. Fred laid his hand on the nape of Michelle's neck, making her shiver a little, a frisson of fear and anticipation rippling along her spine, raising the hair on her arms. She swallowed hard, closing her eyes to deny her nerves, reaching for Fred's other hand as they rode the elevator up to the penthouse. He turned to nuzzle lightly at her hair, brushing her veil out of the way.

"Did you bring a bathing suit?"

"No." She blushed a little.

"Neither did I." His smile deepened.

"Good."

They entered the apartment, giggling a bit from nerves. Michelle sat down to tend her hair while Fred undressed in the bathroom. When he emerged, he started water flowing into the tub. He tried various foaming gels and adjusted the temperature until he had it precisely as he liked. Then he turned his back to slip off his robe and step into the water, easing himself down with a sigh.

Michelle kicked off her too-pointy shoes, rubbing her squashed toes. She managed to grab the zipper of her dress to tease it down, then let the black velvet drop over the back of a chair. She had to hope her clothes wouldn't vanish before she was through wearing them; she had nothing else to put on.

From the corner of her eye, Michelle could see Fred glancing at her in only her panties and bra. He ducked his head away, bashful, making her chuckle a little to herself. A shy incubus? Truly a contradiction in terms.

She turned to him, shrugging off her bra, then stepped out of her panties before walking over to the tub. Fred lost his battle with propriety. The tip of his tongue darted out to moisten his lower lip. She watched it with envy, wanting to taste him herself. He looked positively edible, the steam from the water bringing out a faint sheen of perspiration on his face and curling the fringes of his hair against his neck.

He'd chosen bubble bath with a hint of vanilla, the sensual scent welcoming her into the water. She stepped into the tub slowly, enjoying his admiration, and sank down, immersing herself to her collarbones, stretching out her legs until she encountered his. She smiled at him, flirtatious, over the mounds of bubbles, slowly stroking the sole of her foot against his ankle.

Fred's eyes closed. He exhaled slowly, with evident longing; his knuckles went white where his hands lay over the lip of the tub. "Mmmmm. Talk first?" he asked.

"I think both of us did whatever we had to." She removed her foot, considerate of his wishes. "I know you'll do your best to take care of me. What else is there to say?"

Fred considered, biting his lip. "I could tell you what to expect."

She smiled softly. "I think I know the basics. For the rest...surprise me?"

He laughed ruefully, shaking his head. "I don't understand why you aren't terrified."

She was, a little, if not as much as she ought to be. "Because I know you love me." Michelle sat up a little, bubbles swirling around her. "We'd have decided to try this anyway, given time. We both want to make love, Fred." She reached, her hand covering his on the lip of the tub. Water and suds streamed down. "We both need to."

He swallowed hard, his adam's apple bobbing, looking down at the bubbles instead of meeting her gaze. "Yes. You're right." He lifted his chin and opened his arms.

# Chapter Thirty-one

Michelle seated herself astride Fred's thighs, draping her wet arms around his neck. The soft hiss of popping bubbles and the frothing of the jets filled the air as they sat for a moment, settling in. Then he lifted his chin, offering her a kiss. She sank toward him, accepting, his chest slick against her breasts. His cock rose between them, hard and eager, as her belly pressed against his.

Him. Truly Fred, at last. He felt real, vital, impossibly good, though her perch was precarious at best, her knees uncomfortably balanced on the slick plastic of the tub's bench seat.

He kissed her slowly, exploring her mouth. His arm slid behind her neck, bracing her against him as if he feared she would change her mind and try to flee. "We're going to go out of control very fast as soon as I connect to your energy," Fred mumbled a warning against her lips. "We should be in a safer spot when that happens, I think." He groaned as her hand slid between them to wrap around his cock, her thumb tracing a circle around the tip.

Michelle felt pleasure begin to sparkle through her: the psychic backwash of his feelings.

His eyes opened, pupils dilated, huge and dark. "Can't," he gasped. "Can't wait long." He struggled upright, clutching her against him. She wrapped her legs around him, hanging on for dear life as he climbed out of the tub, ignoring the cascades of bubbles sluicing off them onto the floor. Michelle giggled helplessly, clinging while he steadied, then slid down to stand on her feet.

"Race you to the shower?" She fled across the tiles, leaving damp footprints. Fred laughed, falling in at her heels. She barely made it through the bathroom door before he caught her, wrapping his arms about her waist, leaning in to nip at her neck.

"We'll be eating bubble bath all night if we don't rinse." She wriggled in his arms, very much liking the feel of his cock nestled against her ass. They were still slippery, so she managed to break free, darting into the stall to start the spray.

He pursued, catching her in his arms, nuzzling at her throat and pressing her up against the wall. "Michelle," he muttered, a hoarse husk of need, pushing his hips forward insistently. His hands slid between her nipples and the tiles; she whimpered at the contrast between his warm fingers and the cold ceramic. Hot water slid down her back, tickling her skin as he pinned her in place and bit his way down along the tendon in her throat.

They weren't going to make it to bed. His need pulsed through her mind. She was no longer sure where he ended or where she began. She let her head fall back on his shoulder, moaning. Everywhere he touched her crackled, electric, like the water streaming down over her breasts and belly might boil right off her or even flash to steam.

"Yes," she whimpered as he reached to lift her thigh. She squirmed, clinging to the grab bar. Finally, he managed to find the right angle. Michelle cried out desperately as he sheathed himself inside her.

She shattered immediately...writhing, pleading, and cursing, clinging desperately to the grab bar to keep from falling, she lost consciousness of self, consumed with a supernova of sensation. Pleasure swelled without receding until her vision started to gray around the edges.

Fred's left hand on her breast branded her with sweet heat; he mouthed at her neck, groaning, holding her on tiptoe as he poured himself out into her, his hard, lean body shuddering.

"Fred!" she managed to gasp. He withdrew a little, easing her down, pulling out. His hands trembled as he forced himself to draw back until the sensations were tolerable, until she could breathe again.

"Sorry. Too damn fast! I've waited so long. So long, Michelle...." He fumbled for the showerhead to rinse them both. His hard cock bounced awkwardly as he moved. Michelle slumped onto the bench of the shower, waiting as he groped for towels. The driving force of his need lingered unabated, warming her like sunlight. He wrapped her in one of the towels, trying not to touch her skin. "I'd forgotten how good it felt." His expression looked dazed, his hands trembling a little with the force of his restraint.

"Take me to bed," she breathed. He scooped her up, carrying her to the bed and laying her down on top of the coverlet. She'd never realized he was so strong, but she was easy for him.

He dropped his towel, then reached for hers. Michelle rolled out of it, playfully grabbing a corner of the coverlet. She rolled up inside it instead, swaddling herself like a burrito. He pounced, coming down on top of her to kiss her fiercely. He plucked at her braid, extracting the hair stick before starting to unravel the strands. "I love your hair," he growled softly. "I want to touch it."

She purred, arching to feel his weight on top of her. With less of their skin in contact, she could still feel his lust, but the mind-consuming sensual bliss of touching him reduced enough she could think. "You're putting us in a feedback loop," she murmured before he silenced her with a kiss, nearly driving the thought out of her head again. "You feel what I feel and I feel what you feel. Too much could short out the system," she managed to mumble between kisses. "We'll have to pull back when the strain becomes too strong."

"Mmmmm," Fred rumbled. "There might be something to that." He dove in for another kiss, silencing her, burying his hands in her hair. He rolled her on top of him so the long strands tumbled around their faces, enclosing them inside a tangled curtain. He was so warm she could feel his heat burning into her even through the coverlet; his hand on the nape of her neck sent sweet tingles of fire along her spine.

He pulled her down and kissed her, their tongues sliding sweetly together. Michelle's toes curled. Her whole body vibrated with heat, melting against his. She was already eager to hold him inside her again, hoping he could last longer this time. He'd never lost his erection, and he didn't seem to have a refractory period in dreams. Maybe he didn't need to rest at all.

He was kindling again, his pupils dilated so widely only a thin rim of blue and gold showed around the irises. He tugged impatiently at the coverlet, refusing to surrender her mouth as he struggled to unwrap her. By the end she was helping, thrashing until she was free.

He fell onto his back and she gazed at him, lying naked amidst a ruin of tumbled sheets. His cock stood up straight and proud, eager for her. She rose, walking toward him on her knees, then threw one leg over his waist, mounting him slowly. Pleasure zinged through her with every touch. His hands settled on her waist as he paused to swallow, pink tongue licking his lips. He waited, quivering, as she arranged herself. Then she reached to steady his cock, sinking down.

She shut her eyes and seated herself, taking him fully inside. The concentration on his face revealed his struggle not to come as she engulfed him. She could feel herself enclosing him with tight, slippery heat at the same time he stretched her open, filling her. Then she couldn't think of anything else but him inside her body, thick, perfect, and hot. Her mouth fell open as she braced her hands on his chest, her fingers sliding through his thatch of chest hair. She rotated her hips very slowly.

"Fuck, Michelle!" he gasped through gritted teeth, sweat gleaming on his face, his fingertips digging into her skin.

"You're a nymphomaniac," she shivered with the resonance of his pleasure, then drew a deep breath and squeezed.

Lightning shot straight down her spine. She writhed, poised on the crest of orgasm, her flesh not quite ready to go again so soon. Fred rolled her under him and began to thrust, his hips pumping fiercely. Every fresh thrust brought a new wave of bliss. She gasped for breath each time he drew back and Fred breathed in time with her, hoarse groans rumbling deep in his throat.

She didn't know how long they made love before she crested abruptly. The pleasure was like a live thing possessing her. Michelle erupted without warning, thrashing, going mad in his arms. He bucked up as he came, lifting her off the bed. She would have the bruises of his fingerprints imprinted over her hips the next day, but she didn't care.

He pulled out and cradled her against him, moving off her. He settled her to lie against his side, pillowing her head on his shoulder. His cock was still hard even though he'd come twice, tenting the bedsheet.

"Are you always ready?"

"Mostly." His voice rasped, hoarse; his fingers danced a light, tickling caress along her skin. "After I connect, I respond to your state of mind as much as my own." He didn't seem able to stop touching her, his free hand drifting over to caress her arm, pulling her palm to the center of his chest.

"You were never this tactile before." She nuzzled at his collarbone.

"I have to be careful. Once I start to sense a woman's desire through touch, I have to struggle not to connect. If I fail, the effects can be very embarrassing." He grinned a little, turning his face to hers, giving her a gentle nuzzling kiss with the tip of his nose. "Not to mention dangerous. How are you feeling?"

"Good." Michelle couldn't even begin to feel weary, not with his fingertips painting brushstrokes of pure ecstasy across her skin. "Better than good." She nuzzled a kiss against his jaw, nipping her way up to his earlobe to take it between her lips, breathing softly into his ear.

He shivered, goosebumps prickling on his skin as all his hair stood up. He groaned softly. Her skin whispered with delight, echoing his. She nestled close to him deliberately.

"Once more, then we rest?" he husked. Michelle nodded. He turned her beneath him and slipped between her thighs, filling her in a slow, smooth stroke.

"So good," she nuzzled the words against his throat, quivering with joy.

Fred was finally ready to take it slowly. The sweetness of his touch glowed like the warmth of a fire sunk to coals, baking deep into her, tingling all the way to her fingertips and lapping her in waves of pure bliss. He moved slowly, playing her nerve endings like a violin. Every sensation vibrated through her without ending, replaced by another before the pleasure could fade.

She heard herself moaning his name, not sure where he ended or where she began. She couldn't bring herself to care. This must be what heaven was like: an eternal floating peace incapable of disappointment or even urgency, pure joy perfected in both mind and body. She moved instinctively underneath him, knowing what was needed, her lips sliding open to admit his tongue. He buried his hands in her hair, humming bliss into her mouth, rocking her slowly until she thought she might dissolve into perfect happiness.

Orgasm arrived slowly, an almost unnoticed crescendo whispering through her on his breath as he murmured her name against the skin of her breast. His fingertips glided softly over her clit. He kissed his way downward, lips and tongue on her nipples, trailing over her belly, drifting down between her legs. He lifted her knees over his shoulders, keeping her at the peak of pleasure with slow liquid swipes of his tongue, each one intensifying the sensation of floating in ecstasy. He kept on until her heart began to race, straining. Then he softly eased away before she could gather herself enough to remember they should stop.

"Rest," he whispered in her ear, his skin damp, smelling of her.

She could sense the way he loved having her scent on him, echoing the way she loved the slickness of his seed between her thighs.

He wrapped her up. "So good, Michelle. I love you so much. Better than any dream," he murmured. Her eyelids closed, her breaths lengthening as she slid toward sleep, tangled in his arms, sated, feeling safer than she ever had.

## Chapter Thirty-two

Michelle woke slowly, reluctant to stir. Fred had wrapped around her like ivy, their arms and legs tangled together. The coverlet felt blissfully warm, soft as a cloud over them. They'd never even pulled back the sheets. Fred's breath warmed her throat at regular intervals, reassuring her she had survived the night. She turned her head to nuzzle lightly at Fred's forehead, then gently extricated herself from his arms to crawl out of bed and take care of business.

She checked the windows, pushing back one of the curtains. Sunlight peeped over the horizon, gilding the tops of the skyscrapers with soft radiance. Michelle hummed a little to herself, shuffling across the carpet. The tiles in the bathroom floor were warm, so she stepped out of her slippers, closing her eyes with pleasure to feel the radiant heat against the soles of her feet.

By the time she finished, she could hear Fred stirring. His joints crackled and popped, alarming her a little. She stood up, going to the sink, glancing in the mirror. Her eyes went wide, then her smile grew a little deeper, a faint blush coloring her cheeks. Fred had marked her: little purple bruises from his lips lingered on her throat and the faint marks of his fingers dotted her hips. She wished she could take a selfie to remember this moment, so she could always treasure the evidence of Fred's passion.

He came in behind her while she was still looking. He nestled up against her back, his arms sliding around her waist. "Mmm, g'morning," he mumbled, nuzzling below her ear.

"Someone's not a morning person," she teased him gently, wrapping her arms around his.

"That depends on what I have to wake up for." His hands

wandered upward, fingers curving to cup her breasts. Michelle sighed, luxuriant, tipping her head back against his shoulder. "We should eat some breakfast."

"Eventually." He nipped his way down to her collarbone, pinching lightly at her nipples. "Shower first, I think." His eyes met hers in the mirror. For the first time, he looked truly relaxed, completely happy.

"I'm relieved," he murmured in her ear between nibbles. "You don't seem to have taken any harm."

Michelle chuckled, nestling her bottom against him, unable to help herself. "No, I don't think so. But I'm starving," she teased him. "I definitely can't wait for two showers before we have breakfast."

"Then we'll have to take one together."

"You read my mind." He tugged her toward the shower with him. They wound up giggling as he twisted the showerhead to spray them both, her body pinioned between his hips and the wall. The water came out in a glorious hot torrent, caressing warm trails down Michelle's skin, steam beginning to billow around them.

Fred reached for a bottle of body wash, still trying to hold her pinioned against the tiles. Michelle squirmed playfully, batting at him with her fingers, making sure she treated his cock to plenty of her wriggling.

"Oh, you're asking for such a washing," Fred chuckled. He poured a healthy dollop of vanilla-scented soap onto a bath pouf and lathered her shoulder. Michelle purred, still pressing her bottom against his cock.

The suds began to stream down over her wet flesh, turning their bodies slippery. Fred gave a low hum of satisfaction, moving the pouf over Michelle's chest, circling her breasts, adding more soap. Far more than was needed, actually. He spread the stuff over her skin, then dropped the pouf, his hands sliding delightfully through the slippery liquid. He pushed her up against the wall. "I could fuck you here, like this," he said, his voice as velvety smooth as the touch of his soapy hands. "But I think I'll make you wait." He slid his cock against the cleft of her ass. His flesh glided smoothly, eased by the sweet-scented suds. His skin felt nearly as hot as the water wherever it touched hers.

Michelle pressed back against him, meaning to tempt him to change his mind, but he chuckled. "Not yet."

Fred stroked the soap over her skin, dropping the pouf, letting his palms do the work. He pinned her lightly against the wall as he stroked her arms and shoulders, spreading the lather everywhere: her forearms, her wrists, between her fingers, up over her elbows, all the way to her throat. Michelle made an impatient little whimper, but he chuckled, his chest vibrating delightfully against her spine as he reached for the shampoo.

He massaged suds into her hair, then carefully stroked the lather down through the length of her hair without tangling. "Close your eyes," he whispered, reaching for the showerhead. He adjusted the spray to a gentle mist, then rinsed her hair until it was so clean it squeaked under his touch, the water trickling over her face and her tight-shut eyelids like a thousand caressing fingers.

He handed her a towel to pat her face, then steered her to sit on the bench. She finally opened her eyes to find him retrieving the pouf for more body wash. He knelt down in front of her, his eyes dancing, his soaked hair plastered to his head. He looked adorably bedraggled, reminding her again of his geeky disguise. Michelle smiled, reaching out to push a hank of hair off his forehead. She parted her knees, suggestive, extending the tip of her tongue to touch her lower lip.

"No, not yet." Fred's eyes sparkled with mischief as he raised the pouf, rubbing small circles on the outside of her thigh, patiently building new lather. "I have to scrub you clean all over, first."

"So you can mess me up again?"

"You've guessed my goal." Both his hands caressed her thigh, slippery-wet and sensual, working their way up to her body but then retreating down to the back of her knee. He picked up her foot, placing it in his lap. She slid the sole to lie flat against his cock, making him lick his lips as she caressed him, very carefully, with her toes. He laid his hand over her foot and lathered them both with the pouf, wearing a smoky half-smile.

"One more leg," he chided her after a moment, his voice husky. He replaced the right leg with the left, washing her with thorough patience. He rinsed her again with the dangling showerhead, then hesitated, gazing up at her, beads of water clinging to his spiky lashes.

"Open up." His hands slid to her thighs, thumbs pressing softly, encouraging her to spread herself wide for him.

Michelle obeyed, watching the heat build in his eyes as she did so. He didn't look down, his hands sliding along her skin, still slick with soap. "Have I done a good job cleaning you up?"

"Definitely." Her voice was ever so faintly unsteady; she slid her hips forward instinctively, positioning herself at the edge of the bench.

"Then I deserve a treat." He bent to nuzzle his way in, not bothering to use his hands. Michelle squirmed, gasping a little as his nose tickled at her. His eyes danced, gazing up at her. He slid his hands behind her ass, pulling her forward. Michelle curled her hands around the grab bar to brace herself.

His hands urged her to rock herself against his tongue, so she did, tipping her head back. The showerhead shifted, clunking around the basin of the shower, then found a corner, arcing a hot spray of water over them both. The steam billowed up in clouds, bringing beads of sweat out on Michelle's throat as Fred worked his tongue into her, nibbling and licking by turns.

He tasted her eagerly, his blue eyes avid as she squirmed for him. She tried to spread herself even wider and he purred approval, humming against her, the faint vibration making her gasp. He positioned his hands under her knees, then lifted her legs, pushing her shoulders against the wall. She adjusted her grip on the grab bar, muscles straining, perched precariously on the very edge of the seat.

Fred flicked his tongue against her, strumming hard pulses of pressure against her clit, nearly driving her mad. The enclosed shower amplified her cries, sharp desperate yelps and plaintive little whimpers nearly drowning out the hiss of the spray and the patter of water droplets raining down. He pushed her knees up further. Michelle groaned, surrendering herself to his strength. He moved down, pressing his tongue inside her, tickling at her clit with the tip of his nose. She writhed for him, her arms trembling with strain as she bucked, desperate for more sensation.

He kept up the sweet torture until she couldn't bear it anymore. "Please, Fred. Oh god, please...." She didn't know how long she could hang on, her arms quivering with strain.

He moved up swiftly, his mouth sealing over her, suckling as his tongue circled. Michelle came so hard she saw stars. She felt herself falling, but his arms bore her up; he cradled her against his chest, his body blocking the warm rain of falling water. She felt as boneless as a ragdoll, helpless in his arms. The wall of the shower chilled her back, but his body burned hot against her. He picked her up when she settled, his cock sliding into her like a hot knife into butter. His lean, strong body braced her against the wall as he thrust into her, his mouth fastening onto her throat, suckling a new passion mark there.

She was exhausted, but she didn't care, enflamed by the resonance of his rising excitement. It thrilled through her nerves. She moaned, draping her arms loosely around his neck, and held on as his powerful arms supported her. He mumbled against her throat, but she couldn't understand him; the words weren't English. She floated on his love, so soaked with endorphins she hardly knew which way was up.

Michelle cried out softly as he came, an echo of Fred's urgent groan. She slid to the floor, still within the circle of his arms, hardly able to hold her head up.

He placed her on the seat again, cradling her face between his palms to study her anxiously. "Are you all right?"

"My legs are wobbly. That's all." Michelle stretched, luxuriant. "God, Fred! Last night was worth every penny, even if I'd spent my own money."

Fred flushed with embarrassment, pleased but still a little worried. "Let me finish my shower."

Michelle rested, recovering. She watched with pleasure as he washed himself rather more briskly than he'd cared for her, lathering his dark hair. She loved seeing the rivulets of water stream over his back and ribs, glistening on the tempting curves of his ass.

He insisted on helping her out of the stall, then wrapped her in one of the soft terrycloth robes. She twined a towel around her hair to squeeze out the water, then brushed her teeth, smiling to reassure him, aware he was hovering in case she still felt weak. She put her feet into her slippers, rising to leave the steam-filled bathroom. She felt better already: loose-limbed and well-fucked, completely content.

"You take it easy. I'll make breakfast to take out on the patio. Would you like that?"

"It sounds heavenly." Michelle strolled out onto the patio garden, where dew still lay heavy on the grass. A few curls of steam rose from the pool. She pulled the wet towel off her hair, draping it over the back of a lounge chair. She sat down lazily in the sun, closing her eyes. She let the morning warmth bake into her for a long moment, then sat back, reaching for her hairbrush.

She began teasing tangles out of her hair while Fred cooked breakfast. She was about out of gas, with the beginnings of a low blood sugar headache. The sushi last night had been good, but the night of sex had burned a lot of calories, so she was starving now.

"Crepes with whipped cream, fresh berries, and powdered sugar okay?" Fred called. "There's crepe batter in a carton in the fridge. I think that's what this big flat iron is for. I hope I won't mangle them too badly when I turn them."

"Sounds wonderful, even scrambled," Michelle called back. She shifted her legs, the soft terry robe falling open around them. She felt delightfully sensitive, even a little sore—something she'd always missed after the dreams, no matter how intense. She smiled lazily, savoring Fred's tender passion.

Fred started singing to himself in the kitchenette, his voice rich and mellow, a pleasant surprise. Feeling happy, she worked her brush up the length of her hair toward her scalp. Finishing, she leaned back, opening her robe to let the sun kiss her pale skin. She wouldn't be out in the sun long enough to burn before Fred brought breakfast.

A shadow fell over her eyes, and Michelle blinked sleepily up into Fred's smiling face. "Breakfast is served," he murmured, his gaze caressing her hotly. She blushed a little, realizing she was all but naked. She shifted her legs, enjoying the way his appreciative look followed her every move.

He set a plate in front of her: folded crepes, a little torn, with raspberries, blueberries, and plenty of whipped cream—the good stuff, real, not the partially hydrogenated imitation from a can. He set down a canister of powdered sugar next to a jug of maple syrup. She applied the sugar liberally before digging in.

Fred put a glass of juice next to her plate, then sat down. "We should rehydrate soon, but there's good champagne in the refrigerator. After we finish eating, I'll make us mimosas." He cut himself an apple, spreading the wedges on a saucer for them to share, then savored a forkful of his own breakfast. His plate was topped with strawberries. She snitched one, passing him a raspberry to compensate.

"I have to confess, I'm waiting for the other shoe to drop," Fred admitted, a faint furrow creasing between his heavy brows. "That was too easy."

"We stopped the feedback loop," Michelle protested. "Any time things intensified too much, you pulled back to let me rest. Saakaar couldn't have planned on us coming up with a solution."

"Maybe not." He brooded at the distant skyline. "I didn't think to limit skin to skin contact when I killed Mishti, I admit. I did whatever felt best for as long as I wanted. I wasn't in tune with my partner's body, except for taking pleasure. I didn't hold myself back to take care of her." He pushed the bite through the syrup with his fork, but he didn't pick it up to eat.

"Her death wasn't all your fault, Fred." Much though Michelle hated to think of him with another woman, he needed to put his guilt in the past. "You didn't know."

"I suppose. But why didn't I? Someone could have told me. Someone should have told me. My father, my mother...." He stared at his fork with a scowl. "My father was long gone before I was ever born. I suspect my mother didn't know any more than I do. There are too few of us supernaturals, and most of the time it's every man for himself. We should support one another, but instead, we're fearful, jealous, and stay isolated." He finally put the bite in his mouth. Michelle smiled at him, gentle.

"You can start to make the difference you want when we have a son."

His gaze darted up to lock on hers. He stopped chewing.

"Shit, I didn't think to use a condom!"

"I forgot, too. I'm on the pill, so we should be all right." She couldn't help but ask. "Would it be so bad if we had a baby?"

"No, I...of course not!" Fred shook his head sharply as if to clear his mind. "But we should wait a while first, build our relationship, enjoy being a couple...."

"And here I thought I'd have to persuade you we should stay together." Michelle laughed, giddy with happiness despite her fatigue. She took another bite of her crepes. "These are really good. You should quit designing electronics and pursue a career as a pastry chef." A lock of her damp, clean hair fell forward over her face, threatening to trail right through her sticky plate.

"You wouldn't say that if you'd seen the mess I left on the kitchen counter." He reached to her forehead, laughing, pushing back her hair. His fingertips trailed across Saakaar's mark, all but forgotten.

Michelle's world went dark.

When she woke, she lay half-supported in Fred's arms, collapsed over the lounger. His fingers felt cold and wet; she realized he was dipping them in her water glass before patting her face to revive her, carefully avoiding her forehead.

"Michelle? Michelle? Fuck! Where's the phone? Michelle...."

"I'm OK," her tongue responded thickly, her voice slurring. A flicker of motion distracted her; a hose on the lawn behind Fred stirred, dark green against the grass. Not a hose, a snake. Saakaar.

"Fred!"

He whipped his head around, following her gaze. Spitting a curse, he set her back against the chair and leaped to put himself between Michelle and the huge king cobra rippling toward them on the lawn. Its sinuous body stretched ten feet or more, all the way to the rail on the balcony. Fred's hand groped on the table and came up clenched around the fruit knife, a pitiful weapon against the gleaming, scaled menace.

The snake reared upright, hood spreading. It began to weave from side to side, hissing. Saakaar's forked tongue flickered from between his lips as he scented the air. The hissing resolved into sibilant laughter.

He shifted, scales melting, flowing into golden-dark skin, his hood receding to leave its imprint across his shoulders, his tongue darting once across his lips before retreating into his mouth. He stood stark naked but unashamed, his black curls gleaming. His arms separated from his sides and he reached toward Fred with his palm open.

"My jewel, if you please."

"Release Michelle from your spell first." Fred faced him, defiant.

"My spell is released." Saakaar laughed. "What's wrong now is none of my affair."

"What have you done?" Fred didn't stir, his knuckles white around the knife handle.

"What have *you* done, incubus?" Saakaar smiled wickedly. "Look to your own magics."

Fred turned half aside, studying Michelle through slitted eyes. His face went pale. "This is what you intended all along, when you attacked her. You arranged for the theft of your own jewel as a distraction. This was all a mind game."

Saakaar's mouth twisted with malevolent satisfaction. "You are a fool, incubus. You don't know how to use your own powers. To mark a woman without claiming her? All you did was leave her vulnerable." He reached to take a slice of apple. Fred circled to keep facing him, still brandishing the knife.

Saakaar chewed, smirking. "You seduced her, you persuaded her to let you in, you opened her mind, then you left a welcome mat waiting for other immortals to see. You singled her out as a target." He ran his hand along the top of a marble railing, stripping leaves from a vine of ivy. "I claimed her as mine to dispose of, yet I am not without mercy. If you had been able to control yourself, she would not be in danger now."

He stepped off the grass onto the patio, smooth as silk. "You did not respect my marking. You bypassed my spell and connected your energy to the mortal woman's when you fucked her. The energy required to neutralize my sigil solidified the channel between you. You can't shut it now."

Saakaar smiled. "My spell would have dissipated harmlessly when the jewel was restored to me. If not for your impatience, you might have done as you liked once my spell was gone."

"You've made a mockery of our bargain." Fred's eyes narrowed, his expression dangerous.

"Your choices brought about this outcome." Saakaar looked more smug than wise. "Even before I intervened, you set yourself on this path. The connection would have happened eventually in any case."

"I chose to feed from Michelle, but I wouldn't have risked sleeping with her. You're the one who put an innocent in danger when you cursed her to take revenge on me. You set us up, then sent Robin to convince Michelle to bid on me!"

"You were the one who brought Robin into this, Fredric, if I must remind you. But you are mostly correct. I had her intervene because matters were too delicate to entrust wholly to you. I may also have had her suggest the geas to Mr. Smythe," Saakaar agreed with false friendliness, his smile too wide, a suggestion of fangs indenting his lower lip. "However, what happened afterward was none of my doing. You were too cowardly to fuck the girl on your own terms, but when you had an excuse...you couldn't even wait to have me remove the spell before you fulfilled the geas. You might have contacted me at once last night instead of wasting your time at dinner, you know. I was at hand after the sale; the transaction could have been handled conveniently. You lack self-discipline."

"Bastard." The curse sounded out of place on Fredric's lips. "You wouldn't have come. If not for the geas, I wouldn't have..."

Saakaar's white teeth gleamed mirthlessly. "The girl knows. The two of you would have had sex eventually. I merely encouraged it to happen faster."

"So you could be sure to have your revenge."

"If you wish to stand here all day arguing semantics," Saakaar's smile deepened, "then yes. But the outcome will be the same, sooner or later."

"Release Michelle. I'll do whatever you want, but release her."

Saakaar laughed. "You release her, Fredric. My spell is ended. The only power on her now is yours."

"Twisted by your meddling."

Michelle tried to sit up, but dizziness surged through her. Panic swelled in her heart, fed by Fred's desperation. "Fred, what does he mean?"

"The sibyl asked me not to kill her. I will not. You will do it yourself." Saakaar turned his gaze on Michelle. He raised his arm, his hand clenched in a fist, and flung his fingers wide as if casting a spell. Fred lunged toward him with the knife, then hesitated, turning back to Michelle, his eyes wide with fear, as a few crushed ivy leaves rained down on her upturned face.

Saakaar shifted abruptly, his arms attaching to his sides. He fell forward, fully a snake by the time he reached the ground, darting past Fred quick as lightning. Fred knelt next to Michelle, brushing the leaves off her tenderly, searching for signs of harm.

"I'm fine," she managed to speak as Fred brushed back her hair, gazing anxiously into her eyes. He released her and tore after the snake.

Glass shattered and Fred cursed loudly a moment later, agonized. Banging and thumping still going on behind him, Saakaar emerged from the open door, still in his snake form, the jewel in his mouth. He darted past Michelle like a streak of lightning, ignoring her completely, and flowed up over the wall, rippling quickly down the side of the building.

A moment later Fred charged out, limping on a bloody foot, barely in time to see the tip of the serpent's tail vanish down the waterspout.

"Fucking hell." Fred fell onto the lounger and began picking glass shards out of his foot. "He broke the glasses I put on the counter. That slowed me down." He laid a bloody shard of glass on his plate, his face pinched with misery.

"What's wrong with me, Fred?" Michelle managed to sit up, but her head spun, her stomach rolling with nausea. "What did he do?"

Fred paused for a long moment, looking at her, his eyes vague, before he refocused. "I can't disconnect," he muttered hollowly. "He's right. The energy channel between our minds is still there, Michelle. I thought I'd closed it after we left the shower, but it's still open. I can't disconnect." His voice sharpened with fear. "He means for me to drain you to death, slowly."

"Oh," she remarked intelligently, then her vision went gray around the edges, closing down to a pinhole. The cold lattice of the lounge chair was the last thing she felt before reality swam away.

# Chapter Thirty-three

Michelle awakened to the sting of a needle, finding an unfamiliar face bending over her. Fred hovered behind the stranger, anxious. Slowly she understood she must have collapsed.

"Miss Jones, glad to have you back with us. Follow my fingers with your eyes." The doctor began moving his hands. She obeyed. Things seemed a little fuzzy around the edges, but both her vision and her stomach were settling down.

"Her reflexes seem fine. Her heartbeat is strong and regular. Her color is good. I'm not sure why she collapsed." The doctor shrugged. "I gave her a vitamin injection; it should do her good. Miss Jones, how do you feel?"

"Tired," she mumbled, truthful.

"I suppose that's to be expected." He thumbed open her eyelids to shine a light inside. "You look all right; there's no sign of concussion. Your pupillary response is perfect. Can you tell me what day of the week today is?"

"It's Thursday, I think. The Thursday after Labor Day."

"Where are you?"

"Penthouse at Superlatives. With Fredric. Manhattan." She tried to push herself upright. Both Fred and the doctor hastened to help her.

"She seems quite lucid." He felt her pulse, falling still for a moment. "Perhaps she experienced a momentary drop in blood pressure; these things happen sometimes. Miss, if you experience any other symptoms of distress, you should see your personal physician immediately. You shouldn't be left alone for a while, I think."

"Yes, certainly I'll see a doctor." She swept back her hair, pulling her robe closed.

"I'll escort Miss Jones home," Fred announced firmly. "I'll stay with her till I'm sure she's well enough to take care of herself."

The doctor gave him a wry, suspicious look, causing Fred's brows to pull down into a glower. "Because I want her to recover, not because I'm going to continue preying on her," he informed the man sharply. "This isn't a stage play for the *Grand Guignol*." He offered Michelle his hand, supporting her when her legs wobbled as she stood. "Not dizzy, are you? Good." He slid his arm around her waist. "Let's dress."

The doctor hovered, watching her as she stepped away. She made her way into the bathroom, skirting the broken glass with care, remembering to pick up her dress along the way.

"Is this a typical reaction?" She heard the doctor ask quietly. "I've dealt with several cases involving vampirism, but that's easier to diagnose and simple to treat. All the victim requires is blood replacement. This time, I don't know precisely what's wrong."

Michelle closed the door, shutting out the worried voice. She glanced at herself in the mirror. Shadows sagged under her eyes. Her half-dried hair resembled a rat's nest. She repaired both problems. The black dress slipped on over her head with a bit of struggle. She settled it around her body with a quick shimmy. She looked acceptable, she decided, if a little peaked.

After she finished, she went out to find her shoes. Fred had swept up the broken glass and dressed himself, also. Their meager collection of things lay on the bar, ready for departure.

She stepped into the painful pumps, wincing as one rubbed at a blister on her heel.

"Shall I call you a car?" The doctor inquired, polite, one hand on the house phone. "I don't think either of you will want to walk far."

Michelle grasped her purse to peek inside, managing to suppress a grimace as she snapped the clasp shut to conceal the writhing mass of frogs waiting there. "No, we'll manage for ourselves." She gathered Fred with a look, suddenly desperate to be gone before Mr. Smythe and Mr. Barton opened their vault.

Fred caught up with her in haste, casting a last look around the room before snagging his suit coat. The doctor departed on the third floor, but Fred and Michelle stayed inside until the car stopped at ground level. As they descended, Michelle tilted her purse toward Fred, opening the clasp.

The distinct sound of croaking drew his attention, making him grimace. "We'd best hurry," he muttered. "Robin is invariably a master of poor timing."

# Chapter Thirty-four

After they left the building and melted into the crowd on the sidewalk, Michelle started to feel a little safer. "There's a subway station," Fred muttered. "Are you up for a ride?"

Michelle grimaced at her uncomfortable shoes, but gave him a brave nod. She trailed after him, trying not to limp on her blisters. The stairways to the platform seemed endless even though he gave her his arm to lean on. The crowd buffeted her. At rush hour, the hot, noisy tunnels were jammed with people. She felt the humid heat sucking energy out of her as they descended, then climbed again to catch their connecting train.

Fred watched her with concern, trying to support more of her weight. "This isn't all caused by your shoes," he fretted. "You're exhausted already."

"The subway is hot." Michelle swiped a strand of sweaty hair off her forehead. "And crowded." A large man pushed past her, nearly knocking her off her feet. "I'll be fine once we're in the room."

"I don't think we'd better stay in the hotel for long. Superlatives may have adequate resources to penetrate their security. I'm going to need to go underground for a while." Fred grimaced. "I was afraid I might have to. But that was before—" he halted abruptly, then began guiding her onward in silence.

"Before what?" Michelle wasn't going to let him evade her so easily. "What, Fred?"

"Nothing." His expression looked grim.

"Before what?" She dug in her heels halfway down a staircase, refusing to budge. "Before you were stuck with me? You planned to disappear, didn't you, after you did your duty and saved me from Saakaar."

She could feel she'd guessed right; his state of mind bled through their connection. Waves of sorrow, guilt, and resolve mingled in his mind.

"I would have left to protect you." Fred reached to stroke her cheek, but she jerked her face away.

"You'd have left me to wonder what the hell ever happened to you. You'd have gone on to feed off some other woman, someone who didn't know what you were."

"To keep you alive? Yes. I'd have gone." His face looked hard, almost alien, his eyes ice-blue. "You should live safe from Saakaar, away from all the fucking bullshit that goes along with supers. I want you to be as safe as Jenny or Elise."

Michelle pulled away from his supporting arm. She reeled a little, catching herself against the grimy tile of the wall.

"We'll argue about this later." Fred reached for her, steadying her when she swayed. "Let's keep moving for now." He was still limping.

"Are you all right?"

"I had the doctor clean the wound and bandage me while you dressed." He grimaced. "It's nothing."

A busker with a trumpet was playing on the other side of the tracks when they reached the platform. The mellow sound of the horn made conversation impossible. The train rattled in a couple of minutes later, the hot wind of its passage tugging at Michelle's hair. She pulled away from Fred to board the train by herself, but she let him nestle up behind her. He wrapped his hands around the bar above hers, his body cushioning hers, keeping her from falling when the train lurched forward.

The ride didn't take nearly as long as the interminable climb out of the subway station. The effort left Michelle dizzy and staggering, clinging to Fred in spite of herself as he led her into the hotel, past the sneering pixie.

He settled her on the sofa in their room, covering her with a blanket, then began throwing their things into bags. "You should change into some better traveling clothes." He tossed her a T-shirt and jeans. She scrambled wearily through her bag for a change of underpants, feeling too tired to leave the couch. "I mean to board a plane before they find out we used false gold."

"That'll require us to show our ID. If they figure out your everyday identity, won't they have police waiting wherever we set down?"

"You're right. I'll rent a car, then."

Exhausted, Michelle struggled to pull the dress over her head. Fred tugged her dress up and tossed it aside, then eased her out of her underthings. He replaced them with clean ones, dressing her like a doll.

A resonant croak startled Michelle, who lifted her head to see no sign of her dress on the floor. Instead she spied a suspiciously dark frog hopping away toward the bathroom. Fred set her legs down to pursue the frog, snatching the amphibian up in mid-leap. He deposited it into her purse with its brothers. Then he spent a frantic five minutes chasing her former shoes out from under the sofa. Michelle giggled at his antics in spite of her exhaustion.

"Robin and her tricks!" He chuckled. "At least your clothes didn't transform while you still needed them, or we'd be at the NYPD right now trying to find a lawyer to clear you of public indecency charges. Let me help you; I can move faster right now than you. I know you can do it yourself. Hush." He persisted with his efforts until she was dressed, then stuffed the remainder of their things into the cheap traveling bag he'd bought at the airport.

Fred ransacked the bathroom next. "They shouldn't be able to track me back to Robotidata. I used a false tax identity there. It isn't linked to my other documents. However, I still wouldn't want to stake our lives on the assumption that finding a billion dollars' worth of frogs in their vault won't prompt Superlatives to mount an enthusiastic search. Worse, I can't rule out the possibility they'll seek competent psychic assistance. Still, the sibyl isn't far. She'll know what we ought to do. At least she can suggest someone to ask for advice."

Fred frowned at Michelle unhappily. "I'd like to let you rest a few hours, but I don't think it's wise. At least we have cash. Superlatives can't trace us directly if we spend that instead of using my card. I think I can manage the rental without having to show identification."

If the attendant at the rental lot turned out to be female, Michelle was certain he could. She chuckled a little in spite of her weariness.

"The subway ride was too much for you. We'll hire a taxi to take us to the rental company." Fred stripped out of his suit with haste, changing into casual clothes. Michelle gazed in dismay at the bloodstained bandage on his foot as he changed his socks. It looked considerably worse than he'd let on.

"Fred, you're bleeding." A rush of terror seized her, her hands turning cold, the skin clammy. Her whole life was collapsing. She couldn't even be sure Fred would stay with her. She felt sick, exhausted, and vulnerable.

"Hmm? Oh. It isn't as bad as it looks." He hesitated, gazing gently at her, moving to sit next to her for a moment. "About what we said in the subway: I love you, Michelle. I won't leave you. Not like this." He tilted her chin up to brush his mouth against hers, butterfly-soft. "I would have left you to protect you, to keep you safe."

She could feel the fierce tenderness filling his heart, warming her through their connection, easing her panic. "We'll find a way to fix this. Don't be afraid. I'll rent a car you can lie down and sleep in." He shouldered their bag and reached for her hand. "Just a little farther, then you can rest."

Fred was as good as his word. He hired a taxi to drive them to the rental company, where he procured an SUV with a wide back seat. He tossed their bag into the trunk, then settled her in the back, bundling his suit jacket under her head for a pillow.

"We'll do a little better than this when we find a department store. I'll buy you a pillow, a blanket, and a car-seat air mattress, if I can find one." He drove them out of the parking lot. The obstruction of the speed bumps made Michelle's stomach lurch queasily. She closed her eyes against the sudden bright light as they turned onto the road.

"Sleep," he soothed her. The compulsion of his voice washed her under into dreams of him nestling her against him, safe from everything, lulled by the beat of his heart.

# Chapter Thirty-five

For Michelle, the day passed in a haze of sleep disturbed by a few brief stops. Fred built a cozy nest for her, then halted them at regular intervals to rouse Michelle, encouraging her to eat. She didn't feel hungry, but when she nibbled a little to try to please him, she discovered she was ravenous. She devoured her burger and fries, then drank her entire milkshake.

"Your body's compensating for energy loss," he guessed. "Eat all you want, if you can keep the food down."

Michelle felt better for a couple of hours afterward, remaining awake to watch I-95 flow by, an endless river of cars, trucks, and congestion.

"I'll stop us for the night somewhere near Raleigh/Durham," Fred told her before she drowsed off again. "We'll eat some more food. Then you can sleep in a proper bed."

Fred carried her into the hotel despite his injured foot, overriding her protests, breezing past the wide-eyed counter clerks with a brisk order for one to come operate the key-card for him. He asked the girl for take-out menus, and she quickly returned with a handful.

"Mexican, Chinese, pizza, pizza. Italian, but they don't deliver. Have a preference?"

"I want a burrito, wonton soup, fajitas, and dumplings. And some churros. And beef with broccoli."

He laughed gently. "Will you leave me a fortune cookie to nibble? Let me write all this down."

They spent half an hour debating over the menus as they assembled their list, then Fred ordered enough food to feed a small army. Dinner arrived in two big batches, and Michelle was already out of dumplings by the time the delivery man arrived with her burrito. She still felt starved, so she tore into the food, pausing when she was done to burp. Too late to cover her mouth, she glanced at Fred guiltily.

"Eat," he said gently, pushing forward her soup and doughnuts. He was about halfway through his own carton of lo mein. He helped her polish off her chicken fajita plate when she ran out of steam about halfway through.

"Does eating do you any good? I mean, do you need to eat food to survive?" She managed to swallow her mouthful before asking, loosening the top button of her shorts.

"I enjoy eating. I also need to eat for health reasons." Fred smiled a little. "I have to do a great deal more psychic feeding if I don't eat regularly, or if I don't eat a healthy diet."

"So you have to do both."

"To be healthy in the long-term, yes." He cracked open a fortune cookie. "You will be met with success in your endeavors." He regarded her with a crooked half-smile. "A good omen."

"Mine says 'You are going to have some new clothes.'" Michelle chuckled at the fortune, tossing the little strip aside. "If I keep eating like this, it's going to be right." She stood up to wander over toward the bed, flopping down with her arms and legs flung wide. "I'm sleepy."

"I'm not surprised. Pythons have to sleep for a month to digest a meal like that one."

"Asshole." Michelle giggled, lobbing a pillow at him. "Bringing up snakes at a time like this."

"Sorry." Fred caught the pillow and tossed it aside, then came over to lie down next to her, propping himself up on one elbow. "Sleep. I'll watch over you."

"You'll need to feed."

"No, I don't think so." His eyes clouded a little. "I feel very good, energized and alert. I seem to be drawing energy off you in spite of everything I can do." He stroked her arm lightly. "I'm worried. You're sleeping so much...."

"I don't feel bad. Just tired. We had a busy night last night."

"Having sex drained you. We emptied your reserves. You don't have them to draw on now you need them." His palm brushed her cheek, pushing back a wisp of hair. "Saakaar was right. I don't have enough self-control."

"After five hundred years of physical celibacy, the man doesn't think he has self-control?" Michelle implored the ceiling. "You have more self-control than Mr. Smythe and Mr. Barton have frogs." She glared at him, more amused than angry, not able to feel very cross with a good hot meal in her belly.

"That's a lot of self-control and frogs." He started to grin in spite of himself. "I wish I could have seen the look on Smythe's face."

"Those poor assayers will be in trouble."

"It doesn't much matter what kind of magic preventatives they try if the trick is good enough, and Robin is the best trickster under the sun. I've been thinking about the gold we paid Superlatives. It probably wasn't taken from a leprechaun's hoard. The assayers used magic devices that would have detected any fakery of that nature, and leprechaun gold wouldn't have been cast in nice tidy bars, each one stamped with the imprint of the Bank of England.

"I suspect Robin used a relocation spell. What we paid them was genuine gold, non-magical, so it satisfied their tests. Robin must have opened a portal to a storage vault inside the purse she gave you. Later she made another one inside the safe at Superlatives and transported the gold back out again. Afterward, just as a thoughtful touch, she replaced everything with frogs— including your clothes, just for a laugh." Fred rolled his eyes. "Humans are helpless when she's involved; none of their protective measures can keep her out. She's damned sneaky." Fred snuggled up to Michelle. "She's too clever for me, too, I suppose."

"Maybe she can do something about my problem."

"That idea might actually be worth an attempted guilt trip."

"Don't you mean a 'gilt' trip?" Michelle waited patiently till Fred got the joke; he flopped over on his back, groaning loudly.

"That was awful." He levered himself up off the bed to slouch into the bathroom. "You want to brush your teeth, or are you planning to have Mexican breath in the morning?"

"Brush." She followed him into the bathroom and fished in their bag for her toothbrush. Even though she was still sleepy, she could push through her weariness like she had on the subway. She just didn't want to overdo it again.

"I think the subway wore me out." She giggled as he spat minty foam into the sink. "Gross." She sorted through her things, still looking for her toothbrush. "Maybe I can ride up front in the morning."

"If you want to." He wrapped his arms around her waist, nuzzling rough stubble at her neck. "I would enjoy the company."

"When do you think we'll reach Atlanta?"

"Sometime around mid-afternoon. I want to meet with the sibyl as soon as possible. I'll need to send Erik a text before we turn in."

"Maybe I should tell Elise what's going on."

He raised an eyebrow at her in the mirror.

"Yeah, maybe not." She sat down on the lid of the toilet, starting to brush her teeth between sentences. "She's having to handle the Marcuses without us."

Fred grimaced. "I have a feeling we're both going to be hunting another job after this is over. I'm sorry."

"Can we find jobs with a shorter commute?"

"Anywhere in the world you want to go." He reached, catching her free hand. "I may not have had enough money to buy Saakaar's jewel, but I'm not entirely without resources."

"The commute would be fine if we could ride in the car together." Michelle blushed a little at him. "That is, if you're not still planning to leave as soon as I've recovered." She stood to rinse her mouth.

"I don't want to leave you." Fred breathed the words against her earlobe, capturing it between his lips and giving her a gentle nip with his white teeth. "If we can figure out a way to keep you healthy, and if you're willing to run from Superlatives with me, I know a hundred countries that wouldn't extradite us even if we kept our original identities. I hope we won't ever need to be apart again."

"All right," Michelle answered him softly, feeling ridiculous with her wet toothbrush in her hand and foam on her lips. "I'd like that."

He kissed her neck once more. "Good. But for now, I prescribe a nice long dose of bed. You can sleep on my shoulder while I watch a little TV." He led her into the bedroom again and pulled back the coverlet. Lying down, he opened his arms for her.

"That sounds perfect." She settled her cheek comfortably on his shoulder and fell asleep within a few minutes.

# Chapter Thirty-six

Michelle managed to sit up a little longer the next day, but still felt sluggish. She dozed off around Lavonia, not rousing until they entered Gwinnett County. Yawning, she began to quiz Fred. "Did you hear back from Erik?"

"We're to go straight to meet with the sibyl." Fred frowned. "He says she isn't feeling well. The convention put a great deal of stress on her."

It surprised Michelle a little to hear a supernatural being was subject to illness, but she reminded herself Fred was still limping from stepping on broken glass. Supers might be more than human, but they were still closer to people than gods. "I hope she isn't seriously ill."

"She's lived a long time." Fred grimaced a little, helpless. "Unfortunately, even supernaturals don't live forever. Still, there's no reason why she shouldn't have another few hundred years in her. Legend has it one of the Greek pantheon granted her immortality, but she forgot to ask for eternal youth."

"That rumor must have helped her live several consequent lifetimes in her own identity." Michelle stretched.

"Yes, it can be inconvenient having to pretend to age and die, then re-establish yourself in another way elsewhere, or maybe return posing as one of your own offspring a few decades later."

Michelle chuckled. "Elise, Jenny, and I always used to speculate Dick Clark was a vampire. He never seemed to age. Then all of a sudden he looked terribly infirm. Pretty soon afterward he was gone. We figured he had to reinvent himself before people figured him out."

Fred grinned at her. "Dick Clark wasn't one of us, but I bet you've seen those internet memes about how closely some modern celebrities resemble dead actors. Most of those are coincidental, but a couple of them are supers who didn't want to take up a different career choice." He merged them onto I-75, squinting into the setting sun. "Could you find my phone and turn on the GPS app?"

She did, typing in the address he quoted. The unit's flat monotone voice soon directed them off the freeway into a seedy neighborhood. Most of the stores had bars on the windows, and gang graffiti decorated every available flat surface. Michelle resisted the temptation to palm the door lock as they reached a stop sign, glancing with worry at the men lingering near the corner.

"We'll be all right," Fred reassured her. "The locals here know better than to harass anyone who might be a super." He headed down a narrow road, then turned left into a vacant lot where shards of white and green glass glinted on the ground. He parked next to a dingy four-story brick tenement with a wrought iron fire escape winding its way down the side.

"We're to climb up on the outside." He got out of the car, then stepped around to her door. "I'm carrying you," he told her flatly. "That's a tough climb even under the best of circumstances."

He boosted her up onto the first level, where she let the last segment of ladder down for him to climb. He pulled it back up after them and gathered her in his arms. Then he carried her up the narrow steps, holding her tucked against him with one arm, sure-footed in spite of her weight. They stopped on the very top level, where a window lay open to the late-afternoon air, tattered lace curtains moving slightly in the hot breeze off the rooftop. Fred set Michelle down.

"She keeps her apartment hot as an oven inside. The sibyl grew up in ancient Greece, so she doesn't hold with modern air conditioning. Let me know if it bothers you."

The heat radiating out through the window closed around them with dull, oppressive solidity as they climbed inside. They stood up in a chintzy little parlor, Fred resting one protective hand on Michelle's waist. Erik rose to greet them, setting aside his newspaper. "She's tucked up in bed with a glass of retsina," he said drily. "I'm to bring you in."

He opened a narrow door decorated with pale green, cracking paint. The room inside showed no light other than the flicker of an old-fashioned black-and-white television screen. The sibyl lay beneath a tattered patchwork quilt, holding a bulky old television remote. She glanced up, then clapped sharply, activating her bedside lamp. The bulb pushed the gloom into the corners of the room. "Humans may say supers are magical beings, but they're the ones who've achieved the unnatural," she muttered, hardly seeming aware of them.

"Sibyl," Fred addressed her politely. Michelle echoed him, slipping her fingers into his hand.

"Fredric. Michelle." The sibyl reached onto her bed-table for her glass. She sipped, making a face. "I was expecting you. Erik told me Saakaar's gem is back in his possession. Has he kept his part of the bargain, as agreed?"

"Not entirely." Fred inclined his head respectfully to the sibyl. "Michelle was released from his mark, as agreed, but Saakaar engineered the situation in such a way she is still in danger."

"What was done?" She set her wine aside, blinking up at the ceiling, looking old and tired. Michelle felt a pang of regret. Such frail shoulders shouldn't have to bear the burdens of others, but there was no telling how many times different beings had consulted the sibyl for help with their problems.

Fred told their story as clearly as he could, making no effort to spare himself when dealing blame. He summarized in haste, trying not to exhaust either the sibyl or Michelle, who eyed the room's single spindly chair with longing.

"Sit, child." The sibyl waved one frail hand at her. "A thing like this will bring ill to our community, regardless which of you does the killing." She inhaled the bouquet from her glass, seeming to take strength from the scent. "You can't buy good retsina anymore. It simply isn't strong enough." She made a face at the dregs of her drink, extending her trembling arm toward Erik, who accepted the glass.

"You would think your drink too weak unless the fumes could peel paint," he commented without rancor. He carried the glass out.

The sibyl fidgeted with her remote control. "Fredric, you should consult one of your own kind. An elder, if at all possible. You will need to consult a medium, as well. Some supers are able to reverse the flow of energy through a psychic connection; maybe you can manage to learn the skill. It is not without risk. You could end up the one who dies, drained past your ability to endure."

"That is acceptable." Fred lifted his chin, his jaw set with determination.

"No!" Michelle rose to her feet, agitated. "I don't agree, Fred."

"Or your attempt could fail. If so, both of you might die. Energy manipulation is not a thing to be done without guidance." She sighed, deflating so much she hardly seemed to make a lump beneath her quilt. "Come here, child." She reached toward Michelle.

Michelle approached, hesitant, taking the old woman's groping hand.

"You love our Fredric. I am sorry you have reason to regret it. He is a good lad who loves you deeply." She patted Michelle's hand, her fingers hot and dry. "Maybe Saakaar has another part to play in this. His people are neutral by habit, and they value justice. If he can be reminded he has violated his neutrality and acted against an undeserving innocent in the name of vengeance, you may move him to remorse." She gestured wearily. "Seek your answers in lands far from this one."

Her eyes closed. Erik slipped back into the room, tilting his head to urge them toward the door. "The sibyl must rest," he murmured. "The convention exhausted her." Michelle heard a faint snore before the door clicked shut.

Michelle's t-shirt was plastered to her body with perspiration by the time they climbed back out the window onto the fire escape. She held onto Fred's neck with both arms, the view on the way down making her so dizzy she shut her eyes. He leaped the last few feet, wincing as he stumbled a little on his sore foot before setting her down on solid ground. Behind them, Erik pulled up the last segment of the ladder.

"Good journey, my friends," he called. They waved to him before returning to the car. Michelle shivered in the sudden blast of the air conditioner.

Fred's forehead crinkled in a grim frown. "It's as I feared. We can't resolve this quickly enough to save our jobs. We should probably resign, even without giving two weeks' notice, so you won't get a firing on your work record, Michelle."

"Exactly what I was thinking." A trip to Europe? Michelle suddenly felt tired. "I think I need to eat."

"My apartment is closest, I think. Here." They stopped at a light, where he fished in his pocket for his phone, hastily thumbing up a menu of restaurant numbers before handing the phone to her and driving through the intersection. "You like any of these places? I can stop to pick up takeout on the way home. Order whatever you want."

# Chapter Thirty-seven

Michelle drowsed after Fred picked up the food, opening her eyes at length when she felt the car park. She gazed out at a pleasant little courtyard filled with small trees, bark mulch, and monkey grass. The clean little apartment building beyond looked inviting, warmly lit, with cozy balconies outside each unit.

"Home sweet home." Fred gathered the bags. He hurried to Michelle's side of the car when she climbed out, helping support her as they walked up the sidewalk between tastefully arranged clumps of little topiary shrubs. They paused while Fred collected the post, making a face at the assortment of junk mail stuffed into his mailbox. "I'm afraid my apartment is two flights up."

"I can handle the stairs." She followed behind, leaning on the banister. The food smelled divine. She helped him ferry the bags inside, then looked up, curious, to inspect his home.

He'd furnished the living area in leather, most of the chairs upholstered in hues of gray or black, but he'd highlighted with enough colored pillows and fuzzy throws to make the place feel inviting in spite of the severe color scheme. A Christian Bale *Batman Begins* one-sheet faced off with a Gandalf the Grey from *The Fellowship of the Ring* across the coffee table, commanding opposing walls.

The dominant feature, though, was a huge computer set arranged on a brushed aluminum desk in one corner: a quad processor Mac tower, Bose speakers fit to make an audiophile's mouth water, and dual widescreen monitors the size of flat screen TVs. "Good lord, Fred. This thing must have cost a year's pay." Michelle approached the computer with awe while Fred rooted around in the kitchen, dragging out plates, napkins, and cutlery.

A neat aluminum tower next to the desk sported a digital clock on the top shelf over a selection of DVDs and books, some of them read nearly to tatters. Michelle found herself smiling at the familiar, welcoming titles: *Spaceballs: The Movie. The Matrix* series. *The Princess Bride. Hot Fuzz. Star Trek IV.* All of the *Star Wars* movies plus a boxed set of the *Clone Wars* cartoon. She spotted the obligatory copy of *The Lord of the Rings* sitting beside some scattered pieces of Robert Jordan's *Wheel of Time* series. Fred even had a couple of John Norman's early *Gor* novels. Now that was a topic they'd have to discuss later, when Michelle was feeling her proper self again.

She decided she could forgive him for watching Keanu; there wasn't a boring movie in the bunch.

"I needed a powerful computer to run my CAD suite for work. I was able to write it off my taxes as a business expense." The kitchen wall muffled Fred's voice. "I don't have a television; I stream whatever I want or watch DVDs on one of the screens."

"You were ready to leave all this behind?"

"I still am." He emerged with some of her food on a white ceramic plate. "My computer's not the best lady in my life. She comes in a rather poor second to you."

She picked his tablet computer off the coffee table, part of her mind tallying the cost of the electronics. Fred apparently hadn't been lying when he said he had money.

"Dinner's ready." He brought their loaded plates and set them down on the coffee table, interrupting her reverie.

They both ate heartily, sharing their meals and competing with dueling forks for the last bites of his steak. After they finished, Michelle insisted on helping clear away the mess. She found his kitchen as obsessively neat as the living room.

"Let's not waste any more of your energy than we can help." He pried the last fork out of her hand to tuck it with the others, then started the dishwasher. "I'll show you the bathroom and we'll go to bed—" he blushed suddenly. "That is, if you want, you can...we've been sharing, but I could take the couch."

"Your bed?" Michelle belatedly understood his shyness. "Not without you, Fred."

"It's a little small." He cleared his throat, looking nervous. "I've never brought a woman home to my own bed, I confess."

Michelle couldn't help but smile. She laid her palm against his chest, caressing lightly. "What's there to be ashamed of? Do you have Ninja Turtle bed sheets and a night-light? If you do, I'll feel right at home."

She made him chuckle; he leaned in to kiss her cheek. "No, but my room is a mess. Nobody ever sees the back of the house."

He wasn't kidding. The back bedroom was a disaster area of discarded clothes, shoes, and fannish paraphernalia. What had probably started life innocently as a nice collection of models and action figures posed neatly on shelves had expanded, spreading to all available flat surfaces. The place looked like a hoarder's wet dream, complete with a logjam of books and comics stuffed willy-nilly into empty shipping boxes stacked in teetering heaps.

Michelle couldn't help but smile. Standing inside this room, she felt as if she'd finally been given a glimpse of Fred when all the walls came down. He was her adorable geek boy after all. He even owned a lava lamp.

"You probably have Action Comics #1 buried in here somewhere, but you don't even know," Michelle giggled, patting one of his red cheeks. "This is what my whole apartment looks like lately, so don't be embarrassed." She considered his half-open closet. "Not even by that," she pointed at a Weird Al Yankovic concert T-shirt peeking out of the chaos. "Weird Al is not acceptable work attire by the standards of the official Robotidata dress code. Therefore, I approve of him."

"I do have a life outside Robotidata." He grinned at her. "I just don't let my co-workers know."

His bed was made up with pastel blue cotton sheets under a wild tangle of light, fluffy blankets and pillows, smelling acceptably fresh in spite of their disarray. The bathroom looked sterile, as neat as the front of the house. He set their bag where she could reach her things, fetching some clean towels out of the linen closet for her.

Michelle indulged in a shower, but decided not to bother with clothes as she patted herself dry, shyly opening the door to his room. He did have a nightlight, probably so he wouldn't stumble and impale himself on any part of the mess if he had to visit the bathroom in the middle of the night. The light was a disappointingly mundane blue seashell covering a single LED.

"I know what to give you for Christmas," Michelle murmured, teasing, but a pang of dismay shot through her as she spoke. Would she still be around by Christmas? Would Fred still own these things he loved, or would they be abandoned, scattered, forgotten after he moved on?

Fred sat on the edge of the bed, wearing a tank tee and boxers, his laptop balanced on his knees. He glanced up as she spoke. "A maid servi—?" the words died on his lips when he realized she was naked. He swallowed, his tongue flickering across his lips.

He shut the laptop, setting it atop a stack of papers, standing hastily. "Michelle." His voice melted with tenderness. "I don't need to feed, not yet."

"Nonsense." She lifted her chin firmly. "Besides, I want to make love. I feel good."

He stepped over to her, stroking her hair back behind her shoulders, then settling his palms on them, his thumbs caressing her collarbone. "A quickie, then. For you." He tried to smile, but his eyes were dark with worry. "One dream. I'm not risking anything more intense, not now."

"All right," she agreed. She stepped around him, lying down in his bed and stretching. He stood still by the bed, staring at her a little like a college freshman confronted by an unexpected opportunity to lose his cherry. She guessed he must be imprinting the sight on his memory so he would never forget: her lying in his bed for the first time, offering herself in spite of everything. Guilt flickered across his face even as she sensed the feeling through the connection lying open between them.

"Don't, Fred," she breathed, reaching to pull him down next to her. "You aren't to blame for Saakaar's choices."

He came slowly, settling next to her as if she were made of fine, fragile porcelain that might shatter if he handled her too roughly.

"How is your foot?" Michelle stroked his hair out of his eyes, which proved a fruitless gesture; the strands fell right back again. "You're limping more than you were."

"I hurt it a little when I jumped off the fire escape," he admitted, lying down next to her.

"I want to check it tomorrow. We don't want to let you get infected." She nuzzled at his face, tracing his cheekbone with her nose. Weariness had begun to creep up on her again.

"Yes, ma'am." Fred's mouth covered hers, his tongue parting her lips, as he kissed her to sleep.

The setting didn't change, except his room suddenly turned tidy, the books tucked away neatly on shelves, the profusion of memorabilia neatly dusted and arranged, the dirty clothes and the battered shipping cartons banished, the closet and all the dresser drawers tidily shut. There was a carpet, Michelle realized. She chuckled at it. The dreadful beige shag rug must have come with the apartment.

"Nice," she teased. He nipped her lip, laughing. The sensations from reality didn't quite match her dream, disorienting her until she understood she didn't just feel his arms. She could also feel herself inside them.

"Feels weird," she mumbled against his mouth.

"Let's try something," he purred softly. "Tell me if you don't like it."

He began to nibble his way down along her throat to her breasts, kissing and nuzzling softly. After a moment, she realized he was doing the same thing to her sleeping body.

He settled between her thighs, opening her. She moaned, feeling the soft flutter of his breath at the same time as she scented herself. His tongue drew patterns on her in sweet, liquid fire; she tasted of warm salt and smelled faintly of the sea.

Michelle whimpered, giving herself up to his lovemaking. She'd always thought a man must find it vaguely unpleasant to give oral sex, but she could feel Fred savoring the flavor of her under his tongue.

The way Fred genuinely loved touching her made Michelle quiver with delight all the way down to her toes with an incredible rush of mingled adrenaline, sensation, and tenderness. She'd never had many lovers, and she didn't think any of the few she'd allowed into her bed had truly enjoyed giving pleasure in the way Fred did.

A cynical person might think Fred was different in bed because he was an incubus; to him, giving brought the same reward as taking. Michelle didn't think his motives were so selfish. He'd always been kind, acting out of a generous spirit both at the office and in her dreams. He'd acted the same way at DragonCon, bringing her drinks, providing food for the group, and taking care of her with a genuine sweetness she'd never before experienced from a man.

That was the real reason she'd come back to him, not any half-assed logical thinking she'd done regarding Saakaar's curse. She wanted to nurture Fred's shy devotion, to accept his love. She wanted to love him and care for him in return.

She sank into sensation, not trying to figure out where her feelings ended or where his began: smooth skin covered the curve of bone under her palms, soft heat under her lips meshed seamlessly with the slow glide of his tongue awaking every nerve. This must be why Fred could feed from either gender. Michelle had no inclination toward women, but in spite of that, experiencing both sides of his lovemaking brought nothing but bliss.

His thumbs stroked her hips, liking the texture of her skin, then he trailed his fingers down. He slid two inside her, curling them delicately, making her buck with soaring pleasure. The delicate flick of Fred's tongue made her writhe, suddenly unable to contain any more. Every muscle stretched taut, lifting her in a perfect bow. Fred clasped her waist, supporting her, lifting his gaze to watch her come, enjoying her flushed skin and her desperate cries.

"Too fast," she complained fuzzily when she could finally talk again. He slid up so he could reach her face, then shushed her with a kiss.

"We'll do more another time, when you're feeling strong again," he promised, soothing her deeper into sleep.

# Chapter Thirty-eight

Michelle pried her eyelids open, blinking up at an unfamiliar ceiling. Fred's head was a warm weight on her shoulder; his hand rested possessively on her breast. He was snoring softly and his leg lay between her parted thighs.

Michelle glanced around, spotting the blue glow of his nightlight and orienting herself at last. Location didn't matter anymore, not with him holding her. She could be anywhere, but as long as she lay in his arms, she would feel at home.

She wriggled out from under him, trying not to disturb him any worse than she had to. Her bladder demanded a trip to the bathroom. Another night-light glowed there: five minutes after six. When she roused herself to wander back into the bedroom, Fred sat up and scratched his chest.

"How do you feel?"

"A little sluggish. Okay." She went to him, stroking her fingers through his tousled hair. "I enjoyed last night, Fred." She kissed the crown of his head. "I don't want to stop living because I'm afraid of the future."

"I understand." He pulled her close, pillowing his head against her breasts and closing his eyes. "I have some eggs in the refrigerator. I'll make us two omelets. Do you want ham in yours?"

"And cheese and mushrooms." Michelle let him go and reached for his computer, discovering he'd been composing his resignation letter to Robotidata. She cut and pasted his for a template, then changed a few details, but delayed sending. She'd discuss the letters with him first, then they'd take the final step together.

His other browser windows were interesting, too. He'd been

researching companies who would pack up and store your belongings. She sat still for a few minutes, considering. No matter what happened next, the previous phase of her life was definitely over. She didn't want to go back.

"This is a good idea. Let's have them do my apartment, too." She pointed to the screen when he emerged. "I want to pick up a couple of things first, though."

He hesitated, biting his lip a little. Taking the laptop, he set it aside on the bed. He raised her to her feet and crushed her to him, burying his face in her hair. "Michelle." His voice was gruff, hoarse with emotion. She knew he couldn't articulate the complex mix of feelings inside him, but she could feel them too, so she understood.

"You're my home now," she said, squeezing her arms tight around his waist. Her choice might not be wise, but she knew it was right. "Let's move, shall we?"

They made breakfast together, very domestic, sitting down to omelets and microwaved bacon and some orange juice he'd found in the fridge.

"Ready to send our letters?" Michelle looked Fred steadily in the eye.

"If you are." He opened the laptop. "After this, there's no going back."

"I'm ready to go forward." She kissed him and watched as he clicked send.

They lingered long enough for Fred to pack a few things in a larger suitcase, then called the move-and-store company, leaving their keys and paying in advance for the two pack-ups.

"We'll need to pay our last bills. Don't forget to cancel your utilities," Fred murmured. "Then that's taken care of."

They drove to Michelle's apartment next. She took a bit longer than Fred to gather her things. She had to sort through her belongings, reluctantly leaving photo albums and keepsakes to go into storage, but she packed her favorite jewelry in her carry-on bag.

"Almost done? Good. Make sure you bring your passport," Fred reminded her, pausing between phone calls as he canceled their utilities. Michelle grimaced at her own thoughtlessness. Digging the document out of a drawer, she tucked it into her purse next to her emergency cash.

She was folding a sundress when the doorbell rang. Fred looked up at her with mild alarm as she went to check the peephole. "It's Elise."

Fred groaned. "Let her in if you like, but we can't stay long. I've booked us on an afternoon flight to Heathrow."

Michelle loosed the security latch. Elise marched in, steaming.

"Michelle, what in Christ's name are you thinking? There's gossip all over saying you both mailed resignations to HR this morning. I bribed Joe to show me the letter. The IP address in the header was the same as Fred always uses when he writes in from home, so I knew you were back in town. When his apartment was empty, I figured you had to be here. Who the hell do you think you are, fucking up her life like this, Fred?"

"Good morning, Elise." Fred had found Michelle's coffee maker and brewed a pot while she packed. He set down his steaming mug. "Want a cup of coffee?"

"What? No!" She glared at him, so angry she hadn't even realized Fred wasn't wearing his normal dork disguise. "You're acting like this is nothing. Michelle," she turned her back on him, still in full rant. "if you call HR right now, they can stop the process. Think about this. You don't want to give everything up for dorky little Fred."

Fred cleared his throat, sounding a bit irritable. Michelle tittered, and her laugh brought Elise up short. She glared at Michelle, visibly searching for more to say.

"Elise." Fred's voice was firm. "Michelle is an adult, perfectly capable of making her own decisions. You are the one treating her like a child." He retrieved a second mug from the cupboard and poured her a cup of coffee. She rounded on him, clearly prepared to shout, but the words trailed away as she stared at him, blinking.

"Fred and I made this decision together," Michelle confirmed, but Elise wasn't listening. She was staring at Fred, who held the mug out to her. She didn't move to take the coffee, her eyes skittering over him in disbelief, her mouth falling open in a perfect O.

"You're going to catch flies," Michelle warned her drily. Fred wasn't dressed up, but he hadn't put on his glasses or his dork disguise. His hair was free of goop. His dark blue T-shirt highlighted the powerful, lean muscles of his arms and chest, the color making the pale blue of his eyes turn striking. His jeans lovingly cradled his ass and his package. If he'd been wearing a suit, Elise might have toppled over; as it was, she couldn't find her voice.

Michelle reached for the coffee, pressing the mug into Elise's empty hands. "You'd better have a sip of this." She was hard-pressed not to laugh at the stunned expression on Elise's face.

Elise accepted the cup and sipped without thinking, burning her mouth. "What the fuck!" The pain woke her from her daze. "Who the hell died and made Fred hot?" she demanded, outraged, as if some fundamental tenet of her universe had been violated.

"He was always hot." Michelle winked at him. "You just didn't have the right eyes to see it. But sex isn't why I'm leaving Robotidata." She sobered. "I'm sorry, Elise. Please tell everyone goodbye. Give Jenny my love."

"But you can't just vanish. You're my best friend." Elise turned to Michelle, imploring. "And the Marcuses...."

"The Marcuses will have to deal. You have all my files." Michelle shrugged, feeling sad. Elise's best friend? She hadn't ever thought of their friendship in quite such fond terms, but Elise was terribly upset. Still, she was resilient and she had Jenny. She'd be fine.

"I sent copies of all my work files to HR this morning. It'll be reassigned." Fred finished his coffee, carrying the mug to the sink. He rinsed it, then set it to dry in the drainer.

"I'll keep in touch as much as I can." As she made the promise, Michelle knew she wouldn't call Elise often, not even if she and Fred solved their problems quickly. This phase of her life was over. "You and Jenny will be fine; you can hang out with Joan and Annie down in the data collection center. You know, Joan was gossiping about how Billy wants to go out with you, but he's too shy to ask." She gave Elise a sly wink.

"If every half-baked tech geek at Robotidata has the potential to clean up like Fred, maybe I ought to ask him myself," Elise said slowly, glancing back at Fred, who flashed her a megawatt grin that set her back on her heels all over again.

"We need to go, Elise. We have a plane to catch," Michelle said gently. She reached for Elise, giving her a quick hug. "Rinse out your mug and the coffeepot. Lock the door when you go?"

Elise hugged Michelle tightly, then turned half-away, wiping at her eyes, glaring a little at Fred. "You handsome bastard, romancing my best friend and sneaking her off right under my nose." Elise couldn't suppress the admiration in her voice. "How long were you hiding under the radar, waiting for your chance at her?"

"Six hundred years," Fred told her gravely. He reached for Michelle's hand as Elise's eyes went wide with sudden comprehension. "Good day, Elise."

# Chapter Thirty-nine

They fled the apartment before Elise could recover. Fred couldn't stop laughing as he hoisted the suitcases into the trunk, then started the car. "Poor Elise. Jenny will be furious she didn't come along. Her first and last chance to inspect a real super."

"She'll never believe you're a super; Elise was too shocked to snap a picture of you before we went." Michelle was glad to settle into her seat. She felt worn out already. "I need to call my mom to tell her I've met a man, quit my job, and moved out of my apartment. That won't be as simple as dealing with Elise."

"Better call her now. Calls will cost a fortune during the flight." He laid his hand on her thigh, comforting her with a caress. "If she's too difficult, tell her you have to go because the plane's taking off."

Michelle kept her end of the conversation as calm as she could, but the discussion didn't go well. Fred kept giving her sidelong glances, reaching to pat her knee. "From work, yes. I've known him for months, mom. Yes, he's very nice. I'll arrange for you to meet as soon as it's practical. Yes. Soon. No, I don't know when. ...I can rent a new apartment, mom, as soon as I need one. We'll probably rent one together to save money. We're going to be traveling in Europe for a while first, though. No, I'm not pregnant. ...I can find another job. Don't worry about me. Mom, I have to let you go. My flight is boarding. I love you. I'll be in touch." She shoved her phone in her purse and leaned back against the headrest, closing her eyes. She felt completely drained.

"Sometimes I think I didn't miss out by not spending lots of time with my family." He gave her a wry grin. "Your mother will probably take a few bites out of my ass when we meet, but maybe I can talk her around."

"I'm the only one in my family who has permission to touch your ass," Michelle informed him, cracking an eyelid to give him a sidelong smirk. "I'm the only person on the planet who gets to touch your ass, in fact. By special decree."

The skin around Fred's eyes crinkled with amusement. "I'm agreeable to including that as part of our contract."

They rode the shuttle to the airport. Michelle felt herself starting to flag as they retrieved their suitcases. She pushed through her fatigue, staying at Fred's side, accepting his help whenever he offered, but refusing to ask for more. Finally, they boarded their plane and she collapsed into her seat with a sigh, her eyes closing.

Fred woke Michelle whenever the stewardesses brought snacks. She roused again for the in-flight meal, but she was spent. By the time they landed in Heathrow, the worried wrinkle in his brow had sunk deep. He hovered over her anxiously until she was off the plane, then called for a wheelchair to carry her to baggage claim. The attendant pushed her out to the curb, where Fred took over, helping her into a cab. He managed their luggage on his own.

"Time for you to have a good supper and a sleep." He stroked her cheek, encouraging her to pillow her head on his shoulder, where she lay gazing out the window at the London streets passing by. "I want to call Karl. He's a genealogist by trade, so he keeps track of any number of European supers. Maybe he'll know someone we can talk to."

"I feel useless," Michelle murmured unhappily. "I'm a burden on you."

"No," Fred denied stoutly, nuzzling his nose gently against her face. "Never a burden."

She doubted that. Part of her mind burned with resentment against Saakaar. Right now she and Fred should be enjoying the first incredible flush of being in love. They should spend their time getting to know each other, exploring the good, learning slowly how to deal with the bad. Thanks to Saakaar, instead of enjoying being in love and making her first trip to London, she was barely able to keep awake as she lolled on Fred's shoulder.

Scratch that; she wasn't.

Michelle awakened already tucked into a crisp, sweet-smelling bed with a flower-print coverlet. Unfamiliar paintings surrounded her, one on each of the four walls. Fred had brought up fish and chips from a stand next to the road. He propped her up in bed, then fed her bite by bite until she was able to take over.

"Do you want some more? I can get us something else," he offered when she'd polished off the last chip and the newspaper wraps lay crumpled in the trashcan. "There's a takeaway Indian place on the corner, but I didn't know whether you'd like spicy food."

"I'll eat anything but kidney pie," Michelle giggled wearily, subsiding onto the pillow. "My aunt used to make the stuff. It smells like pee."

"It tastes like it smells," Fred confided conspiratorially. "I'll go buy us curries in a few minutes." He paused. "I'd like to settle here for a day or two so you could rest now we're out of the States. Superlatives would need time to trace us this far, if they can manage to track us at all. But I don't think we can afford to waste any time." He kept his tone light as he stroked her hair, his warm palm slightly rough. She could feel his worry, a strong, sour note of anxiety.

He spent a minute or two typing on his phone, then sent his text. "I'll be right back." He brought back lamb and rice curry, chutney, biryani rice, chicken tikka masala, some poppadoms, and samosas. Michelle found herself eating as ravenously as if she'd never touched the fish and chips. She felt a little better afterwards.

"You're losing weight," he commented unhappily when she rose. She looked down at the waistband of her shorts, disbelieving him at first. They were the same ones she'd been forced to unbutton a couple of days ago after dinner, but now they hung loose around her body even after a heavy meal.

"If we could bottle your influence to sell as a weight loss solution, we'd make a fortune," she tried to joke, escaping into the bathroom. He was right. In the mirror her face looked thin, her color sallow. She'd need to start using makeup if she didn't want to resemble a zombie. She stuck her tongue out at herself, then brushed her teeth to remove the lingering spices.

"No sex tonight," he admonished her with gentle sternness when she emerged from the bathroom in her nightie. "We shouldn't have last night, either."

Michelle pouted at him, but he was right. She was already tired again in spite of her meal. She sat down on the edge of the bed, wrapping her arms around herself, trying not to shiver. "I have some jet-lag," she

195

insisted when he came out of the bathroom with his hair damp, wearing fresh boxer shorts. "I'll be fine tomorrow."

Not looking convinced, Fred located the thermostat so he could turn it up. His phone buzzed, interrupting the uncomfortable moment, and he checked the readout. "It's Karl," he murmured to her. "He says I should call back."

He settled into bed next to her, sliding one arm around her shoulders. He punched in Karl's number with one thumb, turning on the external speaker so Michelle could hear.

"Karl, thanks for the quick response."

"Fredric." Karl's voice sounded tinny through the speaker. "I understand you find yourself in a desperate situation. Fortunately, I may be able to help you. There is an elder incubus living in Ireland at this time."

"That's great, Karl." Fred's voice filled with relief.

"Perhaps, or perhaps not. He has resisted contact with other supernaturals for longer than my lifetime, invariably declining to attend any conclaves or gatherings, regardless how urgent. The records I inherited say he has always been so."

"I'll persuade him to help if I have to nail him to a wall," Fred vowed. Michelle felt a shiver go down her spine at the determination in his voice.

"There are others, though not so old. They are farther away, but they may be more approachable. You are a rare breed, Fredric. I can't list more than three who may be knowledgeable enough to help you."

"The sibyl suggested I consult a medium, a powerful one skilled in energy manipulation."

"Fortunately for you, those are more common." Karl paused. Michelle could hear a rustle of flipping pages. "I have to transfer these records onto a computer file system somehow, Fredric; half my books and parchments are crumbling at the edges."

"After this is over I'll personally come scan your entire library," Fred promised. "I'll make your documents searchable by keyword and author, too."

"That would be ideal. I'll email you the elder's last known location along with the rest of my information, which is sparse enough. The medium is a more pressing concern at the moment, I assume. Here we are. You're in London?"

"Yes."

"Excellent." Karl's already-precise tones turned fussy. "She calls herself Madame Defarge, like the character from the book. I know the name doesn't fit her vocation. Maybe she likes to knit. Don't make faces at me, Fredric." Michelle tittered a little in spite of herself; Karl was right.

"She chose a dickens of a name, you have to admit," Fred smirked. Michelle rolled her eyes at him.

"I wouldn't make those sorts of jokes around her, if I were you. Mediums can be abominably sensitive." He recited her address so Fred could scribble it down. "Here's her number, too. She might still be up. Many of them keep odd hours."

"I'll give her a call, Karl. Thanks." He looked hopefully at Michelle. "Feeling well enough to go out again?"

"For a little while, but we may be buying another dinner when we come back."

"If you want, I'll buy you a seven-course banquet fit for the queen."

# Chapter Forty

Fred and Michelle took a cab toward the east end, crossing the Thames and passing the Tower of London. The neighborhoods gradually grew dimmer and the height of the buildings less. As they turned off the main street, their path narrowed through streets of mingled residences and warehouses. When the taxi stopped, Fred paid the cabbie, pausing to offer Michelle his hand. She was glad she had enough energy not to lean on him as they climbed the steps up to the door.

A flickering neon sign in the shape of an open hand advertised a variety of services, palmistry apparently the most popular. The door buzzed, opening to allow them inside. They followed hand-lettered signs up a single flight of stairs, then down a dingy corridor. The whole place smelled of pungent smoke: cloves, tobacco, and marijuana.

"That's hashish," Fred made a face when she asked what she smelled. "Mixed with opium, if I'm any judge. We probably shouldn't agree to smoke anything she offers." He tapped cautiously at a door painted in psychedelic runes, which swung open with an impressive groan.

"Enter," commanded a woman swathed in ludicrous harem pants, gauzy veils, and a wild assortment of bangles. Fred and Michelle exchanged a dubious glance, but Fred led the way inside, the draft from the door making candle flames flicker wildly.

"The spirits have much to say regarding your problem." The woman gestured dramatically at the dancing flames, further endangering the imperiled candles, nearly igniting the synthetic fabric draped over her arms.

Fred cleared his throat politely. "The two of us have come to consult with Madame Defarge, if you please."

The woman's eyes went wide. "Oh. That's quite another matter." Suddenly businesslike, she passed them in the narrow space to latch the door, flipping an assortment of switches. Half the lights in the room went off, including a cloudy glow from a half-covered crystal ball. Another, brighter light came on, showing the tawdry decor for the tattered, dusty junk it was.

"I have to keep up a show for the proles, or they don't think they've seen a proper psychic." She pushed back her bangles, then shed half a dozen layers of veils and shawls. Underneath them she looked pleasant enough except for the heavy rings of kohl lining her eyes. Her turban had flattened her hair into a skull-clinging snarl of natural red ringlets.

"The proles are ridiculous, really. I always tell them they're going to meet someone tall, dark, and handsome, or short, blonde, and busty. That's all they want to hear. If I give them a realistic prediction, they sulk. They say the future is too dull." She reached into a box, extracting a hand-rolled cigarette, then offered the container to Michelle and Fred, who shook their heads politely. "But a girl's got to eat." She lit up, inhaling deeply, the scent of cloves filling the room. "Madame Defarge is me, I should say. Now, what can I do for the two of you?" Her eyes flicked keenly from one to the other of them. She settled on Fred. "I don't see many of your kind in here, incubus."

He smiled a little thinly. "We need more than parlor tricks, I'm afraid." He clasped Michelle's hand in his. "The story is a long, involved one. I'll repeat the most relevant part. Circumstances have led Michelle and me to connect telepathically. I discovered I cannot break the link. I'm draining her energy constantly. Unless the flow can be altered or stopped, she will die."

The medium turned her gaze to Michelle, taking a drag on her cigarette, its tip glowing bright orange. "Not your desired outcome?" Her hoarse voice turned wry.

"Not for either of us," Fred said smoothly. "A reliable source tells us you're renowned throughout Europe for your energy work. Can you break the connection, stop or reverse the flow, or teach us how to balance the exchange?"

"We'll have to go down to the cellar." She wrinkled her nose at the room, rejecting the cluttered, stuffy ambience. "This place is full of vibes from all the proles. I need to study you someplace clean." She stood up, stubbing out her cigarette, then led the way down a back stair, shedding miscellaneous garb as she went until she wore only a simple black sheath, almost a slip.

Michelle was startled to realize she was very young, perhaps still in her twenties. She opened a door into a small antechamber with a bench on one side. "You should take off anything that absorbs emotional associations. In other words, lose the jewelry and the clothes." She gave Fred a sly wink. "For business reasons, you understand. Nothing personal."

Fred rolled his eyes. "We'd better do as she says," he murmured to Michelle. They stripped to their underwear.

"All of it." The girl pulled off her own slip, revealing a body entirely clad in an elaborate lacework of tattoos. "Protection," she winked at Michelle, noticing her glance. "You don't need to draw a magic circle every time if you're already contained within one." She scratched at her hair, removing the ties binding it to the back of her head. She shook her head and let the damp mass tumble wildly around her shoulders, but didn't bother to hide herself, giving Fred an appreciative once-over before bringing them back to business.

"Let's go before you freeze." She led them into a surprisingly clean room. The cellar walls had been made neat and tidy with white plaster. Michelle saw no sign of dirt or dust. The floor was done in simple triangular white tiles, but the pattern formed an intricate five-pointed star reminiscent of a Hollywood-style magic circle.

"I need you to lie here, incubus. You go over there, lady." She positioned them carefully with words, taking some time to arrange them to her satisfaction on the chilly floor. Then she dug through a chest in the anteroom, emerging with a clear quartz crystal in her hand. "This will work as a focus. Lie very still—you moved, incubus. Put your hand back down right there. Yes. Now clear your minds. Think of a waterfall, a clear, pure stream of water. Feed any extra thoughts or emotions or doubts or fears into the flow. Let them wash away." Her voice droned on, hypnotic, until Michelle felt herself drifting toward sleep in spite of the cold floor leaching heat out of her skin.

"I can see the channel now. You're right, incubus. You're killing her by inches." The woman's voice remained calm, quite casual. "Try to close the channel now. I said, try to—you are? Oh. Hm."

Michelle cracked an eyelid and watched the woman wave the

crystal. "No, stop. The attempt is counterproductive. Lady. Michelle," she said abruptly, though neither of them had given her a name. "Can you see the channel?"

"I can feel Fred's emotions. He's upset."

"Hm," she said again, uninformative. "Feeling his emotions is a start. I'm not sensing a lot of clairvoyance from you, though. Can you pull for more of what he's feeling? Incubus, fix a feeling in your mind. Don't push it at her yet."

"Worry," Michelle said after a moment, confident.

"Good. Now think of a sentence, incubus. Michelle, you try to hear what he's thinking. Pull the thoughts out and bring them to you, like picking berries."

Michelle struggled but came up with nothing, obeying the medium's occasional terse instructions. "No luck with words? Picture an object in your mind, incubus, something neutral with no emotions associated. No? Push the thought to her gently, incubus. Still no?"

Michelle tried until she was sweating, but the most she could pick up was a vague sense of Fred's emotions and his physical sensations, when he consciously tried to send them. Contacting his mind felt as if she stood outside with her eyes shut, able to sense the warmth of sunshine and automatically know which side of her face the light was falling on. She could no more see images or overhear the specific verbal thoughts in his mind than she could reach up to pull down the sun.

"She can't pull from you, incubus, or read your mind," the medium said at last. "She doesn't have the talent. Michelle, stop trying before you wear yourself out, honey. Rest." The medium moved toward Fred, her bare feet pattering on the tiles. "OK, incubus. You were trying to push your thoughts at her. Try again. This time, focus on your core energy. Picture yourself gathering your energy into a ball. You see the connection? Form the ball and push it along the connection."

Michelle suddenly felt dizzy, as if the room were spinning; she managed to moan.

"Much smaller!" The medium snapped suddenly. "Make it the size of a pinhead, not the size of a fucking beachball. No, stop." Her feet pattered again, bringing her back to Michelle. "You drew a ton of energy out of her for that; I have to feed her now. Sit up, honey. Any allergies? Good." Her hands were warm, supporting Michelle with kind intent. She put something small and round between Michelle's lips. She crunched down, tasting familiar chocolate: a peanut M&M. She devoured the candies as quickly as the medium could feed her, then lay back, relieved when the room settled down around her ears again.

"Okay, let's try again. Pinhead sized." The medium resumed her position to one side. "No, you're still pulling. Let's try this instead. I'm going to feed you some of the same candies I gave her. When you swallow them, picture them forming an energy ball inside your stomach. Keep hold of the idea: your mouth and esophagus is the intake channel. All you put into the ball is the M&Ms coming in through it. While you eat, your stomach is an isolated chamber that doesn't connect to her. The M&Ms create heat as they enter. The only way in is through your mouth. When you start to feel your stomach warm up to the point of discomfort, stop eating. Open a pinhole in the chamber and send the warmth down the connection to her."

Michelle waited quietly, trying to keep awake, listening to Fred crunch the candy. She was starting to feel a little warmer; maybe she was growing used to the cold tiles.

"That's it," the medium said quietly. "Sustain the transfer as long as you can. Focus on the channel. Don't think about anything else. When the heat is gone, close the pinhole."

After a while the warmth faded. Michelle started to shiver; the medium pursed her lips. "You've made a start, incubus, but it's not natural for you to transmit energy. You were still pulling on her at a low rate even while you fed her. I don't think you can give her enough to keep her alive indefinitely, not even if you spend every waking moment eating and sending her what you ate."

"But I can l keep her going while we seek a better solution." Fred's voice sounded a little lost at first, but firmed with determination as he spoke.

"Can you touch my energy while you're connected to hers?" The medium sounded a little wary. "I mean, without connecting to me. No fucking around with me or you'll get a nasty shock; I didn't have these wards inked for nothing. Just a tendril."

"I can't," Fred said quietly. "I already tried to see if I could reach someone else. I tried to reach you, too. I couldn't touch you. Not even enough to sense the wards."

"Figures. So you won't be able to feed from anyone but her. I know enough about your kind to know you need her pleasure. If you're going to feed off her, you both should eat like crazy to generate as much spare energy as you can first. You feed her everything you can from your meal before you get it on. Draw the pleasure she generates. Then feed her again afterward. She'll need to recharge as much as she can before she sleeps."

Madame Defarge raked a hand through her curls again. "Your skill at making the transfer should develop a bit with practice. After you learn, she'll receive more benefit whenever you feed her." The medium rose, cracking her neck, producing an alarming series of pops and snaps.

"Could you sever the connection?" Fred asked.

"Theoretically." She popped her finger joints next, a rhythmic series of quiet crackles. "I'd have to kill one of you to complete the process, I think."

"Unacceptable."

"I wasn't exactly digging for the ritual knife. But whatever you say." She paused. "The more you starve yourself, the harder you'll pull on her when you finally do feed. I don't think you can help it. But you can try to manage how much you take. Eat a balanced diet and get plenty of rest. Feed her as often as you can, but you should take a minute to meditate in order to calm yourself before you try. Then feed her exactly the way you did a minute ago. Regulate the size of energy transfers by imagining the transaction visually. Limit the size of the ball you draw in and maximize the size of the one you push out. God, that sounds awful." She reached for her slip, signaling the end of the session.

"Girl, you need to carry lots of quick energy food. Nibble on something all the time. Your body will try to compensate for the psychic expenditure by drawing on your physical reserves: first fat, then muscle. Eat as much as you can to slow the deterioration."

"What you said earlier." Michelle struggled to sit up. Fred hurried to help her. "You mean we should have sex."

"I mean he's going to pull what he needs from you whether he wants to or not, whether you have sex or not. So yeah, but stick with dream-sex. Dreams shouldn't pull nearly as much physical energy from your body." She patted Michelle's shoulder. "He's set up to take what he needs; it's automatic. He can't consciously make himself stop."

She eyed them both, a sad smile forming. "Besides, you may as well have a little of the sweet along with the bitter. At least you'll have a chance to enjoy getting drained. Come back upstairs. This bag's empty, but I have some cake in the pantry. I can give you a sugar fix."

"How about energy drinks?" Fred looked thoughtful.

"Yeah. Try any kind of high-nutrient food; pack it in. Sugar's fast, but the energy fix you get doesn't last long. She should eat a lot of all kinds of things, and so should you." She led them into the anteroom where their clothes waited.

Michelle wrinkled her nose. "I can't stand energy drinks."

"Choke them down." The medium gave her a sympathetic look. "Let me guess. You fell in love with the sex god here, literally the man of your dreams. You never had a clue what he was until it was too late?"

"Fred and I are in love," Michelle affirmed a little stiffly, fastening her bra, then pulling her T-shirt over her head. The medium nodded absently, watching Fred with obvious enjoyment as he stepped into his boxers.

"Incubuses don't have a reputation as reliable partners. They usually don't stick around for long. This one's still here, though, which is worth a lot." She didn't quite manage to pry her eyes off Fred as he vanished bit by bit, first into his shorts, then into his jeans and shirt.

"How come everyone knows all kinds of things about incubuses except me?" Fred muttered, a bit sullen.

"Because they don't stick around to raise their own kids, natch." The medium shrugged sympathetically. "I think your kind is hard-wired to take off. It makes sense for them not to stick around, given they tend to kill their mates. They need the human woman to survive, give birth, and raise their offspring." She led the way up the stairs.

After Michelle wolfed down a huge slice of chocolate cake and washed it down with a foul-tasting energy drink, she felt almost human again. Fred was eating too. She realized he must be channeling the energy to her. He sat still, his eyes closed, chewing slowly.

The medium gazed pensively at them while they ate, her eyes a little hazy. "Oh wow, that's some backstory." She shook herself at last. "Maybe I was a little harsh with the moral judgments down there. Looks like both of you caught a tough break with the naga." She pulled her fingers through a strand of her hair, working out a tangle. "They can be nasty customers sometimes. They like to think they're neutrals, but they just rationalize the hell out of whatever they do until they're doing exactly as they please."

Michelle blinked at her for a moment, surprised by the woman's sudden knowledge. "Yeah. That's how he seemed to me."

Madame Defarge patted Michelle's hand, then transferred her attention to Fred. "Too bad about the girl you killed, incubus, but some of your kind do a hell of a lot worse things deliberately." The medium cut Michelle another huge piece of cake. "Eat up, don't be shy." She gave Michelle a kind little smile and turned back to Fred. "I hate to be a bitch, but we need to talk pay. I've lost a whole evening's business with the proles helping you two."

"Of course. This shouldn't turn into a frog," Fred passed over a thin sheaf of bills. Unfamiliar with British currency, Michelle couldn't begin to guess how much. "It's legal tender."

"The guys upstream somewhere are the ones whose pockets croak? Right." She laughed, tucking the money into her top. "Stick it to the man." She sobered. "I don't do future readings for real, or I would. I make up fantasies for the proles, but they're all based on cold reading shotgun bullshit. But I'll be rooting for you two. You know where to find me if you need what I can do."

"Yeah." Fred snagged Michelle's cardigan and held it for her. "Thanks for your time; being able to feed her will come in handy."

"Glad to help," she answered, her expression grave. "Move fast finding your answers, incubus. What I showed you won't keep her going forever."

Fred swallowed hard, giving her a curt nod.

# Chapter Forty-one

Fred led Michelle down the steps to the street. "We'll go back to the hotel and book a flight into Shannon tomorrow, early. I want to talk to this elder incubus as quickly as possible."

"What if he doesn't want to talk?"

"I'll find a way to persuade him." Fred hailed a taxi.

They stopped on the way back to the hotel to buy Italian food, then stocked up on candy at a small market. "It's harder to find good hard junk food here than in the US," Michelle commented wryly, examining a packet of biscuits. "I never thought I'd miss the stuff."

Fred gestured her toward the chocolate shelf. "Britain has better chocolates, though. Actually Britain has lots of junk food. Sometimes you can get the same thing with a different name. This one is sort of like a Snickers." He picked up something labeled a Curly-Wurly. "And it's also sort of like a rope ladder."

"That sounds encouraging." She tossed a handful into her basket anyway. "It looks like every country has trail mix, too."

"Trail mix should be good stuff," he agreed. "Lots of different nutrients."

The snacks proved surprisingly expensive, prompting Michelle to make a nervous count of their cash, but Fred covered her hand with his. "We'll have what we need."

His intention to pay for everything rankled a little, but at least there was something productive she could *do* now, even if it was just stuffing her face. She hated letting other people act while she waited. Fred better not expect her to sit on her ass over the long-term.

"Maybe I can charm the other incubus into talking." Michelle lifted her chin. "Fred, I may be dying. I can't sit back and let you handle things. I have to help."

Fred bowed his head and swallowed hard. "I should have let you go with me to Superlatives in the first place. Maybe we could have done things differently. We might have avoided all this misery."

"No guilt trips." She reached for her phone and did a little poking around online while he looked for a cab. "The first flight to Shannon is at eight tomorrow. I'll book two seats, shall I?"

"Of course."

She did. When they arrived at the hotel they ate, then she slept. Fred made brief, gentle love to her in her dreams, all too careful for her taste. Restraint was becoming a habit of his, one she would be glad to change.

She woke in Fred's arms. He stroked her hair gently, kissing her forehead so delicately tears prickled the corner of her eyes.

"If I weren't so exhausted, I'd pounce on you. I'd love to give you something to think about," Michelle murmured, lifting her chin for a kiss. "You owe me a bout of serious acrobatic sex with lots of sweat, yelling, and at least a dozen climaxes. I mean, I want the neighbors to call the police."

"I'll take a raincheck," Fred agreed, chuckling in spite of himself. "But right now, you need a snack." He stroked his palm along her arm once, savoring her skin, then withdrew, reaching down beside the bed for a sack of candy and a can of Coca-Cola. "Shall I fill your cup with ice?"

"That would be perfect."

He poured her some Coke and sat cross-legged next to her on the mattress while Michelle chewed her way through most of the Curly-Wurlys. He meditated afterward, sending her as much energy as he could.

"Midnight chocolate bars in bed. You sure know how to treat a lady," she sighed happily when they were done, tossing a last wrapper into the trash. "Sorry about the crumbs." She tilted her head back for the last drops of soda and crunched a piece of ice.

He smiled, though his eyes were dark with worry. "Don't worry about them. I'm going to call Karl. If the Irish guy doesn't pan out, I want to be ready to move on immediately."

"Okay." Michelle settled back on the pillow. "Don't be long."

"I won't." Fred grabbed his phone and a key-card, letting himself out quietly.

Michelle lay awake, flush with new energy, though it was a

relatively thin veneer over the core-deep fatigue starting to settle permanently into her bones. Still, she didn't feel like she could sleep right away, so she finally gave up. On her way to the bathroom, she overheard the soft tenor of Fred's voice outside the door. She hesitated. If he was making notes on their destination, they were certainly taking him a while.

Maybe he was still trying to do everything without letting her have any input?

Michelle hesitated, but the door was almost close enough to reach out and touch. It didn't fit very well in the frame. The edges very loosely sealed, with a wide gap at the bottom.

She stepped softly across the carpet and leaned against the wall, pressing her ear to the crack.

"I'm worried, Karl." She could easily make out Fred's voice echoing in the empty hall. "She's fading away in front of my eyes. I swear she's lost twenty pounds in three days, even though she's eating as much as she can hold several times a day. At the same time, I've never felt better. And I'm supposed to keep feeding off her on purpose, because if I don't, I'll pull harder on her reserves when I'm not actually doing it deliberately. It's driving me mad.

"No, the medium was helpful, but she didn't have a lot of good news. Even with us doing everything she could suggest, Michelle is still going to die unless we can find some better answers." His voice rose as he grew more upset.

"The worst thing about this is it's all my fault. Fuck Saakaar; he's loving every second of this. I'll kill him, Karl, if she doesn't survive. You think I can't? I'll die trying, then." His voice turned bitter. "I don't care what the damned sibyl says; I'll find a way to let the whole world know everything he's done."

Fred's voice faded as he moved farther down the corridor to keep from disturbing her through the door.

Michelle reluctantly returned to bed. She heard Fred come in not too long afterward. She closed her eyes, waiting for him to slide under the covers next to her. At last she snuggled close, finally able to relax and fall asleep.

# Chapter Forty-two

They woke at five. Michelle stretched, pleased to feel alert and energetic. Even so, Fred wouldn't let her leave bed without eating breakfast first. Room service brought a tray so she could sit right where she was, eating bacon and eggs, black pudding, toast with marmalade, and juice. She glanced at the wastebasket, now running over with wrappers. She looked at him suspiciously.

"You got up early and channeled food to me," she guessed. He flushed a little, nodding.

"I feel good," she smiled shyly. "Thank you, Fred." She set aside her empty tray, kissed his cheek, then padded into the bathroom for a quick shower.

"May I join you?" Fred's face appeared around the shower curtain. Michelle beamed at him, stepping back to make room.

"I thought you'd never ask." She reached for him when he stepped in. He let her soap his back and his hair.

"That tickles," he laughed a little, squirming, as Michelle ran her hands along his ribs.

"How about this?" She slid her hands down to curl one around his cock, sliding her soap-slippery palm along his length.

"We shouldn't."

"Fuck that." Michelle refused to give this up. "I want you."

Fred opened his mouth to argue, but she shook her head, fierce. He firmed quickly, filling her palm, and she wrapped her free arm around his belly. "Don't fuss," she murmured. "Let me."

She felt him relax slowly, his head tipping back as he let himself enjoy her touch. She nuzzled at his warm, wet shoulder, pleased with the slippery feel of him in her hand—thin skin over the hard core of his cock.

She could feel his pleasure, glowing with increasing strength in the part of her mind he now occupied.

She listened to him, carefully adjusting her strokes, trying to sense any differences in what he liked. She stroked a little faster, loosening her grip. Fred groaned, his muscles rippling inside the circle of her arms. He began to push his hips forward. Her sense of him blossomed into bliss as her slick wet grip activated every nerve in his body. He gasped, his hips jerking forward. Perfection. She knew without asking: he'd never had a woman take him in her mouth. She smiled, letting go.

Michelle tugged at his body, half-turning him, then lowered herself to sit on the lip of the tub. He blinked down at her, his eyes hazy with startled pleasure, as she slid her hands behind his ass, opening her mouth and tugging him forward. He whimpered low and deep in his throat, obeying, reaching with one trembling hand to steady his cock for her.

"Fuck my mouth, Fred," she told him, sultry, licking a gleaming droplet of water off the tip of his wet cock. "I want you to."

The lightning bolt sizzle of his arousal flooded them both as she flicked her tongue against the slit. He trembled with the sudden fierce need to thrust. She lifted her gaze to his face to meet his burning gaze; his trembling hands slid around her cheeks and his fingers threaded into the wet strands of her hair as she pillowed his cock on her tongue.

"Michelle." His voice vibrated with a soft growl. He slowly pushed forward, his cock moving between her lips. Michelle sucked softly, welcoming him. She tilted her chin and his cock entered her throat until he was fully sheathed inside her mouth, his wet hair tickling her nose.

"Holy fuck," he swore. His hands tightened, holding her still. He thrust again a little faster. Michelle sucked harder, urging him on wordlessly, savoring the spare, taut curve of his ass against her palms.

He began to rock tentatively at first, then with increasing confidence. She found his rhythm, breathing in stuttered gasps between his thrusts. The shallow breaths made her a little dizzy, but she loved the feeling of his strong hands steadying her head so he could push his thick cock between her lips.

He tasted saltier now, his cock rigid and quivering. She moaned softly, purring around him. A shudder thrilled along his spine, vibrating under her palms. Clouds of steam rolled into the air from the hot water collecting in the bottom of the tub, bringing out a sheen of sweat all over his body. She pulled him forward, urging him to thrust harder. He surrendered, riding her mouth hard, his fingers pulling at her hair.

It hurt a little, in a good way. She loved feeling him abandon himself, trusting her to take whatever he gave. She moaned her satisfaction, trying to communicate her love. His eyes fluttered open, his gaze fastening on hers. He made a low, throttled cry and his hips jerked as he spasmed, coming on her tongue. The bitter taste of his seed filled her mouth.

She swallowed, eager, moving one hand to milk his shaft gently, kissing pearls of creamy white from the tip.

"God, Michelle," he whispered, his voice husky. "So fucking good...."

"Wash my hair for me?" She licked her lips. He washed her hair slowly, reverently lathering the long strands and burying his hands in them, his fingertips firmly massaging her scalp. She helped him lift the heavy mass of hair so water could sluice through, rinsing it all the way to the roots.

"Here I thought we'd save some time if I showered with you," he murmured, sliding his arms around her waist and rocking her against his body.

"Mmmm, I loved every minute." She squirmed against him, loving the slippery velvet of his skin against hers. "But I guess we'd better catch our plane."

# Chapter Forty-three

The flight to Shannon turned out to be quick. Luckily, Michelle still felt good when they departed the city in their rental.

"We want to go north. Ultimately, we're heading for the Burren," Fred muttered, handing her his phone. "The incubus Karl mentioned doesn't have a proper address, just latitude and longitude, but Karl said the place was near Corofin."

"We'll want the M18 to the N85. Then look for the 460," Michelle decided at length. "Some of these may not be very fast roads, though."

"Ireland doesn't have many four-lane highways." Fred shrugged helplessly. "Unless we want to charter a helicopter, we'll have to drive slowly. How are you doing?"

"Fine. The constant food is helping." She smiled at him with determination, popping a few chocolate-covered peanuts into her mouth.

They ate lunch deep in the Burren. Michelle inhaled deep breaths of the fresh, clean air, tipping her head back so the sun could warm her body. She sat perched on a hot limestone rock carved into almost a perfect rectangle by centuries of flowing water. Deep cracks scored the land everywhere. Smaller flakes of the gray stone lay piled into rough stacks. Near her, a circular pool had formed where the water had eaten into the slab. A few pebbles lay in the bottom. Luxuriant ferns grew in nearby cracks. Small pink and yellow flowers bloomed between the rocks. Bees droned sleepily through the air, gathering pollen. Though the sunlight shone brightly where they sat, heavy clouds massed on the horizon, threatening rain.

"It's beautiful here," she murmured as their gazes locked.

Fred smiled. "Maybe we can come back when we have time to enjoy Ireland properly." His hand sought hers and their fingers twined.

Fred leaned in to kiss her cheek, then stole a bite of her sandwich.

"For that, you can give me the last of your Coke." She felt stuffed, but she lifted her plastic cup anyway. "Even Coke tastes better here."

"Irish Coca-Cola tastes better than Coca-Cola from the fount of all things Coke in Atlanta?" He teased her gently. "They still make soda with cane sugar in the UK, not high fructose corn syrup." He poured the rest of the bottle of soda into her glass. She tipped her head back and swallowed, then held out her hand to let him pull her up.

"Let's drive some more." She helped him pack their picnic back into its bag. Already she felt ready to rest.

"I can't concentrate deeply enough to send you energy while driving," Fred apologized after a moment. "I'm sorry."

"Don't worry about it. Just get us where we need to go." She sat back. The rocking of the car lulled her to sleep while they progressed toward Corofin.

She opened her eyes again when the car began to vibrate unsteadily, rocking from side to side. They'd left the pavement, traveling along a cart path so narrow the witch hazel bushes on either side knocked solidly against the car's side-mirrors.

"The GPS says these are the coordinates we want," Fred said. She blinked at the windshield wipers, a little surprised by rain pattering on the glass.

"I'm worried about rising water. They have temporary lakes in the valleys around here after rain. All the water drains off those limestone hills in a hurry. Look." They emerged from the thicket of witch hazel. Fred slowed to a stop. A silver-grey lake gleamed before them, its edges lapping at the verge of the road. A cottage lay on a raised spit of land not far away. Even through the mist Michelle could spy roses, small dots of red, pink, and yellow hanging from trellised green bushes. Smoke rose from the chimney but settled back into the hollow again, oppressed by the steady, soft rain.

"Let's go while we still can." Fred put his foot back on the gas. "This cottage is right on top of the coordinates Karl gave us for the GPS."

Michelle roused herself to dig out some peanut butter crackers. "Let's hope he's at home."

A black and white border collie emerged from the cottage as they drew near and ran through a gate in the stone fence, barking ferociously. Michelle hesitated, her hand on the car door. A man followed close after the beast, glaring at them with no welcome. He caught the dog by the collar.

"You'll find no tourist accommodations here; you've taken a wrong turning. Water's rising. Best turn around now and head back before the turlough cuts you off," he snapped, pecking at the glass of the window on her side of the car and gesturing sharply back the way they had come.

"Fred, look at him." Michelle gasped in shock, gazing up into the man's scowling face. His short, roughly trimmed beard obscured his face from a distance, but up close the resemblance could not be mistaken. From his ice-gray eyes to the line of his jaw, from his heavy brows to the shape of his nose and forehead, the man was a dead ringer for Fred. He looked a little more grizzled, slightly more worn. If the two men were human, she'd have guessed his age at about forty-five compared to Fred's thirty, but she had no idea how supernaturals showed their ages.

Fred sat still for a moment, his eyes wide; his adam's apple bobbed in his throat as he swallowed. He reached for the door handle, climbing out of the car to face the man over the top.

"Good afternoon...father." She could hear the tremor in his voice, though he tried for calm.

# Chapter Forty-four

"I'll be buggered." The man said slowly, still hanging on to his dog. He studied Fred, startled, but his frown stayed right where it was. Michelle could see no sign of softening in him.

"May we come in? We have matters of some urgency to discuss with you." Fred didn't wait for an answer, closing his door and stepping around the car to open Michelle's.

"Rosie, go lie down," the man snapped to his dog. "I suppose I can't be stopping you." He glared at Fred, his eyes narrowing. "But mind you, don't step on my flowers."

Fred and Michelle followed him up the cobbled path, stepping with care to avoid the lush green moss between the stones. The roses had all been neatly pruned and tied to their trellises with a loving hand. Was there more to the man than his short temper? Dense, sweet-smelling peat smoke eddied around their shoulders as they walked through the rain.

Fred ducked his head to avoid the low lintel of the door The interior of the cottage was dim but cozy, with a thick rag rug on the floor and a comfortable-looking leather chair next to the hearth. A hard-looking horsehair sofa held down the other edge of the rug. The dog lay in a cozy padded basket within reach of the armchair, looking up at them apologetically as they entered. Her tail thumped lightly on the floor at the sight of her master, who neglected to offer them either a seat or any refreshment.

"What business do you have with me?" The man flopped down and put his feet up on the hearth, still scowling. "I'm very busy. I don't have time for youthful nonsense."

"My name is Fredric, and this is Michelle." Fred gracefully seated Michelle on the sofa, but remained standing by her side, maintaining

215

social courtesy in the face of rudeness. "We've come to consult with you because I need information about my natural abilities."

The older man studied him keenly, sharp eyes intent. "So you want me to play the attentive father to you? Make up for missed years? Pat you on the head and say what a fine son you are?"

"I had no idea we were related until I first laid eyes on you." Fred had regained his cool. "I was referred here by an expert who thought you'd have the information I need."

"What do you want to know? I'd like to have you on your way by teatime."

Fred's lips narrowed, going white. Michelle laid her hand behind his knee, trying to help him keep his temper.

"Believe me, I'd like to learn what you know as rapidly as possible. Your knowledge would have been useful centuries ago." He bit out the words with knifelike politeness. "I've inadvertently connected to this woman permanently, and am dr—"

The man spat out a derisive laugh. He opened a drawer in the little end table next to his chair, pulling out a pipe. "Draining her to death, yes, yes. Very tragic." He stabbed the stem of his cold pipe at Fred accusingly. "You're not young. You ought to know by now you'll kill them whenever you draw too much. Visit a pretty human a single time in a dream, then forget her. Don't fuck them unless you can move on afterward—or unless you want to breed. But even then, you shouldn't fuck them too often."

Michelle lowered her gaze to her lap, biting her lip at the casual contempt in his voice. She pulled Fred down next to her, stroking his shoulder to calm him.

"If you fuck them, you'll kill the ones you grow to care for." Fred's father insisted, ignoring Fred's thunderous look. "If you keep feeding on one over and over, even in dreams, you'll eventually wind up connected to her permanently." He snorted. "You're pretty old not to have figured that out on your own by now, but it's apparent you have no self-discipline."

Fred's face crumpled with hurt. "I know that." He drew a deep breath and steadied himself. "I want to know how to disconnect or, if possible, how to balance our energy exchange so we can be together without danger to her."

"How to disconnect? Leave her far behind and let her die." Fred's father opened a pouch. He slowly thumbed sweet-smelling tobacco into the bowl of his pipe. When he was finally satisfied, he pulled a straw out of the drawer, leaning forward to the fire to light it. He sat back and sucked on the pipe, drawing the flame down into the bowl until he had it going well. Then he flicked the straw into the fire. "Proximity is a problem."

Michelle could hear Fred taking slow, measured breaths, struggling to govern his temper. "And the other?"

"Can't be done." His father looked up, exhaling smoke through both nostrils. "Why do you think I left your mother, whelp?"

"She was a cambion."

"She had enough human in her she'd have died, exactly like this one will. I barely left her in time." He took another deep draw from his pipe, blowing the smoke out again in one long stream. "I have no more idea how to stop it than you do. Death is part of our nature, boy." For the first time, Michelle thought she sensed something like compassion in his gruff voice. "Don't ever let yourself grow to love them, that's my advice."

"Breathe, Fred," Michelle murmured urgently. He sat very still, his hands clenching into fists, his knuckles going white. Her heart began trip-hammering and her mouth tasted as if she'd bitten a copper wire when she heard the casual assertion she was simply going to die.

"So we're supposed to seek out a succubus to breed with? A female version of our own kind?" Fred spoke slowly, through gritted teeth; Michelle sensed his internal struggle, his desperation to make sense of things.

"Absolutely not." His father scowled at his pipe. "They're too like us; they need a human to draw from. You can't connect to one of those at all."

"Would Michelle be saved if I died?" Fred asked slowly.

That caught the elder's attention; his eyes kindled to a blue blaze of fury as he snapped them up to glower at Fred. "Don't be a fool."

"Would she?" Fred demanded, rising to tower over his father. The dog growled low in her throat.

"She'd die along with you. You'd pull her right along as you went down." He cleared his throat and spat into the fire, his face sullen. "Have you found a lodging?"

"No." Fred stared at him coldly.

"There's a bit of a pub in Corofin. They don't usually let rooms to tourists, but they'll let you stay the night if I vouch for you." Fred's father sucked on the pipe. The tobacco glowed fiercely for a moment.

"You'd do that? Thank you," Fred said evenly.

"You're blood kin. I suppose you have that much claim on my kindness." He scowled out the little window. "Dark already." He rose, transferring his pipe to his left hand before extending his palm for Fred to shake. "I'm Bradan. I suppose your mother never told you my name. She was Maire, no?"

"Yes." Fred hesitated, taken aback by the sudden change in his father's temperament. "She died when I was around a hundred and twenty."

"You have a touch of red in your hair. Doubtless that was from her." He knocked the dottle out of his pipe on one of the andirons before tucking it away in its drawer. "We'd best be moving out before the lake comes up any farther."

# Chapter Forty-five

The rain fell, unrelenting, but Fred's father insisted the turlough was still low enough to manage. Cautiously, they plowed through the edge of the lake then wound their way out through the witch hazel thicket, headlamps illuminating a curtain of falling rain as they rode toward Corofin. Once again, Michelle surrendered to fatigue.

Fred nudged her awake to go inside after he and his father negotiated successfully to rent the back room at the pub.

Supper consisted of hearty Irish stew served in deep dishes, poured right into a nest of mashed potatoes, with parsnips, carrots, and broccoli on the side. Michelle ate as much as she could. Bradan had left them, preferring to take his meal with his pub-owner friend.

"I'm going to spend some time talking to my father. We'll probably sit up until the pub closes." Fred gathered the empty dishes, piling them on the dresser. "Perhaps he knows something he isn't telling. At any rate, we can't go any further tonight, so I want to spend a little time with him while I have a chance. We'll move on to Karl's next option first thing in the morning. But first...."

Fred sat down, composing himself to serenity. Michelle felt the soft flush of heat as he began sending the energy from his food to her. She lay quietly, watching him as he worked. She loved the curve of his lashes against his cheek, the perfect narrow line of his sensual lips, the rough stubble on his face and neck where he'd shaved carelessly, going with the grain, the way a few wisps of hair tumbled down over his forehead in spite of all combing, now that he'd abandoned the horrible styling gel.

"Thank you, Fred," she said when he finished. She lifted her face for a kiss, touching his tongue with hers briefly before he withdrew to stroke a thumb over her cheekbone, his expression gentle, terribly helpless.

There were no easy answers. If there were, someone would have known them. Karl, the medium, Fred's father...the sibyl herself, for Christ's sake. If she didn't know, what hope did Michelle and Fred have?

Michelle knew only one supernatural being who might have the power to help her.

She reached for a bag of Cadbury Clusters and put a few chocolate covered raisins in her mouth. "Where are we off to next?"

"Karl sent me the address of a medium in Qatar. She may know something Madame Defarge didn't."

Michelle eyed Fred narrowly. Judging from the wrinkle between his brows, he didn't have much hope.

"I want to talk to Saakaar about this again, Fred. The sibyl suggested he may have an answer for me."

He lifted a brow at her, surprised. "He won't talk to us."

"We should try. He has his jewel back, so he may have calmed down."

"He's always calm." Fred lifted the curtain, looking out into the night. "He's implacable."

"Maybe so, but I believe he has answers we need."

"One answer, maybe, but he won't be inclined to cooperate."

"I could appeal to his sense of justice."

Fred spread his palms, gesturing helplessly. "He was the one who set you up to die, Michelle. He isn't going to help save you."

"You're being fatalistic."

"We'd be wasting valuable time and resources to seek him out. We don't have enough of either to spare on a wild goose chase." He tried to paste on a cheerful expression. "I'll go grill my father to find out what he knows. Maybe there's something he isn't telling us. Getting him drunk might loosen his tongue a little."

Michelle curled into herself unhappily, wrapping her arms around her knees, watching Fred reluctantly turn away. He fished his wallet out of the pocket of his rain jacket, then tucked it into his jeans. Taking the dirty dishes, he went out to the pub.

~ * ~

Fred hadn't been gone two minutes before Michelle heard a tap on the door.

"Come in, Bradan." She ignored his forbidding expression. Returning to sit on the bed, she left him the room's single rickety straight chair. "I was expecting you."

"Were you indeed?" He didn't sit. Folding his arms over his chest, he leaned against the dresser, looking anything but friendly.

"You seem very opposed to any kind of long-term relationship between a human and an incubus. Why?"

"There aren't enough of my kind remaining to risk Fredric's life on romantic foolishness." Bradan scowled at her. "You humans think your kind are the normal ones, but you're the demons, if you ask me. Running around killing anyone who isn't like you, making up nonsensical claptrap about gods and devils when you aren't blathering gibberish about true love? Then you expect us to take up your ways of living instead of keeping our own. Your kind always think you have a right to whatever you want. You mean to have your selfish desires; to hell with the cost."

Michelle could hardly contain everything she wanted to say in response, but she focused on the most critical point. "Risk Fred's life? Cost? What do you mean?"

"If he's with you when you die, you'll pull him right down with you," Bradan spat. "If you valued Fredric at all, you would travel as far away from him as you can." His brogue thickened with his anger, his eyes flashing at her.

"You want information? I'll give you plenty. Think of your connection as a vortex. The closer to the center, the stronger the pull. A boat on the outskirts of a vortex can escape, but one in the middle will be sucked down. There's nowhere on Earth far enough to escape the pull entirely, but he has a better chance to live through your death if he isn't right on top of you."

"You came with us to see if you could convince him to leave me," Michelle said slowly. "You don't want him to die."

"Got it in one." Bradan thrust out his chin. "But he's a damned fool who won't agree to go. He ought to have been born human, he takes your moral system so seriously. He holds himself responsible, as if preying on humans to survive were cold-blooded murder. Your foolish human notions of love are even worse. He's convinced he has to go down with the ship instead of saving himself." He glared at her, a bitter challenge. "I hope you're less of a fool than he is."

"You shouldn't have left him to grow up on his own. If you wanted him to learn your value system, you should have stayed with him."

"I care about my race!" Bradan thumped his fist on his knee, furious. "I left his mother so we wouldn't kill one another—or our unborn child. Do you know how few of us are left? Do you?"

She shrank back into the chair under the force of his anger. "No. How many?"

"I am aware of six incubuses who remain alive today. Six! How many of you infernal humans crawl the world now? Seven billion. What is the life of one human next to my son, girl?"

Michelle couldn't answer, wanting to know how you bred an incubus, how long they lived, and what else could kill them, but this didn't seem the right time to ask.

"Take your romantic human ideals and apply them as you should for once. Let Fredric live," Bradan advised her bitterly. "That's what I'd have you do. Leave him. The next time, he'll know better." He left her abruptly, closing the door with a sharp snap.

Michelle sat very still for a moment, startled by the heat of his anger. Bradan must care more deeply for his son than he wanted to admit.

She went to the door and watched Bradan stride through the pub, his head held low between his shoulders, his hands jammed into his pockets. Her heart ached to see the strong resemblance to Fred: the shape of him, the way he moved.

He was right. Fred should leave her for the sake of his own safety. He must be off to spend the evening trying to talk Fred into saving himself, but they both knew better: Fred wouldn't leave her.

She remembered the sibyl's enigmatic words: "Saakaar may have a part to play in this yet."

Her gut instinct agreed, but even if she persuaded Fred to speak with Saakaar, he would only infuriate the naga.

Michelle returned to the room, her mind racing. Fred's rain jacket lay tossed casually across the top of the dresser, the car keys gleaming inside the half-open pocket.

Her heart felt as if it were being squeezed inside a giant's fist. She sat still for a long moment, trying to breathe. She could feel the tension in Fred as he dealt with his father, an icy lump where warmth and welcome usually waited.

She moved very carefully, keeping her breathing slow, very even, as she took the keys. His passport lay tucked inside the pocket as well. She bit her lip, then removed it. Losing his papers would slow his pursuit.

Moving deliberately, humming to herself, Michelle wrote a short explanation on a pad of paper from their London hotel. She tore it off, leaving the note on Fred's jacket. Forcing herself to remain calm, she gathered the remaining snacks from the room, pouring them into a single shopping bag. She hadn't unpacked any of her clothes or toiletries, so all she had to do was shoulder the shopping bag, grab her carry-on, and pull it after her. She abandoned the suitcase with most of her clothes. Travel light, move fast.

The worst part was sneaking through the back of the pub. She paused, forced to wait for a girl to take chairs down off a table and set them on the uneven floor. She glanced aside, nervous, to see if she'd been spotted.

Fred sat by the bar, perched atop a barstool next to his father. His boot hooked casually over the footrest, reminding her of her first dream of him. He didn't look in her direction, focused on Bradan, who reached across the bar to accept two foam-capped glasses of stout.

"She's a lovely girl, Fredric. I'm sorry." Bradan's gruff tones had vanished, replaced by quiet compassion. "I have been where you are."

"Where, precisely?" Fred still sounded distrustful, his shoulders stiff.

"In love with a human, killing her." Bradan swigged his beer, wiping the foam from his upper lip with his sleeve. "Our folk are as we are, Fredric. We mustn't let ourselves love. Maybe the cattle are right to call us damned things and kill us whenever they can."

Cattle? Michelle pursed her lips, angered as the reverse psychology hit Fred right in the gut, making him fold up and hunch his shoulders, leaning over his beer. The old incubus might be no more than a master manipulator, but he cared for Fred, even if he hadn't raised him. He was right; she had to go. It was her best chance— and Fred's.

Would Bradan have been able to convince Fred to leave her? Unbidden, her brain presented an image of Fred in her place, suitcase and belongings in his hand, sneaking away without so much as a last goodbye.

Her eyes filled with tears and she clamped down hard against the image before it could shred her heart and alert Fred to her distress. She needed to be far away before he discovered she was gone.

Michelle stole out into the rainy night, fumbling the key into the door of the car. She dumped her wet bags into the passenger's seat, then sat behind the steering wheel. Other than being on the wrong side, the driver's array was more or less what she was used to. Now if only she could negotiate the intersections without forgetting which side was hers....

The car started with an obedient purr and Michelle drove into the night, programming the GPS for the Shannon airport.

# Chapter Forty-six

After about an hour, Michelle started to weave on the road, wandering over the center line and back again. A quick check on Fred's emotions revealed the cause: he was buzzed from the beer. Fine. If getting drunk kept him from figuring out she was gone for another couple of hours, then she hoped he would drink deeply.

By the time Fred found her note, his emotions exploding with distress, she was nearly to Shannon. She ignored the frantic buzzing of her phone, letting him go to voicemail. By the time she dropped her car at the rental dealership, it fell still. She shuttled into the terminal, riding the van alone.

"I want to be on your next flight out of Ireland. I don't care what destination," she marched up to the all-night desk for Aer Lingus, presenting her passport.

The bored, sleepy clerk raised a brow at her, then tapped at a keyboard. "It's headed to Paris in half an hour."

"Give me a ticket." She mustered all her remaining energy for the quick hustle to the gate. With any luck, she'd be moving too fast for Fred to catch up with her before she found Saakaar.

Michelle reached the gate with a few minutes to spare, stopping in the duty free area to load up on chocolates. She was nearly done when she spotted a little box of chocolate bars with a frog on the label. Her hand rose to cover her mouth as tears sprang to her eyes. "Freddo," she read aloud, touching the wrapper.

She tipped all of them into her basket, then took it to the checkout counter, startling the cashier. "Nieces and nephews in France," she lied, passing over her credit card.

After boarding her flight, she fastened her seat belt and fell asleep before the plane ever finished taxiing to the runway for takeoff.

A stewardess roused her later, offering her a drink. Michelle made herself sit up and asked for caffeinated soda. Fred's presence, tucked away somewhere in her mind, was so agitated she had to struggle not to cry, but she forced down two of the frog-shaped Freddo chocolate bars and drank an entire can of cola. Before she finished, she could feel the faint warmth indicating Fred had stopped whatever he was doing to feed her.

Overcome with love and regret, she sat sobbing silently with her hands wrapped around a plastic cup of melting ice, tears running down her cheeks.

"Are you all right?" Michelle hesitated, puzzled by the stewardess's thick brogue, then dug up a plausible fib.

"Death in the family."

The lie earned her gentle treatment and a free Irish coffee. She warmed her hands around the cup, sipping until the coffee was gone, then drowsed until they touched down in Paris.

She didn't dare linger. Fred might be a few hours behind her, but he'd soon dig up alternative documents or simply use his glamour to bamboozle a female customs agent. She bit her lip, annoyed with herself for failing to write down Karl's number before she fled. How was she going to find out where Saakaar lived?

She picked up her phone and thumbed it on, but before she could key in the security code, the screen lit up with a phone number listing. A single word flashed: "Robin."

She groaned, but her heart lifted with hope as she tapped the dial button.

Robin's shrill voice came on the line at once. "I thought you'd never call! Do you *know* how long your phone's been sitting waiting for you to call me?"

Michelle tried without success to squeeze a word in edgewise, waiting till Robin's tirade finally wound down. "What do I need to know? Why couldn't you just come tell me?"

"I can't offer the information without being asked." Robin began to pout, her voice sullen. Michelle could imagine her round-cheeked face pulled into an expression of resentment.

"Okay, I'm asking." Michelle forced herself to remain patient.

"New Delhi."

"What?"

"Buy a ticket to New Delhi," Robin exaggerated her patient tones, an audible eye-roll. "That's where you want to go."

"Are you helping Fred?"

"I haven't spoken to Fredric since the afternoon I met you both at La Guardia." Robin sounded so innocent Michelle could practically hear her glowing halo. In other words, she'd be going to Fred as soon as Michelle hung up the phone. Great.

"Why do I need to go to New Delhi?" Michelle tried again, feeling exasperated.

"You want to see Saakaar, of course. Even Fredric knows that."

"Don't help him." Michelle angled her path toward a ticketing desk.

"If I have to, but only when the time is right. I know the way to Saakaar's heart." Robin's tone practically dripped smugness. "It sure as hell isn't through Fredric. But I've said too much."

The connection went dead.

"When is your next flight to New Delhi? *S'il vous plaît*?" she asked the ticketing agent, relieved when the girl answered her in heavily accented English.

"An hour and a half, *mademoiselle*."

"Can I buy a ticket?"

"*Bien sûr*." The woman accepted her credit card and scanned the magnetic strip, then printed a boarding pass. "*Merci, mademoiselle*."

Michelle bought more junk food, wrinkling her nose. She was sick and tired of endless greasy, salty snacks, so she wandered into an Italian restaurant near her gate, ordering a big bowl of pasta, glad to have a real meal. She was running on fumes. Even Fred's attempts to send her energy were muted, as if the distance between them had weakened their connection.

Michelle chose to take the faded connection as a good sign. If she gained enough distance for him to survive her death, at least she could die with a clear conscience.

Passport, boarding pass, bag tag. She endured the long slog down the jetway into the plane, wrestled her carry-on into the overhead bin, and ignored the inevitable lecture from the flight attendants on oxygen masks and safety belts. Michelle closed her eyes, thinking wistfully of Fred, and willed herself to wake up in India.

# Chapter Forty-seven

Night dominated Michelle's dreamscape. She found herself wandering the darkened corridors alone at Robotidata, the dull plexiglas windows revealing squares of darkness broken by the orange glow of sodium vapor lights in the parking lot. Emergency lights cast pools of illumination at intervals to relieve the gloom. She kept moving, looking for her office, unable to find the door.

Michelle winced. One of these offices would be Fred's. She began to creep as quietly as she could, trying to avoid him. He would visit her dreams if she wouldn't answer her phone. She should have anticipated it before.

She peeked cautiously around a corner, checking to see if he was waiting for her in the cafeteria. The empty room was too exposed, so she turned to go back the way she'd come.

Fred stood behind her, his hands in his pockets, his shoulders sunk low.

"Come back, Michelle. My father is wrong." Fred's handsome face twisted with grief. He reached out for her, imploring.

Michelle couldn't bear to let him touch her. She raised a forbidding palm, keeping him back.

"I'm sorry, Fred." Michelle turned her back, not wanting to see how miserable she'd made him. "I don't want to hurt you, not any more than you wanted to hurt me, but I refuse to drag you down with me when I die. Anyway, this is something I have to do alone." She struggled for words to persuade him, to comfort him, but there were none.

"What are you doing?"

"You know I can't tell you." Michelle wiped tears off her cheeks, feeling weak and horrible.

"You mean to try your luck with Saakaar." Fred reached out to her, pleading. "Michelle, you don't even know where to find him. Come back. Karl can help us figure out where he is. Then I'll hunt him with you."

"You'd just piss him off, Fred. I have to do this by myself."

"Then leave me in the hotel while you go talk to him. Just take me with you." Fred laid his hand on her arm. The corridor wavered, fading; for a moment Michelle was aware of a stewardess bustling past, jostling her. Then she was back with him again. She stepped aside, letting his hand fall.

"It's hard enough talking to you here without having to try to convince you in person." She went to him, kissing his cheek. His skin tasted wet with salt, nearly breaking her resolve. Michelle drew back and rested her forehead against his shoulder. "If you keep coming into my dreams to argue with me, I won't be able to let myself sleep. Please don't come again."

Fred tensed as if she'd slapped him. "I won't give up. Karl is researching every entity who might be able to help us. I'm right behind you."

"You should go back to Ireland and get to know your father." Michelle forced herself to step away. "I love you, Fred."

"I love you, Michelle."

She jerked herself awake, blinking out the tiny porthole window at an ocean of puffy clouds far below the wing of the plane. Fred wouldn't be able to feed properly if he didn't visit her dreams. She'd just have to hope he'd be all right until she fixed things on her own or her death freed him.

She made herself eat crackerjack mix as the plane made its final descent, sliding back and forth between consciousness and sleep, half-dozing, the box propped in her lap.

# Chapter Forty-eight

The New Delhi airport teemed with chattering people. Michelle's head felt like a helium balloon, loosely attached to her body on a string. People jostled past her, nearly knocking her down. She clutched at her carry-on bag, dreading the challenge of trying to find a lodging without understanding the language. She had no idea where to start her search for Saakaar.

Michelle sank down into a chair, meaning to figure out how best to proceed, then found she didn't have the stamina to stand up again. Incomprehensible announcements blared on the PA as she stared helplessly out at the milling crowd.

Eventually, she realized Robin stood leaning against the opposite wall, staring at her.

"Mortals." Robin pushed herself off the wall. The crowd gave her no trouble as she weaved through the press to sit at Michelle's side. "How your race ever managed to put together a civilization without magic is beyond me."

"Maybe we're the ones who came up with civilization because magic made supernaturals so lazy they thought they didn't have to work for what they wanted." Michelle closed her eyes. She swayed dizzily, feeling sleep press in on her.

"You shouldn't be rude to someone who has the resources to help you. New Delhi isn't a very good place to be a sick woman, alone, who doesn't speak the language." Robin curled her lip, smug.

"Point taken." Michelle fished a chocolate bar out of her purse, eating it slowly. Fred was trying to feed her again; she could feel the growing warmth of him through the connection. His efforts, combined with the chocolate bar, pushed the dizziness back to a faint gray speckle at the edge of her vision, but Michelle wasn't going to make it very far without a real meal and several hours' sleep.

"Where do I find Saakaar?"

"He has a temple in the mountains."

"The Himalayas?" Michelle giggled a little, feeling punchy. A temple? Of course Fred had managed to piss off a god.

"Yes. The pilgrimage starts at Rishikesh. All pilgrimages start there. It's traditional."

Everything shifted, disorienting Michelle. She blinked, reaching out to touch the surface where she sat, orienting herself. A cow bellowed in the distance. Bright sunshine dazzled her eyes. The airport seating area had vanished. She sat with Robin on a low wall, looking down at a wide, brownish river. A suspension bridge crossed the water, with a steady stream of pedestrians traveling back and forth across the narrow span.

"In ten minutes Fred would have found you sitting there in the terminal," Robin informed her tartly. "He booked a non-stop flight to New Delhi out of Shannon."

She should have known. Michelle exhaled. Instead of holding her carry-on, she now wore a backpack slung over her shoulders. Her shorts and canvas sneakers had transformed into jeans and sturdy hiking boots. She blinked at the improvements with a weary lack of surprise.

"Is that the Ganges river?"

"The Ganga," Robin corrected.

"I need food and a place to sleep."

"The longer you sleep, the sooner Fred will catch up." Robin pursed her lips.

"Why didn't you take me directly to Saakaar?"

"Why are you complaining about the way I choose to help? I might not help you at all." Robin sighed, very put-upon. "This has to be done properly. To ask the god for a favor, you must undertake your pilgrimage with a repentant heart. You need to make the traditional sacrifices."

Michelle blinked at her, filing the words away for later, when she'd have more ability to think.

"You're fortunate the shrine is near the river. Would you like to try to climb the Himalayas? He could be ten thousand feet up, buried in snow. You're lucky cobras don't like the cold. Get up now, come on."

Robin chivvied Michelle until she rose. They wandered down a narrow street into a small building, apparently the local equivalent of a hotel. Robin vanished while Michelle wasn't looking, but a smiling native woman with a reddish-brown caste mark on her head led Michelle down a corridor to a small room. The amenities consisted of a cot with suspended mosquito netting, a pitcher of water sitting in a chipped basin, and a chamber pot shoved out of the way under the bed. Michelle didn't care; all she wanted was food and sleep.

The same local woman brought Michelle a tray: flatbread and a bowl of unidentifiable vegetable curry, and another full of soup. Michelle fumbled in her purse. Knowing nothing about the currency or the cost of her meal and lodging, she offered a handful of money. The woman selected a few coins, then left the tray.

Michelle ate until the food was gone, then collapsed onto her cot, sleeping so deeply she never dreamed.

# Chapter Forty-nine

Michelle woke in darkness. People wandered up and down the halls, talking quietly. She yawned, wondering where she could find breakfast. She hadn't taken off her clothes, so she didn't have to dress. She used the chamber pot, strapped on her pack, then ventured out timidly. Families sat on the ground eating in a little courtyard where a kettle bubbled over an open fire. She took a bowl and offered to pay again, but the little woman by the fire shook her head, smiling.

"Do you know where I can find the naga? Temple to the naga? Saakaar," Michelle tried to communicate.

"Naga," the woman nodded emphatically and pointed down the road to the left, toward the suspended bridge.

Michelle smiled thanks at the woman and followed the pointing finger, crossing the bridge before she faltered, no longer sure of her path. The streets baffled her, with people milling everywhere. Cows wandered lazily through the crowd, given right of way as though they were respected elders. A number of people, some of whom looked like westerners, wandered down the street in front of Michelle. She ambled along with them, listening for anyone who might speak English.

She finally located an English-speaking couple, stolid Brits by the sound of them, standing at the edge of the way, arguing over a map. The man wore khaki shorts and dark socks with sock suspenders; his wife had on a fussy sun hat. Both looked sweaty, quite bothered.

"Excuse me, please." Michelle approached them diffidently. "Can you direct me to the shrine of the naga?"

They looked at her briefly, with mild dismay, then politeness kicked in. "I don't know of one. Is it a Buddhist temple?" The man frowned at his map.

"I don't think so."

"A naga is a king cobra, Reginald." The woman fanned herself impatiently. "I heard about a snake temple on one of the tours, but I think that one is in Tamil Nadu."

"This says there's one in Nagercoil."

"Thanks anyway." She smiled.

"Do you know of a lodging across the river?"

"It's not fancy like a western hotel, but I stayed in a place inside the town." Michelle directed them there, drawing a map in the dirt beside the path, then moved on. The road led down to the river. She hesitated there, wondering where to go next. The water lapped at the shore, a restless, lonely sound. Michelle gave up and pulled out her phone.

The display showed an arrow, refusing to give her anything else. No matter which way she turned the phone or what part of the screen she pressed, the arrow always pointed up the river. Shrugging, she followed it.

Shortly after she left town, the path narrowed. No one walked close enough for her to hear voices; the only sound came from monkeys chattering and shrieking in the jungle. Michelle hesitated at a fork in the trail. The path away from the river looked faint, very nearly overgrown, but she spied a sign next to it displaying two entwined serpents. In the absence of any other clues, it seemed a logical guide.

Michelle glanced behind, wondering how many pilgrims walked this trail, then surrendered to the inevitable. Ducking through the overhanging branches that shaded the sign, she hoped there weren't any poisonous spiders lurking between the leaves.

She slapped a mosquito, hitching her belt a little tighter. Weight was melting off her, and her shorts threatened to fall right off her body even with the belt. She paused to eat a chocolate bar, startled halfway through to find Robin sitting in midair at her side, wearing a ridiculous gold lamé turban and curly-toed shoes with harem pants, an elaborately embroidered vest, and a wide cummerbund.

"One who thinks the body to be the self and the land of his birth worshipable, who desires an everlasting relationship with wife, relatives, etc., and who goes on pilgrimage simply to take a spiritual bath, is no better than an ass or cow," she intoned as Michelle blinked at her uncertainly. "That's from the *Bhagavat Purana*."

"I don't think Hindu religious texts apply to me."

"You want to be with Fred forever," Robin pointed out.

"I don't want Fred to die." Michelle corrected her firmly.

Robin produced a clipboard from thin air, making a tick mark in an ostentatious manner. "Good motive," she said. "I figure you have a burning desire to see things; all Americans seem to. That'll take care of *darshan*. How's your karma? Are you in harmony with the divine?" She snapped her fingers and vanished.

The questions lingered in Michelle's mind as she pressed forward, climbing a stony ridge where the river cut a narrow gorge through the foothills. She didn't think she'd ever done deliberate harm to others, but as an American she'd lived a privileged life, enjoying significant advantages in a wasteful way. One of the articles she'd read about nagas said they responded personally to offenses against the environment. Remembering that made her uncomfortably aware she hadn't always been as careful as she should about recycling or turning out lights.

How could she atone for waste? It wasn't enough to boast she didn't always kill spiders inside her house. Not unless they were in her bed or in the bathtub. Any spider in those areas was an automatic casualty of war. Death by paperback, athletic shoe, or possibly showerhead.

Feeling ashamed of herself, Michelle wiped sweat off her face, squinting up toward the top of the ridge. She had to hope she was still headed in the right direction. If the journey was going to take more than one day, she was in trouble. She didn't have so much as a jacket in her bag. Just candy, her identification, and a few pieces of jewelry.

By the time Michelle reached the top of the ridge, the sun hung directly overhead. She sat down on a sun-warmed stone to eat a few of her candy bars. Hiking took a lot of energy. Fred kept trying to feed her, but he couldn't support her effectively from a distance.

Michelle squared her jaw, looking upriver. She couldn't let Fred catch up with her. Surely, she could walk and chew at the same time. She rose, packing up her things, but the back of her neck prickled and she turned to see a half-naked brown-skinned child looking at her soberly.

What could a little sharing hurt? Michelle smiled, fishing out a candy bar. "Want some?"

The little girl darted forward, snatching the candy from her hand, then vanished into the foliage before Michelle could speak. Shrugging, she slung the pack on her back and headed down the trail, determined to make good speed before the next climb.

That was the steepest ascent, but walk as hard as she could, the sun westered and the air began to turn chill before she found any sign of a town or shrine. Michelle's energy faded with the light, leaving her plodding, half-asleep. Finally, she slumped to the ground next to the trail, watching dispiritedly as the sky turned black in the east.

In the forest, a bird called. She had no idea what sort, or whether there might be predators to trouble her in the night. She stared aimlessly across the river. A tribe of pale-furred langur monkeys cavorted at the opposite edge of the water, their long tails curved high over their backs.

The air was turning cold; goosebumps popped up all over her skin. She didn't have the energy to keep moving, and she had no way to cover herself for the night.

Her cell phone, amazingly enough, showed three bars, representing both rescue and failure. If she called for help now, she'd never make it to the shrine.

Swallowing hard, Michelle tucked it away again without dialing. Huddling into herself, she wrapped her arms around her knees. She could feel Fred, a constant presence of burning frustration and worry in the back of her mind.

She was about to pull out a handful of trail mix when the measured pad of footsteps approached, the first sign of human habitation since lunch. A man walked down the trail toward her, carrying a lighted torch. He carried a crude rucksack on his back, filled to overflowing with sticks of firewood. When he spied her, he shrugged the pack off his shoulders. He beckoned, carrying it along in one hand.

The man led her back from the path under the heavy canopy of a tree. Cascades of branches, or maybe roots, trailed from its crown to dig into the ground. At the base of the tree the earth had been packed flat. A charred black patch of ground indicated a fireplace. Someone had left a brightly colored woolen rug hanging off one twisted branch nearby.

The man set down his bulging pack then poured his firewood into the ring. Michelle gasped a protest, guessing the wood represented his entire day's work. He ignored her, touching his torch to the wood and tending the fire until the flames took hold. He said something unintelligible, then turned to leave.

Michelle dug into her pack. She hesitated over her stash of chocolate bars, but she felt silly offering candy to a grown man. Instead, she reached into the pocket containing her jewelry. She sorted out two pearl earrings set in gold and the matching necklace, a birthday gift from her favorite aunt, and offered them on her outstretched hand. The man spoke an unintelligible phrase or two before he accepted her gift, revealing bad teeth when he smiled and tucked the pearls away into a convenient pouch.

He beckoned her to one side of the clearing toward a plant that reminded her of a bromeliad with a funnel-like crown, where a pool of rainwater had collected. He reached in with cupped hands. Lifting them out he drank, then gestured her toward the reservoir. Afterward, he shouldered his empty pack and went away.

"Maybe my karma is okay after all," Michelle said shakily. She could feel Fred calming a little, responding to her improved mood. His presence in her mind was still faint. Maybe he'd been delayed in New Delhi. She crept back to the fireside, wrapping herself in the rug and huddling near the blaze. She devoured her bag of trail mix, then curled into a ball against the trunk of the tree, falling immediately into a heavy sleep.

# Chapter Fifty

Michelle woke to the gray of dawn, her woolen rug heavy with dew, the last of the fire nearly sunk to ashes. One branch still burned, propped over a rock, its charred, ashy end glowing with coals every time the breeze freshened. Unfamiliar birdcalls echoed through the forest and the ever-present monkeys chattered not far away.

Michelle stirred. She frowned down at her forearm, swatting at a mosquito. She had a nice assortment of bites. She spared a belated worry over the possibility of contracting malaria or dengue fever. She grimaced. The bugs were going to have to race her body to the finish line if they wanted to kill her.

She felt heavy-limbed, weary. Under any other circumstances she wouldn't have even tried to crawl out of bed.

Michelle made herself sit up, then froze as a weight slipped off the blanket and fell into her lap: a black snake marked with narrow pale bands, sluggish with the lingering chill of the night. She sat absolutely still as the thing uncoiled itself and slithered slowly off her lap, its body rippling.

Michelle's spine crawled as she watched. The near end of the smoldering branch caught her eye. Her palm itched with the desire to close around a weapon she could use to strike the snake. But she didn't dare move, not until...*now*, it was off her lap. She reached out, stealthy, and her trembling hand closed around the cool part of the branch.

She didn't pick it up.

It wouldn't do to kill the snake, not even if Saakaar would never know. It was leaving on its own without harming her. It had needed warmth and shelter to survive the night, just like her. This place was its home, not hers.

Michelle didn't move, watching her unwelcome sleeping companion vanish into the forest. She checked gingerly around herself for other unexpected company, grateful to find none.

Her belt wouldn't tighten far enough to keep her shorts up. She had no way to make a new notch in the leather. Instead she picked up a bit of limber vine to tie around her middle.

Michelle ate, not liking the growing lightness in her pack. If she didn't find the shrine soon, she wasn't going to find it at all. After a moment's indecision, she hung the woolen rug back where she'd found it. The rug wasn't hers. Besides, she didn't think she could handle the weight. She could barely manage to move herself.

She hesitated to leave the cozy little shelter under the tree, but given how little energy she had left, she'd better move while she could. She didn't want to end her life here.

At least the near-empty pack was easier to carry.

Michelle filled her water bottle from the plant, then returned to the path again, feeling the faint warmth of Fred stubbornly trying to feed her. She tried not to notice. Any thought of Fred was nearly enough to reduce her to tears, but she didn't have the energy to spare for weeping. Instead, she focused on putting one foot in front of the other, making sure she was on even ground. If she kept her eyes directly on the path in front of her, she didn't have to think about how much farther she still had to walk.

The river widened, growing shallow. The path meandered through a broad valley with wetlands on either side. It remained relatively level, if a little swampy. Michelle was being eaten alive by mosquitoes, but it was too late to buy bug spray, so she endured the itching without complaint.

By noon, Michelle couldn't take another step. She flopped down by the road, heedless of the damp ground seeping through the seat of her shorts, and devoured several of her remaining chocolate bars. The air was miserably hot in the humid river valley, so only a single twenty ounce bottle of water remained in her pack.

Sleep beckoned, her head swimming with the need to rest, and angry, swollen mosquito bites dotted her body. Her hair hung in tangled snarls. She wondered if Fred would even know her if he found her now; she was tattered and muddy, withering away to a skeleton. The British couple she'd met a day ago would be startled if she talked to them now. She could just see them backing away, refusing to speak with her.

Capitalizing on the rush of energy from the candy, Michelle lifted herself back onto her feet and began to trudge again, staggering from side to side on the path, not sure whether she was awake or asleep. The road before her eventually began to tilt upward. With reluctance, she pulled her gaze up to see where she was headed.

A structure clung to an outcrop on a cliff several hundred feet up. The path ahead of her climbed out of the marsh, switch-backing its way up the steep face toward the low building of white brick and its terraced roof of red tile. The cliff faced west, catching the light of the setting sun.

Whether or not the shrine was Saakaar's temple, Michelle was nearly finished with her journey. The certainty sank all the way to the bone as she stood shivering under the hot sun. Some kind of mosquito-borne fever was catching a foothold, making her legs even wobblier than fatigue and starvation. Her body was beginning to shut down.

Michelle refused to give up without reaching the shrine. She moved one foot, setting it down, then the other, over and over again. The path grew rough, sharp-edged rocks rolling underfoot, making her stumble. She leaned against the cliff as she went, trying to keep an eye out for snakes or scorpions or jagged bits of rock that would shred her hands. A stone rolled under her foot and she fell to her knees, then struggled up again.

No other pilgrims walked the path with her. She felt grateful for solitude, not wanting the guilt or embarrassment of diverting others to help her.

Michelle stopped and pulled out her last half-melted Freddo chocolate bar. She carried nothing else but an unfamiliar small package wrapped in sealed foil. The contents felt squashy and heavy to her inquisitive fingertips. A gift from Robin?

Her scraped knees and palms bled, staining her pack. She still had about a cup of water, but the shrine was still at least a mile distant. At least she could see twined snakes on the pillars when she squinted up toward the temple, shading her eyes with her hands.

She might be dying, but her goal would not elude her.

Fred's anxiety hammered at the back of her mind. He had closed the gap a little; he felt closer now.

Michelle drank the water and dropped the bottle, panic driving her on. She had to stay ahead of him, to protect him in the one way she still could even though she no longer hoped to save herself. She must not stop.

Michelle heaved herself to her hands and knees. She began to crawl forward, ignoring her abraded knees. Her fingers clenched on the stones ahead of her, dragging her forward. The sun beat down on her shoulders, but its heat slid off without warming her shivering body. She bit her lip until she could taste blood, forcing herself to keep going.

The sun had sunk level with the temple by the time she dragged herself to the threshold, her hands and knees bloody, caked with dust. She raised her chin to blink at the stone pillar entwined with snake carvings. No other mark or sentinel welcomed her; there were no attendants, no live snakes, nothing.

Behind the pillar she located the shrine, a single low altar with a carved cobra statue sitting coiled in the center, its hood raised. Pilgrims who had come before Michelle had left necklaces of flower petals to wilt on the statues. Little dishes of curdled milk or spices or other offerings sat untouched on the altar. A single woven rattan basket, shaped roughly like an urn, squatted in a dusty corner.

Michelle crawled up the single step onto the smooth dirt floor of the temple, dragging herself the few remaining feet to the altar.

Of course her trip was foolish; the place was empty. Except her pilgrimage wasn't entirely purposeless, not if she'd succeeded in fleeing far enough from Fred to save him when she died.

She let her pack fall off her shoulders, startled by the sight of her bony arms as she reached inside. The foil container awaited her bloody, groping hands. Trembling, she pulled it out and reached to the altar for a tarnished brass knife. Cutting the top off, she poured the contents onto her lap: a zip-top plastic bag of some sort of pungent yellow-orange spice and a silvery vacuum packet labeled "Grade A milk."

Milk and spices for the god. Why not?

Michelle didn't know any ritual words or prayers. She wouldn't have had the energy to utter them if she did. She fumbled the packets open with shaking hands, pouring them out to mix on a platter in front of the statue.

She sat back, waiting, but nothing happened.

So this was it. This was how she would die. Michelle laughed once, a dry croak, too weak to move any further. The roaring in her ears overwhelmed her and her vision faded beneath a gray tide.

# Chapter Fifty-one

The afterlife appeared to be located in a lavish, ornate hall with stained glass windows reaching all the way to floor level. Gilt-embellished embossed diamond designs crawled over every inch of the ceiling and geometric patterns adorned the walls at tasteful intervals. Michelle could barely stir, but she managed to see she had been laid out on a flat, square cushion on the floor, her head pillowed on a round bolster covered in plush velvet.

"Thissss room isss modeled after a room in the Moti Mahal. The decorations ssssuit me."

Saakaar. Michelle tried to panic, but could not. Her capacity for fear had vanished along with her ability to move.

She cast her gaze about desperately until she spotted the naga. He lay coiled on another cushion, his head lifted and his hood spread. His forked tongue flickered out, scenting the air. "The cushionsssss are rather larger here, of courssssse." He did not move, but his skin flowed. After a mind-twisting moment, the man replaced the snake, his legs crossed in a perfect lotus. The cabochon of his jewel glowed on his brow, blood-red.

"This form is preferable for speaking." He stretched out his hand. Michelle lay motionless while he waited, still as a statue. A faint sound echoed through the still room like paper sliding in uneven surges across a marble floor. Then a snake crept into her vision, raising its head to butt under Saakaar's palm. It lifted, twining about Saakaar's wrist, creeping smoothly up his arm.

It was black with narrow yellow-white bands.

"This is a banded krait, the second most venomous snake in India. He is a familiar of mine, as are all serpents in this country." Saakaar smiled humorlessly as the snake settled across his shoulders. "I overheard your thoughts about killing spiders in the shower. Allowances can sometimes be made when a visitor tests a hostess's hospitality too far, of course. A humble spider should not enter a lady's bed or bath without permission."

He stared at her, his dark eyes almost mocking. "You were tested for the sincerity of your morals: whether you would be merciful and kind to those around you, within reason. Your test involved several situations. I prevented Robin from interfering in them."

His eyes glittered in a ray of golden light from the window. "You gave the most necessary means of prolonging your existence away to others: shelter, food, wealth. You gave them freely, without begrudging them, and expected no return. Three gifts you gave, and once you spared the life of my friend." He stroked the snake's head with one fingertip. Its little forked tongue flickered out, tasting the air.

"If you had failed your tests, you would not have survived to come here." Saakaar's matter-of-fact tones convinced Michelle. She licked her dry lips. Where was she? How long would she stay alive? How long had she been unconscious? How far away was Fred?

"Where are we?" She rasped, then swallowed.

"In my basket."

"Inside the shrine?"

"After a manner of speaking, perhaps."

She reached out to gauge her sense of Fred, but he felt distant, his presence muted, as though he had been put behind thick glass.

"Water?"

"Yes." He snapped his fingers to summon a servant. "You have contracted dengue, but it is still in early stages. The fever will not kill you before the incubus." A male child with a shaved head entered, carrying a glass. "You would be dead already from your link to the incubus if I had not brought you here. You are shielded from his predation in this place."

She had grown so frail she was easy for the child to lift. He held the glass for her as she drank two gulps, but he pulled back at Saakaar's gesture, though she was desperate for more.

"Too much too quickly and you will vomit on my floor." He made a low grunt of distaste. "You have come here to ask me to let you live."

Too sick and weak to move, lying helpless at the mercy of her enemy, Michelle acknowledged the inevitability of her death. "I meant to beg for mercy, yes. But now I only want to be sure I won't drag Fred down with me when I die." The child offered Michelle another swallow of water. She hesitated. "I've accepted my own death, not his."

Saakaar raised an elegant brow, doubt plain to read on his handsome face.

"You say I am cut off from him here, at least a little. I can still feel his presence, but it's faint. Will he be sucked down along with me if I die here?"

"He will not." Saakaar's voice remained flat, emotionless.

The child held the glass of water to her lips, tilting it so the cool liquid touched their cracked surface, but Michelle turned her face away. She closed her eyes, relieved. Fred would be safe so long as she died here. She would do nothing further to delay that.

"Drink, girl."

"Let the fever take me here. Count your revenge paid in full."

The krait hissed, its tongue flickering in and out, yellow eyes fixed on Michelle. Saakaar frowned, extending his arm, and the snake descended with as much silent grace as it had climbed, rippling onto the floor. Saakaar rose and the krait slithered onto his cushion, coiling itself meticulously in the warm impression left by his body. The naga stepped to Michelle's side, lowering himself to one knee, lifting her himself. An impatient tilt of his chin warned the boy to step back.

"I will not let an innocent waste away here in my palace. Think of the mess." He smiled, his eyes cold.

"Then kill me, or send me somewhere far from Fred to die." She glared at Saakaar with the last stubbornness in her. "You win, but you won't have us both."

He laughed at her. His mouth opened impossibly wide, fangs distending, the brilliant crimson of the jewel on his forehead catching the sunlight, blinding her with blood-red radiance. She closed her eyes and felt his fangs break her skin, pumping in venom. She lay in his arms for a long moment, floating in the scarlet darkness behind her eyelids, but no pain came.

~ * ~

"Michelle!" Fred's frantic cry roused her, and she realized Saakaar no longer held her. She lay against Fred's chest instead, the welcome heat of his skin warming her as he tucked her close, rocking her against him.

The sun wasn't where she remembered. No light poured in through the front of the temple. Had she spent more than one night in Saakaar's palace? Fred looked terrible, ragged and unkempt, covered with plastered-on dust as if he had swum the river instead of taking the bridge but never stopped to dry himself, racing down the dusty trail after her. She tried to speak, but couldn't croak out any words. He lowered her carefully to the ground, then fumbled in his pack for water and food.

She drank, then lay back to let a square of chocolate melt on her tongue. Her neck began to throb, two pinpoints of intense pain where she had been bitten. Her scraped knees and palms ached, but her mind felt oddly calm, quite clear.

"I'm calling for a rescue helicopter." Fred picked Michelle up gently to cradle her against his chest, wrapping one arm around her. He was finally forced to go through Karl as an intermediary before he could locate the proper authorities, and it took a while to communicate his needs to them, but at last he put his dying phone away.

Michelle blinked wearily at the altar; something wasn't right. The difference had been niggling at her mind vaguely for the last half-hour. Now she finally realized what it was.

"My offering," she husked suddenly. "It's gone."

"What?" Fred squinted at the altar, confused. "Your offering?"

"Milk and spice. I put them on the platter, but now it's empty."

"Maybe the god accepted your offering," Fred said, his voice trailing away into doubt. "But Saakaar wouldn't...would he?"

Michelle let her head rest against his chest.

"Fuck, you've been bitten in the throat!" Fred's anxiety went from overwhelming to white-hot in the flicker of an eye, but he could do nothing except hold her as they waited for the helicopter. Michelle lay still, glad of Fred's solid, comforting presence as the familiar whir of rotors became audible. Finally, a rickety old chopper appeared, navigating with care between the treacherous cliffs enclosing the river. Fred pillowed her head gently on her pack, then went out to signal the pilot, waving his shirt frantically in the air.

# Chapter Fifty-two

"Mr. Fred-er-ik, patient Michelle Jones' husband, yes? Diagnosis is contusions to knees and hands, insect bites, snake bite, exposure, starvation, dehydration. Gods have spared her. No malaria. No dengue. No venom in bite. Able to leave hospital in three? four? days. We feed her, give fluids, treat wounds for infection." A nervous doctor consulted his clipboard as he recited Michele's symptoms. "She not talk. Damage to throat. Not talk," he warned. He could do nothing but repeat his halting recitation when Fred tried to question him further.

Michelle reached her hand out to Fred, lacing her fingers into his. He looked haggard and pale. He hadn't been able to feed, and she was willing to wager he hadn't slept since Ireland, either.

"As soon as they let you speak, you're going to have to tell me everything." Fred returned to his seat at her bedside, stroking a wisp of hair off her forehead.

"No need to wait so long." Robin appeared, sitting cross-legged in mid-air, wearing her harem outfit. She looked quite smug, so much so Michelle rolled her eyes with exasperation.

"Well?" Fred demanded impatiently. "I'm sure you're going to say this is all your doing."

"No. Your human did a little of the work, I suppose." Robin grinned cheerfully. "The boring parts."

"What happened?"

"I made the customs officers detain you while they checked your suitcase and documents. I siphoned the gas out of your rental car. I was behind the landslide that closed your road. Oh, and I caused that bridge to give way too."

"I mean what happened to Michelle?" Fred's face turned red and

246

his knuckles went white, but Michelle thought he showed remarkable restraint under the circumstances.

"Oh. Saakaar isn't evil by nature. It goes against his grain to hurt those who haven't wronged him, or who won't do harm to the undeserving. Plus, he's a sucker for a pretty girl in distress. I knew he wouldn't let an innocent woman die in his shrine. All I had to do was get her there without you hanging around to piss him off."

"So, this is only a reprieve until we're away from him?"

Robin put her feet down on the floor. She walked over to Michelle, tipping her chin to one side to study the bandage covering the half-healed bite. "She had the dengue. Between the pilgrimage and your own tender mercies, she was all but a skeleton. He knew only a single spell that could keep her from dying." She traced her fingertips over the rectangle of taped gauze covering the bite mark on Michelle's throat.

"He used his jewel...?" Fred's voice trailed away in disbelief.

Robin grinned again. "Guessed it in one, incubus. You may have settled your debt with Saakaar—possibly—but he still doesn't like you. Oh, that reminds me. You might be interested to learn Superlatives decided not to pursue their case against the two of you. A reliable authority informed them they would be countersued twice over: once for selling stolen goods and once for trafficking in prostitution." She preened, winking.

Fred's happy whoop echoed down the hall, flustering the duty nurses, who came bustling in to check on their patient. They gabbled irritably at him for making too much noise.

Robin sat through the commotion, her grin never fading, patiently waiting until the stir settled. "Now, both of you owe me the mother of all favors. I'll be calling in my marker one day, you can rest assured." She snapped her fingers, vanishing like the Cheshire Cat, her satisfied smirk lingering for several moments after the rest of her faded away.

Fred reached for Michelle's hand, looking shell-shocked. "I don't know whether to laugh or cry."

To hell with doctor's orders. "Love you," Michelle whispered. Fred smiled, his eyes shining too brightly. He climbed into her bed, lying down very carefully to avoid the tubes and bandages. He slid his arms around her.

"Rest," he advised her. "I'll watch over you while you sleep."

# Chapter Fifty-three

London seemed much larger than before, full of life, color, and bustle Michelle didn't remember from her first visit. "I was pretty far gone by the time we arrived here, wasn't I?" She craned her neck, trying to look through every one of the cab windows at once. "All I remember is the curry."

"You ate enough of that for three grown men." Fred goosed her lightly as she climbed out, making her giggle.

"Is this the place?" She eyed the garish neon signs doubtfully.

"None other." Fred led her up the stoop. They buzzed in, entering the hall where the medley of sharp scents reawakened Michelle's memories.

"Welcome to the parlor of Madame Defarge—oh, it's you, incubus. Is your girl still...? There she is." The medium peeled off her elaborate headdress. She tossed the thing away, squinting at Michelle with interest. "Let's go down to the cellar. I've never seen anything like this before. What happened?"

"We were hoping you could tell us."

"Isn't that always the way," she grumbled a little, unlocking the door to the stairs.

"I went to talk with the naga. I was dying. Then he bit me." Michelle touched her throat, where the bite wounds still ached a little.

The medium's eyebrows lifted. "And you're still walking around, which rules out a number of possibilities."

"Such as?" Fred put a protective hand on Michelle's waist.

"He didn't use poison, for one." She ushered them into the antechamber, stripping off without prelude. "You too, honey." Her gesture included them both.

"Me?" Fred objected mildly. "We aren't here to find out about me."

"I'm not going to delve you yet, incubus, but you should still shed all the vibes bound up in those clothes. They could interfere with her reading." Her eyes twinkled with mischief.

It was colder than Michelle remembered. She lay down in the center of the magic circle while the medium rummaged through a drawer to select a crystal from a padded jewelry box.

"Stay back, incubus. Try to quiet your mind." The medium shot him a reproachful look. "You're thinking so loudly I can't hear myself."

"His name is Fred," Michelle thought her a bit rude. "And mine's Michelle."

"My business is easier if my clients don't turn into friends, honey. Sorry. Now button your lip." She waved the crystal over Michelle, humming tunelessly as she stared into space. Michelle tried to lie still.

"Interesting." Madame Defarge clucked her tongue, making indistinct murmurs as she moved the crystal over every part of Michelle's body. "How about that?"

Michelle traded exasperated glances with Fred. "How about what?" she said at last, unable to stand the suspense any longer.

"You said you were dying before. From the incubus draining you?"

"That, plus Saakaar said I had dengue. He claimed it would kill me if Fred didn't."

"Did the doctors give you medicine for fever?"

"No. The Indian doctors said I wasn't sick. I was just severely malnourished and dehydrated."

"Hmmm. Let me get this straight. You had dengue fever, dehydration, and malnutrition. Then the naga bit you. The doctors said no dengue, but you remained weak even after you were bitten?"

"Yes. The doctors rehydrated me with an IV, then put me back on solid food."

"Looks like you've started gaining back some weight." The medium frowned a little. "That's interesting." She set her crystal aside, fetching a blanket to wrap around Michelle. "Have you and the incubus been intimate since then? Waking, not sleeping."

"We've been afraid to try anything." Michelle looked a little sheepishly at Fred. "He didn't want to injure me."

"I think you should try it," the medium said. "I want to see the energy channels."

Michelle raised a brow at her. "You mean now? Here?"

"I can hardly watch your energy exchange if you run off to a hotel somewhere, now can I?"

"She has a point, Michelle." Fred, once so bashful he'd blushed at the mere mention of orgasm, drew a deep breath and composed himself with an effort. "I'd feel better about making love if we can be sure it's safe for you. She can tell us." He rose, scooting across the cold tile to sit at her side. "Can we at least lie on the blanket? This floor is icy."

"I can tell. Your John Thomas has drawn up halfway to your bellybutton." Madame Defarge tittered a little as Fred went scarlet to the ears, shooting her an exasperated glare. "Yes, you can lie on the blanket. I promise I won't kick back to eat popcorn.."

Michelle bit her lip, reluctant, then chuckled at herself, feeling rueful. "After everything we've been through, I'm not going to stop now."

Fred stroked a wisp of hair out of her face, his fingers a little clumsy, before leaning in to kiss her. "We'll focus on each other. Everything will be all right." He helped her to her feet, then spread the blanket for them to lie on. He knelt back down again, tugging at her. "Lie down."

Michelle obeyed. He settled awkwardly between her thighs, then reached to pull the blanket to drape over his back.

"Luckily I can still see most of the energy flows through that thing," the medium grumbled. "You'll both need to come, though."

"Understood." Fred firmed his jaw, his cheeks still red. "I must ask you to be silent from now on, unless it's absolutely necessary to speak." Fred reached to stroke Michelle's cheek, resolute, smiling to reassure them both.

Michelle smiled back, but her skin crawled from the sense of someone watching. She felt terribly shy as she tried to lose herself in the pure crystal blue of Fred's steady eyes. They reeled her in, inviting, so she concentrated on them, willing her nerves to subside. His warm, pliant skin welcomed her hands and she carded her fingertips lightly through his chest hair, trying to get in the mood.

Fred made a soft little hum, responsive. "Remember back at the convention when we played the daring game with Elise and Jenny?"

"We've come full circle," Michelle realized.

"Yes," he murmured. He bent his head to nuzzle at her throat, working his way down. His lips trailed along her breast, then settled over her nipple.

Michelle expected lightning-bolt devastation, but this time pleasure came gently, slow warmth building at the site of his touch. His tongue swept around her nipple, bringing it to a stiff peak. She whimpered, the floor hard underneath her through the blanket. The medium gave a stifled cough, which made her tense in spite of Fred's sweet kiss.

"I think we'd both benefit from a drink or two to loosen our inhibitions," she whispered.

Fred chuckled against her skin, pressing her nipple between his lips in a teasing love-bite. "You don't say." He tried again, suckling harder. She could feel him reaching out to her through their connection, coaxing her to respond.

Michelle reached back as she ran her palms over the sinewy muscle of his lean shoulders, closing her eyes to focus on the soft press of his mouth, echoed by the warm presence of his mind. His teeth grazed her nipple. She inhaled, low and quick.

Fred was hers. No matter how much anyone else wanted him, he belonged to her. So Madame Defarge liked looking at him? Wanted him, even? Then let her eat her heart out with envy. This was as close as she'd ever be to Fred, but after tonight, Michelle could have all of him she wanted, as much as she could ever desire.

She let her palms wander, savoring the slow burn of pleasure beginning to glow through her. His muscles rippled over his ribs, flexing as he supported himself over her so he wouldn't trap her uncomfortably against the floor.

He lavished patient attention on her nipples. His breath on her wet skin sent a tingle of chill thrilling through her, making her arch with a sigh. He nestled against her, his cock swelling slowly against her, responding to her blossoming pleasure. Michelle dragged her short nails up his back, making him purr a low growl against her breast. He hitched a little higher, dragging his cock against her, then reached to nip at her lower lip, sucking it into his mouth. His chest hair tickled at her sensitive nipples. She arched, pressing up against his body, catching him off-guard as he shifted.

Fred nearly toppled off her, but he caught himself, huffing a soft laugh at her enthusiasm. He eased more of his weight onto her, pressing her thighs apart, his cock nudging at her center with new insistence. She heard a low sound from the edge of the room, but she was able to ignore the interruption as Fred slowly dragged the tip of his cock back and forth over her clit, barely touching her. He lifted himself on his palms, his arms quivering with the strain of his careful motion.

Michelle shivered, a gasp escaping her throat; she lifted her hips, shifting to trap him on the downstroke, guiding him into her. He smiled, a faint sheen of sweat starting to gleam on his skin as he slid deep, nestling their bodies together.

"Stop holding back," the medium murmured. Fred flicked an aggravated glare at her, then returned his gaze to Michelle, his eyes softening.

"I can take more," Michelle murmured against his lips, issuing both an invitation and a challenge. She felt strong, energized, eager for him. She twined her arms behind his neck, dragging him down for a deeper kiss.

This time she felt the two twenty volt crackle as he reached for the energy channel between them. She reached to stroke her clit, making him gasp. His mouth fell open and his pink tongue flickered out to touch his lip, making it gleam. Michelle moaned; she glowed white hot with the sense of him inside her, his arms surrounding her, his lips kissing her, his tongue plunging into her mouth, echoing the powerful thrust of his hips. Every touch of his skin ignited pure, fiery bliss. She writhed, not sure whether she meant to escape or cling to him, desperate for more.

He kept moving, nipping at her throat, as he pulled her hand away, slowing her down. Michelle whimpered, pleading, but he persisted, long, slow strokes, teasing without fulfilling. The pleasure swelled in her until she had to come or explode.

Fred didn't stop, gathering and building the pleasure until she lost herself, her vision whiting out, her nails digging into his skin. She could hear shrieks, possibly hers, but all she could comprehend was an overwhelming tsunami of sensation, his cock lighting her up from within until his thumb finally trailed over her clit, releasing her. She went supernova, dragging him along with her, clinging to him as an anchor while the unbearable bliss flared, bursting outward, a billion sparkling fragments of infinity sifting down through the void to fill the entire universe with love.

She blinked, not sure who or where she was, a wild tumble of limbs, sweat, and joy, tangled with Fred, who lay gasping against her throat, his body trembling.

"Holy shit." She should know the voice; really she should, but the concept of speech seemed foreign, as did the tangle of ductwork overhead.

A face appeared between Michelle and the ceiling, long dark ringlets of hair hanging down. "I hope you know I'll never be able to purify this room." The medium's voice sounded peevish, a little shaky. Michelle ignored her.

A toe nudged her thigh. Fred stirred atop her, lifting his head to gaze groggily down into her face. His hair hung down over his forehead, so she reached to brush it out of his eyes. He leaned into her palm, then sank down against her again.

"How do you feel?" The voice persisted, aggravating Michelle like the dancing, elusive whine of a mosquito buzzing in her ear. "Tired? Hungry?"

"Good" was completely inadequate, but it rose to her tongue anyway. Fred echoed the word, his lips velvety-hot against her skin.

"Then you guys have to get up at some point. You've been lying there in a trance for nearly half an hour since the fireworks stopped. I have some clients scheduled for a reading at nine o'clock. *Damn*, but I need to shower first." This time her toe nudged Fred.

Fred rolled off Michelle, scrubbing his palm over his face. "Fuck, these tiles are like ice." He sat up, tugging the edge of the blanket across his lap. His voice sharpened with worry when Michelle didn't move. "Are you okay?"

She considered. "Never better." She felt blissed out, content, satisfied with the entire world. Aside from feeling so peaceful she never wanted to move again, she thought she could take on a grizzly bear—and win.

"What did the energy exchange look like?" Fred prompted Madame Defarge impatiently. "Is she going to be all right?"

"I can't exactly compare it to last time because I didn't see you do this before." She helped him lever himself to his feet, then gave Michelle a hand. "But whatever you did, the flows didn't look like anything I've ever seen. Usually a supernatural who feeds on a human diminishes the human's limited store of energy. That causes a strain on the human's entire physiological and psychological system. When you two plugged in, she started pulling from outside herself somewhere."

"Outside? Where?"

"I don't know. The cosmic chi? The heart of the sun? Both of you lit up like a fusion reactor. I don't know how the hell all that power didn't burn you both right up, but you were grounded somehow, so it dispersed into the environment instead. Look at this place." She waved her hand at the room. "It's crawling with sex; the psychic residue of what you did probably made every clairvoyant in London pounce on the nearest available partner. I'll never be able to clean all the lust out of here. I'm going to have to find a new office and set up my wards from scratch. You burned out the dispersing tiles in my magic circle; they popped like overloaded transformers."

Sure enough, half a dozen tiles were missing from the design. Black-burned fragments lay scattered across the rest. "If I hadn't been able to release all the sexual energy I absorbed the old-fashioned way, you'd have burned half my tattoos right off my skin." She shook her finger under his nose to illustrate her method. He recoiled from the digit as if it were poisonous, his face a study in dismay.

Michelle felt the laughter welling up, shaking her chest, unstoppable. Fred glanced at her with concern, but then he started to chuckle too, the two of them stumbling into the changing area. They half-fell onto the bench with her leaning against his side, giggling helplessly like a little girl.

"We'll compensate you for your trouble," Fred finally promised when he had hold of himself again. Madame Defarge stood irritably in the door, glaring at them with her arms crossed over her chest, one toe tapping an impatient cadence on the floor. "Give us a verdict. Is our lovemaking safe for Michelle?"

"I don't think your lovemaking is safe for anybody within a mile's radius *except* your partner. You should open a fertility clinic for psychics; if you stay together, any clairvoyant neighbors will conceive more children than they can count." She raked her fingers through her hair. "The proles probably will, too." She relented, losing her scolding tone. "Having sex seems to be safe for both of you, yes. Her system has changed. She won't succumb to stress the way she did before."

"Am I immortal?" Michelle asked, hesitant. Fred's arm tightened around her, his expression anxious.

"I can't say. It's certainly a possibility. The naga bit you, after all, but you aren't dead. You two would be a psychic researcher's wet dream in more ways than one."

Michelle felt a shiver go down her back as a memory flashed across her mind: Fred explaining mortals never had to dread centuries of solitude, reassuring her how she need never live as a vague figure of terror to humans, afraid to reveal herself enough to fall in love with someone...but she could console herself knowing Fred would live for many years yet, many centuries. She could live them with him, now.

She forced her worries out of her mind, reaching for his hand. "Let's dress, Fred." She squeezed his fingers tightly. "I want to go home."

# Epilogue

Michelle tore a strip of duct tape off the roll, sealing the top of a small cardboard carton. She grabbed a black permanent marker to label the box with Kevin's address. Finally, she sat back, smiling with relief at completing a long-overdue job.

"Ready to be rid of those movies?" Fred handed her a glass of iced tea with lemon. He plopped down on the sofa by her side, sliding his arm around her shoulders as she leaned back.

"Yeah. If Kevin doesn't get his DVDs back pretty soon, he's going to swear out a police warrant." She stuck out her tongue at the box in disgust. "He has an unhealthy fixation with these movies."

"I hope he and his action heroes will be very happy together." Fred grinned at her, watching her take a deep swallow of the cold sweet tea.

"Not as happy as me." Michelle set the glass onto a coaster to spare Fred's spotless aluminum coffee table, looking around the living room with satisfaction. She still had dozens of full boxes to deal with, but so far the move was a success.

"I found my stockpot," Fred reported. "Now we can make soup. Someday soon we'll find a skillet, then we can stop using the grill all the time."

"I like cooking out, though." Michelle snuggled under his arm. "And I love our house, Fred." She felt a little shy about saying the words. The one-story brick siding home nestled in an established subdivision with plenty of tall, leafy trees, alongside several dozen nice older-model houses faced with brick or stone, not the new particle-board and aluminum siding abominations overtaking so much of Atlanta.

"I'm glad you do." He kissed her hair softly. "Anyway, we won't eat hamburgers tonight. I splurged on some ribeye steaks. It's our one month anniversary, you know." Fred nipped softly at Michelle's ear, amorous. "I bought an apple pie, too. You still need to gain some of your weight back. You've been working too hard moving us in."

"I wanted to finish the move so mom can come visit. She thinks you're some kind of subversive new-age lunatic, maybe a homicidal maniac just waiting to happen. I still haven't even mentioned you're a super." Michelle grinned, sheepish. "She's still upset about my sudden resignation and our unexplained trip to Europe. She can't decide whether it's worse we bought joint property without getting married, or that we did it before either of us found a new job." She nuzzled into a deeper kiss, trying to ease the sting of her mother's suspicions.

"About that. I've been thinking." Fred pulled back after a few sweet moments to gaze into her eyes, his expression a little anxious. "Karl wants me to digitize his library. Lots of other supers need access to the kind of information he keeps. Others need more permanent records made of what's in their heads.

"I was thinking we could open our own consulting business. We'd start small, helping Karl, but over time we could build up a library of information and clients, then start selling access to our knowledge base. I can do both coding and hardware assembly. We can hire any other skills we need. Then the supernatural community can turn to us to learn things they need to know, find resources they can use for legal or emotional help, anything really. My community needs a solid core, a place to go when we need help."

"Our community." Michelle kissed him again. "Will Karl pay?"

"Of course he will. There's a place for your skills on the ground floor, too. Hundreds of supers have valuable information stored inside their heads. You know how to make their information easily understandable, Michelle. As part of the fee for our services, we'll interview our clients, then transcribe your notes. Afterward we can sell access to the information.

"We can offer an incredible service to all the species by keeping records of what supers know." His face clouded a little. "I think we should approach the sibyl first. She's so frail. If she dies without sharing her knowledge, we stand to lose an incredible amount of crucial knowledge."

"Still wanting to be more responsible than your dad?" Michelle stroked back an unruly wisp of his short hair, teasing him a little.

"I'd like him to contribute too, if he'll agree. Anyone who has data about supernatural customs, culture, or physiology would be welcome. We can collect it, then index and cross-reference it, make it searchable. What's most important is for us to start putting together definitive information so others won't have to go through what we endured." Fred smiled at her, still with a little sadness in his gaze. "I came so close to losing you."

Michelle blushed, ducking her head. "I think your plans might turn into a job much bigger than two people can handle."

"We can expand the business as demand grows." Fred lit up with enthusiasm, his excitement kindling. "Do you think you'd like to try, Michelle?"

"Of course." She stood up, pulling him to his feet. "Karl will provide a start, if he'll give us free access to his information so we can form the foundation of our database."

"I think he'd like that," Fred beamed, swinging her into the circle of his arms. "He may even want to partner us in the venture."

"There'll be some resistance. You said yourself, supers are leery of letting themselves be known for what they are."

"They won't have to leave identity traces if they don't want to." Fred's couldn't sit still, rising to wander around the room, full of enthusiasm. "As we grow, they'll learn to trust us. We'll build a good reputation, like the safe-house where we stayed in the Village."

Michelle let him grab her hands and dance her around the living room, laughing breathlessly, clinging to his arms.

"It's a wonderful idea, Fred. I love it. Let's finish unpacking and setting up our house first, though." She squeezed his hands. "I'm starved."

Fred stole another kiss before he let her go. He went to ready the steaks and light the grill while she put the potatoes in the microwave, then shucked corn to toss in the pot when it boiled.

Michelle glanced through the patio window as Fred readied the grill, smiling to herself. He was still so careful with her, so sweet....

They still weren't inclined to test her stamina too harshly; the consequences of failure could be terrible. However, her nights with Fred didn't exhaust her anymore. Yet they remained careful, proceeding with caution. No matter how healthy she felt, Fred still feared he might harm her inadvertently.

She couldn't help wondering whether her new life was too good to be true. In spite of the medium's advice, they weren't precisely sure how far Saakaar's gift extended. More worrisome, Fred doubted Saakaar counted his debt paid in full. He might be right, but if the naga meant to continue his quest for revenge, he'd gone back to biding his time.

She was grateful. Saakaar had given her mercy and the chance for a future with Fred. That was what mattered most. They had a chance now to test their limits with care, caution, infinite sweetness, and more pleasure than Michelle could ever have imagined.

She found the steaks off the bottom shelf, then leaned against the doorframe, smiling, ready to hand Fred the plate.

She trailed her fingertips across the two tiny round scars on her throat while she waited for Fred to finish adjusting the gas. Deep in her heart, Michelle believed Saakaar would choose a different tactic if he tried to hurt Fred again. If that happened, they'd just have to face his anger as best they could.

She passed over the plate, listening to the meat sizzle on the hot grill. Humming, she went in to set the table.

Fred hadn't gone back to the bedroom this afternoon, but Michelle had prepared a surprise in there, too, between unpacking cartons and filling garbage bags. She grinned a little to herself, hoping Fred would find it just intriguing as she did.

She put shucked ears of corn in the boiling pot, then started the microwave. The oven dinged as Fred came in with the steaks. She juggled the hot potatoes onto a plate, serving them next to the steaming sweet corn. Grabbing a stick of butter, she sat down across from him. Eating together in their new house, sharing cozy domestic comfort with Fred— it was all still a novelty. Michelle hoped they could look forward to many more meals shared in peaceful contentment.

Michelle polished off her steak and vegetables in record time, then enjoyed a generous wedge of apple pie with cheddar cheese. The hour was still early when she finished putting the dishes into the dishwasher, but....

"What do you have planned for this evening?"

"I wanted to see if I could find the rest of my cooking gear. Maybe they packed a skillet in with the bedding, or possibly the bathroom linens. You?"

"I need to write to mom. Then I'll turn in." She gave Fred a flirtatious glance from under her lashes. "Don't wait too long before you come to bed," she purred as she hit the button to start the dishwasher. "If you do, the second course will get cold." She lifted her hair off her shoulders, stretched luxuriously, then padded off toward the bedroom, aware of his eyes following the sway of her hips.

She closed the bedroom door softly, trying to estimate how much time she had. Fred could be stubborn; he'd probably crack open at least a few boxes before he gave in to temptation. He'd want to give her enough time to write to her mom. That had been a fib. Nothing could be farther from Michelle's mind.

Hastily she opened the shopping bag she'd tucked next to the bed, blushing a little at what lay inside.

She stripped hastily, buckling on the array of leather straps with some difficulty. This kind of fetish gear wasn't exactly user-friendly. The leather felt cold, smooth against her skin, bringing her senses alive to the caress of the air as she stepped across the carpet to turn out the light. She hoped tonight would be the kind of treat for Fred his lovemaking always was for her.

She listened for him with half an ear, hurrying to arrange herself in the center of the bed. One last piece—the *coup de grace*. She clipped a velvet-padded handcuff around one wrist, looping the bit of chain behind a rung in the headboard. Prudently, she left her other wrist free, ready to shut the latch, waiting until she heard his footsteps in the hall before she snapped the latch shut. Her heart leaped, racing when his soft tread approached. She closed her fingers around the cuff, ready to lock it the instant his face appeared in the door, and turned her head aside, so her hair fell over her face.

Fred never heard the soft click of the cuff when he opened the door. He blinked into the darkness, pushing the door open so far the light from the hall illuminated the bed, a soft shaft of illumination falling across her body. She did her best to look vulnerable and helpless, laid out waiting for his pleasure.

She heard his breath whistle between his teeth in surprise. Silence followed. She lay very still, waiting; he could move silently when he wanted.

She sensed him an instant before he touched her: a soft breath of air, a prickle of anticipation on her skin. She lifted herself into his touch as his palm curved over her belly, making a tiny, responsive moan.

He paused, his hand warm, then stepped aside to the bureau, where she'd laid out an array of toys for his convenience. Her heart hammered with eager anticipation as he surveyed them; she could hear a rustle and soft thump as he considered his selection.

He turned back to her, one hand hidden at his side. His palm covered her face, keeping her in place with gentle, firm pressure. Her nipples tightened in response to him; a soft tickle began against her calf as he touched her with a feathered wand, teasing her.

Michelle moaned at the maddening sensation as the feathers tickled across her skin, then slowly worked their way up to her hip. They teased her where she was most sensitive, inside the hipbone, making her whimper.

He took pity on her after a moment, moving the feathers up, softly dragging them against the curve of her breast, then her nipple, then her collarbone. He tickled them slowly up the insides of her arms, which lay exposed, drawn up over her head, her wrists now firmly manacled behind the bedstead. Michelle breathed quickly; he was in a mood to draw out every sensation.

"I love how sensitive you are," he murmured. She knew he could feel every pleasure he brought her, soaking them up and savoring them as much as she did. He followed the trail of the feathers with a slow fingertip, circling her nipple, which tightened so much she ached.

He lifted his hand off her face, so she lifted her chin to see his expression. He smiled at her, his eyes dark with lust, turning away from her into shadow as he returned to the bureau.

This time he came back with a pair of scarves, flipping one of them into a neat roll with a twist of his wrists. He pressed the cloth to her lips and she opened her mouth to accept it. He lifted her head to tie the gag behind her neck, then eased her down again. The next scarf covered her eyes. Michelle shifted a little, feeling vulnerable. He made a low sound, a murmur of reassurance, his fingertips petting her cheek.

She didn't know what would touch her next, or where. He might use the cool loop of a leather flogger, the hot velvet of his fingertips, or the maddening tickle of the feathers. He kept her in suspense, varying the sensations until she grew accustomed to them, then startling her— something cool and unyielding nudged at her, opening her to press inside.

She made a soft, startled cry as the dildo slid inside her to the hilt, swiftly warming. She squirmed and moaned, liking the fullness. The toy was solid, pleasantly thick. He kept teasing her, stroking it in and out, then let the tip trail over her clit before plunging it back inside her again. He left her briefly, and when he returned, he carried a clip, flicking it lightly against her nipple. He applied the clip, fastening loosely, just a tease of pressure. She licked her lips; he could tighten it until she was left shrieking, panting for mercy.

He gave her another few strokes with the dildo, then withdrew the toy, replacing it slowly with a ribbed one. Michelle gasped aloud as the new object went in, shivering. He reached to lift her, positioning her on her knees.

"That's good," he purred, his hands sliding across her back. He pressed her face down, setting her cheek against the pillow. The position put a little strain on her shoulders, making her conscious of her captivity. He stroked the dildo in and out of her again, very slow, every rib stretching her open as the thick length penetrated her. The dildo began to move, its heavy length vibrating deep inside Michelle, sending a ripple of pleasure surging up her spine.

Without warning, the strap of a broad leather flogger cracked across her ass. Michelle jolted, yelping with surprise. Fred's hand on her back steadied her. The strap landed again on the opposite cheek, leaving matching stripes of heat printed across her skin. Michelle moaned, pushing her ass up into the air for him. He reached down to her nipple, tweaking the clamp a little tighter. He paused to regard her, then tightened the clip again, making her quiver and moan around the gag.

Her fists clenched in the restraints as she anticipated the next strike. He didn't disappoint her; the strap fell lightly along the crease of her ass and thigh. Michelle keened, digging her nails into her palms. The vibration of the dildo hummed sensation through her, maddeningly close to her clit, but not quite close enough. The slow, measured blows of the flogger woke a soft glow in her ass. Fred continued to build the sensation patiently, pausing from time to time to stroke his palm over her reddened skin to feel the heat he'd awakened there.

He tweaked the nipple clamp again, to the point where tightness neared discomfort. Every sensation fed into the others, pain mingling seamlessly with pleasure. She was whimpering and squirming constantly now, craving his touch on her clit.

"Greedy girl," he scolded softly, his voice warm. "Patience."

Michelle drew a deep, shuddering breath, hearing the thump as he tossed the flogger aside. He moved to the bureau. When he came back, he put a second clamp on her other nipple, tightening it down immediately to match the other. Michelle quivered, moaning. The air chilled her warm bottom. He brushed against her occasionally, the flutter of his open shirt tickling the sensitive stripes from the flogger, tormenting her.

Fred leaned in to brush a kiss against her bottom, testing the heat there. His thumb settled against her clit and swept around in a slow circle, making Michelle keen for more. He withdrew, swatting her lightly, his chuckle rich with lust. "Not yet." Fred moved her knees, pushing them wide apart, then turned up the vibration so pleasure fluttered insistently along her spine. She trembled, feeling the strain on her wrists, clutching at the head of the bed with both fists.

Michelle waited, anguished with impatience and need, as he paused. She could heard a silky sound of skin on skin as he handled himself, taking the scene at his own pace. She licked her lips, wishing she could see him, but the blindfold kept her in darkness. Her ears strained to make sense of the soft sounds.

"Gorgeous." His voice rumbled deep in his chest, husky with lust. She heard a strange artificial sound—the snap of a pop-up lid?—before something cool touched her ass. He carefully pressed one lubricated finger into her ass, making her squeak a little with surprise.

He did not hesitate, thoroughly lubricating her. Michelle quivered, sensing his pleasure in watching her adapt to the unaccustomed penetration.

Michelle blushed. It felt odd at first, strangely full, but he moved very slowly, letting her grow accustomed to his touch. He added more gel, teasing the sensitive flesh with light touches, making her moan with growing arousal.

Fred's enjoyment was contagious; Michelle began to push back on his finger, asking for more. He added another finger, pushing a little deeper. Michelle made a low, involuntary noise. He purred in response, kindling a flare of wanting in her belly.

"That's it," he breathed as she squirmed, needing more sensation. "Trust me." She basked in his pleasure, trying to obey, letting the slow burn build, savoring the anticipation he created.

Finally, she could take his fingers easily, rocking back on them with urgency as she moaned deep in her throat. Patient, Fred reached to remove the dildo, slow inch by slow inch. She quivered, anticipating his cock, but then the dildo returned, cool with gel, pressing at her ass. He pushed it into her in place of his fingers, gradual and gentle.

Michelle tensed a little at the unaccustomed size, but he was careful, murmuring soothing words, stroking her flank. The dildo went in bit by bit, not hurting her. She panted for breath, air whistling through her nose. The buzzing felt odd; good, but frustrating, too far from where she needed it most.

"Patience," Fred breathed again, a chuckle in his voice as he rocked the dildo slowly inward. Soon he was fucking her the same way he'd used his fingers to open her. The rhythmic press and retreat of the solid thickness excited her, the ribbed surface stimulating her ass as it moved in and out. Before long she was rocking into his thrusts, taking more, enjoying the unaccustomed fullness. She liked being able to take whatever he gave her; it made her feel strong and capable despite her bonds.

She was starting to glow with pleasure now; she could feel how much he liked watching her take it, liked sensing both her trust and her helplessness as she let him do whatever he pleased with her. He was so turned on his arousal made her feel even hotter. She shifted her hips so he could watch her squirming as the dildo pushed in and out of her body.

"There," he said at last, sliding it deep. "Good job, sweetheart."

His cock teased at her next. He pushed it into her, filling her with a quick, firm thrust. Michelle moaned, deep and throaty, her body stretched full. What had been startling at first had turned maddeningly hot. The buzz of the dildo combined with the pressure of Fred's thick shaft to make her feel as if she had taken a cock twice Fred's size. Sweat misted on her skin, and she pushed back against his cock, begging to be fucked.

He chuckled, rich and deep, then obliged her with firm, hard thrusts. He stayed away from her clit, tweaking the nipple clamps instead. She whimpered, sensation starting to overload her nerves.

"Give in, yes. Let yourself feel," he murmured, speeding the pace. She swayed, unable to brace herself, her nipples rubbing against the coverlet, emphasizing the pinch of the clamps. The gag kept her from pleading, but she couldn't throttle the broken whimpers filling her throat. She could feel his pleasure keenly now his cock was inside her; the extra layer of sensation made her quiver, her legs threatening to collapse.

"A little longer," Fred tightened the clamps again, his fingers sure and swift. The red-hot pain lit up her nerves, overloading her brain and transmuting to pleasure in its intensity. Michelle heard herself shrieking around the gag. Then Fred's fingers finally touched her clit, swift slick pressure. She went off like a rocket, her orgasm triggering his. He pumped his hips twice more before seizing her waist to hold them still, spasming inside her with a shout.

She collapsed, whimpering, needing the clamps off. He recovered quickly, releasing them, then withdrew both himself and the dildo from her body.

Michelle lay shivering, coming down from the mix of orgasm and endorphins. He stroked her belly softly, then went for a cloth to clean her up a bit. When he was done, he turned her onto her side and wrapped himself around her back, not releasing her from her bonds or removing her blindfold.

"My pretty Michelle," he crooned, licking a droplet of sweat from her shoulder blade. He was still hard, his cock prodding her ass. He lifted her thigh, then slid back inside her, moving his hips very slowly. He maintained his rhythm as she moaned low in her throat, squirming against him.

Michelle felt no fear or weariness, floating on a pillow of bliss. He wasn't finished with her yet. Time to push the limits.

Fred waited for a few minutes, then set his fingertips against her clit, moving them as slowly as he pumped his cock inside her, lighting her on fire with subtle strokes.

She came suddenly, a sweet rush of melting pleasure. He didn't stop stroking her, so she went off again at once, harder, clutching him tight. He growled softly against her shoulder as he rolled his hips, measured and strong, never pausing. She came yet again, the squeeze of her body around him triggering his orgasm. The feedback of his pleasure washed into her. Then she lost herself, thrashing and wailing, as the crest swelled beyond bearing, whiting out her vision, sending her half-mad.

When sense returned to Michelle she was free. Fred cradled her against his chest, lipping soft kisses against her eyelids. Both blindfold and gag had gone. Her throat felt raw from her cries. He gazed at her, his eyes worried.

"All right?"

Michelle was beyond speech; she wrapped her arms around him, holding him as tightly as she could, her face wet. "F-fuck," she managed at last. He laughed, almost a broken sound.

"My Michelle." He kissed her forehead fiercely, holding her with careful tenderness. "So good. How did you know I'd like that?"

"I saw your books." She tucked her head under his chin, feeling shy.

"Books?" He blinked at her; she could see his eyelids starting to droop in the aftermath of orgasm.

"Those old-school geeky books about slave girls in sexual bondage." Michelle blushed. "I saw them back in your old apartment. I shouldn't be the only one in this relationship who gets the kind of lovemaking I enjoy, Fred."

"You're too good to me," Fred whispered, his voice starting to slur. Michelle could feel sleep gathering as well, wrapping soft, thick gauze around her mind and his, binding them together in gentle lassitude.

"You're stuck with me anyway," she told him. "Forever."

They fell asleep in each other's arms.

The author would like to acknowledge the following artists and holders of brand names, intellectual properties, and copyrights. No infringement or negative association is intended through mentioning these properties.

IMAX (IMAX Corporation)
DragonCon (Dragon Con, Inc.)
Marriott (Marriott International)
Peachtree Center
*Firefly* (Mutant Enemy Productions)
Hyatt (Hyatt Hotels Corporation)
Hilton (Hilton Worldwide)
Totoro (Studio Ghibli)
Crüxshadows
*The Hobbit* (Metro-Goldwyn-Mayer (MGM), New Line Cinema, Wingnut Films)
*The Rocky Horror Picture Show* (Twentieth Century Fox Film Corporation, Michael White productions)
*Revenge of the Nerds* (Twentieth Century Fox Film Corporation, Interscope Communications)
Voltaire
Sheraton (Sheraton Hotels and Resorts)
Superman (DC Entertainment, Time Warner)
Clark Kent (DC Entertainment, Time Warner)
Sotheby's (Sotheby's)
Christie's **(Groupe Artémis)**
Brooks Brothers (Retail Brand Alliance)
People of Walmart (Three Ring Blogs Network)
Wal-Mart (Wal-Mart Stores, Inc.)
*Star Trek* (Paramount Television)
BBC America (British Broadcasting Corporation (BBC), AMC Networks)
*Dr. Who* (British Broadcasting Corporation (BBC))
"Michelle (Ma Belle)" (The Beatles, Paul McCartney, John Lennon)

The Grand Guignol (Le Théâtre du Grand Guignol)

*Batman Begins* (Warner Bros., Syncopy, DC Entertainment, Legendary Pictures, Patalex III Productions Limited)

Gandalf the Grey (New Line Cinema, Wingnut Films, The Saul Zaentz Company d/b/a Tolkien Enterprises)

*The Fellowship of the Ring* (New Line Cinema, Wingnut Films, The Saul Zaentz Company d/b/a Tolkien Enterprises)

Macintosh (Apple Inc.)

Bose (Bose Corporation)

*Spaceballs: The Movie* (Brooksfilms, Metro-Goldwyn-Mayer (MGM))

*The Matrix* (Warner Bros., Village Roadshow Pictures, Groucho II Film Partnership, Silver Pictures)

*The Princess Bride* (Act III Communications, Buttercup Films Ltd, The Princess Bride Ltd)

*Hot Fuzz* (Universal Pictures, StudioCanal, Working Title Films, Big Talk Productions, Ingenious Film Partners 2 LLP)

*Star Trek IV* (Paramount Pictures, Industrial Light & Magic (ILM))

*Star Wars* (Lucasfilm, 20th Century Fox Film Corporation)

*The Clone Wars* (CGCG, Lucasfilm Animation Singapore, Lucasfilm Animation, Lucasfilm)

*The Lord of the Rings* (by J. R. R. Tolkien, published by Houghton Mifflin)

*The Wheel of Time* (by Robert Jordan and Brandon Sanderson, published by Tor Fantasy)

Gor (novel series by John Norman, published by Open Road Media Sci-Fi & Fantasy)

Teenage Mutant Ninja Turtles (Lowbar Productions, Nickelodeon Animation Studios)

*Action Comics # 1* (Detective Comics, Inc., DC Entertainment)

Weird Al Yankovic

M&Ms (Mars, Incorporated)

Snickers (Mars, Incorporated)

Curly-Wurly (Cadbury, UK)

Coca-Cola (The Coca Cola Company)

Coke (The Coca Cola Company)

Cadbury Clusters (Cadbury, UK)

Aer Lingus (Aer Lingus)

Freddo Frog (Cadbury, UK)

## About the Author

For years, college professor Olivia Fields has been writing romantic tales to pacify her muse and entertain her friends. She believes in making her characters work for their happy endings. When not at her keyboard, Olivia enjoys nature hikes, photography, and the constant companionship of several rather irregularly trimmed Shih Tzu dogs. Olivia's first published novel, *Her Heart's Liege*, is also available online.

# Coming soon from Rogue Phoenix Press

Dream Makers II
Sequel to *Jewel of the Naga*

An Excerpt

"Briony!" Ken Stockman appeared at the cubicle door, his wavy brown hair slicked down, his conservative blue suit perfectly pressed. A shaft of morning sunlight glowed over his shoulder, making her long to be out of the dingy little office in the fresh air, soaking up the sun.

He grinned, his eyes twinkling, as if he could read her mind. "You passed the annual fitness survey with flying colors. I have a new assignment for you." He extended the fat manila folder he held in one hand and took a sip from the steaming cup of coffee he clutched in the other. "I know you'll be happy to get out in the field again."

Briony pushed back her curly red hair as she straightened up from her computer, her back cracking. She stood up and stretched. Ken was short for a man, but she was so petite the top of her head barely reached his nose. She returned his smile as she inspected the folder. "I sure will. I hate riding a desk. Thanks, Ken."

"No problem. Justine turned up the lead, so you should thank her whenever she gets in." He stepped into her cubicle and inhaled the steam rising out of his cup, sighing with pleasure. "The mark is an old codger living out in the Burren. He doesn't have a current deed. He has no licences or registrations on file, either, and the preliminary investigation turned up some intriguing rumors nearby. If he's a super, he could turn out to be a class three predator entity."

Briony whistled through her teeth, surprised and pleased. She loved a challenge.

"Be careful with this one. You know class threes can be trouble." Ken laid a fatherly hand on her shoulder, his hazel eyes narrowing with concern.

"I've handled class fours without backup, Ken. I'll get him." She reached for her highlighter and marked an intriguing passage for later review.

"That's my girl. You always do good work— enough of it for two." Ken beamed his approval. "I've told equipment to ready a standard surveillance equipment package by eleven. You want a ride out?"

"Sounds good. I'll phone when I'm ready for pickup." She frowned a little, studying a map showing the location of the man's home. "Looks like the guy lives a few miles out of Corofin. Could you ask John to prep me a bicycle?"

"Will do." Ken dug out his phone and sent a text, his lips moving as he plied his thumb. "Done."

"Thank you." Briony's heart lifted when she gazed out at the bright sunny morning. It was a perfect day for hunting.

"Don't forget to check in every day." Ken grinned at her again. "You look just like a kid at Christmas."

"That's because I love my job." Briony chuckled. "Don't worry. I'll keep in touch."

"Worrying's my job— and I love it, too." Ken laughed along with her. He began whistling as he moved on, a spring in his step.

Briony turned back to her computer. She'd wrap up her current research before eleven and leave Justine a note about her findings. With any luck, she'd be on the road by noon.

~ * ~

Bradan packed his stone-cutting tools into the bed of his old Land Rover, shoulders feeling the comfortable stretch and burn of a hard job well done. The mortared stone fence outside the garda station should stand for ten more decades, bar another clumsy tourist running off the road. The week's work had earned him a tidy sum, enough to fill the pantry for the next month, give or take.

He whistled and held the door as his dog jumped up. "There, now. Let's be off home." He paused, attention caught by a young woman marching down the sidewalk. She was petite and pale, with an unruly head of flaming red hair and a strong, tilted chin to match her patrician nose. She was a pretty little thing, but she had a determined look, as if she knew how to get her way. A handful, just his sort— that kind was always full of ideas. The saucy tilt of her chin reminded him he hadn't had a *real* meal in more than a week.

Bradan licked his lips, intrigued, but shook his head with resignation. Probably local; she looked absolutely Irish. Off-limits, if so. He ought to get home.

He delayed, letting her draw near while he pretended to have trouble latching his tailgate. He bent forward over the side of the truck to rummage in the bed, grumbling a little, extending his leg into her path as if to balance himself.

"Excuse me." Her bright little voice reproached him, right on cue, and her hand settled briefly on his ankle, steadying her as she was forced to step down into the street to detour around his foot.

An American accent. Bradan straightened up in triumph, keeping his voice surly, turning his face away from her. "Aye, there's not any excuse enough for some."

She huffed and kept going, but the moment of contact had been enough for him to sense the shape of her thoughts: purposeful, driven, with that same fierce determination he'd seen stamped on her face. She was a woman on a mission.

He had the scent of her mind now, so he ought to be able to find her again if she had a lodging nearby. He stared out across the road, pretending to watch the football pitch full of players in bright red shirts and white shorts. He observed her from the corner of his eye as she approached the police station. She moved just fine, with a sassy twitch of slender hips in tight denim jeans. It looked like she'd already forgotten their encounter, preoccupied by whatever goals drove her.

Excellent.

He climbed into the cab of the Land Rover, reaching absently to fondle Rosie's ears. "We'll both have a fine dinner tonight," he predicted. At least, they would if the pox-bottle who'd staked out his house didn't try any damned fool shenanigans and get in the way.

Bradan growled softly as he started the truck. Humans were a meddlesome lot, always prying and poking, putting their noses where they had no business. If the headcase who was spying on him didn't sod off soon, the bastard was likely to have himself a nasty accident.

He frowned, maneuvering into the road. It was smart to lay low while he was being watched, but he couldn't risk weakening himself too badly. He had to eat soon. A dream would have to be enough. It wouldn't give him all the sustenance he needed, but it was enough to keep him going, and it would be safer than going out on the prowl to find a girl.

He reached out with his mind as he drove, extending his senses back toward Corofin to find the girl again. She was still at the garda station, in a perfect tizzy of righteous fervor, upbraiding some poor peeler who wasn't doing to suit her. He laughed to himself. She felt young and strong, passionate, with plenty of energy to spare. A dream or two wouldn't hurt her at all.

## Also by the Author
at
Rogue Phoenix Press

*Her Heart's Liege*

Tomboy Alex Bonham has fought her male peers tooth and nail to prove herself worthy to become captain of the king's guard. When her country is invaded by Danes, she is ordered to take the king's younger son, a charming but irresponsible rake, away from the front lines for safekeeping.

Alex walks a difficult line, trying to balance her growing attraction to Prince Holden with her dedication to duty and her responsibility to keep him safe from robbers, Danes...and even himself. But when they are drawn into the struggle to defend East Anglia from occupation, both the prince and his captain must grow. Can spoiled Prince Holden evolve into a good man who could lead the kingdom—one Alex can trust with her heart?